Parts

A novel by
Shoney Flores

Texas Review Press
Huntsville, Texas

FIRST EDITION
Requests for permission to acknowledge material from this work should be sent to:
Permissions
Texas Review Press
English Department
Sam Houston State University
Huntsville, TX 77341-2146

cover design: www.ebooklaunch.com
author photo: Linda Naila Ruiz

Library of Congress Cataloging-in-Publication Data
Names: Flores, Shoney, 1985- author.
Title: Parts : a novel / by Shoney Flores.
Description: First edition. | Huntsville, Texas : Texas Review Press, [2017]
    Identifiers: LCCN 2017026608 (print) | LCCN 2017027956 (ebook) | ISBN
    9781680031386 (ebook) | ISBN 9781680031379 | ISBN 9781680031379q(pbk.)
Subjects: LCSH: Stores, Retail--Texas--Fiction. |
    Automobiles--Parts--Fiction. | Mexican Americans--Texas--Social life and
    customs--Fiction.
Classification: LCC PS3606.L624 (ebook) | LCC PS3606.L624 P37 2017 (print) |
    DDC 813/.6--dc23
LC record available at https://lccn.loc.gov/2017026608

For Linda and Samuel—
for being the best parts of me

Parts

PART ONE

The Part About Chains

Some years ago—October 2006, to be precise—I either quit or didn't quit working at the auto parts store, so call me unreliable. I remember leaving the phone ringing, calls coming in from other workers from other chain stores from nearby towns, wearing the same red shirts, double-checking if we had a certain Ultima starter for a '98 Jetta or a Cardone rack and pinion for an '01 Ranger to sell and make extra commission.

Our auto parts warehouse was set near the heart of McAllen, Texas, by the clogged artery known as south 23rd Street, where traffic attempted to flow north and south, and probably could if there weren't street lights fifty fucking feet away from each other. To our right, a Catholic church with disorganized chain-linked fences that seemed to be protecting nothing. To our left, a used car dealership run by a man who specialized in acquiring repossessed cars from auctions, big yellow flags with *Buy Here, Pay Here* and *Se fía* poled up front.

Shoe Guy knew there was something up when I snaked through the piles of merchandise boxes waiting to be stocked. He quit scanning the new orders, something he did every five or ten minutes anyway to do anything else—sell some shoes, take a payment from a coworker who had previously purchased shoes from him, wipe the sweat off his pinched mouse face, or to hold his vending machine cherry pie to his

1

lips and teach a younger employee how to properly eat pussy. This time, he stopped scanning to know what the problem was because we always wanted to know. Everything was our business.

These were my coworkers, and I never wanted to be like them.

In Spanish, Shoe Guy said to me, Phone's ringing. I responded, in English and in auto pilot, that his wife couldn't take a hint.

While he laughed behind me, Quique helped stock Borg Warner switches in the aisles for old times' sake. Another coworker, some new guy from the front counter, snatched a switch from the shelf to sell and rattled it at Quique's face, mocking him for his lost commission. I pressed through the green double doors leading to the front of the store and the rush of cold air made the sweat on the back of my head coagulate like bacon fat on a baking pan. The boss hugged his office phone with his face and shoulder, most likely trying to make another problem go away, probably a customer who witnessed Quique or someone dry humping another coworker in his unnaked ass.

He gestured for me to wait, which ended up looking like the same OK sign employees under him usually used when talking about an asshole. There's a vowel sign language game the guys at work play. They say *A* and form a pussy by pressing both forefingers and thumbs together and stretching them apart. They say E and form a masturbating hand, I and throw the middle finger, O and form the asshole sign, and then say ooh, as in the Spanish for *U*, and with arms to their sides, yank them backward as if pulling a woman's ass towards their dicks. And there's no acceptable context for this either. Someone will randomly ask if you know the vowels with no invitation. The boss crossed his long, right leg over his left, forming a wide letter T, his foot hanging in the air shaking up and down as if he were conducting in allegro, something I always noticed about him since my childhood. That's probably where my own version originated from. I lay my own feet flat on the floor, raise my heel a bit like I'm tiptoeing, and shake my leg like I have to take a leak, probably due to some unknown anxiety or something in our blood.

The chair nearest him had upholstery that was peeling off, revealing stained memory foam and spring coils that stabbed into the back of your thighs. I started doing my knee shit which slightly grazed the bottom of the computer desk where some of the guys would sneak to during a break to play Minesweeper. I introduced a couple of them to Solitaire once—even the crappy Spider one anyone can beat—but it seemed easier for them to click little gray squares at random until the sad face appeared. The manager patch on the boss's shirt was beginning to peel off as well, with his embroidered first name beneath it. How many different words could I come up with using the first few letters? Rambo. Ramifications. Rambunctious, a commonly misspelled word found in elementary letters from absent teachers to their substitutes, as in "Watch out for fourth period. Their [sic] the most rambuctious [sic] group."

What's up, bro'? he said, covering the speaker with his hand.

I want to quit, I said. Or something along those lines. I had planned saying it right in my head for almost three years, but the words never come out like you hope.

The fuck up, he said, and get back to work, then returned to his call. I remained seated—Rammstein—taking careful notice of his omission of the word *shut*. If I were to quit, everyone would probably think the pressure of running the hub was too hard to handle—rampage—or say I am an ungrateful piece of shit for throwing away the job my own brother pulled strings for me to be bumped up on the application pile, a favor and sense of obligation that had me chained to this dump for three years. Not like hundreds of men were that desperate to work with assholes—ramshackle—the kind that stayed planted here forever, raising fat humans on dollar-menu cheeseburgers and leaving pissed-off wives at home, staring out windows, with their failed dreams of being interior designers or CNA's, assholes that needed second and third jobs to be able to afford prostitutes or pot or beer or whatever vices they had, jobs like selling stolen shoes on the side and having to pretend your seventy-five-cent lunch was a cherry-jelly-filled cunt to escape judgment of only having that to eat because the reputation of being a dumbass by far surpassed the reputation of being poor. Rambling.

Listen, I said, getting out now would—

The words escaped my grasp again like bills in a money booth, like I needed dollar words to communicate and the only ones in my hand were ten-dollar ones. I wanted to tell him about what happened a few minutes before, and about becoming—what's the opposite of evolve? Regress? Degenerate? Would he even know what that means? I wouldn't want that for him if it were the other way around. But he was already gone.

You can't fucking wait? he said. You can't wait until we can train a new supervisor? The hub can't run itself, you know. He went from looking at me to studying me, judging me with those half-squinty, brown Mexican eyes. Besides, he said, what are you going to do if you leave now? How else are you paying for rent? Your classes?

I didn't know. So I said that.

We didn't say anything to each other for a while, and I could actually feel the phone ringing four hundred feet away, the ink ribbon of the old printer sliding left and right, vomiting order after order dipping in dot matrix ink, some of the hub drivers back from their routes seeing their unsorted orders and starting to panic.

What do you want? the boss asked. How can I get you to stay?

There was nothing he could give me. He couldn't give me a raise, even if I actually wanted one, because the fact that we shared the same DNA alone was reason enough to get him fired if the regional manager found proof the store stank of nepotism, along with old oil and faint battery acid, as if that were the worst crime around here, and an extra dime every hour doesn't make a difference.

You've been running the hub for one stupid day, he said, and you can't pull your own weight or what?

One day, officially, I said, and that's not why I'm quitting. Rick couldn't pull his own weight.

That's not funny.

You weren't there.

To exit the store, it was required to pass through the counter area, trying to escape all the stares from the workers there, a large Q stitched on my back. Entering the store, it was usually a forced "good morning" because it was expected of me to respond, but on the way out, the laughter and the whispers from the counter salesmen followed me out the door like a hallucination in a ghost film, and even if they were imagined, knowing that deep underneath that layer of laughter, they knew it wasn't my scheduled time to punch out, and they'd be pissed like when I got dibs on scheduling my vacation the last week of

December, they never complained because of my relation to the boss. We never complained. We thought, and I thought as I slid into my small truck and used my short, left sleeve to wipe the tears and sweat from my face, thought some more as I punched the steering wheel four, five times, thinking on one layer of the thought stack how hilarious I must look to people passing by because my stupid truck horn sounded like a Lollipop Guild midget being kicked in the stomach, staring at the cars cruising on 23rd Street in humid South Texas, the sun sucking up all the air like when you get a pen cap stuck to your cheek, and on the layer above that, wondered, before opening the door again to go back inside, how the fuck I got there.

Maybe I only needed to catch my breath.

I took a break on the half flight of loose wooden stairs that led up to the loading dock to smoke a cigarette, a habit no one outside the auto parts walls knew existed and no one inside suspected was a secret. I smoked so naturally that anyone would believe I'd been smoking since I was four, my age when I lit up one of my dad's Raleighs and walked into my mom's hair salon to announce, in front of all her clients, that I had finally learned how to smoke. Sixteen years later, I thought I finally needed the cigarettes since smokers had longer breaks than non-smokers, and I'd kill for longer breaks, even if it was myself.

Rick's funeral was happening in the Catholic church next door, though he wasn't even Catholic at all. They allowed the workers to go to the funeral during their breaks that day, but most of them had to choose between Rick and food. Two ended up attending. I had to choose between Rick and a cigarette.

Halfway into the smoke, Plato joined me, cleaning his ears with a metal file from a nail clipper. He ran the distribution center in front of the hub, where they stacked hundreds of buckets of oil and paint, which was its own separate business, like a McDonald's inside a Wal-Mart. We called him Plato all the time, as in the Spanish word for *plate* since his flat face was shaped that way. Not after the philosopher.

Do you know what the difference is between half-empty and half-full, he asked.

Can't you cut your ear doing that shit?

Well, I have to keep them clean, he said. He pulled out the file from his ear and wiped the wax by his jeans pocket. I tried to look the other way and listened to his voice add, No one wants to have dirty ears. They itch. And you don't want to scratch in there with a dirty finger.

I pictured getting grime and engine grease on our hands, washing them over and over and being unable to get rid of the dark in the permanently inked finger tips. I asked Plato, Ever heard of Q-tips?

Don't like them, he said. They leave residue behind in the ear. Even the ones that are wrapped up tight. Fucking hate them.

Don't expect my help if you end up bleeding out of your ears, then.

So, tell me, he said. You know the difference? Between half-full and half-empty.

There was probably some sexual innuendo going on with the question or some dumb joke as it was to be expected from anyone here. That was our ever-dick-referencing culture. So I tried thinking of possible punch lines, maybe something having to do with ejaculation, but that was a long shot for a setup like that.

It's a simple question, he said. I have this bottle of Coke here. Drank half of it. So which one is it?

Half-empty, I said, and he looked surprised and asked why. Because it all depends on the previous action that took place to determine which one it is. If you're drinking out of it, it means you're emptying it, so that would make it half-empty, but if you were filling it up with God knows what, then it would be half-full. Is that right?

Yeah, he said. That's it.

Seriously?

He nodded and pointed at the people going in and out of Rick's funeral across the street. Are you going? he asked me. It's messed up, what happened to him. Not the way to go. You worked for him. You should go.

I didn't like him, I said, and it would be hypocritical to put him on a pedestal now that he's dead. Dying doesn't make you less of an asshole. It just makes your asshole stop working. Sometimes.

You liked him once, he said. Besides, your brother's going.

That's because he'd look like a dick if he didn't. The company paid for the whole funeral, and all because he was an idiot who couldn't watch his step because his extra large beach ball gut was in the way.

Shouldn't speak about the dead that way.

Which is why I'll leave milk and cookies out at night in case he decides to continue haunting me.

Way to honor the dead, he said, and then he left.

A woman in a black dress stepped out of the funeral, dabbing her eyes as if she had been crying but didn't want her mascara to run. She lit a cigarette and sat on a bench by a statue of the Virgin Mary, crossing her legs and revealing most of them beneath her dress. I felt like her cigarette buddy, and I probably even raised mine in the air like a wine glass. I couldn't tell who she was from across the street, but I could notice her parts, her legs which looked smooth even from thirty yards away that suddenly made me want to put my lips to them, there, right on the bench, in front of the Virgin Mary, in front of God's house, and He could peek out the window to watch if He wanted to for all I cared. I found myself desiring her completely, or at least wished I were out on the road delivering parts so that I could stop on one of the empty farm roads south of Edcouch, surrounded by fields of corn and wheat, and jerk off at the thought of being with her, imagining what the rest of her parts looked like under her dress, the real shape of her breasts without her bra's support, what color her panties were, if she shaved down there, and maybe even her name. The thought evaporated when she sunk her face into her hands and continued to cry, or when the end of the cigarette burned my ring finger right after that. I don't remember which one it was, or want to remember. I didn't know why she cried, who Rick would mean so much to, the pathetic man. I spun my wedding band with my other hand before I climbed the stairs to get back to work.

Shoe Guy and some other guys stood by the loading dock garage door, checking her out, too, and he started mumbling some sexual words as he humped the rail part of the door while the other guys laughed and rubbed their dicks like they were hurting, or like they were literally trying to keep them in their pants. Hey, Shoe Guy yelled out to her, hey, *chiquita*, can I have your number? He never stopped humping, an action sequence I pictured in slow motion as the girl on the bench wiped her tears and took refuge inside the church, leaving the guys whining as if they had not won the lottery that time, and one by one, they went back to work.

Spider Man—an acne-plagued nineteen-year-old with thick glasses and skinny like he did crack and blow for breakfast, lunch, and dinner—had been running the hub while I reviewed applications. He handed me the cordless phone while mumbling something I didn't understand and left the office. The phone rang as soon as it left his hand.

"Hey, this is Jim from Donna. Can you check to see if you have a CV shaft for me? Part number A1 60-365."

Hold on, I said, and sighed as I clung the phone into my side pocket. No one liked fetching parts on the second floor of the warehouse, the story closer to the sheet metal roof that invited and multiplied the heat from outside, the one that forced you to limbo sideways through the oil-covered rack and pinion boxes sticking out of the aisles as dust rained on you and danced in the rays of sunlight secreting through the cement wall vents like molecules in a microscope. Brick-sized holes on the wall, other than the ones forming naturally from pockets of air trying to escape, left you doing your best to find some way, from any direction, to gasp for oxygen. But it wasn't that much of an improvement downstairs, anyway.

Yeah, we got it.

"Can it make the next trip?"

Yeah. You still have time.

"Thanks a lot, buddy."

On my way back to the hub office, James stepped out of the commercial department and casually asked, What's up, faggot? The least he could do to better his reputation around here since everyone else thought he was the faggot for having that long hair tucked underneath his Pantera cap and for painting his fingernails black from time to time, using his desire to look like a rocker as a defense. His nickname was Pansy, and he couldn't do anything to change that.

Just because I let you suck my—

I stopped myself before finishing. He wouldn't have heard me anyway as he turned right and disappeared into the starter aisles. The phone rang in my hand again, and I let it ring that time as I walked back towards the hub office.

This is how you eat a girl's pussy, Shoe Guy was telling Spider Man in front of a coworker audience who looked entertained as much as attentive. As I passed by, he told me the phone was ringing.

I know, I said. Your wife can't take a hint.

More laughter. It started to sound exactly like the phone ringing.

I thought about the girl by the church again, who was probably in someone else's arms being comforted now, and I felt like vomiting, like a fucking idiot.

I remember the phone ringing while it happened, I told V-Lo in the commercial department, which he ran and basically dealt with delivering and selling parts to local mechanic shops. He had been asking me to repeat Rick's story and telling different versions of it to different people over the phone. He wanted to hear the real version again.

You're the only one who saw it happen, he said to me. Those who were right there pretended not to be interested. San Peter, the old man who dealt with Mexican accounts and made a lot of commission by selling parts in bulk, would turn every once in a while. V-Lo had been waiting a long time for him to retire or die to take his accounts. Pansy was in the room, too.

There's no story, I said. Rick went to get a few parts upstairs, probably lost his balance, and fell down. The chain happened to be in the way of his head. It was an accident that could happen to any one of us.

Lost his balance?

Yeah. It actually happens to fat people a lot, usually because of the uneven matter in the front and back. Miracle the impact of his body hitting the bottom floor didn't kill us all.

Everyone in the room laughed, and there was a sense of comfort in knowing we all shared this cynicism, except I wasn't finding it funny despite the material was coming from me.

Still doesn't make sense, Peter said.

Why don't you go show us how he fell, then, San Peter? Pansy said. V-Lo would love that.

More laughter. That's what was interesting about working with idiots who didn't understand the concept of emotions, that a coworker dies one day and we joke about it the next, which no one considered immoral or abnormal. Earlier that morning, a homeless man pretending to be a customer escaped with a fuel filter to probably sell for drugs, and Hesse (Jesse, really, but he must have been too gringo to embroider Jesus or Chuy on his uniform), one of the counter men, tried to catch up to him but failed. After that incident, people forgot Rick died.

V-Lo seemed to be the only one interested in Rick. Probably because Rick had christened him V-Lo because, Rick had said, his ass was tight in his pants. No one questioned whether or not V-Lo's ass resembled J-Lo's. They just liked the sound of V-Lo, so it caught on like most of the nicknames at work. Oh, shit, he said, I forgot to tell you. Yesterday, when you were with La Polla, one of your writing friends came looking for an oxygen sensor for her car. She had these nice tits, man.

He put his hands up to his chest and started pinching invisible nipples, and I returned to reviewing applications to replace Rick, picking out the idiots who made it obvious they filled them out for a signature to prove to the government that supplied them with food stamps that, yes, they had, in fact, been trying to find work. The boss had asked me to fix the problem of hiring a replacement while he cleaned up the whole death mess and worked on getting matters back on track.

What about this one? I had asked him.

I remember her dropping it off, he said, so it's a no.

Her? It says his name is Alex. He's thirty-eight.

She's thirty-eight, and I can't hire a woman again.

You know that's sexism, right? And illegal.

I need to make sure all the jobs here get done, he said. If I hire her, you know what's going to happen to everyone. Same thing that happened last time.

He opened and closed every drawer of his desk, looking for any more misplaced applications and disappointed that out of all the ones I had reviewed, I chose a female with a background in auto parts retail.

What's going to happen, I asked. Back to caveman times? Everyone's going to fight for the love of Alex? What if she's ugly?

You think that'll matter to them?

It kind of mattered before.

Take a break, he said, and then look through the same pile. Lower your standards a bit. I'll get Spider Man or someone to work the hub a while.

For the most part, I think he was right. I settled for the stairs by the loading dock and pulled out a cigarette from my shirt pocket. Plato joined me after a while, cleaning out the inside of his ear with a nail file, and he asked what was the difference between half-full and half-empty.

Quique walked in the hub office while I tried to catch my breath, a few minutes left in his lunch break and what should have been the middle of mine, eating from a bag of mixed nuts which he offered me as his gesture of saying hello. I refused, wondering if the guys had made fun of him already for eating nuts, probably saying something like, Yeah, you like the feel of nuts in your mouth, don't you? He would've been better off with a cherry pie. He sat in the only chair we had in the office, facing the printer and the fan circulating the room's hot air, but air nonetheless. We stared out the plastic window held together by shipping tape, overlooking the distribution center for a while, watching some of the guys from that department smoking cigarettes underneath a palette of batteries, a step up from when they used to do it by the buckets of oil. One of them, Red, who enjoyed cheating on his wife despite the fact they'd been together since they were twelve, laughed the most at their jokes, almost choking on smoke several times. Güero, who always parked his piece of shit motorcycle where the delivery trucks were supposed to be loaded so no one would steal it, was the quietest. He always looked like he was listening. The other one, Brown (because why not?), always looked like he wasn't listening because he didn't understand anything, just looked off to the side and would laugh every time everyone else would, hoping to piece the events together with the little Spanish he would get sometimes.

Rick not back yet? Quique asked. He chugged down a mouthful of nuts and sucked the salt out of them for a while before chewing them. Hasn't he been gone for more than an hour?

It's like you're following a script, I said.

Alright. Calm down, asshole.

Sorry, queer.

Now, just because I let you suck on my dick, he said, don't mean I'm queer.

I waited for more orders to come in to take five or six with me on every trip to the warehouse instead of walking back and forth for one order at a time. Quique grabbed a can of Coke and started spitting the desalted nuts into it like a mother bird regurgitating into its babies' mouths. Perfect lunch, he said, like always. What, you don't like Coke and nuts? Man, everyone loves Coke and nuts. His thick Mexican accent would get the best of him sometimes and he'd end up pronouncing *Coke* slightly different. Fucking fat ass probably eating everything in the fridge, he said about Rick. Probably eating the fridge, too. His wife and kids. The dog. He's eating everything, the fucking fat ass.

He clocked back in and left the office. Through the small window by the computer, I saw him run into Rick in the warehouse. He tried to lecture him, but Rick kept walking straight to the office, a blank look on his round face, and he let the door slam shut behind him, clocked back in, and looked at the three orders on the printer, apologized for being late, looking more serious than usual. I know there's no time for you to go to lunch, he said, looking at the clock, but I'll try to make it up to you this week. I'll let you leave an hour early on Friday.

We're shorthanded on Friday. Lou has the day off.

Oh, yeah, he said. Fuck. Well, we'll work something out.

You okay? I asked, not knowing why.

I think my wife's cheating on me.

And?

He expected me to care about his situation, but I wasn't interested in his problems, not because of the lunch issue, which had turned into an every-day occurrence, but because I actually didn't care. Don't you cheat on her like all the fucking time, I said.

This is different, he said. A wife is supposed to be loyal to her husband, at all costs. No questions asked. Regardless.

You sound like a dealership commercial.

It's okay for us, men, to cheat because it's good practice to use on our wives. But when a wife cheats, it's like someone else had her, you know?

I didn't say anything.

Look. When you have sex with another woman, you can wash the pussy off of you. Clean up dick. Good as new, right? Like nothing happened. But you can never wash the sex off a woman. Because that shit's inside her now. It's impure. And adultery. You know what I mean, right?

The chair's steel legs creaked a bit when he sat down. It surprised me he still fit between the armrests. He shuffled the orders with his pudgy fingers, breaking a sweat. You know, he said, changing his tone a bit. One day you're going to get out of this place.

I don't know about that, I said, cutting off his stuck-in-a-small-town speech. I mean, it's a miracle if I can even get out of this place for a lunch break.

Nah. You're different than the rest of us. You're smart. You're gonna get out of here, and maybe one day you'll write a book about all of us.

No offense, but you guys are idiots. Don't get me wrong. I'm not saying I'm not one, even if you don't think so. God knows I'm a fucking idiot who probably deserves to be hated. After all, I'm an employee here, right? It probably rubs off. I don't think anyone would want to read a book about a bunch of pieces of shit.

He sat there for a while longer, thinking hard about it. I hated him more than any other person in the store, not only because he always fucked me over with lunch or taking the routes away from me or being late in the mornings or picking me to be assistant supervisor so he'd have it easy, but because I genuinely hated who he was as a person, how he pretended to be more important than everyone else in the store, how he pretended he was smart because he used the word *flabbergasted* once and surprised himself like he scored a three-pointer with his back facing the net, how he'd pretend to be religious except for the part about infidelity.

Everything about that guy sucked.

Take a break, he said in the office after a while. I'll go get these parts. It took him a while to stand up and the chair actually came up with him for a moment, attached to his hips. He exited the office and stepped into the warehouse, and I kept looking out the window, watching him fumbling with a few parts on the second floor as the phone started to ring in the office, followed by the cordless phone hanging from his side pocket. I remember the phone rang a third time when I watched him grab the chain attached to the forklift we used to lift and load engines and wrapped it around his neck. A fifth time when I saw him jump off.

I picked it up on the sixth ring, right after the head came off, unable to tell blood from burnt transmission fluid.

"Can you check to see if you have a filter?" the voice on the other end said.

Hang on.

PART TWO

The Part About Ropes

The way in which my involvement with the writing group began was somewhat unusual. I sat and shook my right foot up and down in the air, waiting in Dr. Lima's office. No doubt he had an obsession with vampires. He owned more Dracula-themed decorations in one room than my mother did crucifixes in her entire home. A framed Béla Lugosi picture stood by his Dell computer where a family picture should've been. Lugosi with a fancy suit and resting his face on the palm of his hand while holding a cigar. All it needed was a love note followed by an autograph. Several Dracula posters stuck thumbtacked to the four walls, practically acting as wallpaper. One of them, an image of a graffitied brick wall, read *Dracula Sucks*. By Lugosi, a white ceramic mug held black pencils with bat-shaped erasers attached to them. The inscription *If You Don't Like Vampires, Suck It*. To my left, a diptych wall scroll of Tom Cruise on one side with the quote, "Your body's dying. Pay no attention. It happens to us all." On the other side, Brad Pitt looking upward at dim lighting with the quote below him, "I'm a spirit of prenatal flesh. Detached. Unchangeable. Empty."

"Pretty damn psycho, huh?" the girl next to me said, pointing at a violent, illustrative poster of a man driving a stake into his own heart and turning into dust starting by his feet. I sucked in my lower lip, surprised the office decor disturbed *her* considering she looked like she flew out of the posters herself in her goth costume. Not a bad-looking girl once you moved past the fact there was more ink and jewelry than flesh. More ribbons and bands than hair. More black than white. More artificiality than originality. As was the case with a lot of goths.

She sat in the middle row at the back of Dr. Lima's Stoker class, hoping to be called on the least. I tried to hide in the corner of the room farthest away from the door. To be honest, it didn't seem like she read the material. Always drew pictures of anime cats. Probably thought a Stoker class was another goth accessory.

"You're in my stalker class, right?"

"Sorry?"

"The Bram Stalker class," she said, "with Dr. Lima. Yeah, I re-member you. You sit in the back. Always answering questions about—stuff?" She spoke somewhat like an elementary student overacting a reading of *Casey at the Bat* for a UIL Prose competition. Though mixed with monotone. Like she kept forgetting which word came next in the string. Or like she needed a PA to hold up cue cards for her. Or like she made it up in real time.

"Yeah," I said. "I always get called on to say stuff in that class."

She laughed. Or cackled. Not sure what it was. A friendly display of white teeth and metal hoops sounds right.

"It's 'cause you said that smart—thing. About ex- exenophobia? Anyway, that thing at the beginning of the semester. That's why Dr. Lima calls on you all—the freaking time. Would've been better off not saying anything. At all. Now he probably thinks. That anything you have to say—is going to help the class." She nodded and added, "So why are we even here, man?"

I shrugged.

"You're a cool dude. What's your name? I'm Aparición. Total weird name. I know. My friends call me Apari."

"Shit."

"Shit's right," Dr. Lima said as he entered the office with a stack of papers in his hand. Even upon closer inspection, nothing about him suggested at his obsession with the literary vampire. Tall. Skinny. Bald. Thick glasses. Black tie with a plain white shirt. Then again, maybe he had coffins buried in his basement. A lot of professors did. He sat on his side of the desk, adjusting the Lugosi frame before saying anything else. A compulsion.

"So you two thought I wouldn't find out." He took the paper sitting on the top of the stack. Flagged it around in front of our faces too fast for us to be able to make out anything from it other than a few red slashes across it and a circled *F*. "You know what this is? It's a copy of Tuesday's quiz with the name 'Aparición' written on top. 'Number 2: What *does* Van Helsing first tell Mina to do on their quest to kill Dracula?' Answer: 'To seduce him because she, the long, lost love of Count Dracula, is the only one who can.' Really?" He tossed the paper towards us, even though, in a quick murder of the dramatic effect he sought, it flipped back in the air in his direction.

"It's from the movie, huh?" Aparición said looking at me. "Right?"

I muttered, Oh my God. My face buried in my hand.

"Funny to think," Dr. Lima said, "that the same student making comments in class on psychoanalytic interpretations of texts would write answers as thought-provoking as this one."

"Oh, but he didn't write that," Aparición said, scratching the side of her head with one hand and pointing at me with the other. "That's my quiz. You think I copied—" She stopped and then laughed again. "How could I possibly copy from him if he sits all the way in the corner? That's dumb."

"I want to know one thing," Dr. Lima said, ignoring her completely. "I already know which one the real Aparición is. I want to confirm that you have not been turning in work for her, whoever you are, since the start of the term. Have you been pretending to be her to help her get her grades up?" I shook my head. "Then who the heck are you?" He opened his roll sheet on his computer. "I tried matching people in class with names I do recognize, and I can't seem to pinpoint you even though I remember calling you Aparición at the beginning of the semester. A name like that is not hard to forget, even in the Rio Grande Valley. Are you even enrolled in the course?"

"I'm sorry," Aparición, the real one, said, "but I'm free to go, right?"

Dr. Lima motioned for her to leave, holding up her quiz to take with her. She disappeared from the office, taking her name with her. A name I had stolen when seizing an opportunity to sneak into the class. She either hadn't shown up the first day or was too used to people calling her Apari that she forgot to answer when Dr. Lima checked his roster. I took a chance to avoid the $1,400 I would have to magically conjure after rent, electricity, and gas to pay for tuition, and raised my hand. No credit. No GPA. Only knowledge.

"She had nothing to do with this," I told Dr. Lima. "I wanted to be in your course, but I just—. Your class was full. So I couldn't register for it."

"You can't be showing up to people's classes like that," he said. "Especially in a university like this one. There are issues with meeting fire code, and not every classroom is set up to sit two-three hundred students. You'll wind up in one that sits forty and eventually get caught again. And while there are more official ways to audit a course, some professors won't go for it."

"Right," I said. "I'm sorry. I won't be returning to your class anymore." I started to leave, hiding my trembling hands from his field of vision.

"You're not doing this with other classes, are you?"

"No," I lied. I had also been frequenting Literary Criticism, Milton, Civil War Through the Ages, and a Contemporary Mexican Novel course in the Modern Languages Department.

"Tell you what," he said. "Why not stick around? Finish off the semester. I could use the class discussion. You don't understand how difficult it is to get people to like Bram Stoker nowadays. Vampires aren't what they used to be. So, what do you say?"

"Sure," I lied again.

"Oh, and here," he said. "I don't know if you're interested in writing, but some of my old students are starting a writing group. You should check it out. They're looking for members. Good news is you don't have to be registered to participate."

In the beginning, when I got myself hired at the auto parts store, Quique literally showed me the ropes. Red ones. White ones. Yellow ones. Covered with dust and oil and grime and eroding like dry dead leaves. They hung behind an empty shelf on the second floor of the warehouse. Quique said they should've been thrown away years ago, but no one ever got around to it. In that moment, it wasn't clear why he showed them to me. Why he proceeded to tell me the stories of their lives. How the guys used them to tie around cardboard boxes so they wouldn't open and let the parts inside fall apart. The first full five minutes of my first day on the job talking about the ropes. Until he stopped and said, Anyway, these are the ropes.

My first impulse was to be rude. Say, And you're showing me these because . . . ? After all, Quique was one of two (now three, with me) stock boys, whose list of duties consisted of scanning hundreds of incoming parts, sorting them into three piles—downstairs, upstairs, and the air-conditioned front of the store—stocking them in their shelves, checking discrepancies, and, with time left (and there usually was), clean the restrooms and mop the aisles.

In other words, as Quique put it later, stock boys were shit. The most replaceable employees in the building who stepped aside to let other workers who actually made the company money pass.

The stocker test during the interview process clarified this with its long list of true/false questions like, "The number 148921 is the same as 148291." So I didn't have a problem accepting the fact that my new job lacked meaning. Like the ropes. And even though being rude to Quique probably wouldn't cost me the job, it wasn't the best foot to start with either. I settled for middle ground and asked, *What's* with the ropes? Somehow, his dark-complected face managed to turn a darker shade of red, like he had forgotten to say something important. Or to be more specific, like he gave the punch line to a lame joke before taking the time to set it up.

The thing is, he said, *usually*, when we hire a new inventory specialist, your brother'll say something like, "Quique here will show you the ropes so you can get your bitch-ass to work."

A horrible impression of my brother's voice. He only deepened his own pitch, which I managed to notice while still trying to get past *inventory specialist.*

But he didn't say that, I told him. He just said you were gonna train me.

Anyways, he continued. It's kind of like a personal insider's joke of mine that I came up with. Your brother says to show him the ropes, and I bring the guy upstairs to show him the ropes. I guess I assumed he had said it out of habit this time. So fucking stupid, I know.

How many times have you done this bit? I asked.

Not that many. I'd say like seven or eight times. Maybe nine.

Well, I said, it's a good thing he didn't say, "Quique here will get you acquainted with the warehouse" or else we wouldn't get any work done. Not to mention the awkwardness of being properly introduced to all the parts.

He smiled. I guess the morning isn't ruined after all. He told me his real name was Enrique, but people called him Quique.

Why is it spelled with K's on your uniform, I asked.

I don't know. When they asked me what I wanted my uniform to say, I just said Quique. Guess I didn't really spell it out. It's pronounced the same way, anyways.

At least it's not your birth record, I said. But the misprint on his uniform was the least of his problems. If everyone at work took the same IQ quiz, it would prove that Quique's intellect didn't surpass anyone else's. From spending a few minutes with him, it was apparent that he liked to pretend to be smarter and cleverer than everyone else in the warehouse. Like a lot of the other coworkers did. Liked to wish to believe his half-semester of college sufficed to make him the last drop of wit in this desert of idiocy. Whether he did it for respect, acceptance, or both, or to feel like he could lead his fellow coworkers out of the desert, it didn't matter. Though the common sentiment in that regard was "Let them die of thirst instead."

This is the area we work at the most, he said, extending his arms as if he made the loading dock appear behind a curtain. Truck comes in the middle of the night, unloads the pallets. We scan the parts. We stock the parts. I usually scan Monday-Thursday. Shoe Guy scans Fridays and Saturdays. That way we both know how to scan in case one of us gets sick or goes out on vacation.

Shoe Guy?

Shoe Guy, Quique called out to the short man removing parts from one box, scanning them, then dumping them into a different box. He's our older, Quique continued, and therefore slower, inventory specialist.

We call him Shoe Guy because he sells shoes on the side. Hooked me up with these Nikes. Fifty bucks. In payments, too. Shoo is also the last word he hears from his wife in the mornings. So, Shoe Guy. Get it?

Quique introduced me as *new guy*, and Shoe Guy pulled me off to the side before saying hello. It's important, he said, to call Quique La Gata.

How come? I asked. La Gata is Spanish for *the female cat*, a nickname Quique later said has no particular significance, which I can get behind since, if anything, Quique reminded me of a duck more than a cat. He said Shoe Guy decided to call him that one day, thinking that if he did so enough times, then the rest of the guys would do it, too, and it would stick. It did. There's nothing these guys like more than a funny nickname, Quique said, except maybe fucking other women.

Because he's a pussy, Shoe Guy answered.

Anyways, Quique said. New guy, let's go back upstairs so I can introduce you to the racks and pinions.

Where do we fix cars? I asked him. He mirrored my confused look. I thought people brought their cars here so they could get fixed. We don't do that here?

No, man, he said. We don't fix anything here. We only sell replacements.

I did not know exactly what Quique wanted to be before becoming La Gata. He didn't remember either. He did remember the moment he started becoming La Gata, long before he even earned the nickname, before he met Shoe Guy and everyone else at the auto parts store. The memory went like this: He was sitting on a university bench with Tracy under the shade of a fruitless tree. There isn't a more romantic place to break a heart, and minutes before he did—not months—he had everything in his life aligned. A career path for the both of them fully paid by financial aid. Eventually get married. Eventually get rich. Eventually have two kids. Travel. The works. Everything. He told her, We have to break up, and started crying before Tracy even had a chance to react. He told me Tracy's the best-looking girl in the world. Hot. If he had to compare her to a Hollywood actress for comparison, he'd pick . . .

No. He couldn't. Because Hollywood actresses wished they were as hot as Tracy.

The day they broke up, she wore a blue dress, the same one she had worn a couple months before on their one-year dating anniversary. He had taken her to Red Lobster that day because in the Rio Grande Valley, he said, you can't do better than Red Lobster. So he sat there on the bench, covering his wet eyes with his fingertips as if he were trying to apply pressure to keep the tears in. Then he had to spill the beans.

Six months before, an ex-girlfriend, Luci, had come down to visit from Oklahoma. At that point in the story, he said, Tracy starts to cry, too.

Luci was fucking crazy back when they dated during junior year of high school—the kind of crazy that called in bomb threats to skip wood shop and make out with other guys in the fields behind the school—and someone he'd known since they were kids. Old family friends. So the families were always in each others' business, always looking to see what each family was up to even after Luci and her family moved away. During a get-together at Quique's parents' house, they started talking, remembering the times they used to have until they had to break it off because they couldn't stand to be in the same room anymore. In his flashback, he called Luci a cunt fuck. They talked about memories they laughed about as they recalled them. And then, in a moment of weakness, they fucked.

Now she's coming back here, Quique told Tracy. Now she's going to have my baby, and, I don't know. I think I need to raise this baby and marry Luci.

Tracy didn't say anything back to him. She only sat there. Thinking. Not even looking at him. Looking at the ground, at the tree, at the sky. Anywhere else. When she finished crying, she left. Quique said he considered stopping her, end the relationship a little differently. But in the end, it was done. Could've been worse, he said. Could've been way worse. Could've punched me in the face.

He called the moment he broke up with Tracy—not the moment he conceived a child with someone else—the day a man's life changes because if nothing would've happened with the other woman, if she wouldn't have gotten knocked up and shit, then a man can have the life he always wanted and wouldn't have to tell the actual woman anything.

I took notice of the psychic distance he added to the situation and played along, adding, But that would mean the man would live the rest of his life with this secret. Knowing that every time he looked at Tracy, he would be reminded of his infidelity. That shit's tough to deal with, especially with time.

If Tracy never knows, he said, then I pretend it never happened. No changing anything now, though. It is what it is. Now I'm a month or two away from being a father. Luci came down from Oklahoma, has a job selling car insurance at an agency no one's heard of, and I got myself a night job cooking at Pizza Hut. Rick works there with me, too. He delivers the pizzas and is the one that put in a good word for me.

And that's how my life got fucked, he said. Well. That's lunch.

If there's one thing you have to understand about this hell hole, Quique said during my training, it's that you want to make life as easy as possible for the salesmen up front. Even the store is set up to fit their needs by looking at where the parts are stocked. In the front, the air condition, we have the parts that sell the most—spark plugs, oil filters, air filters, fuel filters, fuses, wiper blades. Hell, even air fresheners and cell phone accessories. This is so they don't have to come to the back so much, where it's fucking hot. So fucking hot that I bet you people in hell buy their heater cores here. The conspiracy continues back here, too. First floor, we have gaskets, alternators, starters, brake pads, computers, switches, rotors, and stuff. Second floor, we have CV shafts, rack and pinion, gas tanks. In other words, the less we sell them, the further they are from the people in the front.

Farther, I said.

Yeah, that's what I said, he continued. Guys up front get everything handed to them. They make the most commission because they actually sell parts. They get to stock the parts that go in the front while there are no customers because the people upstairs don't want us, rear inventory specialists, to get used to the air condition over there. And the salesmen even fucking complain about having to do *that*, the lazy bastards. So. Anyways. Best way to learn where everything goes is to make it up as you go along. I'll give you a quick run-through of the place, and we'll start stocking the merchandise. If you're wondering where something goes, let me know. Most people I've worked with get the hang of everything by the third day or so. There'll be some days when we'll get weird parts you've never seen before because we rarely sell them. Guess where those go.

Quique started by showing me the front because it would be the quickest. There was no need for him to show me that area, but he did to feel the cool air for a bit. Or to feel like he worked that area. High fluorescent lights lit up the front counter in the areas that the natural light seeping through the thick glass door and windows with cling displays couldn't reach. The difference in temperature and cleanliness between the front and back at the store might as well have included a sign that read *Coloreds Only* on the doors leading to the warehouse in the back where I'd be working. The front area even smelled cleaner—which was a necessity considering that's where the customers were—but also in the sense that you actually smell. You couldn't breathe in the back without sucking in some of the dust stuck to the cardboard boxes filtering the scent of your own sweat. Even the old computers in the front counter with software that looked like it hadn't been updated since the 70s still smelled as if they had barely been unboxed. The salesmen at the counter stared at me as if I were the new guy in prison. Not sexually, as I later came to find how they were up to their heads in homophobia. They were much more comfortable feminizing other men, giving them female characteristics through joking, to make themselves appear more manly. They didn't look at me like new prey, either. But more with a sense of curiosity. Who's this new guy? What will we talk about? What's his deal? What's a good nickname? Since it was still around the end of lunch hour, there were only three workers waiting for customers to appear.

A short fat man with the name Larry embroidered in cursive under his *Assistant Manager* patch wore thick glasses that rested on some of the pre-popped pimples that permeated on his face. In the few minutes Quique showed me around, Larry raised his jeans five or six times to keep them from falling off.

A tall guy named Bill, who, Quique said, was a halfie (half Mexican, half White) could hook me up with any movie I wanted on DVD for

$2. Got me *Anger Management* last week, Quique said. When it wasn't Bill's movies, we could find them at any flea market—Alton, Alamo, Palmview, take your pick. The movie would premiere on a Friday morning, and that weekend, we could buy the DVD from a Mexican man who barely knew how to work a printer to display a cover the studio would never use for the movie. It wasn't the best quality of film. Sometimes the audio didn't sync with the lip movement, and other times, you could see the shadow of someone in the theater walking over to take a piss. But to everybody, it was the same as watching the real thing and quality didn't matter.

Back there behind the counter, Quique said, is the manager's office, which you already know 'cause he's your brother and all.

We prodded through the set of double doors and descended into the warehouse again, Quique repeating some of the same parts he had already mentioned. There's a lounge, he said, on the second-and-a-half floor. Not really a third floor. No one uses it because when they do store food in the fridge there, it always disappears. So we eat in our cars or in the departments where we work, keeping to ourselves because if anyone sees us eating, they'll either ask for some and guilt us into sharing or end up snatching it as we're eating. It's not that we work with jerks or anything. It's just that they're assholes.

We passed a set of steel stairs with chipping mustard-colored paint, passing through a row of alternators and then another shelf of bushings and ball joints in blue and yellow boxes that never seemed to fully close and a second set of stairs before stopping by an office stationed halfway between the front of the store and the loading dock.

This is the hub area, Quique said, which pretty much delivers parts to other branches so their customers don't have to drive all the way here. V-Lo runs the hub, but not for long. He's dying to make more money and move up to the commercial department, which sells parts at special discount prices and delivers them to mechanics around the area.

Quique mentioned that most of the drivers in the hub kept to themselves, which seemed to be the case for the most part. They didn't look too bright. Reminded me of old cartoons from the 60s where robotic people would punch in at work, act dead all day, and then punch out.

Dago drove the McAllen and Mission route because it was the shortest so it didn't require too much thinking. He had a habit of walking up to people, limping with his left leg, and grabbing their shoulders instead of using his words. He didn't use them with Quique and me. He placed his hands on our shoulders, waiting for us to finish what we're doing and address him. When Quique stopped talking, Dago said to me, So you're the brother's boss? Strangely enough, it sounded right. I didn't correct him. Didn't answer him either. It was probably something people shouldn't know about. But then Quique said, Hell, yeah, motherfucker. So you better behave, bitch, or else it's your ass. Out in the grass.

Mario did not say much because he did not give a shit as far as I could tell. Quique said he had been doing the same routine since way before the warehouse was even purchased by the company, back when it was still a mom-and-pop auto parts shop, and that routine was drive the Pharr and Edinburg route. Same damn shit for fifteen years. There are some moments, Quique whispered, where I notice Mario does everything the same way. For example, the way he retrieves a part for his route. He walks up to the printer as the ticket's coming out, rips it off, holds it up to his face with one hand and adjusts his old glasses with the other, and at that point, if it's not for his route, he places it in the box next to the printer. Even if that route's scheduled to leave in the next two minutes and its being on time depends on Mario's help. If it's a part for his route, he sighs, places one hand (the one he's not holding the ticket with) in his pocket, and then takes it back out of the pocket to go out of the hub office to get the part. Waiting around, hoping to die.

When I saw him do this, he did it exactly as Quique described. You want to know what's the saddest part about him, Quique said after Mario left the room.

You mean there's more?

The saddest part about him is that every so often the minimum wage goes up, which means that what you're getting right now, he was probably making last year. Back when he had fourteen years working here. Isn't that funny shit?

There are a couple of other guys that work here, Quique continued, that you won't see as often because they drive the longer routes. Ray goes all the way to Raymondville and Brownsville in the mornings, and then all the way to Rio Grande City and Roma in the afternoons. Then there's Rick, the one I work with at Pizza Hut. He goes to Donna, Weslaco, Mercedes, and Elsa. He's cool. But fat.

Way over here in the back of the warehouse is the distribution center. Or DC. Like DC Comics. You like comics? Now, we may wear the same uniforms, DC and us, but we're separate companies. They basically use our company as a front to distribute big buckets of oil, paint, batteries to the stores around this region. That way the hub doesn't have to carry a bunch of boxes of oil on every route. That would take forever. So, we have Güero who's blond, Red who's red, Homer's Brown, and John is really brown. His real name is Juan, of course, but we all call him John because a couple of years ago, the little bitch cried during 9/11.

How does that make him John?

The fucker was born in Matamoros. Thinks he's fucking American. Anyways, Homer got a write-up the other day because Red caught him pissing in the back of DC by the batteries. Guess he didn't want to walk all the way to the restrooms. Which are by the front area, of course.

Then there's Elias, who runs the show here in DC. But we all call him Plato. As you can tell, almost everyone here has a nickname. It's part of the whole cultural thing we have going on here. If you don't want one, all you have to do is try to be like Mario. As boring as you possibly can be. That's why he doesn't have a nickname. Maybe I should start calling him Mother Teresa.

Why Mother Teresa?

Because she's boring.

The commercial office shared a plastic window with the distribution center and it was home to a sad collection of men that worked with the lights off. An old man who, Quique mentioned, was one of the original investors of the mom-and-pop shop before the company bought it punched away at a keyboard with only his index fingers. He actually had thirty years working with the company when you added it up but didn't complain because he made a lot of commission by selling parts in bulk to Mexican companies in Reynosa. Sometimes up to five hundred rotors at a time. We were supposed to call him San Peter.

Because he's boring? I asked Quique.

No, he said. Because he's old. Check out this faggot right here, he said and pointed to a younger employee walking out of the office with a couple of invoices. We call him Pansy because he has long hair. Like a girl. Hey. Pansy.

What do you want, fag?

Come on, Quique said. Just 'cause I let you suck on my dick, don't make me a fag.

Fuck you, Pansy said.

Yeah, keep walking, Pansy. Shaking that sweet ass. We fuck around like that. And this right here. This entire huge room with that piece of shit metal box for recycling oil in the corner. This is the area you already know as the loading dock.

He paused for a moment and then pointed at an old pickup backing into the loading dock filled with oiled up, used parts. Check this shit out, Quique said. A man exited out of the driver's door and walked around to open the passenger door for an older man who was completely blind. The blind man, Quique said, is a mechanic from Reynosa who can tell what's wrong with a car better than any computer can. All the other person has to do is turn it on and let it run for a while, or try to turn it on. Blind man tells him what's wrong and tells his employees how to fix it. Funny thing is he was born blind. He comes by every other week or so to dump these old parts so we can send them back to Houston and get them refurbished. So you know what this means, right? Means *we're* getting a pretty nice commission next paycheck.

How does that work? I asked.

You know what, he said. I have no fucking clue.

I flashed back to senior year in high school. We were reading *Spoon River Anthology* and working on analyzing each poem, when the girl sitting next to me started singing a loose interpretation of Train's "Drops of Jupiter" and probably only getting the "nah-nah-nah" lyrics right. The teacher overheard her singing and said, "You know that song is an extended metaphor."

"For what?" I said.

"I really don't know."

Quique walked me back to the front to let my brother know I was good to go. His official training, Quique said, is officially done.

Did you show him the ropes? my brother asked.

Sure did, Quique said, winking at me. Well. We should be getting back to work now. Those parts aren't going to stock themselves, right? He laughed, tapping me on the shoulder blade, and we left the office. Before heading through the double doors, Quique stopped me as another salesman, a short man with a crew cut and thick mustache was clocking in. You see that guy over there, Quique said, pointing directly at our coworker. You see him?

He's twenty feet away, yes.

That guy over there. A few months ago, he killed a little girl.

PART THREE

The Part About the Pineapple

Near the boiler in the bathroom at work, hidden in the labyrinth of graffiti, by the *gays*, the *queers*, the *faggots*, and the *pussies*, past the *Pete sucks cock* and right below it in different handwriting *Maybe that's why they call him Pete the cocksucker*, someone had written *PIÑA IS A MURDURER*. Piña—as it was stitched on his uniform, otherwise Oscar to his closest friends—had no memory of killing a seven-year-old girl with his Dodge Ram. Quique told me this while we stocked a couple hundred Borg Warner switches together. Said, You know how they say don't drink and drive?

He looked around. Probably to make sure no one was hearing him gossip. I decided against telling him anything. Doing so would only cause him to get sidetracked and prolong the story. Well, he continued, drinking and driving in Reynosa, Mexico . . . He nodded as if everyone knew the rest of the phrase he most likely made up on the spot.

All it took was a few exchanged words with my coworkers to notice how even though half of them lived in Mexico, they had such a media-spoon-fed view of it. V-Lo, who drove all the way from Rio Bravo the days he wouldn't split the night's hotel rate with a woman who wasn't his wife, said Mexico was the place tourists visited to get robbed and killed. That gangsters would wait for them in a dark alley while they walked by to grab them and stab them millions of times in the stomach.

Amateurs, I said. Don't they know all the cool white guys are doing school shootings now?

It's all about the drugs, someone else said.

Great *putas*, no prison, said another.

You can't walk the streets there.

Too dangerous.

Donkey show.

It kills you, you know, Piña said about it. He played with the keys at his station behind the red front counter. One of the *F* keys on top caused the old computers to make a heart-monitor-like beeping tone good for passing the time during customer droughts. Really, he was trying to avoid charging my Diet Coke, which none of the front counter guys liked selling since, at a couple cents over a dollar, it would lower their daily cash ticket average. Every payday, the counter guy with the highest average would get a whole $25 on their paycheck as an incentive to sell more parts. Oh, your brake pads are busted? You should also buy this battery. Most of them liked to pretend they didn't want the bonus, like $25 was meaningless to someone in the auto parts retail profession. To me, that's three or four meals to buy if it wasn't strictly a clerk perk. To them, it wasn't so much that they wanted that extra pay. They only wanted the other fourteen candidates *not* to earn it. So that kept them competing. Company wins.

My coworkers also had a habit of using the phrase "you know" for almost everything they said. It's only an expression, but after a while of taking notice, I started to hear it in the literal sense. Asking myself why they thought I knew everything.

Piña continued, You know how people from Mexico come here with hopes and dreams of becoming someone important?

I just want to pay for my drink so I can go back to work, I said.

He adjusted his balls. He did this in front of anyone when he wasn't playing with his keyboard keys. Though few sights disgusted me, Piña groping his balls every two minutes was one of them. I could understand the need to scratch an itch. Piña wouldn't scratch, though. He'd grope. Like they were starting to fall to the floor and he needed to pick them back up. Like he had lungs instead of balls and if he didn't give them some air, his dick would suffocate and die.

Mexico, he said, killed my hopes and dreams.

I opened the bottle before the drink warmed up and sipped it on my way back to the warehouse.

People like Piña or V-Lo or almost any of my coworkers didn't use Mexico as the wilderness they described. But as an escape. A place to get lost at the base of a bottle of booze. To lay some cheap fuck—which, according to their code, wasn't technically cheating. Take advantage of the poor cell reception where their wives, who they'd been together with too long, couldn't call wondering what time they'd be home. Or if they hadn't been jumped on in an alley and stabbed in the stomach to death.

Piña frequented the same bar in Reynosa, one of the closest ones to the border, less than a half hour from work. He always sat on the same stool to the left side of the bar, overlooking a mirror where he could see himself drink and the girls half his age dancing behind him. You know. To keep his chances in sight. Most of the dancers were college girls from this side of the river. Something my coworkers were jealous of, or otherwise hated me for. I was a college student. Could walk into work every day with a new story to share involving college girls. They hated me more for not having stories.

Every time a girl would approach Piña's bar area to order a drink, he'd listen to the order and try to remember how much it costs; if it was within his range, he'd offer to pay for it in the hopes that she'd go to at least his truck with him, considering it would be too complicated to have to cross an international bridge to take her to his home, where his wife waited. A third girl rejected his offer the night he ran over the little girl. Every time a girl said no, he'd add one more tequila shot to his night limit. A little game he liked to play. By himself. He didn't drink the pussy drinks the girls dancing behind him carried around, sipping them out of some fucking twirly straw. He'd hide his laughter well within the noise of dissonant dance music when girls would go up to the bartender and order drinks like Scooby Snack or Dead Nazi. Sometimes, when he'd start to feel buzzed, he'd make up names and ask for drinks like Cock Fuck or Dirty Beaner. Sometimes the bartender made them. But it was mostly shots of tequila he drank. He considered beer a few times, but why drive there when you can fly for the same price. That's my metaphor. The narrator actually said, Why waste time drinking beer when you can get there with tequila in a ratio of a time?

"I thought girls liked getting free drinks," he told the bartender when the third one ran away. "You know, at least get a little turned on at the fact that I work *en el otro lado*." He modeled the company patch on his uniform like it was an Armani suit.

"Lot of girls here," the bartender said, "come with their boyfriends. They beat them up if they know they're accepting drinks from some guy. They don't like some foreigner messing with their property."

"Property?" Piña said. "No. What? *Foreigner*? I'm a Mexican like every one of you. Just because I happen to live and work in a place where they pay me better doesn't change who I am here." He pointed to the last name on his shirt and added, "I can fuck any Mexican girl I want."

"So would it be okay for one of us to sleep with your woman?" the bartender asked, looking at Piña's ring.

Piña took it off and said, "Can I pay for my drink so I can leave?"

But the bartender continued, "Piña. Can't even spell your name right. Why not spell it with two *E*'s?" His laugh started to drown in the music while Piña left the bar, not bothering to correct the bartender and say it really was his last name. The music did a worse job at hiding the bartender's laughter since Piña could still hear it when he closed his truck door. Or it was still ringing in his ears.

A loud mariachi poured out of his truck speakers from the radio station he usually used to hide the noise of his ringing phone. Or to add to the melancholy of leaving the bar drunk and empty-handed. He changed the station to something in English, a station playing Rupert Holme's "Escape" or some remix of it. He didn't particularly like the song. If he were to sing it at work, the guys would make fun of him for at least two weeks. He simply enjoyed the fact that his last name was in the song. A small pleasure most of us recognized upon finding our names in public places, like an old friend, Jesse, who liked Rick Springfield's "Jesse's Girl" because it made him think that everyone wanted his girlfriend. In reality, no one did because she was a fucking idiot he probably used to make himself look smarter by association.

Every time Piña's name came up in the chorus, he'd sing it louder like most people do when the profanity comes up in the song. He didn't know the lyrics, maybe only the first two lines of the chorus. The rest he mumbled which could be due to not knowing or being drunk. Or both. He mumbled when his truck started swerving to the right. He mumbled when it pinned a little girl against the wall of a school supplies store that had gone out of business. The girl did not survive. I heard the boss bailed Piña out of jail and out of Mexico.

All this was apparently a cliché.

To Toby from the writing group, almost everything anyone wrote was a cliché. It was his favorite word. I could never use it in regular conversation back at work. Otherwise, they'd fall into the same old routine and say something like, Why do you have to say smart words? As far as my coworkers were concerned, cliché was a collection of pebbles local ranchers used to make roads. During the workshop of my chapter, Toby must've used the word seven or eight times.

"So this Piña guy," he said, and then took a sip from his coffee thermos, "which, by the way, I don't even understand the name. I know I sound kind of spiteful, but is there supposed to be some kind of symbolism there? With a pineapple? What's up with the name, anyway? Why can't it be Peña? Though *that* would be a cliché."

Writing group usually happened at night twice a week. Coordinators would find an empty classroom in the building that housed most English department courses. We sat in light gray desks, socratic seminar style, surrounded by white boards none of us used and flyers on pin boards advertising joining the military, joining a performance art school, or adopting one of the many cats that lived and roamed the campus. When no one spoke, I'd focus on the sound of the air escaping the vents right above us, the auto parts store sweat forming a coat on my face. Sometimes there were ten of us, but we usually averaged seven.

In my forced vow of silence, while the group sliced and diced my work, I noted that I should change the names of my coworkers when and if the entire novel was finished. For a moment, I considered telling Toby and everyone else that Piña was actually his real name, but that went against the rule of having to keep your mouth shut while being critiqued. The infamous gag rule. Made sense. Some writers never shut the fuck up and get defensive over every single comment, so we never get any work done when that happens. On the other side of that spectrum, a single hive mind is created on what creative writing is supposed to look like and any attempt to make it look different unleashes the bees of protest. These are the kind of sons of bitches that would probably tell Hemingway to write longer sentences because his short sentences are too weird.

How could I make it work if I changed Piña's name? With the Piña Colada song and everything. Without having to remove the song aspect altogether or having to change his name to Slim Shady since he wasn't slim. So I waited for something constructive. But constructive never showed up.

"Then there's the whole grabbing the balls thing," Toby said. "That is *such* a cliché."

I may be guilty of mouthing cliché with him that time.

"What's the cliché?" Melissa said. One of the quietest members of the group. She adjusted her thick glasses, which didn't suit her freckled face, and tucked her red hair behind her ears. Through her writing, I noticed how she kept trying to understand the true character of the male gender. Every story she turned in every other week or so had something to do with a woman falling in and out of love with a man because, when you break it all down, she didn't understand him. Here I thought it was the other way around. I half-hoped the men in *Parts* would paint a clearer picture of what men are like here, but she'd distribute a different story to us the following week, dealing with the same damn subject. This one: a woman who made a habit of yelling at her sexually ambiguous significant other because he (or she—that wasn't clear in the draft, maybe on purpose [though in writing, nothing's an accident]) dropped his act. Wouldn't open the car door for her anymore. Wouldn't be romantic anymore. Wouldn't be a gentleman. The woman then comes to the realization that she, too, had dropped the act and stopped dressing pretty for him.

Opening car doors. My coworkers drove off and left their ladies behind to walk.

When Melissa spoke during my workshops, she defended my work. Maybe she liked me. Maybe it was the work. At the end of the night, when the people being workshopped received their work back, amidst all of the large *CRAP STORY*'s written over every single page of Toby's critique of my work, Melissa's copy stuck out. Always clear. Always neat. Like she didn't want to damage a copy of my work. Always with happy comments. She never had anything bad or constructive to say about my writing. When I would let a typo slip, she'd draw a perfect circle around it and write something like *Oops! You have a typo here, but don't worry. It happens to all of us.* It was always nice to have someone to balance out the critique with Toby so far on the opposite end.

"Just because men grab their balls," she said, "it doesn't mean it's a cliché."

"It's not a cliché because of that," Toby said. "It's a cliché because Piña is the typical Mexican-American man who's a dumb-ass archetype of lower-class Rio Grande Valley folk. Look at this guy. He runs over a little girl. Cliché. Then he comes back to work like nothing happened? What *is* that?"

"Is it a cliché?" another group member said.

"I don't get what you're saying," Melissa said.

But that was the point. Toby would say sentences almost no one in the group could possibly understand, and then we'd give him credit for being right because we were idiots for not understanding his higher intellect. He'd always win.

They kept talking about my failure to capture the true spirit of a drunk while I drifted off to think about the story. Most of the comments were of little use to me anyway. Somewhere along the middle, someone noticed the semicolon used to separate two sentences; then the entire class started discussing why they're more effective than periods sometimes. That discussion ate up fifteen minutes. For the moments the story did embody the subject of the conversation, it was fascinating to hear them psychoanalyze my coworkers while they all assumed they were fictional characters molded out of clay.

In the fluorescent-lit classroom with a window covered in pigeon shit, the blinds bent and broken in some places, I wondered how Piña could go on after doing what he did. Laughing. Singing some loud

Spanish song like "*Por tu maldito amor*" while searching for a part in the warehouse. Adjusting his nut sack. Waking up in a jail cell and being told that someone, a little kid, was dead because of you. That had to be a lot worse than sitting in a jail cell with the vivid memory of committing the act. Right? I didn't know if Piña killed the girl on purpose. Some of the guys at work thought so, though they made sure Piña didn't hear when they talked about that.

"Does the writer have anything to say?" the leader of the writing group asked. It was anti-productive, yet funny, to keep comments in the third person during a workshop, even when it was me being directly addressed. It felt too much like asking, *Does the defendant have anything to say in his defense?* If we normally got along in the second person, we'd be more prone to honesty. The leader who put the whole group together hardly had anything to say either, as if moderating the conversation was enough work for him to take on. Must be the easiest gig in the world to not have to do shit here.

I said what I always said. "Just thanks, everyone."

When the writers handed back my copies, Toby said what he always said. "No offense, man. I didn't get it this time around. It was too cliché." Sure enough, as I read the papers in bed that night, *Crap Story* was written over the first page, Piña's name trapped inside the *O*.

A paperback was always smothered inside my left pocket at work, but my ego (and superego) got in the way of taking it out when there wasn't much to do after stocking all the merchandise. Quique had said, When that happens, look like an idiot and offer your help to anyone that needs it to pass the time. It wasn't hard the first couple weeks, but then I started searching for *anything* to do, looking for parts that weren't in order, fixing them in their shelves, or putting a bunch of them out of order to stock them again. By my fourth week as an inventory specialist, I resorted to memorizing the order of parts and brands behind the front counter even though we never stocked those. My brother noticed me studying fuel filters, and he came out of his office with a box of brake pads and a receipt.

Do you know how to run a COD? he asked.

I can probably figure it out.

It's simple. Just *deliver* this to the mechanic across the street, he'll give you the *cash*, you give him the part and the bottom copy of the invoice. Cash. On. Delivery. C. O. D. Get it?

So what do I do after I give him the cash?

He didn't get the sarcasm and asked Piña to join me, saying I'd probably fuck up if I went alone.

We passed the two father and son palm trees by the store separating the customer parking lot from the employee one, crunching dried dead palms with our shoes. Every open parking spot featured collections of oil and power steering fluid stains that looked like piss and flea market Rorschach tests. We tried not to trip on the asphalt cracks that formed from the rain and lack of maintenance and always caused everything in the truck to shift when we drove in before crossing the four-lane McAllen 23rd Street, absent a middle one, to deliver the part to an old man who ran a small fruit stand connected to a small garage that served as a mechanic shop. Piña reminded me again what COD meant. "It's stamped right there on the ticket," he said. "Usually the commercial drivers who drive to the mechanic shops handle these tickets, but since this customer is right across the street, we like to make shit easier. Since it's cash on delivery, they have to give you the cash before you give them the part. They sign the receipt to cover your ass, you give them the carbon copy and the part. Then that's it."

"So risking getting killed by a car," I said, "is a lot easier than wasting money on gas?"

He stayed silent for a while before saying, "Right." I should've chosen better words. I never asked Piña—or anyone else—if the incident in Mexico was really true. You don't do that. Different coworkers passed around different versions, all of them willingly throwing themselves at the opportunity to share it.

"This guy's fruit stand," Piña said, "usually doesn't sell a lot of fruit because of the location. There's a lot of traffic congested here and a lot of auto shops and small dealerships, so all the fumes start getting into the fruit. Can't tell if a banana is going bad or if it's all the pollution. But every once in a while, this guy gives you something to take back to the guys. Bag of oranges or apples. A banana bunch. Whatever. His own way of saying thank you when he's bringing us the business."

A man in his late sixties appeared from the back of the room, wiping his oily and greasy hands with a dirty, blue shop towel, limping to his counter area which was made up of old, rotting wood sitting on top of a table. He grabbed on to the cement wall for support and started pulling cash out of some small shelves. Black spots covered the cement wall like a stray Dalmatian. "Let's see here," the man said. He pulled a pair of glasses from his front shirt pocket, the frames also covered in dark grime, and held them up to the name stitched on my uniform. "You're new. Huh. How do you pronounce that?"

"Just like the restaurant," Piña said. He slapped me on the back and added, "Ram's little brother."

"Well," the mechanic said, "I'd shake your hand if I had a clean one, so I'll spare you. Got those brake pads I ordered? Gotta get that car done today."

"That's why we're here," Piña said. The mechanic handed him the money, and he added to me, "In this case, we call the customer before taking off. We ask him what he'll be paying with so we know the amount of change we should bring with us. That way, we can avoid a double trip."

"Tell the boys I said hey," the mechanic said, "and that hopefully they enjoy this." He handed Piña a pineapple who then handed it to me.

"Cute," Piña said. "I'll be sure to send Pansy next time so you can give him a nice, big banana." They laughed together for a few seconds, while I tried to hold on to the pineapple without getting pricked.

We waited for the traffic to stop for a while before crossing the street back to work. He walked ahead of me, talking about how the mechanic had been a customer way before the auto parts store was franchised and was still called Hidalgo Auto Parts. He said, "Thank God they didn't get rid of the people when they changed the name because I don't think this old man would've continued dealing with us."

When I set foot on the final lane and Piña reached the sidewalk, one of the leaves of the pineapple pricked my arm and caused me to drop it. The fall didn't damage it. I kneeled to pick it up, looking out for an incoming car two blocks away. Plenty of time to wrap my fingers around it with care. Piña disagreed.

What the hell are you doing? he said.

I'm picking up—

Hey, come on, man, he yelled. The car's going to hit you. He ran to grab me by the arm, still giving me plenty of time to grab the pineapple by its leaves and pull it with me as he yanked me onto the sidewalk as if he were saving my life in a movie.

A whole ten seconds later, the gray Ford Focus passed by without even the slightest honk of urgency.

Are you okay? I asked him.

The car, he said, it was going to run over you.

It was way the fuck over there, man. And you almost made me drop this shit again.

A puddle of urine began to form by his shoes. He reached down to adjust his balls and more piss flowed down. Are you sure you're okay?

Yeah, he said. Tears started to form in his eyes as he kept staring at the empty road. I'll meet you inside.

Back inside the store, the cool air greeted me more so than my coworkers. One of them said, I hope the old man sent something good this time.

Well, I said, if you like *piña*, and left it on the counter. I walked into my brother's office and asked if it was possible to work in the hub and drive to deliver parts when I finished stocking.

Piña quit at the end of the day, promising my brother he'd find some other way to pay him back.

That night, I dreamt that Toby from writing group didn't have a mouth.

PART FOUR

The Part About Fidelity

I saw Rick for the first time a month after I started working—in late November or early December—when the blind mechanic showed up again to drop off junk parts and Rick jumped into the bed of the truck, placing a tremendous amount of pressure on its shocks, grabbed a long coolant hose, and swung it around in front of his crotch pretending it was his dick. It slapped against Red's ass a few times as he helped unload the parts, who didn't care and carried on while the guys watching from the loading dock pointed and laughed, some of them jealous because they didn't think of doing that with a coolant hose before Rick did. Rick laughed along with everyone else, his laughter blending with the truck's squeaking shocks as he kept jumping around. I tried to look away and continued loading the white and blue boxes of CardOne parts—still mystery boxes to me at the time—into a pushcart to stock them as Quique appeared out of the aisles with his own pushcart empty and ready to be loaded again.

Who's that goof over there?

Oh, yeah, he said, that's Rick. Some of the guys call him Rick The Dick since he's kind of fat.

Kind of, I wanted to say, coolant hose still swinging and truck still squeaking.

Don't take that the wrong way, Quique said. He likes to mess around like that, but he's a nice guy. He has three kids, and a fourth on the way, and names them all after Bible people. Jeremías, Isaías, and Some-other-ías. I don't keep track.

He started to load small switches into his cart. His favorite to stock. Everyone's favorite considering an entire hour could pass by stocking them before you had to come back to reload the cart. Oh, by the way, he said. I forgot to give you one of these. He reached into his shirt pocket for what looked like a cigar, but instead was a cigar-shaped pink bubble gum wrapped in clear plastic with the gold lettering *It's a girl.*

It's a girl, Quique said.

Congratulations. I put the gum in my pocket and went back to loading the boxes, and continued telling Quique, waving my hand in Rick's direction, So with all that shit going on here, all this messing around, how does this store handle sexual harassment situations? Do they not show us a video? I mean, it's funny. I guess. But it seems a bit—I don't know—inappropriate?

There's probably a video somewhere. I personally have never seen it in my time working here. But if I had to take a guess, we don't seem to care about that shit here. We're all guys trying to get through the day and shit. And this is how we mess around. This is who we are. Nobody has yet to speak up and complain about this, so we keep doing it. Whatever keeps the morale up, right? And it's funny. Besides, we're only men.

But what if we hired a woman?

We don't. I've been here a good while. I've seen about ten people get hired during that time and not one of them has had a pussy. Maybe your brother doesn't want to disrupt the harmony here. I bet you that if we did hire some nice piece of ass, we'd probably have like ten sexual harassment the first day alone. Bitches could probably get a whole different kind of rich working in a company like this. With dicks like us.

I rolled the cart into the CardOne aisle and started stocking those parts. Brown, one of the distribution center workers, pushed through the double doors, exiting the front area, folding a printed sheet of paper and then putting it away in his shirt pocket. As he passed by me, he reached for one of the boxes already stocked and pushed it out of the shelf and onto the floor. Probably an easy way to let some anger out. Nothing against me. The previous day, some other workers caught him pissing on one of the corners in DC. Based on Quique's description of him, a repeat offense. The wrong person caught him this time, which led to the write-up in his pocket. I wasn't around that day—a school day—to see how they all reacted, but as far as the motive for the crime, everyone assumed laziness. The restrooms were on the complete opposite side of his piss spot. In other words, too long of a walk for something that takes ten to twenty seconds. Everyone said laziness, but Quique said coprophobia. Truthfully he said, I think he's scared shitless of using the shitter. Maybe, he said, when he was a baby, Brown's mom was so poor that she used to give him his baths in the toilet. Then one day, she "accidentally" flushed it and it started sucking poor baby Brown in, almost drowning him. And ever since then, he could never use the toilet again.

A story that would've been labeled as fiction if not for finding myself waiting to use the restroom a couple days before Brown's write-up and seeing him exit without the lingering sound of a flushed toilet refilling its tank on the other side of the door. Or a running sink. A green liquid settled against the sink porcelain after he came out. I never knew if it was piss or not. Didn't risk finding out and decided against washing my hands that time, thinking it more sanitary not to.

I kept my mouth shut after he dropped the box, picked it up and went back to stocking. Quique, on the other hand, saw him and yelled out, Hey, why don't you go drop something in DC? You fucking pisser.

Fuck you, homo, Brown yelled back.

Yeah, just because I let you suck my dick, Quique said, don't mean I'm a homo.

That was always his comeback for any homosexual attack against him. He never realized how dumb he sounded saying that. The rest of the workers he used it on never caught on either, so to Quique, it sounded like a worthy comeback to be proud of. Several times, he also used "When I ask for your opinion, I'll pull my dick out of your mouth," but not as often since sometimes he'd fuck it up and end up with "I'll pull your dick out of my mouth." But the comeback's victim never noticed anyway. They could never tell the difference. They could even be called handsome and for all they knew, if it sounded like an insult or had the tone of it, it required a comeback.

You do know it does mean that, though, don't you? I finally asked

Quique as Brown disappeared. He squinted his eyes. Getting your dick sucked by Brown, I said. It means you're as much a homo as the guy doing the sucking.

That doesn't make sense, Quique said, because I wouldn't be the one putting the dick in my own mouth, which would make me gay. Know what I mean? Why are you squinting? Look. It's the same thing with two guys doing it. Only the guy taking it up the ass is the fag. Because if I walk into a dark room and I see an ass, I'm not going to stop and wonder if it belongs to a man or a woman. I'm going to fuck that ass. I'm not going to *not* fuck it, right?

But, you see, I said, that's possibly making love to a guy, which, again, makes you gay, or attracted to a male. At the very least bisexual.

That ain't making love.

Well, yeah, not necessarily, but— Do you hear what I'm saying at all, though? Maybe it's not a good idea to keep using that line.

Well, then, what would you say? He started looking more serious, though he still didn't understand the point. But he seemed angry because the actual dissection of one of his common phrases and the subject of homosexuality was making him uncomfortable. He repeated, What would you say if someone called you a gay?

I don't know, I said. I don't think anyone who adds an article before the word *gay* has a good grasp of what it even means to be gay. So I don't know. Your mom?

You see? he said. That's why you always gotta be prepared. This place will eat you alive if you don't get with the program. You need comebacks. You need to strike back at these guys. Call them fags. Compare them to bitches. Show them you have the bigger dick. Don't worry. You'll get there soon.

He returned to stocking switches as a coworker from the front counter came back to search for a part, chewing on the cigar-shaped bubble gum like it was a piece of licorice. I didn't feel too guilty after flushing mine down the toilet later that day.

For lunch, Rick ate tacos of shredded beef in guajillo sauce in panini pressed flour tortillas. He ate them slowly, savoring the meaty flavor, as Fidelia kept bringing them fresh, one after another with a smile on her freckled face. Rick arched his back forward and sat leaning into the table to avoid dirtying his work shirt, his arms protecting the plate at each side. Sometimes, part of the salsa would get stuck on his thick mustache and he'd swab it with his forefinger before putting it inside his mouth, making sure to leave no traces of food behind. "As always," he told Fidelia, "these are the best. Once the restaurant opens, these are going to sell like crazy."

She walked up to him, grabbed a piece of meat off the plate, and pulled it away from him until he kissed her before feeding it to him.

At that moment, as he pressed the fourth taco into his stomach, he asked himself if he really did love Fidelia. She was five years younger than him, and he remembered the first time he saw her, sitting on the front bench at church, curls falling slightly below her shoulders. Rick on the fifth or sixth. She sang along with the choir without even look-ing up at the overhead projector to read the lyrics. She knew all the words. And she sang like an opera singer. He loved her the first time he saw her, before meeting her. That day, despite all the negativity in the scripture reading of Isaiah 47, Rick moved up to her bench to be able to hold her hand during a prayer.

She wore the same dress then. The one she was wearing as she brought him his fifth taco. A navy blue one with black dots scattered from the U-shape above her chest to below her knees. Rick liked that length because every time she came close, he would raise it a bit to see her underwear. Cotton pink. She'd tap his hand away, though always smiling. She asked if he wanted another. "No, sit down with me al-ready." He struggled to pull out his wallet and handed her a fifty-dollar bill. "For our little restaurant fund," he said. "There's no such thing as a free lunch."

"Thanks, baby," she said and then put the bill away in her bra. "So what's new at work?"

"Not a lot," Rick said. "Same old shit, mostly." Fidelia tapped his hand away, that time harder. "Sorry. There's this new guy I'm train-ing on the route in a bit, Ram's kid brother. Quique says he's going to college, trying to be a writer or something. Sounds nice. Anyways. I've seen how he always has this little notebook with him. In his front pocket. And he's always writing in it. It's like one of those little note-pads detectives use when they're investigating a murder. I don't know what the he—'eck he writes in it all day. I'm not up to training him, to be honest. He's quiet. Hardly says anything. To be stuck with that for two hours on the road? At least it's only one route."

"What about that guy that quit? Anything else from him?"

"Well, I'm not sure. I heard it from a friend that after he quit, he told some family member that he was going to Mexico. The only reason someone goes to Mexico is—well, you know. So he drove down there, and people haven't heard from him since. Disappeared forever. Could be dead now."

He stood up to wash his plate in the sink and continued talking about work with Fidelia, short anecdotes narrated in his half-Mexi-can-half-rapper accent that obliged him to replace ask with ax all the time. Stories about Quique 'bout to have a baby girl, and Dago, the Mission/McAllen driver, getting stuck with a broken down truck at a close-by gas station in front of a Jack in the Box, or, as Rick mimicked Dago put it, "The Yumbo Yack." He told her how as soon as V-Lo took over the commercial department, he was going to run the hub. That meant he would make more bank and be closer to opening up the restaurant. "I want all our dreams to come true together," he said. "Ever since meeting that new guy at work, I want to go to college, too. Make something of myself, you know. I think I'm going to apply."

When he finished drying off the plate and placing it on the other side of the sink, he axed her if she wanted a quickie before going back to work.

On his drive back to work, he adjusted himself in his van to fit better under the steering wheel, still feeling the sex as his boxers stuck to him in several places. He started talking to himself, asking if Fidelia was the right woman for him. "How could she not be," he said, making hand gestures at the air. "She's hot, cooks good, waits on me, and for being in her late thirties, actually likes to make love. No. I can't mess shit up now. We got a great thing going on."

He entered the store about ten minutes late, but no one, not even the other workers greeting him, seemed to notice. Some of them did look on their computers and saw that it was 2:10 and wondered if Rick should've been back by 2:00, but then they could've assumed Rick didn't leave for lunch until 1:10, which would make him on time, so fuck it. He walked into the manager's office to shake his hand and say hello, not even thinking about where his fingers had been a few minutes prior to interlocking them with Ram's. So, Rick said, looks like I'm training your bro' in a bit.

Show him the ropes, the boss said.

Yes, sir. Rick paced around the manager's office a little bit more, wanting to hang out there for a while longer, to feel important, as if the work he did for the company meant a lot to him and therefore he deserved a good promotion and raise. No one else in the office said anything, so he started leaving for the hub office in the back. V-Lo roamed the halls with a pile of parts bunched together under one arm and two or three tickets trapped between his lips. Rick snatched them away, ready to get back to work, and sorted those parts out. He grabbed the cordless phone hanging from V-Lo's pocket to give him a break from it and it rang almost immediately.

Hub office, he spoke into the phone, this is Rick.

It was his wife.

Hi, baby, he said, and then waited. No, he said. I'm sorry I didn't tell you. I had little time for lunch today, and I decided to eat at a nearby cheap place. I'll be home soon.

He waited some more.

Soon, he said, I love you, Holly. He made kissing noises into the phone before hanging up.

This new guy joined the writing group. A funny-looking skinny student who always wore a tight black sweater, even on hot days, a beret, and thick John Lennon glasses that looked like they didn't have any magnification on them. He always had a camera hanging from his neck like a necklace, some small point and shoot. I guessed for the same reason I always carried around my notebook in my pocket. Because you never know when the muse is going to open her mouth and put out. Whether it's to sing sometimes or to yawn again. He called himself Jeremy. I tried to camouflage my sighs every time he started to speak.

He didn't seem like a real person to me. More like a figment of an imagination. Seemed too made up, even for all this. People sitting around in a circle talking about writing and shit. He reminded me of an elitist. Always trying to impress someone. Not girls like my coworkers did, but people in general. The kind of person who got wood when he corrected someone's grammar online. Or ejaculated when he corrected them in person. In the writing group, instead of talking about the story, he talked about the state of literature.

I expected Toby to find the cliché I planted for him in my piece. The part with Rick telling Fidelia there was no such thing as a free lunch. Rick probably didn't say anything along those lines, but it would be hilarious to start leaving candy out for Toby. But Jeremy ran with the critique before Toby had the chance to say it was crap. He held the copy of my work in one hand, its pages written on with more comments than there was actual prose from me. He gestured with the other hand while he asked, "Why the surprise at the end? Why wait until then to say that Fidelia wasn't Rick's wife?"

The moderator of the writing group, an older white man with green eyes and a greener Hawaiian shirt, fidgeted in his seat and scratched at the dry skin on the side of his nose. "The author is not allowed to speak during his critique," he said. "Please refrain from asking him questions until after the critique." That was the most he had said since I started coming here.

"Alright, alright," Jeremy said. "Splendid." He licked his fingers and flipped the page, making me cringe in my seat. The silence hovered in the air. Jeremy was testing the rest of the group with his surprise question. When he probably realized it didn't register, he continued, "You see, because I was wondering how this story would've been different if we, the readers, knew right from the start that Fidelia wasn't his wife. That he was in fact cheating on her. I think it would've created a bit more of the *right* kind of suspense? Like knowing a character has evil intentions from the beginning. Dramatic irony."

"What do you mean the 'right kind' of suspense?" Melissa asked. "I thought the surprise at the end made it suspenseful."

"Somehow," Jeremy said, "I knew you'd make that remark. See, if you were familiar with Sir Alfred Hitchcock, you would know there's a huge difference between suspense and surprise. Suspense is good. People like suspense. It keeps them reading. Surprise? I don't know. It seems kind of cheap. Maybe even makes the reader feel stupid for missing it the first time around. I mean, I despise using this as an example. So unprofessional of me, but I need to consider my audience. Look at the film *The Sixth Sense*. We get a surprise of titanic proportions at the end, and then there's a series of repeat clips from earlier in the movie that somehow should've given us clues that there was nothing to be surprised about."

"But the surprise at the end of the movie was what kept people talking about it all these years," another member said. "I know it was *my* favorite part of the movie."

"Yes," Jeremy said, "and I understand where you're coming from. Completely. But let me ask you this: did you watch it a second time? Did you watch the movie again knowing the secret that was revealed at the end? All of a sudden, you're looking for the signs. You're a more active viewer. All of a sudden, the movie seems more interesting because you, the audience, know the secret, and the characters don't. And that's suspense. Damned good suspense."

"Okay," Melissa said. "So then why not read this story twice? People read books more than once."

"It's not as simple as watching a movie again, obviously. And even if it is, keep this in mind: having our work read twice is a luxury we rarely get. I don't think even Faulkner has that luxury even though he should." He sat back and crossed his legs, allowing more silence to simmer between all of us. As if he dared us to challenge him. He looked like he felt happy with himself. If there were no witnesses, he'd probably turn slightly and cock his arm backward in a *nailed it* motion.

Though his explanation made sense to me, I wondered if he meant it, too. Sometimes, while he spoke, it sounded like he was free-writing with his mouth. Like he was hoping it would all make sense and ultimately have some kind of connection with the actual story we were talking about. My story. Which I'm sure wasn't read twice. And based on the comments received, not even once.

In my notebook, I wrote down the words *suspense, not surprise*, and then realized, to anyone looking in my direction, it could pass off as *kill Jeremy.* I wrote down other surprise endings that materialized in the moment. Rosebud. Darth Vader's reveal with a line too popular for anyone our age, in the writing group, to be surprised by. I wrote down *O. Henry*, names of stories I remembered reading by him with surprise endings. *Guy de Maupassant.* Did people call *their* surprises cheap? That was my issue with workshops. We each had a set of rules, ideals, and preconceived biases about what literature should look like. They never matched. I wanted to ask if there was a way to make surprise work. To make it do more than surprise the reader. That's what I wanted to say. But I couldn't speak.

"No one is going to say anything?" Jeremy asked. He waited some more. "I don't believe it, but okay. When it comes to this story, here, surprise is cheap for one important reason. At the beginning, we are led to think by perhaps an unreliable narrator that Fidelia and Rick are husband and wife. How they act with each other, meeting at church, the words they exchange. Typical husband and wife dialogue."

I wrote down *unreliable narrator*, which meant that if I had manipulated that story with Fidelia and Rick to make it sound like they were husband and wife, I wanted the readers in the writing group to re-question everything else they've assumed about the work.

"Then we get the phone call with the real wife at the end, with—" He flipped through the pages. "Holly. And we come to realize that Rick is not only cheating on his wife, he's creating an entire life with someone else. Someone he loves. So Rick is not the person we all think he is anymore."

I wrote down *anagnorisis*, which is when the main character of a work suddenly realizes he isn't the person he thinks he is. I wrote it down again over the same letters. And then I wrote it again, making the word darker on the small page. I liked that word. It sounded more like a diagnosis to me than a plot device.

"So there's the surprise, right? There's something else that surprise leaves us with, and that is this act of infidelity. The fact that because it is a surprise, the narrator is claiming, albeit indirectly, that infidelity is taboo, or something to be surprised about. Something so strange, that it hardly ever happens in real life. And I'm telling you, writers, that I don't think that's true."

Poetic justice. I thought of Harvey, the killer in Sebold's *Lovely Bones* falling down the slope to his death. In Jeremy's case, poetic justice would be having a horrible day and then walking into a surprise party for him. *Peripeteia,* when everything suddenly turns around completely for the protagonist. I noticed the word *suddenly* kept appearing in my notebook. Maybe that's what makes writing cheap. When events suddenly happen even though suddenly happens all the time. You suddenly hit the brakes. You suddenly realize something. Most of the time. Some of the time.

"Did anyone else notice there was a point of view shift?" Toby suddenly asked. "It's a first-person work and then it was third-person? How can the first-person narrator know what's going on in scenes he's not in?"

"On the contrary," Jeremy continued, ignoring Toby, "infidelity is something natural. Something that happens every day. So, I think, by turning it into reality from the start and not a cheap surprise, it says something completely different about this act."

"But what if it's the narrator's way of saying it is taboo?" Melissa asked. "What if he's really against the act and that's why he uses sur-prise to show how horrible an act it is?"

"You don't need surprise to say that."

Deus ex machina, or god out of the machine. An easy outcome to turn a bad situation at the end of a work into a happy one. Greek playwrights used this device when they would write themselves into a corner.

"Oh," Toby jumped in, "and, 'There's no such thing as a free lunch?' Are you fucking kidding me?"

Chekhov's gun . . .

Twin expressways flung across the afternoon as Rick and I traveled east on 83 from McAllen to Donna, passing sets of towns like Pharr, San Juan, and Alamo that all seemed to blend so much into each other, they named two high schools after this collection of towns. He talked about the store in Donna first, the people that worked there, how to get there from our store, and sometimes, he would stop talking to turn up the radio when the party station played a song he liked, usually hip hop, though he'd never sing along to it.

Do you like music?

I nodded and kept writing in my notebook.

"What do you keep writing there?" he asked.

"Directions," I lied, drawing lines underneath the written word *nonlinear* while looking out for exit ramps and turns.

Up until the moment I climbed in the white Ford Ranger numbered 4717 (so that other drivers can tell us apart when they call the company number to complain about cutting them off), my only encounters with Rick had been the coolant hose image of him on the blind mechanic's truck and, moments before leaving with him on the route, him sneaking up on Quique, bear-hugging him from the back and humping him as Quique's leg swung back and forth, trying to free himself of Rick.

What the fuck, man, Quique told him.

You know that's the way you like it, fag.

Just because you like it when I fuck you, don't mean I'm a fag.

"This is the best route from the four," Rick said, "because it's not as quick as the ones for McAllen/Mission and Pharr/Edinburg, and it's not as long as the Brownsville and Rio Grande City one. With this one, you get to see the warehouse, but not as often, and you don't feel like you're stuck in the truck forever. When I start running the hub, I'll personally make sure you get this route 'cause I know you'll like it."

For the following few minutes, before getting to Donna, he explained the entire process of dropping off parts at stores, of trying to get someone in the store to sign off on them as quickly as possible to move on with the route, and the process of picking up parts from those stores to go to other stores, usually when they didn't order from our store on time. The Donna store was newer than ours, smaller of course, and completely air conditioned. Other than that, everything else looked the same. Same parts. Same uniforms. Rick pointed Jim out near the back, who handled the store's commercial accounts and was therefore usually the one to sign off on the tickets. He continued introducing me to anyone else on the way in and out as we left the store, and then he asked me in the truck, while he wrote down the part number we picked up in Donna to take to Mercedes on the clipboard, if I noticed the girl working there.

"Sure," I said. "The one at the front counter."

"Yeah. Her. That's Becky. She's twenty-two. I heard from a friend that she had sex with half of the guys at that store. This one time, man, she even showed up at our store. This was a little before you started working there, but trust me, those who saw her definitely saw her. She wasn't wearing the uniform, but those of us familiar with this store knew it was her. So she walks upstairs, man, where our district manager's office is, and she stays there for like an hour. At least. Story goes that she got a raise the next day. Not big enough for corporate to notice, but still, I bet she got what she earned."

"She could've just been talking to him," I said. "And I don't know. Should you even be talking about that? Sounds like it's none of our business."

"Well, not really. You're like the twentieth person I tell, and everyone else knows about it already. Pretty much. Not like people do a good job at hiding secrets here. Oh, and they were definitely fucking in there. I heard it from a friend that she's had three abortions. Paid for by the employees at the Donna store."

The Weslaco store was planted off the town's busiest street between a Wendy's and a Whataburger and across the street from a pawnshop, an older building with more square footage than the Donna store. Air conditioned. Despite that, it had a bigger resemblance to our store, workers horse playing in the back while customers waited for them in the front, just as busy, not one female in sight (probably fewer dead fetuses this way), and a commercial department manager who lived to make as much commission as possible. The way he handled the phone and his customers reminded me of someone who owed someone else a lot of money, probably someone who had his family tied up somewhere and if he, Mike, didn't pay up by the deadline, the other guy would slit their throats and dump their bodies in the river. From the entire route, he got us out of there the fastest, mostly because he'd be the one selling most of the parts delivered.

Rick said he knew almost everyone in the store, from the store manager that actually weighed more than Rick, to the young stock boy everyone picked on. Said that if I ever needed anything, he knew the neighborhood and everyone in the store would be more than willing to lend a hand.

I was writing a brief description of Mike on the way to Mercedes when Rick asked me if I was a writer or something.

"Something," I said.

"So then why do they call you Writer?"

Earlier that week, Quique caught me writing on the notebook by the loading dock stairs during a break and asked me who *Roberto Bolaño* was and why was *The worst thing about writing* the fact that *you end up being friends with writers*. He had managed to read all of my small handwriting, standing behind me, his dick directly staring into the back of my head. I told him that friends can never be honest with you, no matter how hard they try to help you turn your work into a better work of art. That's why you need people who hate you to read your work, to tell you what they really think, and, if for some reason they like it, then you know you have something good. He scratched his mustache and said, Isn't there a saying that goes something like, a true friend will tell you that you have come on your face?

A frog kept trying to jump into the wall outside by the corner. Sure, I said, but only because it's noticeable, and he won't tell you the best way to clean it off. Because deep down, he'll still feel sorry for— Never mind. The metaphor's not working.

What's a metaphor?

I stood up and dusted myself off.

So, Quique said, are you some kind of writer? Because you're always writing on that little notebook of yours.

Maybe the worst kind.

Then why the hell do you waste all this time writing on that little notebook if you're not a writer?

To waste time.

Walking away from that made me want to keep talking to Quique, probably because of the subject. Because even if Quique didn't know shit about writing and the extent of his literary knowledge was made up of reading *Cliff's Notes* for *To Kill a Mockingbird* his sophomore year in high school, conversations about writing at the auto parts store were as rare as women in them. But I kept walking away, and twenty-four hours later, everyone at work started calling me Writer.

"It's a nickname," I told Rick and continued staring out the window as we passed by an old house with a large, simpering man, being quicksanded by a kiddie pool in the front yard as he doused himself with a hose resting on his hairy shoulder, legs dangling off the rim.

"Well, that sucks," Rick said. "I've always wanted to be a writer. Write books. I got all these *ideas*, man, sitting there in my head. About time traveling, and science fiction, and stuff like that."

"Like Wells?"

"Sure, only in my story— I don't know. I've always wanted to go back in time, and do things a little differently. If I went back in time right now, I'd be the smartest person in my high school class. Have you ever wanted to do that? Knowing everything you know now and be like a child prototype?"

"Prodigy?"

"Yeah, that. And in one of my stories, it's about going back in time to do this, only the time machine messes up and it takes you way back before you were born. You end up meeting your parents before they were married and hook up with your mom. Have sex with her."

"That kind of sounds like *Back to the Future*."

"What?" he said. "Wait a minute." He paused for a while, thinking and running a stop sign in the process, and then said, "No. Because in mine, I actually have sex with my mom. So it's a different story. You see, it's also about the possibility of making events in history change. Like, have you ever wished you could take modern-day guns to the Alamo . . ."

I tuned out the rest. It felt easier to look out the window and think of something else. We were on a bridge connecting Weslaco to Mercedes. I used to be afraid of bridges, crossing every Friday and Sunday to and from Mexico and looking down at the Rio Grande while waiting in line, a fear I never understood and hoped wouldn't come back after starting to drive this route. My hard breathing, remembering back, oblivious to Rick as he rambled on about how he wanted to turn a low-rider truck into his time machine, was the only thing I focused on, and then, once we came off the bridge and off the expressway, I started thinking of something else.

"So, then, you're not really a writer, Writer?"

"No," I said as he parked on the side of the Mercedes branch. "I've always thought you have to be good at it to call yourself one. Otherwise, from the moment we learn the alphabet, we're all writers. Right now, I'm a stocker."

"Yeah, right now," he said. "But soon you'll be a driver."

There was a pattern to the stores, telling the new ones apart from the old ones, starting with the walls outside of them. The newer branches had cream-colored sheet metal bolted around the building. The older branches, cemented walls painted white, cracks forming like spider webs. All the employees in the Mercedes store, which was guarded by a row of six oak trees on its north side and train tracks on its south, were chubby men—again, no women—a chubby store manager named Pepe, a chubby assistant manager named Tato, and a chubby commercial manager named Mingo, and all the fat continued to run down the counter like melting butter in a bent sauté pan. Mingo had Creedence Clearwater Revival playing off a CD player, and when I started mouthing the first verse of "Bad Moon Rising," he asked, "You *know* who CCR is?"

"Why wouldn't I?"

"Because you're pretty young to like something this old. Shouldn't you be listening to—I don't know—Kid Rock or Nickelback?"

"No one should."

We drove peacefully through 491. No expressway. No heavy traffic. Only green farmlands on either side. Straight shot to La Villa, with a curve here and there. A golf course to our right had a broken wooden bridge over a pond hosting geese. Rick took a shortcut through paved roads behind Edcouch, hidden between crop fields of tall corn and wheat that seemed endless. His silence, mostly due to hip hop and R&B seeping from the speakers by our legs, made the situation more peaceful than it would have been with taller tales of abundant abortions and time traveling trucks. The location reminded me of crossroads. The kinds bluesmen traveled on, hitchhiking from place to place and ultimately selling their souls to Satan in exchange for talent. I could probably stop there and stand in that place for the rest of my life waiting to be a published writer.

The Elsa store, white sheet metal, across the street from a Jack in the Box, employed a female assistant manager named Deedee with long black hair and a patch of gray hair growing on the top center like an uglier version of Rogue from *X-Men*. Rick said later that the store manager was never present, only when the district manager or the regional manager visited the branch. Other than that, Deedee did most of the work in the store. Exiting the store made you notice the constant hum of wires running for miles on each side of the street blending with the occasional customized Honda that makes it belt like a dirt bike for no reason.

"So this is how the route basically works," Rick said on the way back to McAllen. "You drive it the third, second-to-last, run while I'm out to lunch. That's 12:40 - 2:45, after you cover the Mission/McAllen one ending at 12:30 so *Dago* can go to lunch."

When we arrived back to our store, he parked on the side with the rest of the trucks coming from their routes and added, All there is to it. If you ever need anything, you know you can ask me, man. Don't question it. Not for a minute. You'll always have a friend here. You believe me?

Okay.

PART FIVE

The Part About Racism, Or Satanism

By the time New Year's had passed, before I finished my first year with the company, my brother managed to pull a lot of invisible strings to get much of our family working there. Hiring family was the best guarantee to keep parts from vanishing considering three people had already been fired for that. Thief One, front counter worker, waited until after hours to steal a compressor for his truck. Compressors are pretty expensive. He used the computer to pinpoint which exact compressor he needed for his truck, went to the back to retrieve it from the aisles at a time when the commercial department, distribution center, and hub were closed and uninhabited. He raised the loading dock door in the back enough to slide the part underneath it, and then closed it back up again and locked it. Had he been caught messing with the door, he would've blamed it on a cigarette. It was perfect. And he didn't even have to be seen walking out the front door with the huge part in his hand. Two hours later, he punched out for the night, drove around the store to find that his part had been taken by a goddamn thief, and he drove on as if nothing happened. When the part number showed up in the discrepancies list two or three days later, it was only a matter of my brother looking it up on the computer, seeing what kind of vehicle the part was for, and knowing which of his employees had that particular kind of vehicle. Simple. It didn't take our empty-handed Thief

One long to confess, certainly not as long as it took Thief Two, one of the hub drivers, when *he* was caught stealing.

Thief Two, otherwise lazy and hesitant to do anything for the department, suddenly began rushing around and gathering all the parts for his stores and even those for other routes, which came to a surprise to everyone since the change was as obvious as a born-again overnight Christian. He decided to start his own auto part business, and his plan for executing this was to add two random parts to each of his routes, have a friend meet him at a designated gas station on the route to give him those two parts, and eventually build up a collection big enough to sell them and make extra money. It could've worked if their first rendezvous wouldn't have been at the same gas station where a commercial driver from another branch was pumping gas.

I don't remember how the third thief was caught. Only my brother slamming his fist on his desk and deciding to start hiring family. Thief Three was in line to be store manager of a new branch opening up in the area. He used that power to walk out of the store with parts in plain sight. To anyone looking, it looked like he was carrying parts out for customers, or anything else except theft. Did it casually, like it was his job, or like it wasn't anything wrong. Rick said Thief Three was in dire straits, that he needed the money or else all these bad things were going to happen. His words. I told Rick, Who the hell isn't? But Raymond could lose his house. Like the two thieves before him, they asked him to confess and return what he owed in exchange for walking away without filing police reports. I half expected cops to be waiting for them, hiding between customer cars, and apprehending them like sexual predators. But that never happened. My brother said forcing them to quit was enough. That way they couldn't file for unemployment. They'd walk away with their dicks retracting like turtle heads. His words.

After hiring me during my first semester in unofficial college, my cousin Bern Bern's envious mother nagged until my brother hired him, too. Because everything I always had she wanted for her son. If I had a certain toy, he needed to have it. She said once that if Bern Bern were ever to lose an eye, I would have to have one of mine surgically removed. Since birth, even though he's three months older than me, he was destined to be worse at everything, like a computer that couldn't upgrade. In elementary and junior high, I'd lose out on *Street Fighter II* time for getting a *B* in Life Science. Bern Bern would have a party thrown for merely not failing. I joined the school band, so he needed to join, too. I played the trombone in the honor band. He played the trumpet with the freshmen. At least he stuck that out, though. I quit before senior year started upon realizing I wasn't going to band for the rest of my life. Had even started turning in silent recorded tapes instead of playing the music selections they wanted us to play to determine which chair we'd be. The fact that I was still first chair proved they weren't listening.

The driver thief getting fired meant more driving time for me, es-pecially after Rick became hub manager and believed more parts would end up at the right places with me on the road. It also meant I'd have a lunch hour. So, naturally, Bern Bern was hired to replace me, and his job was stock and then drive during the lunch routes. Like band, he'd most likely outlast me in a place like this.

My brother hired Ever (short for Everardo) after that—our oth-er cousin and three months younger than me—to fill the spot at the counter. Sometimes they would let him drive for the hub. Even after he earned the reputation of being able to finish two-hour routes in less than one. Ever was the youngest grandson in our family and my grand-mother's favorite. Bern Bern was as competitive with him. I stayed out of the way. With Ever, our familial competitions had more to do with physical ability since his entire side of the family played baseball. So on weekends with grandma, he'd get a cooked breakfast while I had to eat cereal because of my weight problem.

Why do you finish the routes so fast? I asked Ever once.

It's boring out there, he said, returning to stock parts until it was time to drive again.

I took my time while driving, tried to time the routes to the dot. Roll down the window when driving through the cool, rural fields. Stop for a desolate gas station taco where no regional manager would see me since it was grounds for a write-up or worse.

Flask, Ever's cousin's second husband (from Ever's more athletic side of the family, not mine), replaced Thief Three. They called him Flask because he always carried a flask with him with a relief of a naked woman, her arms stretched behind her for support. On his first day of work, Flask walked in like he knew everybody. Or like everybody should know him. Shook their hands all gangster. He even pretended to know everyone's name since they were conveniently stitched by our chest area. At first, I thought it might have been his second day since I didn't work the previous one to fake take Mexican-American Literature, Mexico's First Century as a Republic, and Existentialism and Phenomenalism. So maybe he did know everyone's names. But the name game bit him on the ass when he called a front counter employee Adam because, like some other coworkers, he preferred to have his last name, Adame, on his shirt instead of his first. No one but me seemed to notice this, anyway. Not even Adame. Flask wore the uniform shirt even though it would be another week before he received his own in the mail. He borrowed it from Ever since his name was colored over red with a marker. When he greeted me that first day, he hesitated for a moment because I refused to pull my knuckles back and do a hand dance with him. I shook his hand like a normal person, and his mustache started twitching. He hated me from the start.

Oh, he said, *familia*. We do it the right way when it's *familia*. He noticed me trying and failing to recognize him and then added, I'm your cousin's cousin's husband.

The only flaw my mom hated about me, as far as I knew, was how I got along so awfully with family. When I was eight, Mexican politics divided my family in half when one of my mom's sisters ran for town (if you want to call a ranch with a thousand souls a town) mayor against her sister's husband, Ever's dad, who lost as tensions in the family evolved. Even when he ran again, twelve years later, with his previous victor's support—and against my *dad's* side of the family—the silence lingered if someone brought up politics at a get-together. So I distanced myself from everyone and chose not to be involved. Like in our cousin competitions. I ate my cereal and shut the fuck up. Three months after Flask was hired, when I'd marry my girlfriend in secret, my brother would tell me: "You're supposed to say, 'I'm getting married,' not 'I got married.' But you were always the fucked up one in the family."

I asked Flask, What does that make us, exactly?

Shit, he said, I don't know. I don't know how you stupid Mexicans make your family rules. In Puerto Rico, it means that we're as good as brothers.

The rest of the coworkers laughed with him even though most—if not all—of them were Mexicans themselves, some of them actually *from* Mexico. We didn't share the same reaction. Mine was a slight squint that let the tension linger in the atmosphere after Flask's nonchalant placing of *stupid* and *Mexicans* side by side. But when they all made fun of each other's sexuality every day, any sense of nationalism was nowhere near the top of priorities they gave a shit about. As they dispersed one by one, Flask started showing off his tattoos, pulling up his sleeves, untucking and picking up his shirt, the words *Puerto Rico* needled in at least five different times around his body without counting the ones that read *Puerto Rican Pride* and *Proud 2 B Puerto Rican*. While most of the tattoos hid behind his clothes, I wondered how it was even possible for him to get hired with a rosary tattooed around his hands to make it seem like he was holding one when he would grasp them together. They gave me a write-up my second week for forgetting to take off my earring. Stopped wearing it completely after that day. Flask had the entire Puerto Rican country tattooed on his body—a vejigante mask spreading its horns to reveal several Puerto Rican flags, Saint John (after the capital, maybe) gazing up at rays of sunlight coming from a green sun with a purple face, which I could only guess was a Puerto Rican symbol, too.

That's right, he said, nodding as a way to take in the amazement some of the coworkers showed while observing the ink. I'm proud to be Puerto Rican.

But you also have Puerto Rican pride, right? I asked.

Yeah, he said. What about you? You proud to be Mexican?

No one had asked me that before. It never came up, even in the college classes I pretended to take, reading up on Mexican literature that depressed the hell out of me in a disturbing way because to call it depressing was an understatement. Tears blurred the black ink as I translated Arredondo's "*La sunamita*" from Spanish to English for a hopeful publication only to later find that several other Americans had taken Luisa from me already and taught her English. Carballido's short stories made me lose all hope for humanity. Rulfo, Pitol, even Carlos Fuentes, who our professor told us to skip over in the anthology because he was basically Mexico's Stephen King, made me want to slit my wrists and love literature at the same time, an effect American literature never had. Steinbeck came close. But before the opportunity to form these thoughts into spoken words, before opening up my mouth and saying something like, Based on the fictional lives I've connected with, pride is almost nothing compared to what's inside, Flask said, No, because there's really nothing for your people to be proud of.

Then, more laughter.

Of all the characteristics to hate him for, that was the one. Not the swastika tattoos around his knees or how he pretended to know everyone when he didn't, but how he had this habit of belittling Mexicans when his own wife was Mexican, an illegal one at that, which in the eyes of my fellow coworkers made her more Mexican than any of us, safely hiding in their apartment with their free electricity, which, according to Flask in one of his anecdotes desperately asking for more approval, was made possible when he drilled a hole under the meter cover and then stopped the wheel from spinning by putting a straightened paperclip through the hole every night after 5:00 to make sure the electric company wouldn't catch it. Every time he took a break, he would gather an audience wherever and tell jokes—not dirty jokes like everyone else, but non-stop anti-Mexican "humor" he probably pulled off dumbass websites. He'd wait until there were at least four or five coworkers with him—including myself, writing in my notebook off to the side—before asking them why Mexico never won the World Cup (ignoring the fact that Puerto Rico had never come close to even qualifying for it), and like any professional joke teller, he'd wait a while, expecting everyone to come up with the answer, even though if they did, he'd lose his shit for stealing his thunder away, but the guys at work weren't quick thinkers.

While the laughs were still going, he'd put his hands up and say, Okay, seriously now. Have y'all heard the one about the Mexican who went to college? After more silence, Yeah, me neither. Quique laughed especially hard at that one.

The jokes continued for the next few days, covering every type of

Mexican stereotype he could milk. Poverty, lawn work, even fucking beans. During one of my breaks, he was still at it when I finally asked, Hey, Flask, what's the difference between an onion and a Puerto Rican baby? I waited. Not because I was expecting anyone to know the difference, or for them to jump in and ask in unison, No, what is it, like we were in a fucking game show, or to leave them hanging in fucking brilliant suspense. I waited to see Flask's face turn serious, like a man playing Bingo, thinking everything's going his way until he hears someone else yell Bingo, or, more specifically, a man realizing the jokes he steals from other idiots on the Internet aren't funny after all. Either way. No one laughed when I said, I didn't cry when I cut the Puerto Rican baby.

Man, Flask said, that's racist.

Everyone else remaining in the room looked to Flask as if for approval and didn't say anything. He had a one-year-old. They exited the hub one by one until only I remained. I felt bad for telling the joke. Don't have anything against Puerto Ricans or babies. And I could've asked for the difference between a Puerto Rican and the onion and leave it at that. I considered this while his own racist jokes kept adding and adding pressure, before turning it around on him. But the more I pictured Flask and his jokes, the more the guilt ran out.

I started spending my new lunch breaks not eating and, instead, writing after finding a clipboard someone had left lying around and stealing a notepad with the company logo watermarked on it. The writing group had gone on for weeks without reading any of my work and hopefully by writing at work, in the frontline, material would flow out of me. This time, for some reason, nothing was good. I wrote in Plato's, the DC manager's, office because it was air conditioned *and* the most abandoned from all the offices. Usually only him sitting there, not working, sometimes answering the phone and putting in paint orders for the hub to take to other stores. His team did most of the heavy lifting and hated Plato for not pitching in, but they couldn't complain to anyone about it.

Outside of his poor work ethic, Plato was someone I could actually have conversations with that didn't involve me having to tell him he sounded like an idiot. He seemed to know a lot about the people we worked with, like Piña's habits of going to the same bar and trying to pick up rucas, and we talked about these topics, not because he was being a gossip freak like Rick was a gossip freak, but because, in some way, he wanted to try and understand these habits and people himself. His usual response to this was: Have you ever realized how each of us is like an auto part in this auto parts store? I mean, we have the manager, right? That's the computer, making sure all the other parts are working correctly and doing their jobs and lets them know when they're not, you know. The people in the front counter are the exterior of the car. Retail. They're the parts people see and judge the car on, the ugly ones probably being the reason the customers would ask for a Carfax. Back here, we're the internal parts. We're the alternators that make sure everything's powered up. The starters are the stockers, Shoe Guy and La Gata, because they make sure the store gets going every morning. The hub department—

I get the metaphor, I said. My brother uses it all the time. He doesn't go into as much detail, but I get it.

The commercial department was on the other side of the wall behind me, and someone kept constantly banging against the wall, making moaning noises in falsetto. I told Plato, You know, if we, in fact, are all car parts, it's probably a shitty car.

What are you writing?

The pen stopped moving and Quique entered the office, plopping into the seat by the door, sweat dripping from his forehead, which made me think he was one of the players in action in the next room. As usual, he had a bag of Lance Salted Peanuts in one hand and a Coke in the other, taking turns and mixing them both in his mouth. He said, What is up, my niggers? With the R and everything. Not expecting an answer from either of us. Just going back to eating and drinking.

Nothing, I told Plato. Well, I don't know. Nothing's working lately. Tried different approaches with what I want to write. Starting at the end and working myself back to the beginning again. Nothing's coming out. Nothing I like anyway.

So then it's writer's block?

Nah. It's not that. No such thing as writer's block. If you sit in front of a computer or, with this here, a piece of paper and a pen, and no ideas are coming to you, it's not writer's block. It's that you don't have any ideas coming to you. Or too many at once. When you have them and aren't writing, it's not writer's block. You're being a lazy fuck. It's you not wanting to give them some kind of shape. More like writer's laze. Point is, there's no such thing as block, so I don't have that.

Can't have what's not real, then.

Right. And even if it was, I wouldn't call it that.

At that point, Quique extended his left arm forward, holding the bag of peanuts, and asked if either of us wanted any, obvious he didn't understand a word. We both shook our heads.

Plato asked, So then what are all those black marks on the paper?

Nothing. For the last three days, I've had the same image trapped in my head, like a cell that's not big enough to stand up or lie down in. Every time I try to write, the same image gets in the way.

So then it's a mental block?

Maybe. But not writer's block. The image is of me, walking into a dark room, and the only light in it is coming from a candle on a desk. The light shapes the silhouette of a man, sitting on an espresso chair, flipping through the pages of a book and sighing, growing more and more exasperated as he flips back and forth through the pages. Like when you're searching for an answer you got wrong on an exam. Then I get closer and realize the person is looking at a phonebook, like he's memorizing the numbers, or looking for someone, and then I get closer, I realize it's me, looking for my own phone number.

That's a pretty fucked up image, Quique said.

And you can't get it out?

No, I said. It's starting to remind me of a story I read once. "Continuidad de los parques." You ever read it? It's about a man who submerges himself so much in a book he's reading that it starts becoming about him. So he's finishing up this novel, all cozied up in his favorite green chair in his study overlooking a park, his back to the door. In the book, a man, dagger in hand, walks into a room, ready to kill a man sitting in a green chair with a book in his hands. What it all means—what Julio Cortázar is saying—is that if I'm ever supposed to get any good at writing, I have to be willing to lose myself completely in it. Become part of the world I'm writing about. Share the same conscious with all characters. There's a point in this short story where the reader is supposed to realize that fiction and reality become one, and that the reader himself has become part of the fiction.

Julio Cortazar, Quique said. Is he *raza*?

Cortázar, I said. Well, he's from Argentina. So I guess you could say—

Nah, fuck that. When he becomes Mexican, then he'll be raza.

How does one ever *become* Mexican being dead for more than twenty years? With my lunch break nearly over and Quique wiping away a piece of nut off his Cantinflas mustache, I left without saying another word. Quique jumped to win my chair, which the airwaves from the office A/C hit directly, before the invisible man in the room could take it from him. As I meandered towards the hub office, passing by the all-too-familiar faces that had grown indistinguishable over the months—DC guys smoking cigarettes and playing Liar Dice, commercial guys moping around in their dark room, feeling the A/C, not wanting to get any work done, and then the hub, San Pedro on the CB radio, talking to some of his clients from his Mexican accounts, Rick, now running the hub, holding on to the tickets that needed sorting with his mouth, waiting for Flask to finish another Mexican joke about Mexicans not being so great at barbecues because of the beans falling through the grill, and on the other side of the room, Mario and Dago, looking on and laughing with everyone even though it was clear they had very little clue to what Flask's English spelled out. Details become more magnified when you're suffering. Flask stopped his last joke as I entered, something about Mexican baptisms. He started showing off his tattoos again, religious ones trapped in his leg flesh, raising his black shorts a bit to show a bleeding cross on his right thigh, praying hands holding another rosary on the other. On one ankle, Jesus looking on to the other ankle where Nuestra Señora de la Candelabra looked on towards her son.

—¿*Es la Virgen de Guadalupe?*—asked Dago, cheap unknown brand of cola in hand.

Fuck no, Flask said. Virgen de Guadalupe's a Mexican virgin, which I hear are hard to come by these days, am I right, *o qué?*

That was another phrase growing in popularity. *O qué.* Or what. Attached to the end of practically anything anyone said as a means to—oh, who the fuck knows? Shoe Guy used it all the time when he'd be scanning the merchandise. He'd stop for a second, wait until I'd pass by and say something like, *Mayonesa, o qué?* His code word for semen, which never had any context when he said it. At all. I'm on my way to grab a part to deliver, pass by him, and then, *Mayonesa, o qué?* Other times, he'd say it attached to someone's nickname, even if the person that nickname belongs to was nowhere near his hearing range: La Gata, *o qué?* El Puto Plato, *o qué?* Fucking why?

Why do you have to say shit like that? I asked Flask.

He turned to face me. Three minutes before getting back on the road to make some kind of point. Was that enough? I didn't waste any time. 180. Why make fun of Mexican virgins at the expense of the Virgin Mary, regardless what clothes she may be wearing. White robes. Blue robes. Or green robes.

What? he said. You religious, Writer?

165. I don't have to fucking answer that here. That has shit to do with what I'm saying.

What *are* you saying?

158. Why are you pretending to be religious with all that ink when you make comments like that? You'd think that if you really followed any of the philosophies you can learn from either person on your ankles, you'd want to try to stay away from mocking them. Just saying.

Are you saying I'm not religious, *o qué?* Think I'm not down with Mary and Jesus?

138. No. What I'm asking is why are you *pretending* to be.

But look at all these tats, man?

130. Not everyone who says, Look at all these tats, man, will get into the kingdom of heaven. Matthew, chapter seven, verse twenty-fucking-one.

Man, you can't fucking judge me. He pulled out his flask and took a sip. Two minutes. Only God can judge me, and as God as my witness . . . He turned around to face everyone else and the soliloquy continued. Toby might get a great kick out of "As God as my witness." As good a kick as he'd get from "get a great kick out of." But Flask kept going, reminding everyone how religious he was and how he read the Bible every Sunday, and that God had created him to defend His religion to the death, that if someone ever held a gun to his head and the person with his finger on the trigger told Flask to denounce God or die, that his last words would be *Fuck* and *you*.

So I put it to the test. Not the gun to the head or the making him denounce God, but how willing he was to defend the religion, to see if he'd take the bait. I asked him, So if God did create you, how do you explain evolution. One minute left.

It's not real, he said after a while. Because if evolution exists, then why are there still monkeys fucking around? I mean, if we supposedly come from monkeys, you'd think there wouldn't be monkeys anymore. Am I right, *o qué?*

50. Sure there'd be. Natural selection, man. Those of us with the dominant genes evolve, and those of you with the recessive genes stay as you are. I can tell, for instance, that you have a lot of recessive genes.

The truth was, I had no fucking idea what I was talking about. I had three minutes to get Flask to quit his shit and between whatever I had to work with and the recurring image of walking in on myself reading the phonebook, that's all I had. It wasn't like I had made my way into the science building yet, so my only understanding of Biology was whatever I picked up as a fucking freshman in high school, which, in South Texas, hardly features Darwin.

Flask ran a hand through his shaved head. He started reciting crap, too, saying something he thought would finish the useless argument once and for all: You want to know why I think evolution's all bullshit? Because when we die, we become a star in the sky, which is our own place in heaven. My mom's up there right now, in her star.

Some of the other guys smiled, appreciating the thought.

That's nice, I said, attaching the tickets on my route clipboard. Did you read that in a science book?

Time.

For the second time since he was hired, I angered Flask, made him want to punch me and not give a shit about getting fired. He wanted to hurt me. Still felt the tension while leaving through the door closest to me. It's possible that wasn't the situation. No one understood what

I meant and went about their business. I wanted the tension to be there. I didn't personally believe in some of the bullshit I was dishing. I was only wondering how well he'd defend this religion that physically needed to be a part of him, which is something anyone who makes that claim should do. Am I right? *O qué?*

At night, when Flask wasn't working at the auto parts store, he bounced at some gay club in Edinburg, the kind of bouncer that stood on a pillar at one corner of the dance floor, wearing a tight black shirt with the club logo on it to appear tougher, watching out for anyone drinking and smoking or almost-fucking, and depending on what they were doing, he'd either tell them to stop, or jump off and pick them up by the back of their shirt or blouse and toss them outside. Beyond the dance floor, in the tables set up around the club, there were no limits. Sometimes he'd even sit down with a group and take a hit with them. The club didn't bring as much money as the auto parts store did, but he felt it was some easy money, plus the benefits of luring nineteen-year-old girls with hooking them up with alcohol in exchange for hand jobs, blow jobs, and/or sex in the private restroom for staff. It's there, he told an auto parts coworker once, so why not take advantage of it, you know?

At three o'clock in the morning on the days he worked the club, he'd take a thirty-minute drive home, crawl into bed next to his wife, under the covers because the A/C would be cranked all the way down to its lowest setting since the meter wasn't running anyway. Sometimes she'd stay asleep. Sometimes she'd wake up. The day we argued about religion, she opened her eyes enough to know he wanted to talk to her. Even though he had to be at the auto parts store in four hours and still had that cute fake blonde's saliva drying off on his dick. He stared up at the ceiling, wondering if he should even sleep or not, counting the glow-in-the-dark stars the apartment's previous tenants had left super-glued to the ceiling, trying to explain evolution in his head without disproving we were created.

"You know how I told you about Rosalba's kid from work?" he asked his wife.

"Ram?"

"No. His little brother. Racist guy I was telling you about who said he hated Puerto Rican babies." He paused to scratch his balls. "I got the impression today that he's one of those people. You know. The ones that don't believe in God."

"*Satánico?*"

"Yeah. Only not really. More like the ones that don't believe in anything at all. The ones we would hear about on the radio back in Detroit, people who believe in 'science,' not religion. I think he's that. In fact, I'm pretty sure he's that. An atheist. That's what they're called, and that's what he is. Today, he asked me about how I believe we become stars when we die, that if I read it in a science book. Racist atheist motherfucker."

"His mom is going to be sad to know that," his wife said. "She's a religious person."

"How's the job search going?"

"Not good. You know what it's like for people like me to find work. And it's not laziness, before you say anything. Because I know how you like to say why there are no Mexicans in *Star Trek*."

I tried writing again the next day at work during a small break in the morning and the only words on the page were beginnings of chapters or scenes that ended up torn in eight places so there'd be no chance of uncrumpling them. They didn't seem to be coming out of me, and the same image kept playing in my head, starting to rob me of my sleep the way those images that latch onto your brain do. Intrusive, repetitive, obsessive thoughts that don't make sense, like a closed factory or the same lyric to the same song. And you try to think of something else but the images come right back.

Bern Bern entered the hub office to get a drink of water, breaking a sweat from helping Quique and Shoe Guy stock parts, and he asked me, So, you don't believe in God anymore?

His question surprised me, coming from someone who stopped attending church before I did. He stopped out of laziness; I stopped due to a mild case of skepticism.

That's what everyone is saying, he said. That you're an atheist. Hm a racist. I didn't know you didn't like black people.

On the other side of the room, Rick was on the phone with people from another store, not checking for parts, but talking about yesterday's events, only in his version, Flask needed to be held back as he started to rush after me. Rick said, Let me call you back, to answer the other line, and then to me, Writer, your brother wants to see you.

On my way to his office, Ever lifted his right arm forward, saluting me like a Nazi, before scurrying away into the aisles. For the first time since I was hired, the office door was closed, a paper of a pyramid taped to it depicting the ten most effective ways to be a good salesman, which I didn't read—nor would I use a pyramid to diagram it—and knocked on the sheet. Inside, my brother sat with the same leg crossed over the other, on the office phone with a customer while his new second assistant manager, a tall guy with thick glasses named Ozzy, counted his box before heading to the counter. The safe by his feet beeped every ten seconds or so, an electronic timer to prevent theft, and the computer on the back part of the room spat out the endless discrepancies sheet Quique would collect later. I tried to focus on those noises, the steady beeping of the safe, holder of secrets, the high robotic screeching of the printer, coins being dropped into their slots, Ozzy clearing his throat, my brother alternating between *yeses* and *noes*, letting the customer do all the talking, instead of wondering what the hell was going on or why the hell was I still looking at a phonebook in my thoughts. My brother motioned for me to close the door and sit by the new computer in the room, the one everyone seemed to be amazed by because it was the only black one, the only one that displayed color other than thin letters and numbers of green and orange, the one that wouldn't beep when you pressed the *F* keys, so in other words, a regular fucking computer. When he hung up, he pulled out his cellphone from his pocket and asked me if I had talked to Mom lately.

Not in the last three days, maybe. Why?

He flipped open his phone and dialed a single number without even glancing at it, kept his eyes fixated on me like he was showing off his precious technology. A female robotic voice came out of the speaker, alerting him of one saved message, and then air, breathing, some sniffing, like someone crying on the other side of the line, my mom's voice, begging my brother to find out why I had lost my faith, what happened to me, why was everyone saying I was racist, atheist, all of her five sisters, all of my cousins, why was I so hateful? She was cut off mid-sentence because that's all the time the voicemail gave her to—

So. Care to explain yourself on this one?

No. I don't care to. But I'm not atheist. Nor racist.

Work started to feel like a prison. Almost literally. No escape. I would know. Can't rat out fucking Flask who probably twisted everything and told his dumbass wife, who probably told Ever's family, and then it spread from there like whispering HIV. Can't rat him out because if there's one archetype you can't be prison, it's a snitch. Homosexual, you're okay. Adulterer, even better. I had wanted to continue my conversation with Flask, tell him, Fuck your God, you goddamn bori, and then immediately regret it afterwards. Chose not to. My brother waited for me to say something else, anything, even though he could probably figure all of this shit out on his own, still shaking his foot up and down, and then he said, Guess that's it, then.

Sure thing, boss.

Back in the hub office, there was no need to say anything to Flask.

I know, he said. I know, I know. I'm sorry.

But it was obvious from his tone he didn't mean shit. He rubbed his red eyes together and sat down in the nearest chair, fingers still in eyes. I readied my route to take off to Donna, Weslaco, Mercedes, and Elsa, where all their employees, thanks to Rick, had started calling me Writer, too. One of them stretching his arms forward, gesturing with his hands like he was revving a motorcycle as he called me that. When the route finished, I took the legal pad out of the clipboard from under the sheet for part transfers and decided to spend my lunch hour doing serious writing. In the hub office, Flask and Rick laughed about something, and then Flask approached the microwave and said, They say the pope said that the Virgin Mary was going to appear on microwave plates sometime soon. He took the plate out of the microwave and started examining it, bringing it up close to Rick to see if he could make anything out from it and then held it up to the fluorescent light.

What do you think, Writer? Flask asked me. You think the Virgin Mary is going to appear? He held it up to my face as if it were a mirror. Why are you being quiet? It's a simple question. I'm asking you if you think the Virgin Mary is going to appear like the pope said she would?

You can see what you want to see, I said as I stood up to leave, but I don't need a stupid microwave plate to tell me what I should believe in.

Plato was out to lunch, too, and naturally, all of his team—Güero, Red, Homer, and John—planted themselves in his office and smoked cigarettes, taking turns at preparing orders while the other three rested, having paid one of the counter guys ten bucks upfront to be on look-out and call them when Plato came back from lunch. I settled for the stairs by the loading dock, settling for the noon breeze that showed up every other minute or so. Hot as hell, but the most peaceful place in prison in that precise moment, and then I stopped when the tip of the BIC pen touched the paper.

Writer's block.

Write what you know. Write what's in your head. The recurring image, walking into the dark room, describing the cracks on the walls and floor from the room being abandoned for so long, the heat waves seeping in from the cracks, the feeling of sweat dripping down my left eyebrow and down my cheek, blowing upward to keep it from going into my eye. Describe the chair I'm sitting in, nearly broken with cobwebs collecting in the corners where the bars of wood meet the chair legs. The candle set to the side of the dilapidated desk dripping red wax all around it, collecting into a small red puddle. Kneeling down on the side of the desk to realize that I can't see myself, the one reading from the book, though it's clear he's crying. The phonebook's the only object that doesn't look like it's about to fall apart from age. It's not a phonebook at all, but a compilation of names, names of writers. Some that I've heard of. Sergio Pitol, Juan José Arreola, Emilio Carballido, Inés Arredondo, Juan Rulfo, Julio Cortázar, Mario Benedetti, Jorge Luis Borges, Elena Garro, Adolfo Bioy Cásares, Carlos Monsivais. Some that I haven't heard of. Alvaro Enrique, Pedro Juan Soto, Luisa Valenzuela, Manuel Payno, Juan Carlos Onetti, Ana Lydia Vega, Manuel Rojas. Some that are dead. Ruben Darío, Horacio Quiroga, Roberto Bolaño. Some that are alive. Amparo Dávila, José Agustín, Octavio Paz, Tomás Segovia, Gabriel García Márquez, Carlos Fuentes. Others that won't be writers yet. Mexicans, Argentines, Bolivians, Salvadorans, Colombians, Mexican-Americans, Chileans, even Puerto Ricans. Names of writers whose words I'd die before having the chance to read, powerful words

I'd miss out on, not gain wisdom from because there's not enough time for all of them. Every fucking book in the universe is out there waiting, and you can't get to all of them.

Write that I flipped the pages of the book, making all the names disappear, to find a story, handwritten, in Spanish about a writer, wrongfully accused of being *racista* and *ateo* by his own family. He stands in a desolate phone booth in a small town called McCook, maybe the only phone booth left in all of South Texas, as he flips through the pages of the business section of a phonebook, wishing to take revenge on the people who ruined his life, that woman. When he finds the number, he shoots two quarters into the slot and starts dialing the number. Two rings.

Servicio de Inmigración y Naturalización. Sí, bueno?

Write that he stays silent, an address to some apartment in Mission written on the palm of his hand. And he doesn't do it. Coward? Fear of being a rat? It'll probably sort itself out. He places the phone back in its cradle and walks away from the phone booth, disappearing into the crossroads of 490 and 2058. Then the other me closes the book and puts the lit red candle to it until it lights on fire. Then exit the room, into another darker than the one before. Can't see shit.

Then, sitting on the stairs of the loading dock at work, I ripped the page out of the notepad and then into pieces, then waited for the next breeze to take them with it.

I skipped class that night, stayed home, and wrote 7,325 words without stopping.

PART SIX

The Part About The Training Wheels

In the opinion of those who knew him well, Flaco Perales had two outstanding virtues: he had amazing familial ethics and, though somewhat confrontational, always fought for what he believed was right. To everyone in the writing group, he couldn't even live up to his first name. A large, older man, even larger than Rick from work, he always sat on the larger table. The one intended for handicapped people. He wore a leather vest, like a biker's only without any patches, with a hat to match. He actually may have been in a biker gang, but no one was paying attention. He always set up a microphone at the front of his table for his hearing aid, which either scared the members that were paranoid about government surveillance or pissed them off because it created a subtle, steady beep in the room we couldn't tune out. No one ever asked him to put it away. It would be too much like asking someone with Down syndrome to close his mouth. Like everyone else in there, he wanted to be a writer, leave a legacy behind before the heart attacked. He wanted to publish his book for many people to read, to get rich. Like his hero, J.K. Rowling.

It would be better if his hearing aid was actually a broken vocal aid so he wouldn't speak.

We started with Jeremy's story, his first submission to the writing group. A travel essay, he called it, about when he traveled to Veracruz.

He even included some of his photographs, formatted within the text like a *New York Times* article, photographs he took himself while he visited. The essay itself, littered with colorful descriptions—mostly shades of purple—of clowned and masked Mexicans dancing through the streets of Xico, to me, seemed like it was more of a reflective text than travel literature. About the narrator wondering if he's devoted enough to his religion. As Jeremy read from it (which was part of our ritual before we had to shut the fuck up for the duration of the work-shop), he had a particular way of distancing himself from his work, almost as if someone else had authored it. It reminded me of my high school creative writing class where a magniloquent pupil thought that high vocabulary was what made the story good. So he'd bust out the thesaurus after he finished one of his stories and change about 90% of the words into their fattest, largest, abdominous synonyms. When he turned one in, the teacher, to prove a point, asked him to read it out loud in class. It was a disaster, especially when he read the phrase *It was then that my dog corroborated a perpetual dissonance as he spasmed over the palisade.* "It's not about having an extensive vocabulary," the teacher said. "It's about using the right word, which is often the first one that comes to your mind." Not always the case. Most of the time it's about the word that produces the best image. Or the right word for the right audience.

Same thing happened to Jeremy as he read, that same display of perpetual dissonance. He stumbled through the words, even changed some of them as he read them, proving to everyone that all writing was a work in progress. He read it like he was bored with it, like he didn't care for it, like someone thought it would be funny to turn in a lab re-port in a fiction class. He read it like he hated it, as if Toby were asked to read *my* work to the class.

Flaco spoke first, after that familiar silence that remained every time Jeremy finished speaking. "I have to know something," he said. "Is this true? Like, did it really happen and stuff?"

Melissa answered, "Yeah. I mean, he said travel *essay* before he start-ed reading."

"So what?"

"So, an essay is something that's considered true?"

I stayed away from that conversation and continued to review my notes on Jeremy's essay, listening for an opportunity to jump in and say something.

"No, it's not," Flaco said. "Isn't an essay some term paper you type up for class?"

"That's actually a definition that has been lost," Jeremy said. "You see, before term papers were called essays, an essay was always a true piece of prose, a piece of writing from the author's personal point of view. The word essay means to attempt, and the first person to call his writing essays, Michel de Montaigne, called it his attempt to put his own thoughts down on paper. In this case, this essay is my attempt to understand something, it's autobiographical, memoiresque. You know. Personal." He whispered the last word while looking at Flaco.

Those were the first words spoken out of place by anyone in the writing group. Some of us gazed at the leader, the one who put it all together, waiting for him to say something to Jeremy, but he looked on, implying that it was okay for *Jeremy* to speak when he wasn't supposed to because we always learned something new every time he opened his mouth. Jeremy kept staring at the floor, as if he didn't want to make any more eye contact with anyone, and tried to listen to what anyone else had to say. Part of me believed he didn't care for our opinions.

"I had a hard time believing this," Flaco said. "That's why I asked if it was true, if you must know."

"Why?" I asked him. "It's clowns and a bus ride. Nothing fantastical happens in the essay. It's mostly description and reflection. What is there to make up?"

"What?" Flaco said.

"I said, 'Why make *this* up?'"

"Because maybe something like this can only pass off as truth," Flaco said. "Fiction would probably require for it to have some more action thrown in there. More fun stuff. To me, it sounded like he needed to get the fact that he didn't love God as much as he used to off his chest and made up some crazy clown story to make that happen. I mean, he says it right there at the end, right?" He picked up his copy of the essay and read out loud, worse than Jeremy, "'But I wondered if my life would be better if, um. If I dressed like a clown one week out of the year. And danced in front of a church? For Him.' You see? Right there. He capitalized the *H* in *Him*, so we know he's talking about God."

The silence lasted longer with that. Way longer than any silence Jeremy could produce. Jeremy didn't react to Flaco's words, almost like he didn't even hear them. Lucky him. To Flaco's left, Toby rolled his eyes at least twice during Flaco's critique, not from frustration, but because I think he was physically trying to move his brain into a position where it would actually be able to understand Flaco's words. To *his* right, another college student who usually stayed quiet buried his face under his arms on his desk, trying as hard as he could to hold in laughter. Flaco looked around the room, nodding like he had told a fifth grader about sex during recess. Or that Santa wasn't real.

"So *what* exactly are you saying?" I asked.

"Hah?" he said.

"I said, 'What exactly—' You know what? Never mind. What difference would it make whether it's fiction or nonfiction? That's a more important question."

"It makes a huge difference," Toby said.

"Why?"

"I think it matters to people to know whether they're reading something true or false. If they're reading something they think is true and all of a sudden they're told it never really happened, they'll feel like they were cheated. People need this confirmation. Why do you think the fucking Lifetime channel, at the end of movies, flashes *Based on a true story* post-credits? Because people care about that shit."

"You watch Lifetime?"

"I personally think it's wrong to tell people your work is true when it isn't."

"But what if you're writing something that's fiction," I said, "but then it turns out it's actually true?"

"Still wrong," Toby said. "You're lying to the reader."

"My point is," I said, "what the fuck is truth? You can't say Jeremy didn't lie here at least once. Even if it's a tiny little lie. What if there were no parents making out on the bus, ignoring the child? Even if he were to claim it's all true, we don't know that. Why should we believe him? Hell, he may even believe it to be true. We make ourselves believe something is true everyday, even if there's a part of us that knows it isn't. Even history's riddled with bullshit. How is writing it any different? We put 'quotation marks' around dialogue, claiming that this is, in fact, what this real character said? We say that the events unfolding in our work are described exactly as they happened?"

"What's your point?" Flaco said.

"My point is that you can have four different people present at the same event, and if they all went home and attempted to write what happened, you'd have four different events. All of them what each person believes to be the truth. So again, what difference does it make?"

"It's still a reflection of the writer's mind and what he believes to be true," Toby said. "So it's nonfiction."

"Burroughs was high as shit when he wrote. Was his work nonfiction?"

"So then how do we fix this true or false problem?"

"We don't. There is no problem because absolute truth does not exist. Truth is open to argument, so there's no point in calling it nonfiction. It should only be literature. The only purpose the *Fiction* stamp on the book serves is stopping idiots from going off to England to look for a magic school. Even then that's not enough for some. We leave it up to the reader to decide. That's how we fix it. Let the reader make of the work what they want. Take from it what they want. I'm sure they'll find more truth in fiction anyway."

I stopped talking and let the workshop take its course, letting people give Jeremy feedback that would actually help him with the revision process. Not make it some random conversation about literature like the ones that happened when they critiqued my work. The writers commented on the structure, on the sequence of events, and on the possibility the excess description was overshadowing the plot, to which Jeremy said plot isn't everything. As it died down, I noticed some of the Spanish words in the essay.

"I don't care much for commenting on grammar," I said, "but I thought I'd add this just in case no one else will. If you're using Spanish words in your work and you forget to include the accent when they're needed, it's technically a spelling error. Just to let you know."

"What?" Flaco said, in a different tone that time. Not from needing reassurance, but rather in disbelief. I pretended it was the former.

"I said, 'It's a spelling error when you forget to use *acentos*.'"

"Well that's fucking bullshit," he said. "If you're going to be all fancy about the way you put your pretty little accents on top of your fancy little letters, then I can assume you're a smart ass and throw your paper in the trash. Won't even bother to read the rest of it."

"*What?*" I said. "But why?"

"Because you're being a smart ass, that's why. Fucking pretty little accents."

"But you do know it's grammatically incorrect, right?" Melissa asked.

"No. Because it's in Spanish. And you're writing in English. So it doesn't matter."

I stood up and walked towards the white board, reached for the nearest marker, and wrote *Si puedo*, and right below it, *Sí puedo*, then walked back to my seat.

"What the hell does that mean?" Flaco asked.

"Figure it out."

"Well, I think that covers this workshop," our leader said. "Make sure you give your copies back to Jeremy. I won't ask him if he has anything to add since he's said enough." And then, looking at me, he said, "Whenever you're ready to read from your piece, go ahead."

If for nothing else, my brother decided to train Adrian at our store before sending her off to the smaller branch a few blocks north to get everyone used to the idea of working with a woman, sort of like training wheels. Or floaties. Not so much that she'd only be with us for two weeks while she trained, but because there was little about her to suggest she even was a woman. The manager at her destined store, a meaty woman with excessive makeup and fake blond hair, wanted Adrian to work the front counter since there weren't other options at that store. On her first day, though, she somehow kept ending up at the back with us, talking to Quique, Shoe Guy, and Bern Bern like she was one of the guys. She probably felt more at home, kind of like how restaurants keep the uglies in the back, but the auto parts store doesn't discriminate by physical attractiveness considering the uglies up front. She didn't have a uniform yet, so, forced to wear the closest outfit to it she could find in her wardrobe, she showed up in cargo shorts and a red t-shirt that read *The only job I need is the one that comes after blow*, the words passing for acceptable as they had started to fade, like she ironed them onto the shirt herself. No one ever mentioned the shirt to her, so she blended in. Same attitude, same mentality, same desires, same everything.

She pulled her hair back into a samurai-like tail, which made her forehead pop out like a martian, buff legs and arms like she did MMA after work, and her breasts, observed only for the sake of this description, almost completely absent. There was something there, barely sticking out, asking for that last bit of confirmation to know which way the arrow or cross should point, but it wouldn't take much pressure or surgery to make her look like any one of us. Fuck, Rick had bigger tits than her.

While searching for a part for delivery in the boxes of incoming merchandise, I overheard her talking to Quique and Shoe Guy about her presence there, that they weren't used to having a female around, so it kind of sucked that she'd only be there a short while.

Why am I the first one in a long time? she asked them.

Quique said, I think it has a lot to do with the kind of people that work here. You know. *Men.* We all knew Quique liked to set himself apart from everyone else, calling us men or dogs or whatever he wanted, because according to him, he was nothing like us.

Shoe Guy stopped loading parts onto the cart and approached Adrian to place his hand on her shoulder. If it bothered her, she hid it well. Shoe Guy said, Don't you worry. If anyone in here gives you any shit, tries to put the moves on you in any way, you come tell me. I'll put them in their place. Punch them in the face. And if no one else here feels like sleeping with you, I'm happy to do it.

She stepped back and freed herself from his grasp, told him he had nothing to worry about because she didn't even like guys.

Shoe Guy arched his neck. He asked, What do you mean?

I'm not interested in guys. I like girls.

She started helping him load a few parts, wanting—the why unclear—to remain a little longer in the back with us. She reminded me of my old computer teacher from high school, who was the only other lesbian I had ever met, aside from her married assistant who she'd sneak into her office, closing the blinds for privacy, while we were left with typing-speed activities. Adrian looked proud to reveal that about herself, and on the first day of work. To strangers. Something I would've personally kept from everyone if I were walking in her army boots.

Quique and Shoe Guy didn't share that sentiment, much to my surprise. Shoe Guy said after Adrian disappeared into the aisles that he always thought lesbians were supposed to be prettier, like in the porns, and Quique said, No, they just do that so that guys actually enjoy watching them. Would you watch lesbian porn if they looked like that? There's no such thing as lesbians, though. Not really. Just guys that like to have sex with each other, but not girls. I mean, it's possible for girls to *like* each other, but they pretend.

I asked, Can you elaborate on that?

What?

Explain.

Sure, Quique said. Because let's say these two guys like each other. They're attracted to each other, they want to get with each other, like all of us here do with girls. Sure, we can make the choice to be with a guy, but it wouldn't be the same because we're not attracted to that. Girls, on the other hand, are not wired the same way we are. If they are lesbians, it's usually because they hate us guys and want to live in a world where there are no guys, probably because one cheated on them when they were in high school. They're done with guys. But it's a choice they make. They *choose* to be lesbians. Guys don't choose that shit because, you know, it's in our brains and shit.

Quique returned to scanning. There's a story that gets thrown around in the aisles of brake pads and rotors, one in which he passed out drunk somewhere and someone sucked his dick, and even after being shown the pictures everyone took of them, he would still deny it. But I guess it's only faggy if it's him doing the sucking.

I asked him, And what about bisexuals, then?

It's a choice, he said. Sure, they may go both ways, but they're still attracted to only one of them. It's all in the wiring. Adrian is no exception, probably only likes girls because of the way she looks. She looks like a dude, so she automatically thinks she should like girls because that's what makes sense in her head. That's what feels right.

Because wiring?

Exactly. And probably because no real guy would want to fuck her.

Raúl "Shoe Guy" Mendoza waited until Ángel, his best friend in the world, sat inside his moving Ford Focus before telling him he had kidnapped Adrian. A mixture of tears and sweat covered his face, even with the A/C turned to its highest setting, and began to form miniature puddles around his flat nose. He wore the darkest clothing in his wardrobe, to blend with the night, and drove towards the border, a sudden stop causing a thump sound to come from the trunk.

"Is that her?" Ángel asked.

Earlier that day, Shoe Guy snuck into the manager's office and searched through the applications to find Adrian's physical address. Now the three of them traveled south on 23rd Street, passing by Dicker Road, the basis for a popular work joke since everyone wanted to dick *her.*

"¡*Puta madre!*" Shoe Guy said, slamming his fist into the steering wheel several times. He didn't sound as comical as he tended to. He snorted in some phlegm and started debating whether to spit it out the window or not, but then he swallowed it.

Ángel grimaced and asked, "You're sure she doesn't know it's you, right, Raúl?" (He didn't call him Shoe Guy like everyone else did considering he was as much a shoe guy as Shoe Guy was.)

"Yeah," Shoe Guy said. "Positive. She was facing the other way when I knocked her out. I'm sorry to get you involved in this. I didn't know what else to do. Didn't know how to stop."

"Don't worry about it. You've stuck with me through worse."

Worse what? Shoe Guy thought. Ángel managed a chain of shoe stores in the area and every time he visited a different one in the Valley, he always left the back door unlocked for Shoe Guy. They wouldn't steal a lot. Never did. Enough pairs to keep their own inventory alive. Usually they operated order by order, with a short turn-around time. They'd make it seem like an employee stole them. At the auto parts store, Shoe Guy also kept a pocket notebook, with names instead of author quotes and numbers instead of literary devices, names of people who owed him money since he'd let them pay him in payments, which allowed him to sell the shoes at retail price. Every time a coworker paid him, he'd give Ángel his take and use the rest to buy food for his family, give it to the wife to pay bills, take his son to the doctor, that type of important shit. So in his head, he wasn't doing a bad deed. All he had to do is make himself believe that. All in our wiring.

He set the cruise control to the speed limit to avoid attracting any attention, and still fast enough to avoid Ángel deciding to bail and jump out of the car. Shoe Guy pulled out a gun from under his seat and placed it on his lap, not planning to do anything with it. He took a hard breath and ran his hands around the steering wheel as if he were massaging it and then wiped the sweat from his forehead with the side of his furry arm, apologizing again to Ángel. He drove around an almost abandoned Hidalgo, Texas in circles, south, then left on Coma to turn back north, then back south again, trying to figure out what to do next. He took a turn east at one point, heading to the back farm roads the led to the arena and Pharr, only to turn around and do it all over again. Aerosmith played on the radio, a song he didn't understand, and that's the way he wanted it. He wanted noise, but he didn't want to get distracted from the plan, whatever it was. He remembered a time when he had started playing the electric guitar because he wanted to be in his son's rock band, to have something in common with him, or even use it to woo the hearts of other women, but his son told him to go fuck himself in the face before he ever had a chance to learn the A chord. But enough of that. He needed to concentrate. He opened up ideas with "What if we—?" and "What about—?" but never finished saying anything, and he kept punching the steering wheel and saying "¡*Chingada madre!*" making the car honk in steady staccato beeps.

"That's good," Ángel said. "Keep doing that so the cops can say you're crazy, too. Want me to drive?"

Shoe Guy trusted him, but said, "You're not on the insurance."

Back on the dirt roads, the radio station started turning into static and Shoe Guy turned it off, making the digitized 94.5 turn into an illuminated 3:36 AM. He would need to stop for gas if he didn't decide something soon. Ángel rubbed his eyes and asked what happened again.

"I don't know," Shoe Guy said, wondering if Ángel would even care, but he told him anyway. He told him about Quique at work and the things he said about lesbians. That girls who said they were lesbians were actually attracted to guys but chose to be with girls, that it was impossible for a woman to be attracted to another woman sexually. "And the next day at work," he said, "I wanted to know more about this. I started telling her about blow jobs, because this guy at work, some shit we all call Writer because he writes. Anyway. I overheard him talking, telling someone else that Adrian was wearing this shirt that said something about blow jobs, so I asked her if lesbians liked blow jobs since it really wasn't sex. She said no. That lesbians only went down on other girls. And then I wanted to know more about this, so I went to her house. I wanted to see if it was true."

"Then what?" Ángel asked, but Shoe Guy refused to talk about anything else as he cut through and around the Old Hidalgo Pumphouse to get to the river, convincing himself that people would let it go if he told them they wanted to do some fishing for catfish or bass since dawn's the best time for fishing anyway. Adrian would wake up eventually and think the cartel was involved in some way because of how close she was to the river, right? The car's shocks shook, making Adrian's unconscious body thump in the trunk again, while clouds of dirt glistening red from the taillights formed behind them. Shoe Guy tried to focus on the road, almost putting his chin to the steering wheel as if he were looking out for a jack rabbit or coyote or Flask's illegal wife to come running out of the woods and get in the way of the car, his left foot already on the brakes to slam the pedal just in case. He stopped the car by the river and turned off the engine, listening in for any Border Patrol that might be scouting the area, and they sat quietly for the next twenty minutes or so, and when Ángel tried to open conversations or ask questions, Shoe Guy told him to shut up and let him think. Then, after another ten minutes of silence and Shoe Guy rubbing his chin, salting his black shirt, Ángel said, "Look, why don't you let me go dump her somewhere? She won't recognize me from anywhere if she wakes up. You stay here until I get back."

Shoe Guy nodded and said okay. The smell of algae seeped in through the cracked windows, reminding Shoe Guy of fishing with his son before he started finding it too boring because they'd never catch anything and talked about nothing. He wondered if Ángel felt like an accomplice to this, if he would stick up for his friend until the end or turn him in, but then figured it was probably too late to be having those thoughts anyway, though he still asked himself what Ángel was thinking as they sat in silence a bit longer, listening to the chachalacas and the anis and the kites, asked himself if some part of Ángel had started to freak out about the entire ordeal, or if he was thinking Shoe Guy would shoot him and Adrian to make it so that nobody knew he was involved in any way, but he knew that Ángel knew he didn't have the balls to actually kill someone.

"What are you thinking of?" Shoe Guy finally asked.

"Nothing. Just that we should do this before daylight."

They heard some splashes in the river, and Shoe Guy gazed at the moon's reflection dancing in the only spot of water he could see between some tree branches, turned his body in his seat and started scouting, making sure no one was around in the area.

"Okay," he said. "But I'll do it. *Es mi bronca*. I'll clean this shit up." He grabbed the gun and pointed it at Ángel, though casually, not with violent intentions, and started using it like a baton with every syllable as he said, "You. Stay. Right. Here." He pulled the keys out and took them with him to open the trunk. Outside, he kicked at the ground, thinking it over a bit longer. Before opening the trunk, he picked up the neck of his shirt to cover his nose and mouth, and then he turned the key. A piece of metal came flying towards his face and struck him on the nose. He fell and rolled into a small ditch by the river bank while Adrian jumped out of the trunk and ran north into the woods, not even taking the time to wonder who kidnapped her. Shoe Guy stood up, raised the gun and aimed it at her back, but he never pulled the trigger. Ángel exited the car and asked what happened, and then a plastic bag from Wal-Mart flew out of the trunk, danced around them for a while until the wind pushed it off into the trees on the other side of the river.

Nothing happened at work the next day. Shoe Guy clocked in and started scanning the merchandise like any other day when it was his turn to scan, and Quique walked up to him and gave him $10 before walking away in his new white shoes—a big mistake to wear in that company because *everyone* noticed white shoes and had a habit of pointing them out for no reason at all. Shoe Guy pulled out his note-book, looked for a page with *La Gata* written on top, scratched out *$60* and wrote down *$50*.

Later that day, someone mentioned Adrian had quit.

I pulled my notebook out of my pocket and sat there without saying anything else, flipping its pages to find the first page with the least amount of writing on it. Jeremy stretched his legs forward. We half expected him to start first and tell me that my characters were starting to get too two-dimensional, that all they live and breathe is fuck-up, that there's nothing in my work to say that they have any chance in the world of being at least a little bit intelligent, or capable of making a kind-of-smart choice for once in their dumb fucking lives. Material is material, though.

Flaco spoke first. "So," he said, "tell me, little buddy. Is this nonfic-tion? Or did this really happen?"

"The author is not allowed to speak while his critique is in prog-ress," the workshop leader said. "Stick to what's on the paper for now and ask questions later."

"Also, nonfiction means it really happened," I said. "Sorry."

"What?" Flaco said.

"This piece wasn't very interesting," the workshop leader said, the first time he spoke up to offer some kind of critique. The rest of the class lit up, thinking maybe he will actually teach us now.

"What could the writer have done to make it more interesting?" someone asked.

"Well," he said. "He can make it less boring."

"Right," Melissa said. "But to make it less boring, how can the writing be revised specifically?"

"Well, it can be made more interesting."

Fucking useless.

Toby sighed, slamming my pinnacle of idiocy on his desk like it was the worst words he had ever read, like he'd wipe his ass with it if it were soft enough. Made me realize then I should've taken his wiring into consideration.

PART SEVEN

The Part About The Demotion

Borges said it first: any life is made up of a single moment, the one in which a man finds out, once and for all, who he is. Around the time my relationship with the auto parts store, in which I was the bitch, headed into the first summer, it occurred to me I didn't know shit about auto parts, what most of them did, how long each of them lasted in a car. I knew the boxes. Brands. How much they weighed in my hands and arms. I came to learn this the hard way, stranded in a busy Best Buy parking lot, waiting for my brother to call me back and resuscitate my dead truck. My best friend and roommate waited with my girlfriend inside the store. I sat alone on the truck's tailgate, swinging my legs under it, and kept pressing the side button on the phone to double-check for missed calls even though there weren't any. "Hi, this is Ram," his voicemail said, "I cannot come to the phone right now, so please leave your message and I will call you right back." Right back turned into an hour of staring at the cars, trying to break them down and take them apart and put them back together, like syntactic trees in a linguistics class, but in my head even though it was impossible to imagine all the separate parts. So reading license plates it was, pretending they were acronyms and coming up with phrases. Most of the license plates were from Mexico, Tamaulipas, Nuevo León, Coahuila, Jalisco, D.F., Veracruz. Shoppers who crossed the bridges stippled across the Rio

89

Grande Valley for the latest trends and gadgets. The plates reminded me of the passenger side of my older sister's car and the crumpled
receipts in the hole to pull the door and close it. She'd scream louder
than whatever pop song she had cranked all the way up because all
the parking spots housed cars and trucks with Mexican license plates.
She'd call them *piojos*. I stayed quiet and dug my fingers into the receipts. "What?" she'd say. "It's true. Just look at them in the stores
when there's one shirt left because they will push you out of the way
to take it from you." I'd tell her that they drove a little farther to get it,
so they deserved the shirt. "But they don't even pay taxes." I'd tell her
that's awesome.

I thought about my Mexican History class, the one that became
too boring to go to towards the end of the semester because the adjunct
ran out of material and started showing us news clippings of violence
on the other side of the border, which wasn't history yet.

The cell phone vibrated in my hand when my brother's text came
through: *Not home. On your own. Need a fuse. Get the pack of 6.* The
fuses hung from metal racks in the front of the store, a side still alien to
me, and I had no idea which ones he meant. Then another text came:
Buss Fuses. I called the only other person that came to mind, and half
an hour later, Rick showed up in his green van. A woman he introduced as his friend sat in the passenger seat. I explained the situation
and asked him for a ride.

"Of course, man," he said. "Hop in and let's go get the fuses."

Elle and our roommate said they would wait for me. Rick took the
longer route, staying off the expressway for reasons I didn't understand
or care to ask about since I appreciated what he was doing without
having to.

"So," his friend said after a while. "How do you like working at the
store?"

"It's okay, I guess." I didn't want to tell them the truth. With Rick's
gossip streak, my brother would feel betrayed for getting me the job.
He would start resenting me, even hate me and stop being my brother.
So I stuck with it, bad day by bad day, and I could've told them that,
but I also didn't want Rick feeling guilty for my misery and "okay"
seemed to sum it up in some sense of the word. Either way, he did most

of the explaining for me in the van, telling his friend, who he eventually mentioned by name (Fidelia), about my troubles with Flask, how he started making everyone believe I was someone I wasn't.

"You shouldn't worry about those things," Fidelia said, "because in this world, someone will always accuse you of being something you're not, even if they're saying something as horrible as you not believing in God. You have to remember that you shouldn't worry about what anyone else thinks, only about what God thinks, and if you have faith in Him, then you'll know in your heart that those words aren't true. When you have Jesus in your heart . . ."

The cars rushed through rush hour, people out of work, drained and blue, dying to get home, to be in the only place where all of a sudden work didn't matter anymore. A woman sang along to some song in her car at a stop light, bobbing her head side to side and tapping her fingers to the beat on the steering wheel, and when she noticed me smiling at her, not from knowing her but from being glad she was that happy, she covered her face with her left hand and looked embarrassed, the kind of embarrassment you feel as a kid when you're dancing alone in your room and then realize your parent walked in without knocking and you're a guy. The woman forced herself to turn right to get out of that situation as quickly as she could.

The next driver rubbed the back of his head, worried about something, kept reaching for his phone in his pocket, hitting a speed dial button, and then hung up almost immediately, only to try again within five seconds. He ran a red light and almost crashed.

Elle hated this about me. How I liked looking at people, reading their faces, wondering what they were thinking and who the fuck they were, and she always refused to turn around when I pointed out someone interesting drowning in some type of misery. She'd say it was rude, even though I was probably drowning, too.

"Hey," Rick shouted. "Writer. Lady's axing you a question."

"Sorry," I said. "I spaced out for a bit." We passed the restaurant that shared a name with me, which usually catered to Winter Texans, old, anglo couples from the north who made their way down here during their cold months since it hardly ever dropped below fifty degrees. Then it would be right back to the nineties the next day. License plates from Michigan, Ohio, Wisconsin, Minnesota, Iowa, Oregon, even some Canadian ones. My sister might call them dandruff. We waited in a long line for the 10ᵗʰ Street light to turn green. Fidelia repeated her question, which wasn't a question: "So Ricky tells me you're a writer."

"I'm not."

"If you're not a writer, how come people call you Writer at work?"

"Is Quique a cat? 'Cause they call him La Gata. They give a lot of people nicknames at work, names that hardly make any sense. They think it's funny. This is no different."

"So then what do you write all the time," Rick asked. "Every time I look over at you, I swear, you're either writing on a notepad or in your little notebook. Every time you're there, there you are, your pen all over the place. I'm surprised you're not writing right now."

"Notes for class," I lied. "They're things my teachers said the day before, or ideas I'll eventually write about in an essay for class, so if we're talking about that kind of writer, then, yes. I'm a writer of term papers."

They didn't look satisfied, as if they were hoping I secretly had five books on the national bestsellers list, but they didn't press on and started talking with each other instead. About Jesus. They addressed me again as we were pulling up in the parking lot of the store. "Nah," Rick said. "Not my man, Writer. I don't care what Flask said. Writer loves Jesus through and through, isn't that right, Writer?"

Right, I said.

When we returned to my truck with the fuse, I only needed one to replace one fuse in the box so the truck could start again. Shaking hands with Rick felt like shaking hands with a giant as he fully wrapped his hand around mine with a smile on his face, Fidelia smiling from inside the van.

"Of course, man," he said after thanking him. "You're my friend, right?" He kept standing there for a while, not saying anything, looking at the gravel beneath our feet and then around at the parking lot, anything except back at the van. I apologized and pulled out a $20 bill from my wallet and handed it to him. He thanked me, said he'd see me Wednesday, and then drove off. I didn't mind paying him, probably kept him away from something and he didn't have to do any of this anyway. Elle and our roommate meandered out of the store. I probably would've asked Rick to pay me, too.

Borges said it first. That any life is made up of a single moment, the one when you realize who you really are. I thought about this quote during writing group because there was nothing else to do. Didn't read all of Shane's story, which went all out up to forty single-spaced pages. Didn't have that kind of time, or the patience to search for it. The story opened with a man arguing with his wife, which then turned physical. The fight lasted ten pages, and afterwards, the male protagonist stormed out of the house and called an escort service. I stopped reading it at that point. I wanted to finish reading it for the sake of having context in writing group, but every time my eyes made contact with the words again, I started thinking about something else, as if he constructed his words like that on purpose, in a way that made the act of reading go on and on forever, like he didn't know how to stop, like a car with the brake line cut out, but more like a car with old, rusted brake pads that refused to create enough friction with the rotor to finally stop.

I didn't say this in writing group. But sometimes it felt possible to get dumber reading the first half of the text. As if the part of your brain that already knows how to do something breaks. That's what it was like reading Shane's story.

So instead of talking, I drew sketches in my notebook and let the other writers rend Shane to shreds, which they did with tremendous ease like a pack of coyotes with a fat, white jackrabbit. I read somewhere that's why dogs liked squeaky toys. Because they sounded like a rabbit getting torn apart, and that sound feels good. The people in the writing group were my subjects for sketching—badly, of course, since I was a worse doodler than a writer—starting with Shane, a fat man with curly gray hair, much too gray for his age, though in my pen sketch, it could only be black, hidden under that lame Indiana Jones hat he always wore. He wore baggy, hippy clothes with no brand in sight, which made me wonder if he made them himself, at his house, sitting under oil lamp light, and working the needle in and out of the material. He practiced Buddhism or Hinduism. Wasn't sure which. But I ended up drawing a fat Buddha over his left shoulder and four-armed woman over his right, sitting in the same position. He mentioned reading and loving *Siddhartha* once and said he always had his pocket copy with him. So whatever Herman Hesse told him to believe, Shane believed *that*. That book was his fucking Bible. He liked making fun of Catholics in his stories, mostly pedophile priests, and a poet in the group, who was actually a Catholic priest, called him out on it and told him, "Why don't you ever say anything about pagans in your work?" Other than the entire bad drawing itself, the only other object you'd probably circle in it if you were playing Spot The Difference were the glasses he was wearing. He looked like he could use some glasses.

Flaco was next, in motorcycle gear with a chain in his bruised right hand for a weapon and as if he rode out of a nuclear explosion like an obese Mel Gibson. He often wrote about motorcycle gangs and brotherhood, though grammatically incorrect, and he dressed like he was in one, too, so one could only put two and two together. He was too old to ride a bike, though. Only part of him he refused to let go of. That was why he wrote about those days. He wrote this story once about meeting with a professor, only instead of sitting directly across from him, he lay on a Chesterfield, a freudian couch, so to speak (he called it a "psychologist seat"). In the scene, they spoke of his latest story, the one that wasn't good. The scene ended with the protagonist telling the professor, "Fuck you and the bed you sleep in."

In his story, crushed by the negative criticism, the narrator spent his entire time strolling around the campus in circles, four hours of walking which he summed up in two sentences: "I spent four hours walking around the college campus. I could not believe my story was that bad." After dusk, he waited for the professor to step out of the building, and he followed him to the parking lot. Then he whipped the professor with a chain, forcing him to the ground, and even breaking some bones. After jail, made up of about four or five more sentences (one of which was "Prison life is like a bitch."), he had to go see a psychologist and sit in another psychologist seat. When we critiqued it, nobody wanted to tell him that there was too much going on for it to be a short story. We wanted to take it slow and choose our words right. We still liked our lives then.

One of the most common comments we always had for Toby was that, like Jeremy, he sacrificed too much plot for the sake of description, and though what he wrote and how he wrote it was always aesthetically pleasing (unlike Jeremy), we'd lose out on what the story and characters had to say. It wasn't Tolkien-bad where he'd spend five or six pages writing about the same tree, but it was pretty bad. Toby didn't care much for our comments, though. He felt he was above them and that his stories, aside from putting the accent in the Spanish translation for *banana* in a few places, were perfect as they were and he only wanted assurance of that. He *knew* he was a great writer. I drew Toby on top of a Mayan pyramid because he always wrote about Mexico, Guatemala, and Costa Rica, and meeting and interacting with poor people, and falling in love with a guy. After the third or fourth story like this, I felt kind of defensive about it, asking myself why this *pinche gringo* was writing about my culture, my people, even though he had nothing but great descriptions to write about them. Why didn't he ever write about other *pinche gringos*? But I envied him because I never had the opportunity to go to these places and meet these people.

Daniel joined the writing group around the same time as me, but he didn't say much. During his critiques, he'd sit in his desk, listening to everyone's comments, and then, he would sum up an entire conversation into one cohesive and solid comment, usually adding valuable information of his own. It was a habit of his that pissed me off a little because of how stupid everyone must've felt (including me) every time Daniel opened his mouth, cramming a twenty- or thirty-minute conversation into two or three sentences. And his sentences made more sense than all our fucking rambling.

His pieces were science fiction, but original, almost like he hesitated to write science fiction but couldn't let go of it because he loved it. Like being in love with someone carrying an STD and condoms don't exist. Sometimes he failed to have the same sense of self-criticism he showed when criticizing others' works. He'd run into some problems in his work during the workshop, usually waiting until the end to address them. He was the only professional in the group when it came to that. Behavior-wise, anyway, because it wasn't like any of us would ever publish shit. One of his stories was about a group of engineers working on a spaceship, which he tried to be ambiguous and make it seem like they were working on a regular airplane. He wanted to add another veil to it, to hide it further, and wanted advice on how to go about doing that.

"Maybe you can *not* mention the NASA logo on their uniforms?"

Then he'd nod slowly and move on to his next question, like it never occurred to him.

In the drawing, he sat on a swing in some desolate park. Crying and staring off into the distance at the runway from which jet planes took off. His hands around the swing chains were darker than everything else to emphasize how grounded he was. It would be great if he wrote what he really wanted to write.

In the back page of that drawing, I drew a man and a woman posing naked and Jeremy photographing them. He wore the same clothes he always wore, the tight cardigan, the fucking beret, and the camera for a necklace. He took pictures of everything, he said on three or four or five different occasions, random objects because he never knew when something in the background would inspire him when reviewing the pictures. He wrote short stories for the writing group, but he wanted to be a poet. He said he wanted to do something no one had ever done before, come up with a new form of writing. One time, or two or three times, he said he wanted to create a novel with photographs, like a graphic novel, only with pictures that aren't preplanned or directed in any way. Sort of like a modular novel of random pictures with dialogue bubbles. "Because anyone can preplan and direct pictures," he said, "but I believe it's of great importance to capture human beings at their most human. That's what I want to accomplish."

"Where do the dialogue bubbles come in then?" I asked. "Because that's not what they're really saying."

"No," he said, "but you can always tell what a person is thinking from looking at their face. That's one of the beauties of working with a different canvas. Like going to scriptwriting from fiction writing. You lose out all the internal narration and the thoughts of the character, but you develop creative ways for the actors' facial expression to convey those same thoughts."

I pressed my lips together and stared off to the side.

Melissa was the only one in the group who was unsketchable

because I couldn't figure out who she was. Everyone else made it obvious by the texts they wrote or said during workshops and casual conversations, but I didn't know shit about Melissa. She said different types of comments every meeting, always adapting them to the specific stories. She wrote mostly about trying to understand men, which reminded me of me. Always failing to understand people because people are so fucking complex.

And me, who the hell was I? But drawing my writing group reminded me of the last sketch I drew in high school: an analysis of *Frankenstein: Or, The Modern Prometheus.* We had to draw it instead of write it for our English class. Why, I don't fucking know. I ended up attempting to draw the monster, sitting in a lab, his hand pressing against his forehead, with a harsh look of regret in his eyes. A normal-looking man's body lay on the gurney with his eyes wide open, like he was waking up for the first time. When the teacher asked me to explain my analysis, I told him it would take away from the game in which he would have to analyze the drawing itself to hide the fact I didn't know what it meant at the time. It became clearer once I reflected on it a few years. I didn't know how to differentiate between the monster and the man, so I drew bolts on each side of the monster's neck. The teacher gave me a D because the real monster is not like he's portrayed in the films. That, and I'm a shitty artist.

The thing about the Borges quote, about my life being defined by the moment I realize who I really am is that every single day I am opening my eyes again and the definition is always changing. I'm not someone completely new either, not usually, but I'm not not different either. Everything that is happening one day, everything I'm saying or not saying, everything I'm thinking about or not thinking about, everything I'm remembering and not ends up determining who I'll be tomorrow because every day it's something. So if life can be defined by this single moment, I'm not even sure I'm supposed to be looking or waiting for it to come. At the auto parts store, I am lost for a whole year, a year where nothing is happening, nothing is changing in me, nothing is changing around me. Or that year is my single moment. I am turning into Mario: I am clocking in. I am doing my work without complaints, often without breaks. I am clocking out. I am going home to rest and think of nothing. Then I am doing it all over again. I am turning into the store, trapped in its heat and dust and mold, and I am not writing because there's nothing else to write and because writing feels like another chore.

I'm tired. I am sitting in silence during writing group, not knowing why I'm still showing up. Everyone else is handing out their shit, is writing, some of them getting better, the rest refusing to get better. I'm reading sometimes, but the words aren't going together anymore, like a linguist's worst nightmare where signifiers no longer match the signified. Out of place. Not creating anything. Not saying anything. And then all the little letters on thepagearestartingtoblurintoeachother to become one giant shitty word. Borges said our life is defined by that moment, but Bolaño hit it closer to the head: That's the way it is, a small sense of failure that gets stronger and we just get used to it.

I'm only remembering three memories from that year, three moments, and they are happening right before the year turns into one full year on the job. The first moment is happening when I arrive at work like all the other days, parking on the side of the building before sunrise, knocking on the front glass door with a keychain so the people drinking coffee in the boss's office can hear me and open the door, a half-assed good morning to Jesse, who usually worked day shifts. When I see him, I am thinking of another separate moment, one of me standing in a La Joya court room, pleading guilty to going 34 on a 30 a few feet after the speed limit change, and Jesse waiting to plead guilty to running a red light, and forty other people pleading guilty to petty crimes to meet some stupid cop quota while high school drama students are stabbing each other in parking lots.

I'm remembering not walking in to see my brother since I told him good morning the day before and can only assume it's a good one today again, so I am pushing through the double doors, dust raining from the steel bars that act as the ground of the second floor and the ceiling of the first. Off in the distance, by the loading dock door, a man who looks almost exactly like Rick is stepping out of the commercial office, pressing the side of his nose with his forefinger to close one nostril and shooting out snot from the other onto the cement floor. I'm wondering if Rick lost weight since the last time I saw him the day before because this man is at least 150 pounds lighter. He is looking over at me and raising one hand up to greet me, in a style similar to Babe Ruth pointing at left field, or a Nazi hailing Hitler. His work shirt is darker around the armpit area, highlighting a significant amount of sweat perspiring there. Why does he think he knows me? I'm assuming he's one of my brother's friends. In the hub office, the real Rick is leaning forward on the desk, between two computer monitors, holding the night's part orders in one hand, staring into the store's locked side door. I am greeting him with another half-assed good morning, and he is saying he has some news, his eyes dripping tears like a partially open sink faucet you don't take the time to fully turn closed. I'm thinking he's been caught in the act, that his wife has followed him to Fidelia's house, that his wife has kicked him out of his house and told him he'd never see the boys again, but all he's saying is: I'm not the hub manager anymore.

He is starting to let out his tears and is burying his head in his arms so I won't see him crying. I'm unsure of what to do. Leave or stay in the room? Stay quiet or ask him why he's not the hub manager anymore? I don't like these situations. To perceive is to suffer, right? But why take on more? I am giving up and saying, What happened, man? But he is not telling me, not saying anything, shaking his head from side to side, brushing me away with a don't-worry-about-it gesture, until he's leaving the room. The air condition is humming louder as its other two-thirds sticking out into the loading dock area are starting to get hotter. I'm finding out later from the boss that a customer complained about Rick, some mechanic's wife that stopped by the commercial department to pick up a few parts for her husband, when from across the loading dock, she saw Rick sneaking up on Quique while he loaded some parts onto a cart, bear-hugged him from behind and started humping him, holding him up in the air as Quique tried to kick himself away. Since this is a rerun that gets played every other day, I'm not having a hard time believing it happened, and therefore they're not having a hard time demoting Rick.

I'm remembering Quique quitting to work at an oil rig some time after that. He's telling me, Those kinds of jobs pay you better because of how dangerous they are, so I'm going to be making big bucks to support my family. Not this minimum wage shit they give us here.

He's saying he put in his two weeks notice but plans to leave within two days, hoping I can keep the secret and not tell my brother, and is vowing never to return to the auto parts store.

The other moment is reading one of Daniel's stories from writing group, not once or twice as I usually do, but five times. I am probably able to read it more, but it is depressing me so much. It is making me feel like shooting my heart out the way Rulfo made me want to kill myself in high school when I first read "*No oyes ladrar los perros*" and then went home to hug my dad for five minutes and said sorry a lot. The funny thing about Daniel's piece is that it's not supposed to make me feel depressed, and during its workshop, I'm not bringing it up because nobody else is bringing it up. They are talking about its morbidity, its lack of believability, because it's feeling like he wanted it to be science fiction, but it's turning out to be more psychological than anything else. I'm seeing the philosophical in it, and I'm explaining to him—alone, after the workshop—what I'm thinking he tried to tell me with it, what I'm getting from it, and he's looking confused, as if I'm the only person crazy enough to make that kind of connection, a connection he's ending up liking and then is saying, "Now I know what to tell Oprah when she asks me about that."

His story's making me want to run away, making me have strange wishes I consider irregular from my usual mode of thinking, like I'm needing a big break from everything, take whatever money I have and get the fuck out, restart my life like restoring everything in a computer as a last resort and lose all your important files after they've been crawling with pathogens, leave and start a new life, go from job to job, meet different people, no family, no friends, no school, no name. I'm wanting to erase myself completely from today's work and create a new one, which I don't have the guts to pull off because I'm not feeling alive in this one, like I'm not experiencing anything, anything worth writing about anyway. And I'm confused as to why I'm telling Larry, the assistant manager, this while he's smoking a cigarette on break at the loading dock. We never talked before. Certainly not about subjects like this. We didn't even say good morning to each other, and when I'm telling him about my crisis at 20, he's saying, Man, who do you think you're talking to? And then he's taking a few more puffs before saying, It's cool. I've been thinking the same shit since high school.

He's reaching into his shirt pocket and pulling out two cigarettes from a pack, and, handing them to me, he's adding, Light one whenever you feel you can't take life anymore. This way, at least you know you're doing something about it, even if it's little by little.

Why two?

Because you'll hate yourself the first time. But then you'll light the second.

We aren't saying anything else after that, only looking at the cardboards sticking out like dehydrated tongues out of the recycling dumpster, Daniel's story's bleeding lead in my left hand, and I'm telling myself I need to read it one more time.

PART EIGHT

The Part About The Fiction

So that night, in the reading room, Erick grabbed the butcher knife, set it down on his desk in front of Jennifer, if that was even her real name. He didn't mean to show it to her, and didn't know why he did. If anything, it was stupid of him.

She gasped at first, covered her mouth with her hand as if catching a scream. Erick thought of *Scooby Doo* cartoons and pictured Jennifer offering him her soft fist, opening it, and then emitting the scream from it. But he brushed the thought away and continued studying her as she sat across his desk, her long legs crossed, attentive, a pretty mouth with hushed moist lips stretching and barely revealing sparkly white teeth. All the qualities he wanted to see. Soft smile, not just with her mouth, but with her eyes that were the only indication of honesty in anything she said, gypsy skin tanned enough to suit his liking, long ash blond hair that fell below her shoulders like silk straps to her breasts. That much was true, he thought.

"Do you want me to do anything else for you?" she asked. Even her voice sounded perfect to him when she spoke the simplest sentences. Not too high-pitched, not too low. Like a faint Princess Leia. He heard her singing in the shower once, the door partially open, and he had to sit down on the floor outside in the hallway to listen to her sing, cold chills running up his spine and the few hairs on his arm rising until he cried for the first time since he was a child. The song was "We Will Rock You" by Queen. The first song he learned to play on his electric guitar when he was thirteen. And she wasn't even singing the right words in the verses.

There, in the reading room, she held down her index and middle fingers of her right hand and made them walk and dance on the arm of the chair before uncrossing her legs and repeating the word *anything*. To anyone else, she might sound like a slut offering herself for the pure feeling of sexual ecstasy, but Erick smiled back at her because he knew better. She loved him. She always said she loved him, and those prepossessing eyes said she loved him, too, since the first time she saw him.

"Why don't you meet me in the bedroom?" he said. "Give me about twenty minutes, okay? I just need to take care of something here."

She continued smiling and stood up, not leaving the reading room until kissing Erick on the lips after lubricating her own with her tongue, a habit he found made her kisses even better. Like she knew that's the way he liked them. As she pulled the door closed, she said, "Don't take too long."

Twenty minutes. He figured it was enough time to get up and stretch. Time to turn to face the bookshelf built into the wall behind his desk, study the spines of his hardcover collection. Books of science, astronomy, biology, physics, chemistry. Books one would expect to have to buy for a university class. Books of philosophy, Nietzsche, Voltaire, St. Thomas Aquinas, Sartre, John Dewey. Time to ask himself, "What the fuck happened?" To pull out *Art as Experience* from the shelf to reveal the collection of books standing against the bookshelf with their covers facing forward, hiding behind the science and philosophy collection. Books one would expect to want to buy while taking university classes. Books he hadn't looked at in years but had read enough times as a kid to not have to look to remember them. Science fiction books. Any kind of science fiction. The spaceship kind. The futuristic, post-apocalyptic world kind. Clones. Aliens. You name it. Twenty minutes. Time to let barely enough light sneak in between the empty space Dewey had left behind and illuminate the *FEND* and the *LIP* in the title of the book in the back, a thin book, like a playbill, Erick knew so well. *The Defenders* by Philip K. Dick.

He started removing all the other science books by their spines, letting them fall to the ground like stunned birds after striking clear windows. Some of them landing on his feet with all their weight, but most of them landing around them. When most of them were gone, the collection of science fiction books aligned across the bookshelf looked like old wallpaper, dust and stains, but, like Jennifer, a most beautiful mosaic. He wanted to bring himself to touch them, at least one, but couldn't, fearing that they would crumble in his hands and disappear like dried mud tunnels. In the center of the piece stood a coverless book, one he hadn't thought about in years, way before science fiction started being more fiction than science to him. A book given to him by his priest, a leather-bound journal with a low-relief cross on the front. He slid it out of the shelf, leaving a hole between two *Star Wars* novels from the collection he used to read through high school and first years in college. He opened his journal to a story or an essay or a diary entry—he didn't know anymore—of a teenager traveling to outer space in search of Planet Heaven, where his mother pointed to whenever he asked where Heaven was. He wanted to find it before he died, but Erick never had the chance to finish the story. If he finished it, it would end with the hero dying trying to find it.

He flipped to the last page he wrote and turned to the next blank one. Eighteen minutes, he thought. Enough time to write a little bit more because he didn't know what was going to happen. And that was his opening thought.

I don't know, he wrote, but I need to find out. I don't know if I will be in prison by the time someone else reads this, or if everything will go back to normal because she'll disappear. I don't know if I might die because her blood will melt through my flesh. I don't know any of this, but I have to know because she's my warden.

I met Jen three months ago. It was raining when I was driving back from work. I could barely see past whatever water the wiper blades managed to push out in double time. Enough to slam the brakes before hitting the woman standing in the middle of the road. She fell forward onto the hood as if the rain had started to push her down. I thought I hit her at first. Something like this has happened before. I had driven forward in the garage thinking I had set the shift to reverse and didn't feel a crash or anything. By the time I realized what I had done and actually reversed, I saw the crack on the wall and later the dent in the front bumper as if I had crushed something invisible.

I stepped out of the car, thankful there were no other cars on the back road I always took to avoid the freeways, asked her if she was okay, if she needed me to call an ambulance, and she remained quiet, sitting on the ground, looking up at me, the water rolling down her face.

"I'm okay," she said.

"We should get out of this rain," I told her, offered my hand and helped her to the car. I offered her an extra shirt I had in the backseat, told her she was wet.

"Where is this?" she asked. She wore a gray blouse and a pair of blue jeans. Her feet were nude and soft like Venus's, Cabanel's Venus, not Botticelli's.

"What do you mean?" I asked her.

"Where am I?"

"Are you sure you're okay? You're in Harlingen. Outside of it, anyway. What's your name? Do you remember anything?" She touched everything around her like a child. The door, the dashboard. The window. She followed the water drops falling down the other side with her finger like fish in an aquarium. She yanked at her seatbelt as if everything was new to her. She said she liked my naval ship. I'm sure that's what she said.

I reached for my phone, but she snatched it and begged me not to call anyone. She said she wanted to stay with me, in my home, where it was safe. Something about the way she said she didn't want to be in trouble sounded convincing to me. So I kept driving. Part of me wanted her to stay with me forever. "Well, then, do you have a name? Are you running away from home?"

"My name?" she said. "Jennifer." Even her name was perfect. Fair, smooth Jennifer.

Erick kissed her for the first time that night, and she said she loved him. He wrote that. But he didn't write that he burst with desire. He did write about how she told him everything a few weeks later about who she really was, a girl from another planet. She didn't remember how she arrived, or where she had been before her face came out of the

105

rain when Erick found her. She only remembered being found. Erick pretended to believe her. Went along with it because she was attractive and he had already started to like Jennifer. Maybe even love her. Ten years ago, he wrote, I might've believed her, or believed the possibility of it. It's what I always did. Read science fiction stories and then tell spin-offs to my friends by a campfire, adding my own details and making them seem as if they really happened, or as if they would eventually happen. Because at the time, I believed it could. And with the way the world is going and its advances, science fiction was ceasing to be a genre. But I read enough of them at one point and they started to become too trivial, like rereading the Bible over and over, looking for possibilities of false phrases or misinterpretations. After that point, it all became too fiction-like to me. But I went along with it. For a while.

"So how are you different from the girls here?" I asked her. "Do you have special powers? Or, I guess, they would just be traits to you?" I didn't expect anything real, maybe something like flying or something, wondering how much further the lie could go, but she stayed quiet for a moment, as if she were translating the question into a different language in her head.

She said she couldn't *do* anything, but where she came from, it was easy for a couple to meet and fall in love because people could take different forms. "Everyone's attracted to a certain type of image or images, right?" she said. "Well, where I'm from, we can sort of take the form of whatever the person looking at us may be attracted to. That way they always think we're beautiful."

"But what if there's more than one person looking at you?"

"Oh, it's all perception," she said. "The other person sees what he wants to see. If a male loves for his female to have red hair and blue eyes, then that's exactly what he'll see when he looks at me. If he prefers them younger, then that works, too. Same thing with a female."

"That doesn't make sense," I told her. "So in your home, if a man is walking around in public, won't he see numerous women who all look exactly the same? How can people fall in love when everyone looks the same?"

"The eyes can only be deceived to an extent," Jennifer said. "Have you ever flipped through a lingerie catalog and thought that all those women were beautiful, even if they were different women?" Of course I had. "Hair will change for us. Eyes, shape, age, color, clothes, but there's so much more to us than that."

"Clothes?"

"Sure. Different people are attracted to different styles of clothing."

Sometimes, when I'd ask her questions, I'd start to believe her. That her name was Jennifer only because it was the name closest to my soul. She's beautiful. Everything about her. I try to remember if I ever made a list of what the perfect female would look like, her features, but it's impossible. Probably would have to lie to myself to hide the fact that the potential list doesn't match with everything about Jen.

While we were dining out once, around the time her claims started making me crazy, I started thinking it was time to stop already. The place was simple. Nothing fancy. Mall food court joint. The kind of place you have to get up again to go pick up your food after ordering it, not where they bring it to you on a tray. On my way to get the food, while Jen waited, I asked a large man, scarfing burgers and crumpling the wrappers, hiding them one inside the other so it can look like he wasn't working on his third one. A man probably waiting in the food court of the mall while his wife and kids shopped.

"Excuse me," I said. The man put the burger down and kept chewing what he already had in his mouth with it open. "Sorry to bother you, sir, but can you tell me what that girl over there looks like?"

"What the fuff?" Chunks of food flew out of his mouth, landing on the table and on my pants by my knee. He swallowed hard, not choking, by some miracle, with the consistency of the food. "What the hell are you talking about?"

"It seems like a strange question, I know," I said, "but it would help me if you could tell me what you think she looks like. Hair color. Eye color. Do you think she's good-looking?"

"That chick over there?" the man said, pointing behind his large soda cup to hide his finger. "You fucking crazy, or something?"

"No," I said. "I just need to know what she looks like."

"You a cop?"

"No. I'm a science teacher."

"Right," the man said. "She's pretty hot, I guess. She with you?"

"Can you tell me about her attributes?"

"What does it matter? She's fucking hot. You need me to break that down for you?"

"Yes, actually."

The man took another bite from his burger and with his mouth full, said, "You're serious." He swallowed. "Okay. What do you want to know? She thin. A nice thin. You know. Not like me. She has pretty hair. Pretty eyes. Looks like a full set of teeth there in the way she looking at you. Tits could be a little bigger, but that's cool."

"What color is her hair?"

"Get fucked, guy. Fucking freak." He grabbed his remaining two burgers, still in their wrappers, and walked away.

That night, I mistook insanity for wanting to embrace her and undressed her under the moon, little by little.

My quest for the truth continued. Took her out to public places more often so I could get more chances. But the questions were never right and, like the fat man, most people thought there was something wrong with me. I even tried to take her out to the racetrack once and pretend I was blind, put on a pair of old sunglasses I didn't wear anymore and walked around with a cane, asking people nearby if they could help me find the girl wearing the dark brown skirt and blazer over a white blouse with black linear imprints. But the ones who wouldn't brush me aside like a homeless man looked around a bit and then apologized. One of them said, "You're here with your daughter, right?" I corrected her, but she also failed to help me find her. So they were either not seeing her, or I was the only person there attracted to the professional look in girls. So much for fucking feminism.

Eventually, the results came. I started trying more casual approaches in bars, walking up to other people after they stopped staring, when Jen wasn't looking and pretended to ask them for relationship advice. I told them my girlfriend was planning to change her hair color and asked them what would look good on her. Then, pointing at her, I asked them, "So as it is now, would you call that a red or a—" to test them.

"Red?" one of the guys at the table said. "That's more like a dark blond. *That's* your girlfriend?" And then he'd laugh, trying to cause further laughter like a virus with the other people at his table. Fake laughter.

And it went on like that, day after day. Getting more and more facts. The first thing I found out is that everyone saw the same hair color I did. Then everyone saw the same skin color. The same figure. The same eyes. The same clothes. Everyone saw the same characteristics.

Erick closed the book and placed it back between the two *Star Wars* novels, taking a moment to look at the wallpaper of old science fiction books again. He grabbed the butcher knife from the table and placed it in his back pocket and turned off the light of the reading room before exiting. On his way to the bedroom, he thought about the three months with Jen, the moments outside of the ones when he wasn't going insane and could feel his heart beat on the left side of his head. The good moments. The silent moments. Without questions. Without words. The happiest moments of his life. But every time he thought of something happy, a lie replaced it. A memory of Jen telling him who she really was. Words and phrases appearing in the hallway walls as if he lived in a comic book.

It's all perception, Erick.

That's your girlfriend?

Eyes can only be deceived to an extent.

She slept quietly in his bedroom. She never snored. She wore a large The Fray t-shirt that reached down a bit above her knees, barely hiding her underwear. Of course, he thought. He made sure not to move so much as he climbed on the bed, to avoid waking her. He reached for the knife in his pocket, felt it as it brushed against him over the denim. He reminded himself that he had to make sure, wouldn't know any other way. He put his weight on his left arm and then—

"Erick?" Jen said, tried to open her eyes.

He stabbed her inwards and then upwards in her stomach area, the knife impaling her with swiftness and ease like he had the first time they made love. She didn't scream. Because he didn't want her to scream. She only gasped and then looked up at the ceiling. He waited until it was over to pull the knife back out. He held it up to his face, studied it in the darkness. In the dark, it looked like blood, but there was something about it. Something more black and white than color.

It looked gray to him, not only on the knife, but the pool starting to form on his white sheet.

He stood up and walked to the light switch on the door to make sure. When he flipped it, the light bulb in the ceiling popped like a camera flash and the darkness lingered.

But that's what he wanted to perceive.

Before I stopped going to writing group, I could only guess that Flaco started growing tired of it, of getting all the negative comments, albeit some of them constructive, and already practiced swinging chains at sand bag dummies, their faces covered with index cards with the names of writers who said anything bad about his writing. He was the oldest in the group—at least a twenty-year difference between him and the second oldest there—and an actual college student. Unlike me. One of those people who decided to go back to college before croaking, who either did better than everyone else because they had more ambition and/or wisdom, or couldn't hack it because the world had changed. Flaco always said he liked writing by hand, anyway, liked the feel of his pencil scraping across the paper to form the words. Near the end of my high school years when teachers required us to type our essays, everyone rejoiced, not for the spelling or grammar checkers created later, but because a tool finally existed that could produce words that could catch up with our thoughts, at least until, in my case, about three or four thoughts formed at the same time and the keystrokes couldn't catch up anymore, couldn't keep them from colliding, like skipping letters in words and writing the firstlet ters of the following word on your current one.

That's probably why Flaco wrote by hand. Because when he read stories, he'd notice something in the beginning, and it would ruin the rest of the story for him. He'd focus in on a single word of the whole sentence and then respond to that word, even if it didn't have any relation to the actual conversation. Like taking the word *sentence* in the previous sentence, and all of a sudden, we're talking about sentencing men to prison. This is the first comment he said when we started critiquing Daniel's story:

"I'm tired of this shit. I'm so tired of these oh-so-self-hating Mexican writers who feel a need to give all the characters in their stories white people names. Erick? Jennifer? Can't get any whiter than that. Might as well have named her Tiffany. And Tanner. Thing is," he said, looking at Daniel now, "you are a Mexican writer. You should be proud of your heritage, man. Name your characters after your *gente*. You know, names like Juan. Pablo. Jesús. María. Pedro. José."

"So then biblical characters," I said, deciding not to point out the various smart-ass accents in some of the names he listed. "Everyone in the Bible Mexican?"

"What?"

"This is the first time I actually notice this from Daniel," I said, raising my voice a bit, even though I was sitting right next to Flaco. "Last time, I remember seeing one of his characters with the last name López, which is a Spanish last name. So I'm not sure where you see a pattern to start getting tired of."

"Sure," Flaco said, "the character's name was López, but what was his first name, again? Do you remember that one? 'Cause I wrote it down right here. Yeah. Silas. Total *bolillo* name."

"There might be something interesting about having a first name in English and a last name in Spanish," I said, "if we must talk about the past piece again. My interpretation is that, yes, your first name is who you are, but your last name origin is what you represent, who you'll always be."

At least that's what I liked to believe. When my writing endeavors began in middle school and for a few years after that, I feared for my last name. Was afraid that when and if my books hit the shelves, when people would find them, somewhere by Fitzgerald or Faulkner (if it's allowed to aim that high), that they'd take one look at my Spanish last name and push it back in the shelf before even giving it a chance to see what was in it. The same people who'd approach me in the Donna store overpacked with other customers as I stood there, waiting for someone to sign off on the parts to proceed on to Weslaco, the people who'd take one quick read at my non-Spanish first name and assume away when asking, "Excuse me, but can you help me find a part? Because all of these," and they'd whisper, "Mexicans here refuse to help me." Whisper it like a little kid spelling out *fuck* and *shit* to avoid getting in trouble, or in this case, because it wasn't bad if nobody heard, right? Of course, now the real joke is the idea of a book with my name ever appearing in a bookshelf.

But even after high school, my characters had white names. Barry, Mark, Julie, Stan, Bill, Harry. And I had already made the decision to shatter my father's heart and use a white pseudonym, thinking my book wouldn't sell with a Spanish last name like mine. I figured I'd worry about what the name would be when and if I arrived at that point. An anagram of my real name or some shit, only more white-sounding. I thought it best not to use *palabras* in Spanish and code-switch like Mexican-American writers, talking about Mom's shitty *tamales* and my *tía's* mayoral run. Not give it away, completely hide the fact that I even spoke my dying mother tongue. I convinced myself that my light complexion would help me pull this off.

Then it went away. As a teen writer, you want people to buy your books. You want to make money off of them so you can quit the shitty job that makes you unhappy and write full-time. But then you actually start giving a shit about the words you want to say, and you realize they are better off not being read by the people who'd put the book back on the shelf because of a last name. In that sense, Flaco's reasoning for thinking Daniel was a self-hating Mexican for naming his characters Erick and Jennifer was almost understandable, but if anything, I think Daniel's father hailed from El Salvador.

"May I just point out," Jeremy said, "to comment on what's actually on the page, for a change. This piece of fiction we're talking about here, to me, it lacked a lot of originality, as most science fiction these days does."

"Can we even call this science fiction, though?" Melissa asked. "Because it's only hinted that Jen's an alien by the things she *tells* Erick, but it's left ambiguous for us. She could merely be a crazy person. Which would make this not science fiction. Only fiction. So are you saying it's not original because maybe Jen is not the first person in the world to claim she's from another planet?"

"I'm not talking about content so much as I'm talking about form," Jeremy said. "There are a lot of motifs in the story that are of a science fiction nature. There's the theme of the quest for truth—"

I started to say, "That's not necessarily—"

"There's the science fiction book collection in the reading room, where the story begins. Then there's the whole possibility of the alien aspect of it. The mere idea that the character Jen finds herself in this random situation, that she just happened to be standing in the middle of the road, suggests that maybe what she's saying is true. As the reader, like the narrator, there's a part of us that wants to believe her. There's a part of us that wants her to be an alien, so that Erick and this woman could be happy. . . ."

He trailed off, talking about how science fiction lacked originality, that people who write science fiction were running out of new ideas already. I stopped paying attention and started thinking about Jen, the way I pictured her in the story, the same way Erick pictured her. To be in that situation—to be in Erick's shoes and have something too good to be true happen like that—it started making my mind race, the thoughts either laterally leaving the center, leaving me too worried about catching one that the others slipped away without my knowledge. Or the thoughts coming in convergently getting ready to crash. Daniel didn't intend to make us fall in love with Jen, but the more I read this story, the more I liked her. Would I commit the same act in the same situation? Kill her even though I knew she loved me and we'd be happy forever? I didn't see myself doing it, even if it was to save my mind. I'd rather my mind stay lost.

"Even if it is science fiction," Melissa said, "there's a lot of great symbolism in it. This whole idea of hiding science fiction books behind books of science and philosophy and comparing that to his relationship with Jen is pretty interesting and I think it works. Because Erick is this character who has gone from being a man of imagination to one of science and logic, and that's how he handles the Jen situation. It only makes sense to me that he can't stand living in a universe that dares to debunk what he's already made up his mind about. I don't think many of us can. I loved this story. I liked the ambiguity at the end that hints at the possibility that Jennifer's an alien, even though we already know she isn't."

Goes back to wiring, I guess. Our mind's already made up on so much that anything that challenges that is resisted. We separate years in terms of decades even though 1999 had more in common with 2000 than it did with 1992. We know that Columbus discovered America because that is the narrative we are fed from the beginning and it gets perpetuated every fucking year. We know these are the classics of literature because we are told what they are and these aren't. But who constructed that list? Who decided on it? Who wrote that history textbook? Who decided today was today? Certainly not aliens.

"It's not symbolism, though, is it," I said.

"Huh?"

"The symbolism is the cross in the book, yes. But the bookshelf itself is only imagery. Or a metaphor. To use the right term."

It was already dark when we finished writing group. Daniel didn't say anything about his critique, simply thanked everyone, and that the comments would help him during the revision process. He stood outside in the dark parking lot, looking on like he was waiting for someone to pick him up. We never talked to each other outside of writing group. None of us did, probably. Sometimes we saw each other in passing and our eyes would meet and that was enough for us, this acknowledgment of each others' existences. I decided to approach him, reminding myself of the closing scene of the story, actually picturing myself pulling out a butcher knife from my own back pocket and murdering him where he stood, take my revenge for my Jen, stab him in the same spot so he can bleed in pain for a while. I brushed the thought away with a silent chuckle and said, "She *was* an alien, right?"

He didn't say anything for a while, as if the question caught him off guard. "If that's what you see on the page," he said. But his response sounded like he didn't believe she was, like I was stupid for even thinking it. I thought he wanted, like Erick, to let go of all this science fiction bullshit, to write real, meaningful literature, the kind of literature assholes like Toby and Jeremy ranted about on a weekly basis. He wanted Jen to be human, to be dead. It would make Erick and Daniel normal, wouldn't it? It would make us all normal.

"You want to know what I think?" I said.

"Enlighten me," he said after sighing.

"I think Jen was an alien," I said. "I think she was being honest in the story." Thought about adding, And you fucking killed her, but the conversation was already too strange.

"What about the rest of the world?" he said. "What about all the people who saw the same thing Erick did? Didn't that prove she wasn't?"

"Nah," I said.

"No?"

"The only thing it proved is that we're all the same. We're all trained to have the same opinions about beauty. There's no more originality left in this world. There's no more uniqueness. We're all different versions of the same person. That's why everyone sees the same thing. The protagonist and the fat fuck are one of the same. That's why they all see what they want to see. And if Erick had taken the time to realize that, Jen would still be alive. I mean, he wouldn't have killed her."

"Heh," he said. "Guess now I know what to tell Oprah when she asks me what the book is about. Thanks." He adjusted the strap of his bag to better align it with his shoulder. "But you do know it's only a story, right?" He started walking into the parking lot even though no vehicle pulled up anywhere. "It's only fiction," he called back, and then disappeared between the student cars.

I reached into my shirt pocket and pulled out the cigarette, asking a pedestrian student for a light and lit it naturally as if it had been a habit for years. I entertained the idea of whispering and repeating *Only fiction* like in a fucking movie but thought it stupid so I smoked. It tasted horrible. I coughed and felt an intense pressure in all my chest area. The second one didn't hurt as much.

PART NINE

The Part About The Sentence

Sometimes the dreams went away but never for more than two or three days, dreams where I still played trombone in the high school band, where I hadn't told the director and my instructor I needed to get a job and that I wouldn't be staying after school for marching band, but still wanted to stay in band and participate in individual competitions, for the music, dreams where they hadn't threatened to move me from the first spot in the honor band to the first spot in the shitty band. A friend said a sense of guilt drove me to dream about band, that most likely I never wanted to leave. I just didn't like quitting. Sometimes I dreamt memories that actually happened back then, like my trombone instructor entering the Subway where I worked, greeting him, and then he'd say, "You don't have to call me 'sir' anymore." The declaration of independence penned by my hand while still in band, complaining about the tyranny being practiced by the directors and student officials who pretended the decisions came from them, decreasing break times when Pigskin drew nearer, the unjustified yelling from that baritone section leader bitch tripping on power, the lack of nutritional value in the two dollar Burger King double-cheese burgers they gave us before every practice, and that Ben should be allowed to wear makeup if he wanted to, among other raised issues, and how instead of getting in trouble for its eventual distribution, the head director asked if I wanted to run for band president or try out for drum major because I'd make a great leader and people would listen to me, about telling him no and missing drum major tryouts to go to my girlfriend's prom six hundred miles away, about him asking me, some time later, if the prom was worth missing out on drum major tryouts. Dreams of the auto parts store would come, too, if I ever escaped.

The Wolf set the tone when he took over the hub department by yanking the payroll schedule off the bulletin board and scratching off the *Manager* next to Rick's name with a dark pen, enough for everyone to see the scratch from a far distance, how it almost tore through the paper, and enough for everyone to still see Rick's name underneath the scratch. Then he put Rick on the Brownsville/Rio Grande City route so he'd be away as much as possible. With Rick back on the road, The Wolf placed me back on the lunch routes and sometimes had me covering for people on their days off, and other than Rick and I, no one else seemed to notice the replacement probably because of how similar Rick and The Wolf looked, give and take a couple hundred pounds. Rick had started calling him The Wolf even before the replacement, not because of a fierce personality or the way he ran the hub, but because he always had the top two buttons of his uniform undone, revealing a dark patch of furry hair. No one else at work called him The Wolf.

The Wolf hated Rick. That became obvious right away. He talked and looked at him like an exonerated pedophile he was forced to work with. It wouldn't even surprise me if Rick's demotion was a conspiracy between The Wolf and my brother, great friends, finding it a bit too coincidental that The Wolf suddenly showed up to work after quitting a few months before they hired me. They had promised him a promotion that never came, and he decided to go work for a different auto parts company. A couple of weeks before his return, my brother told him they started construction for a new branch close to the bridge in Hidalgo. He was trying to convince the district manager to give the branch to The Wolf, as long as The Wolf showed signs of leadership first. So a week after his reign over the hub, he stopped me in the hub office on my way in to retrieve more invoices for parts to sort and send out. He put his arm on my shoulder, thinking I wouldn't stop otherwise and said, How would you like to start coming to work at 9:00

AM? Get an extra hour of sleep, focus on your school work a little bit more?

I agreed, thinking he'd let me drive more if I did what he said. He waited until the next day to tell me about the new rule. Every weekday, someone had to be around to answer the hub phone because the people at the front counter had been getting too many phone calls after all of us left at 5:00. Phone calls meant for us. And they're too busy with paying customers to have the time to walk to the back to check if a part's there. He told me, I'm sorry I'm making you do this. We were going to get the new guy to do this, but he has this other job he goes to right after work, Home Depot or some shit.

He asked me to keep a ledger showing how many calls we received that last hour to see if it was even worth having someone stick around. My first day was a Wednesday and the phone rang once. It rang twice on Thursday, and once on Friday, but that one was someone thinking he was calling a place to get your fortune read. Shouldn't have said, Wrong number. Needed to kill time and writing didn't do it for me anymore. And after a while, neither did switching the *N* and *M* keys on the keyboards in the commercial department.

Once or twice a week, The Wolf would bring pork rinds to work in a ziplock bag. Rinds, he said, he deep fried outdoors in a giant-ass wok, and he'd share them with anyone willing to try them, offering his jackknife to scrape the fat off the skin like someone else's gum from your sole. One of the days he came back from lunch, no pork rinds in sight, lungs expanded and face as sweaty as his armpits that turned that area of his shirt from cayenne to brick, he kicked the hub door open and said, I'm going to kill that motherfucker. I knew he meant Rick.

The Wolf said Rick was trying to get him fired. This is what happened and why he wanted to kill that motherfucker: The district manager wanted to change Rick's route, which delivered parts to Raymondville and Brownsville within four hours in the mornings, then to Rio Grande City and Roma in the afternoons. All of this was done from 9:30 to 5:00 every Monday through Friday. Rick clocked in at 9:00, readied his route, left east, returned by 1:30, then immediately left west so The Wolf wouldn't have to see him so much. The district manager didn't want us driving to Brownsville anymore because for two parts daily, it's a shit-ton of gas. And the district manager from the Brownsville area didn't want *them* coming to McAllen for the same reason. The solution was to go to Raymondville and meet the Brownsville guy there for an exchange, then do Rio/Roma twice. The Wolf told the district manager it would be impossible to do that in one workday, but when the district manager caught Rick in the Rio store, Rick said, I can do that route without problems if I continue taking my lunch hour at 5:00 when I leave work.

That fucking fat fuck, The Wolf said. He started pacing around the office, trying to stand in the path of the air condition, waiting for the cold air to put out the fire. He said, looking at me, How the fuck do you tell the DM that you don't have lunch when it's fucking obvious that you have to have a lunch by law? I'm going to kick his fat ass as soon as he gets here. Trying make me look bad.

He didn't kick Rick's ass when he returned from the route, at least not physically. He only confronted him and talked to him. I stood on the other side of the window, not hearing anything said between them. Rick looked at his own shoes, like a submissive dog exposing his belly, refusing to say anything back or defend himself. He'd run his hand against the edges of the signed invoices, risking paper cuts, feeling the bumps from the perforation. The Wolf didn't return to the hub office after talking to Rick. He kept walking towards the front counter, ready to go home now that his day was over, his own fingers rubbing against the nylon knife case clipped to his pants. Rick bounced into the hub office, signed invoices still in hand, and he started sorting them by time to make it a bit easier for me since that's pretty much what I did for the extra hour. And pick up the phone. If it rang.

Rick said, I can't believe he got mad about that shit, pretty stupid, right?

I didn't say anything to avoid choosing sides. Best to stay out of it if I wanted to stay on The Wolf's good side to stop the suffocation in the store and go out on the road again.

Anyways, Rick said. Take it easy, okay?

He exited the hub, and I wondered if he felt happy it was me staying an extra hour and not him.

The summer that came after The Wolf started running the hub, he made us switch offices with the commercial department to prove that he had ideas and could set them in motion. This way, he had told everyone, the commercial customers can come in through the side door of the building instead of the back and the hub is closer to the loading docks, which loads more parts into trucks, anyway, you know. And the first thing he did in our new office was turn on the lights and pin the payroll schedule and a highway map of the Rio Grande Valley to a bulletin board he had purchased the day we moved. Opposite to the bulletin board was a large plastic window held together by a large asterisk of thick shipping tape overlooking the distribution center, which meant it would be more difficult to escape the duties of the job and talk to Plato considering The Wolf took on a second—sometimes a third—assistant to do his job for him. So he always sat at his post, looking on towards the distribution center and talking to anyone willing to stick around and listen to his stories of what it was like to work for a different company, scraping fat off his pork rinds with his jackknife and showing everyone how to curve the scrape perfectly so that no fat is left on them. I'd have to crawl to Plato's office to avoid The Wolf seeing me through the large window, and doing that would cause the entire store to laugh at me until someone sunk lower. And in the future at some point, if there was nothing going on, Shoe Guy, for the sole purpose of making someone laugh and gain meaningless points, would suddenly remind everyone about the time I crawled on all fours like a cheating bitch, and they'd continue talking about it for the next few days after that. Job duties won, sorting out the invoices as the orders came out of the printer, putting them in order on my way out of the hub office to make my trip to the aisles of parts more efficient, mapping out a path in my head, then grabbing the parts and putting them on the route shelves, only to walk back inside the office, the endless sound of sliding on gravel coming from The Wolf's scraping, with five or six more orders waiting for me. It became easier when I stopped thinking about the time, the minutes, the hours, and the months, ride it out and think about random ideas instead, like the other day, when I heard someone at school tell someone else he was out of his fucking mind, and, bumping into corners, wiping muddy dust with my shirt sleeves, I wondered how the phrase originated, what it meant to be out of your mind, outside of your mind, looking at your mind from the outside. I wouldn't like what I saw if I were outside my mind, to see my thoughts as alien, like someone else is having them. Best to look away. Out of my sight. And back into my mind, I noticed suddenly the ten boxes of auto parts cradling in my arms. I arranged them in their outgoing shelves and pulled the white door open to grab more tickets in the hub office. Scraping. Only eight tickets this time. Eight, ate, eating. The Wolf won't stop eating *chicharrones*. Crunching. He spat out grease when he looked at my face and asked, Why are you sweating, as if it's a concept he's never heard of before, as if it's something you didn't do, in the middle of fucking summer, in South Texas, the pit of Satan's fat tit, as if he were demanding some kind of explanation. What do I tell him? It's cold as fuck out there? I don't know. I should get this checked? Too tired to come up with anything to say. Six tickets next time. Six. Sex. Sick. Out of my mind.

I started keeping an online journal at around this time because none of the fiction made it worth clicking the *Save* button. A paragraph or a page, sometimes ten pages, and I'd hate myself for them, and then click the fucking *X*, thinking to myself, at least the practice was there, at least at first this was my thought. So I did the online journal thing for the practice, right around the time people started posting online journals, before blogs exploded and made the BA in Journalism obsolete, during a time when everyone wanted to be heard because everyone had something to say—at least until sexual predators and rapists started reading them, but even then—and I wrote the online journal because there was something humorously oxymoronic about having a public diary. I didn't intend for it to be profound and have the same amount of quality uncritically forced and injected into my creative work, the work intended for hopes of eventual publication. The journal writing and the real writing (if it ever happened again) would be separate—as if the real writing were made up of the nutrients my body absorbed, while the online journal was a fucking sugar cookie. Usually four or five friends made up my main audience, and sometimes it felt like they only pretended to read, or merely browsed through it, or didn't understand it. Sometimes some stranger would somehow find the journal through a search, strange considering search engines weren't that smart yet. He'd comment something like, "What's the point of having an online journal if you're not even going to post gossip? Don't you know that gossip is the best kind of writing there is?" I spent more time than I should considering a response, and opted for none in the end.

I titled an early post "Communication breakdown." This is what it looked like:

The vicinity around my job has been home to a few strange events lately. For those of you who aren't broiling in the Valley and don't know your way around McAllen, the street in front of our business is compact, four narrow lanes without a middle one, so traffic gets packed like a can of smoked sausages. Last Saturday, about two blocks north of work, a truck hit a telephone pole, knocking it down to the street, and the truck was, somehow, left completely upside down. The cops closed that part of the street for the entire morning. One would think this conspiracy stops there, that this type of accident occurs only once in a city like McAllen, or even the whole Valley. But this is a weird place and the conspiracy continues.

This morning, a block south of us, right on the opposite side to a Circle K, a car hit another telephone pole. The pole fell, and the car was also left upside down. Now it starts to sound less like a coincidence. How stupid or drunk can the drivers of the vehicles be anyway? There's a 30-mile speed limit. How do you end up upside down, physics?

When I left work, though, after the Circle K mess was cleaned up, the side of another car hit the pole on the other side of the street from the one the first truck hit, a little closer to our store. So close that there was a police car parked in front of my car, basically leaving me stuck at work for another half hour. I peeked to check out the damage before I had to sit and wait, and this car, if you can believe it, stayed right-side up. The passengers were pulled out safely, but the ambulance showed up, just in case. No other vehicle was involved. I thought some force would cause the car to magically turn upside down, but instead, to make matters more dramatic, the hood suddenly burst into flames.

No explosion, unfortunately. Though that would've been the perfect ending to this "let's see who can knock down the most 23rd Street telephone poles and end up upside down" game. But only simple flames, sadly, like cooking with rum.

I'm thinking the forces of nature are working on my side. Like they'll do anything to make sure I don't have to stick around at work for an extra hour to answer the non-working phone.

Unlike the rest of us downcast ants dreaming of the hour hand striking five (with my own dreams elongated by an extra hour), waiting to escape the misery that kept pulling us to the auto parts store like a magnet attracting lead filings, to arrive at our personal sanctuaries, kiss our wives (or the other woman), drink a beer, watch the game, try to write, simply sit in front of the television because we're too tired to think of anything else because it hurts our heads to form one more thought and so we let the television do it for us, or anything else we do whenever we get the fuck out of work, unlike us, The Wolf escaped from his home life and made the auto parts store his own sanctuary (or everything around it since I would sometimes catch him sitting in his truck with the window slightly rolled down, staring off into nothing, thinking about God-knows-what, or sometimes wait for more people to clock out so they could drive off to the back of the parking lot by the alley and a large wall, an area they called *la palma* because a leafless palm tree rose from the ground and provided a minimal amount of shade, at a time when no one needed it because by then the high wall provided enough, socialize there to talk and drink beers in celebration of payday or smoke weed in celebration of not being young anymore, passing the joint around from mouth to mouth), all of this because he hated being at home and he didn't want to be there anymore ever since his cub was born, didn't want to have sex with his wife, as pretty as she was, and couldn't even look at her anymore, which we noticed whenever she would drive by the loading dock to bring him lunch sometimes, parking her recently-purchased black SUV next to the hub trucks as the drivers loaded the large red, yellow, and/or green plastic boxes full of boxes housing parts, ready to take them out on the lunch routes, and she'd be wearing something sexy all the time, a short skirt that showed off her legs, a tight blouse that showed off some cleavage, her hair straightened and framing her face and bosom into a complete circle, you know, something to make the rest of the guys look at her, to make the rest of the guys want her and be jealous of The Wolf for having a hot chick like that, to see if anything like that would even excite The Wolf, would make him want to be with her again (at least in bed considering she always assumed it was a basic need to want to have sex all the time), but nothing did it for him anymore because he had been there, in the hospital room, the day she went into labor, a day he had been dreaming about for the nine-or-so months she was pregnant, to finally be able to hold his first son in his hands, so he wanted to see everything, to see his wife in a hospital gown with her legs spread open, the doctor with his half mask, arms spread forward like a quarterback hiking the ball, the cries and moans of his wife as she pushed their son out, screaming in pain because The Wolf insisted she not take the drugs, convinced her even as he drove her to the hospital, saying, "What are you going to say when the doctor asks you," like training your kid to say he fell playing soccer, sometimes running red lights, and then the smell of hospital, of steel when you lick it, of fluorescent light, the smell that only a place where people die and are born can permeate, and then the baby, pushing his head out of his wife's pussy, sliding out like a piece of shit on a constipated day, ripping open the walls The Wolf had spent nights making love to, kissing, licking, touching, a place of comfort his son was marking as his territory now, his face touching places where The Wolf's would never reach, his little hands massaging every single inch of her on his way out, his little penis brushing up against her clit before the last of him came out, and that was when he vomited and couldn't look at his wife the same way, when he started loving to work at the shittiest place in the world, so I knocked on his truck window and asked him, Why can't *you* stay until 6:00, if you're still here?

"The four yeses."

If you want to form the perfect writing environment, there are four requirements. And by writing environment, I'm talking about physically and mentally. First, you need an idea—say, the fact that a Mexican-American or Chicano or Hispanic or Latino (whatever tickles your dick) needs to act more American to be accepted into society. We can call this 'The Chican-Dance" or "The 'Right' Side of the Hyphen," if you're not into the whole bon mot shit. You also need inspiration. I have the motivation, so I don't think inspiration is much of a problem. You need some silence, which I can get or get to. And then, you need a clear mind. And there lies my motherfucking problem.

You should also use *dilapidated* at least once. Every writer uses *dilapidated* at least once.

"Three noes. Or is it no's? Nos? Fuck it."

I printed off the syllabus for a creative writing class I'm interested in going to next semester. I pulled it off the Internet and there was a paper attached to the end of it that read something like: "If you ever want to make it as a writer, you must avoid these three things at all costs: 1) no dreams; 2) no smoking weed; 3) no talking animals.

Well, at least I don't have a talking animal.

Unless you count The Wolf.

Other times, being on the road cleared my mind, let me think of stories I needed to work on, writing that needed writing, either by having good music playing in the background or complete silence, listening to the wind as it pressed against the windshield or the air cutting every time I passed a road sign, as if the wind changed its tone for that second, fields of sugarcane and grain sorghum extending at each direction of Military Highway. My skill in mapping out new routes when new stores opened was one The Wolf thought he should exploit to make the district manager think that, in some sense, The Wolf had discovered me and by association was quite the talent scout. We had another branch opening up in Progreso, and The Wolf told me, I don't care how you do it, but I need you to figure out a way to add that store to the Weslaco route and still pull it off four times in the day, so go. Get the fuck out of here. Go do that.

The anger came from the Hidalgo store not opening yet, which was the one he was promised to run. I took the map from the hub office with me on the route and studied its roads like a railroad surveyor, trying to figure out how much time it would take to get from the Weslaco store to the Progreso branch, from the Mercedes branch, from the Donna branch, which could work out if Elsa wasn't twenty minutes north, in the other direction. I did have a passion for maps and studied the Rio Grande Valley one like a textbook chapter that needed memorizing, following down the river that seemed drawn with a squiggle wiggle pen increasing in pressure the closer you flowed into the gulf. The back roads allowed the most solace, especially when timing Mercedes and Progreso, the long stretch south on 491 followed by a long stretch west on Military Highway, the occasional wheat field or wheat fields in the making, John Deere tractors that reminded me of my dad's. At sixty miles per hour, I drew closer to a small white Focus with some writing on the back windshield. *Honk if your hot*, the writing read. Probably some college guy or girl on the way to Nuevo Progreso, ready to go drink tequila off someone else's body. When we came to a long curve, after crossing the bridge over the creek flowing down to the Mercedes basin, I saw the car at an angle and more writing on its side window. *30 and still hot*. Someone in a gray SUV drove right in front of the car, displaying its own messages in the same handwriting. *Single and loving it!* on the back. *Looking for hotties* and *Honk if your one* on the sides. A few miles east of Progreso, both vehicles stopped for no reason, as if they saw a ghost standing in the middle of the road, so I slammed the brakes and honked.

A thirty-year-old hand appeared from the driver's side of the Focus, gesturing "what the fuck?" in an upward direction before morphing into a middle-fingered "fuck you." What the fuck is right. After passing both cars, risking them calling the number on the sticker on the back of my truck to be bitches about the fact that they braked and got honked at, even when their windshields demanded it, I stopped at Circle K in Progreso to fill up the truck with gas. Halfway through the pumping, the two vehicles with the women arrived who I assumed were on their way to Mexico since the bridge was a block away. They ended up not recognizing me from the near accident, or didn't want to. Their faces were wrinkled like neglected cobwebs on ceiling corners, dark circles on their eyes that looked like low-budget zombie movie makeup, or like they smoked too much. They looked like women who had recently stepped out of abusive marriages and now they were trying to get their lives back and ignore the scars and bruises. They didn't look depressed. They looked defeated. And Mexico had the answers.

"One-man race"

It feels like writing is this way. Untimed. Though not necessarily. The story and its characters are always the driver. And you're always sitting in the passenger seat. You tell the driver where the starting point is and where the possible finish line is, and he usually picks whatever path he takes. There are thousands of them. Sometimes you throw in a few obstacles and directions down the road. The story itself does most of the work.

Lately I've been getting the worst drivers.

Like Juan Lozano. He was in the driver's seat when I was taking driver's ed. Trying to sound smart. You know those guys? Tells the instructor, "Not to be mean or nothing, sir, but sometimes, my parents literally piss me off."

"Really?" I ask. "Literally? Do you wash up after?"

Towards the end of the summer, Mario, the depressing robot, went on vacation, and he approached that the same way he approached everything else in his life: without the slightest hint of emotion. If nothing else, he looked miserable leaving work, staring down at the floor as he started to disappear from our lives for the next eight or nine days. What would he do without his routine? A few days during that week, The Wolf let me take over his Pharr/Edinburg route, which ran six times a day (as opposed to four for the new Weslaco route, which I had perfected by reversing it and starting with Elsa). The six Pharr/Edinburg runs, though absent of desolate roads, didn't bother me. It was time away from working with The Wolf and time alone to think about the next story.

Unfortunately, I began habitually calling the rock radio station from my cell phone every day, talking to two different DJs at different times of the day—morning shift guy and afternoon shift guy. I was one of those guys. The loneliness escaping from the vents in the truck was getting to me. But their current music programming was getting to me more. I didn't want to hear other music or call in to request it. I could live my life without having to. My calls had nothing to do with that, but rather I wanted to sort of introduce the Rio Grande Valley to real music with real lyrics, music with at least a little bit of merit in it, even though I knew jack and shit about merit. So the first few times, my calls were usually negative, and I'd say shit like, "You know there are Guns n' Roses songs other than 'Sweet Child O' Mine' and 'November Rain,' right? They don't only do ballads." And "Have you guys ever heard of The Strokes at all?"

After those first few calls, the conversations started to get more serious. I wanted to know why it was that they didn't play music that would challenge the way people here think and interpret them, Judas Priest songs other than "Breaking the Law" and "Living After Midnight," Metallica songs other than "Enter Sandman," or anything at all by The Ramones, which they never played. Good songs. Not Nickelback. I told one of the DJs, "I think the songs you choose to play and overplay says a lot about what you think about the people from here, what you think their brains have the capacity to handle."

"Are you that guy that's been calling us the last four days?"

"No. But there are way better songs out there. Actual hit songs that I don't understand why you can't bring yourselves to play. 'Rocket Queen.' 'Civil War.' Even fucking 'Don't Cry.'"

"Well," the DJ said, "first of all, don't cry. Second of all, we actually do a lot of research. We have a program director who picks the music we should be playing, who actually goes out and talks with people, does surveys, asking them what kind of music or specific songs they like to listen to and why. We look at when people tune out, with which songs. We ask them when they listen. That's how our playlists get chosen."

"Who's he asking? High school students? I've heard you guys play 'It's Been a While' three times in the same sixty minutes. It's never been a while since you last played it. I know you must think Staind is the best thing to happen to rock since The Beatles, but isn't it unfair to the other artists? Don't you think they deserve some play time, too? How is someone from here ever supposed to like a song and get some culture when you force us to hate them by overplaying them?"

"See," the DJ said, "you're not looking at it from a business point of view. Let's say you own a business, a music store. You know, one of those that probably only sells vinyls because you refuse to give in to the man's demands by not going with CDs."

"Yeah, okay."

"Your business isn't going too well, so you decide to buy commercial time on this radio station. Our people do the research here and tell you that right now, most people are listening to this song, so you can choose to pay X amount of money to have your commercial aired right before or right after we play this song, because chances are, if someone is tuning in, they'll leave it playing on that song. And what do you know? Your commercial comes out right after that. And they're thinking, *Hey, I don't have* Appetite for Destruction *on vinyl, and I'm already in a car* (which is where most people tune in). *Let me drive over to Mr. Communist's and buy myself a copy.* Or you can pay Y amount of money to have your commercial air at 3:00 in the morning, when not many people are listening, so it doesn't matter if we're either cranking it to Nickelback's or Def Leppard's 'Photograph' because at that time, no one will be able to tell the difference. When would you rather play the commercial?"

"So it always comes down to money. If you like music so much, why don't you *do* something about it? Stand up to this system. Spike the playlist and play some decent music. Sometimes art has to be more important."

"Not when you get paid like I do. After a while, you start being happy that there are businesses willing to pay a ridiculous amount of money to have their commercial played after a song that doesn't mean anything at all. And people are always listening, making sure we stick to the program, making sure we don't accidentally say *shit* while the microphone is still on. I'm pretty sure if we played a song we haven't played in years, or ever, someone would notice."

"Your morning DJ said that the program director walked in the studio while Hoobastank's 'The Reason' was playing and said something like, 'I guess rock and roll is making a comeback.' It's not. Not with that song. Can you at least stop playing that song?"

He hung up right as I arrived at the Pharr branch, a store hidden off to the side of the road before entering the downtown area, across from yet another pawn shop, by a street light hardly anyone obeyed and with a dumpster graffitied with two or three gang initials marking it as their territory. A fourth artist announcing *You Have Arrived.* The side door used to drop off parts was locked, which was something they sometimes did on Saturdays when they closed the commercial department early because they didn't expect to make many more sales. I entered through the front door, its glass starting to turn white with time and lack of cleaning in the area not covered by the Monroe shocks and struts displays, and was greeted with the odor of mold and old seeping through the store walls like cigarette smoke on furniture. I carried a fuel filter and a radiator box and was asked to take them to the back of the store and get them signed there. Genie, one of the store's two female employees, a dark-haired Mexican with large breasts (trust me, you couldn't *not* notice), stepped out of the manager's office when she heard me coming and said, "Let me sign those for you." She matched the part numbers on the invoices with the part numbers on the boxes and signed them off, adding, "You're kind of in trouble, honey," almost whispering it so that no one else would hear.

"What do you mean?"

Before she said anything else, the district manager exited the same office, finishing tucking in his white polo company shirt, a tall thin man with a thick mustache who looked like one of those guys that could paint your cartoon house. He came up to me, sticking his hands in his pockets as if looking for change, but it seemed more like he was adjusting them so they wouldn't stick out like tongues. He said, "Do you have a cell phone with you?"

"Sure. I mean, you never know when you might need it, right?"

"Didn't you know you're not supposed to carry a cell phone with you on the road, much less talk on it while you're driving? It makes the company look bad. It makes us look like we're careless. Another employee saw you talking on it and called it in."

130

"Sorry. I wasn't aware of that rule."

He disappeared into the manager's office again and Genie followed after him.

It took me about ten minutes to get back to my store—Nickelback liking someone for how they write their checks, apparently—more ready than ever to finish off the day. And the night shift manager had a write-up waiting for me. He was an okay guy, but we never saw each other when our shifts didn't meet. He apologized when he handed the form to me and added, The district manager ordered it and I couldn't say no, man.

I signed it without even reading it, and he said, We're still cool, right?

The Wolf and the rest of the hub people had gone home already, so that room greeted me with darkness. The wire gate separating the loading dock from the distribution center was chained and locked to prevent people from stealing the oil and paints, even though most people climbed the gate anyway. In the hub office, there was a paper for me on the desk, written in The Wolf's handwriting, that read *Stick around until 6 just in case phone rings.* He probably wouldn't let me drive anymore after this write-up. He'd probably also get one for not explaining the rules to his drivers, but his never came.

"Credit"

I was thinking about Frida Kahlo the other day. Two things actually. The first thing was the unibrow. Why she painted it every time. I know you have to paint yourself as you are, but I'd knock a few pounds off if I painted myself. I'm sure Picasso's face didn't look like a rhombus.

On a serious note, the second thing was her paintings. Many of which she owed to all the pain she endured in life. It sounds kind of cheesy to put it that way, but think about it. Think about what would have happened had the pain not been there. In a way, many people would have missed out on good art. Many artists would not have been influenced by Kahlo if she didn't have the life she did. The same can be said for any other medium of art—writing, music, any kind of art. It seems kind of selfish to think of it this way, that one gets to enjoy and be inspired by great art because the artist went through some shit, because the author lived with pain all of his life, or was sexually molested and abused as a child, or is an orphan whose parents died in a war, or witnessed a murder or death. All kinds of fucked up.

Not making sense yet. Still working through it. But think about the rock music that was the offspring of war. Vietnam. I'm thinking about the rock music that was great music *because* of its political-ness and that existed *because* there were people dying. Take the dying people out of the equation and what shit are we left with? What kind of music would the bands of the 80s, 90s, and this new century be left with? I'm not saying there wouldn't be music if bad moments didn't happen. Not every song or poem or story has to be depressing, but what if another songwriter was inspired to write music specifically because of this music? Would he still exist?

All of sudden, everything's connected. Everything's a pattern. So maybe my writing won't ever make shit happen. It won't inspire anyone who reads it, if by some miracle someone reads it. I could write about my idiot coworkers as much as I can or want and it's not going to make them any smarter. But then *maybe* one person reads it, and it could be only a sentence or a phrase that clicks something in his head. And he feels inspired and writes a book or an album. And those songs or that book don't make shit happen either, but someone *else* gets inspired by *that* some years later, and *his* art makes some shit happen. A revolution. A change. Something. At that point, even though I could be dead already, I may be able to realize that it all wasn't for nothing. And it's all because someone I read refused hospital care to finish his last novel or because of something *he* read by someone who went through something even more fucked up.

So who or what gets the fucking credit here?

And what if nothing fucked up ever happens to us? What do we do then? We fuck ourselves up.

PART TEN

The Part About The Backstory

Since I started working alongside The Wolf full time, as he unleashed me into the heat to retrieve parts all day while he conversed with his other assistants in his cool office, I was allowed a lunch break thirty minutes after Bern Bern. My daily lunch diet was usually made up of either a gas station taco or a fast-food-joint dollar burger, not because they were cheap, but because having to return to finish a shift at the auto parts store would be a horrible end to a great meal. A stupid reason, but that was my train of thought.

One of those times, Bern Bern sat in his parked Malibu next to my truck. He ate in his car with the windows rolled down. Microwaved chicken nuggets off a tupperware container with chopsticks, clasping them carefully before dipping them in small pools of mustard and ketchup, coating the yellow in red. He put down his plate as I drew close and adjusted his black cap with the lettering *CARLO* for the hundredth time that week. He wanted to let his hair grow more, which at first was to please his new girlfriend and her infatuation with men with long hair, but then we learned he grew it out because he wanted to style it like a samurai to complement his sword collection. The only way the store let him have long hair—like Pansy—was by concealing it under a cap. He unlocked the passenger door.

"Are you on a diet?" I asked.

"No. Why?"

"I read somewhere that if you eat food with chopsticks, you're forcing yourself to eat it slower than you normally would. So your stomach has enough time to tell your brain it's full."

His eyebrow arched up and he started looking around the car as if a paper with an answer was somewhere on the dashboard.

"But that's not why you're eating with chopsticks, is it?"

Since before we finished high school, Bern Bern had found solace in the Japanese culture. Or at least in what he thought was Japanese culture. It had started with watching anime, dubbed in English because he couldn't stand to read subtitles that quickly (and he never made the time to learn to speak or understand Japanese), before he moved on to collecting katanas and various other types of swords, which he'd sometimes spend entire nights sharpening with a rock while watching anime. The sound of the rock scraping against the steel would provide background music for the horror stories pouring out of my word processor program on a Packard Bell. Why he spent that much time sharpening them was a mystery to me. He was never going to get into a sword fight with anyone, though sometimes he'd go into the woods behind the house to meditate, he said, but if you looked out the window, there he was, swinging his sword around at the tree shadows, trying to cut branches around him as if they were limbs. The branches would get cut only sometimes. Usually they'd be pushed slightly downward before coming back up to their at-rest positions. After he moved out, someone told me he had upgraded to fighting refrigerator boxes.

When they opened the first sushi restaurant in Rio Grande City, he said his life made sense now. He wanted to go every other day to pick up sushi to try out all the different combinations, but he'd forget which ones he had tried and ordered the same ones most of the time. Every time we picked up, he'd reach for the white paper bag with the sushi rolls inside, trapped in a styrofoam to-go plate, with both hands and a slight bow, holding on to the food as if in deep appreciation, and say, "Arigatou," and the Mexican sushi chef would respond, "De nada." Back home, Bern Bern would reach into the back of the Tupperware cabinet to take out his sauce trays and waste about ten minutes pouring all the different sauces in them before locking himself in his room to eat and watch anime.

I only saw Bern Bern cry twice in my life—outside of slipping on mud, landing on his head, and other stupid things we'd do as kids. The first one was walking out of the theater after having seen *The Last Samurai*. He cried with rage and anger because they got so many elements wrong with the cultural aspects. And because of Tom Cruise throwing his sword at the American general, a move Bern Bern claimed that character was not allowed to do.

The second time he cried was about a week after 9/11. We were both juniors in high school and because we're nowhere near and nothing like New York, the shock had died down already—no more interrupting news reports in the morning, no more moments of silence during announcements, no more counselors asking anyone who needed trauma counseling (or rather anyone who wanted to get out of class) to go to the courtyard to talk about it. He jumped in my truck and slammed the door, and, all dramatic like we were in the middle of a day soap, he said, "Just drive." He had never done that before. I asked if it had anything to do with someone taking over his marching band spot, if it had anything to do with the fact that he'd be shadowing someone now, pretending to play the saxophone, an instrument he didn't even know how to hold, so the setup could look right to the band directors, or if it had anything to do with 9/11, and he said, "No, it doesn't have anything to do with anyone attacking this fucking country." And that was when he started crying. "Did you know," he said, "that we atomic bombed Hiroshima?"

"Yes, I did know," I said. "Did you know about Pearl Harbor?"

"That's not the fucking point," he said. "I mean. All those people."

"Antisocial aficionados."

This is an attempt to understand why some people are anti-pop culture. We'll see how we come out at the end of this.

When I was in middle school—worst three years of my life—the band hall had a yellow poster with the quote: "What is popular is not always right. What is right is not always popular." A stupid quote that reminds me of a fortune cookie I opened once: "Do what you should, not what you must." I don't know if "anti-pop culture" is the right way to define this group of people. Here's an example.

I was having dinner with Bern Bern and his girlfriend the other night at Denny's. Some time in the middle of dinner, we (or rather, they) started talking about anime, about how Bern Bern would always try to get me to watch *Dragonball Z*, which I didn't have the patience for, for the same reason I didn't have the patience for *The Matrix* sequels: film fights shouldn't last an hour. At one point, Stephanie said, "I used to like *Naruto* a lot. But then it started coming out on Cartoon Network and a lot of other people at school started liking it, so I didn't like it anymore."

"Fucking why?" is what I almost said, but I didn't want to make life awkward again. During Bern Bern's birthday party, she flipped her long hair over her face, covering it entirely, to put on a blind fold, and I said, "Hey. Cousin It." She started walking away, down the street in a direction opposite to her house miles away, after telling Bern Bern, "I'm not going to stay here if your fucking friends are going to make fun of me."

Example 2. One of the members of the writing group I used to attend said once, "Yeah, I don't read any bestsellers because if they sell a lot, it means they suck." So does popularity automatically mean the book sucks? I mean, it's one thing for you to realize your favorite book is also the local rapist's favorite, which might lead you to adjust your criteria. But if something is universally well-liked . . . I guess what I'm trying to say is you should hate Stephen King if you think he's not a good writer or doesn't write to suit your taste buds. Not because he's making more money doing what he loves than any of us ever will.

If everyone wants to be outside the crowd so much, then no one's outside the crowd. They become the crowd. Maybe you, antisocial aficionado, need to exist. The sole purpose of your kind that hates pop culture has to do with balance. Ying and yang, that kind of shit. If you have a lot of people liking something, then you have to have a group of people hating it. I only wish you had more creative reasons to hate it.

After he downed the last nugget, Bern Bern asked if I planned to go eat somewhere and I shook my head as he reached in the backseat for a small, rolled linen case like the ones chefs used for knives. He pulled the strap off the velcro and unrolled it, revealing a small collection of throwing knives, three-bladed stars, and a cloth rag, which he used to wipe down his plastic chopsticks before placing them in the case. He noticed me staring and said, Well, you never know when you're gong to . . . and the rest of the phrase disappeared into a giant slur. Serious conversations with him were impossible since he always went on like that—stuttering, mumbling, slurring, and refusing to make sense in the long phrases as if he stopped caring halfway. If he were ever cast in a movie, he'd be the extra in the background talking with the caption [inaudible dialogue] every time he spoke.

Sometimes he could multitask, though. When he lived with me and my parents, he could be on the phone with a friend while chatting with another online, sharpening his swords, listening to fast-paced Japanese music as inaudible to me as his speech impediments, and still be able to tell me—while struggling to annunciate half of the words—the basic plot of the anime episode playing on the television behind him. But then I'd ask him where the cordless phone for the hub office was, and he'd space out and say, It's on the—rolling out the *uh* sound at the end. I'd repeat the question, and he'd come back to reality and say, Oh, it's on top of the—and space out again. Even when he wasn't focusing on anything else. So any type of serious conversation concerning his girlfriend and one of my roommates was out of the question. He had twenty minutes left in his break, and it would take more than that to find any kind of resolution to at least bringing the problem forward. It seems we only went backwards when we talked. So we didn't say anything and sat there, by the side of the road, in silence, looking at the 23rd Street traffic traveling north and south.

In tenth grade, a few months before our state standardized test, the school came up with a program where advanced students would work together with regular students so that our passing average would go up. Because we lived in the same house, they assigned me to tutor Bern Bern in English without giving me any type of instruction on how to go about doing it. Bern Bern said, "Well, if you ask me, our teacher really only cares for just one hm."

"One what?"

"Grammar?" he said. "Yeah. That's all our teacher really cares a hm."

"You do know that grammar isn't everything, right?" He nodded but was still staring at an Inuyasha wall scroll in his room. "Well, let me put it this way. If I show you two identical paragraphs, one of them with grammatical errors and one of them free of them, what's the difference between the two of them?"

"One of them sounds dumb?"

"Well, yeah," I said, "but otherwise, the message is the same. There's nothing different about them. It doesn't matter if one of them has a few grammatical errors here and there because people will still be able to understand its message. Now, if it's littered with grammatical errors so much that the message is incomprehensible, then we have a problem. Or even worse, if one message is grammatically correct but has factual errors. For instance, if I wrote something like 'America didn't gain its independence from Taiwan until the nineteenth century' all grammatically correct, it wouldn't be a better sentence than the correct one with grammatical errors. Get what I mean?"

He thought too much about it.

"Point is, I don't know what the big deal about grammar is," I said. "What good it does if what you're saying with it is not even important."

"Well, my teacher said that—I don't know. She said that when people get hired to grade the essays, that all they look for is grammar and that you have five para-hms."

Grammar's not difficult to grasp if you want to be a writer. I was reading books and asking myself why punctuation was where it was, why the author started a new paragraph here and there, what was happening with the text at different points. But that was because I felt like it, back when I thought that if I ever wanted to make it as a writer, all I needed was great grammar skills. I wasn't sure Bern Bern *felt like* learning grammar since most people in our classes had the mentality that they'd never need it, or that they'd eventually learn it in college. Who can blame them? They were telling me in middle school math I'd never have access to a calculator in real-life situations. Bern Bern needed to forget about grammar and start caring more about making a good, important point.

During our first tutoring session, I came up with a sample prompt for us to brainstorm on together, something about validating what schools should take into consideration now that pen ink was turning into computer pixels. He asked me what I meant, and I said, "Well, we're part of this change where instead of writing by hand, we're typing up our essays. So how do you think this might affect how we learn?"

"Badly," he said.

"How come?"

"Well, because it would be stupid of teachers to trust us like that. Think about 'eh. Too many distractions with computers. Instead of doing our work, we'd be chatting all the time. We'd never get any real work done."

"Is that what you think?" I gave him a minute to answer. He didn't. "I mean, is that what you think, or is that what you think the people grading the test *want* to read? Are you thinking, *Hey, maybe if I say what they want me to hear, they'd be more willing to pass me because I'm agreeing with them?*"

"Well, what do you think?"

"I'd say it's a pretty good move. The fact that we write without even knowing we're really writing, even when we're chatting. Then there's also revision, which becomes easier and more effective by giving us the ability to modify in the middle of our text, which is harder with hand-written essays without having to block paragraphs and write notes for raters that read *Read this paragraph second*."

"But what about the grammar?"

He was probably right. In the end, to these people, it won't matter how smart the message is. They would take one look at your grammar and syntax, and if it didn't meet their standards, they'd fail you. So we started with a short story. "Bullet in the Brain" by Tobias Wolff. I told him to write it down, word per word, paragraph per paragraph, period per period, every mark, every letter, everything.

"This is going to basically force you to read the work slowly," I said, "and make you pay attention to all these little marks and what they're doing in the text. When we read, especially when we read silently, we tend to read quickly. We make patterns on how the words look like in the text, sometimes automatically read over them, and then we interpret them and move on to the next set. So while you're doing this, ask yourself what's happening in the text and *with* the text. I think it'll help you."

It didn't. Both versions were the same, only Wolff's was clean and Bern Bern's wasn't. "But you were supposed to copy this down," I said. "You were directly using—What the heck happened?"

"I get messed up with the punctuation."

"Punctuation is easy," I said. "It's all a matter of reading the text out loud. The length of your pause when you come to one determines the type of punctuation to use. For example, I use a comma after this phrase, you see, because now I'll be needing a period after this one. The pause for a semicolon is right in the middle of the two; it's longer than a comma and shorter than a period.

"When you're ready to have a shift in thought, *that's* when you start a new paragraph. So read your work out loud and listen in for the pauses. You'll get them. Now, about the story. Did you understand what it was about?"

"A bank robbery. Some jackass gets shot."

"Yeah, but it's about more than that, right? Otherwise why even write the thing."

"About what happens when someone gets shot in the head?"

"Yeah, but did you get its message? I picked this story because it reminded me of you."

"I'm not good at interpretating stories."

"Well, that's the thing," I said. "There are some stories that are not meant to be interpreted. They're meant to be experienced. Just like when you hear a song that's not about anything. A song that's only about the song. This story. It's about words."

"The thing about rhetoric."

He doesn't visit as much as he used to. Sometimes he'd stop by after work, watch television for a bit, not say anything because it would never take us anywhere, but we'd simply be here, being family, being friends. The other day, he called one of my roommates—a high school friend to us both—a "sumbitch asshole" and hoped for his and his new girlfriend's deaths on *his* public journal. I chose to stay out of it. It would only make matters worse, which is why I'm setting this post to private. It is none of my business, and it's not like anyone would be reading anyway, but it lacks understanding. We write in order to understand and find out how it all works. To see it in text like words in the air. Because we don't know what story to believe anymore. So here's the goddamn story, as I understand it:

I have twelve cousins on my mother's side of the family. Most of them are dead to me from either living so far away that I never see them or hear from them, or I dislike them because they're always around like leeches or because we don't have anything in common, only mothers that happened to have the same parents. Out of those twelve, I only talk to Bern Bern.

He's still dating Stephanie. Been doing so for some time now. Sure, they broke up a couple of times, but I would call those falling outs commas or em-dashes—not periods. She seems like a decent enough person in my book. Treats Bern Bern like the nice guy he is. Ever since they started dating, we see less of him. That's normal. Natural occurrence that happens when a relationship gets serious. It also doesn't help we live in McAllen and Bern Bern in Rio Grande City, which is almost an hour west, into the next county.

During one of the commas, though, I invited Bern Bern over to our house after work, and we all spent a good while chatting, without any interruptions that usually took the form of his girlfriend calling his cell. When midnight neared, Bern Bern's mom called him to suggest driving home already, and we spent another hour or so talking outside.

Then something went wrong. He wrote the shortest journal entry he had ever written, the one condemning our friend and his girlfriend to death. The situation cleared up after that (he even revised some of the wording in the entry), but the tension was always there, from refusing to get down from his car on my birthday to always asking if "the other one" was around before he'd stop by to visit. Here's where I think the mindless drama gets confusing:

Right before my roommate was flying to New York to meet his online girlfriend for the first time, Stephanie asked him if she could—how to put this lightly—suck his dick so that she could be his first. I don't know how the conversation played out exactly, considering I heard both versions from both parties, both of which have grounds to be biased in the way they tell it, but based on how excited my roommate was to go meet his girlfriend for the first time, dancing back and forth like an idiot when his mother approved and agreed to pay for the trip, I think his version, the one where *Stephanie* had the idea, sounded a bit more believable.

It's all fucking rhetoric anyway. Both truths already exist. Even if they're conflicting. Rashomon effect.

Bern Bern turned on the car and made the windows go up before a soft Japanese ballad started playing out of the side speakers. He reached for the power knob and turned it off right away.

"Don't worry about it," I said. "I don't care."

"We have about twenty minutes left, so do you want to drive like, eight minutes tha way and them come meh, not goin' far?" I shrugged and he started heading south towards Hidalgo, passing under 83 as traffic flew east and west above us, truck horns blaring and decreasing in tone as they added more distance between us.

When I knew he wouldn't speak, I said, "Any chance things will go back to normal?"

"I uh-know. Depends on some people. Or person. In particular. If he's—If he'll apologize."

"Even if he has a completely different story about what happened? I know it's hard to take his word over the word of the person you probably care the most about, but can you at least try to see the possibility that his story might have some truth to it? Not to believe it completely, but to believe in the possibility of it."

"What's the difference?"

"Open-mindedness."

When we were eighth graders, we believed in the possibility of spirits from the Ouija board. Deep down, we all knew it was bullshit, but it was nice to entertain the notion like people who read horoscopes to each other and laugh. So we thought it held the answer to all our relationship problems, that it was the only way to know for sure who would end up with Roxy, and so that we could strategize the right way. We always used it in the cemetery behind our friend Jay's house at the top of a hill, thinking it would work better if we were around a bunch of dead people. Bern Bern asked the board if anyone liked Jay as a test question the first time, and even though we all knew the answer already, we wanted to make sure it worked.

The board gave us initials of people instead of names. Someone with the initials *CJ* was interested in Bern Bern which made him question his sexuality before we learned the ghost was too lazy to spell shit out. The one underneath the unmarked grave we used the board on was *NED*, who died when he was *7*, of a *C*, and that his *M* was a *B*. We received initials because it was a bitch to spell out entire names since we made the Ouija out of half a white poster board with a *Don't Do Drugs* design on the back because none of us had the money to buy one and none of our parents would take us to the store hell-bent on picking one up from the toys section. Bern Bern made the oracle, I wrote in the letters and numbers, and Jay drew the sun on one side and the moon on the other as best as his skills allowed him to. It worked like the real thing. At least we thought it did, so we didn't complain. And Bern Bern looked on the bright side of the initials feature, saying it meant we didn't have to keep track of spelling out long names, so, if anything, it was better than a real board.

With his question, it moved to the *B* and then the *G.*

"Of course," Jay said. "It had to fucking be her." *BG* had been getting her friends to deliver personal notes addressed to Jay for several months. Sometimes, they would slip them in through the vents of the locker he shared with Luis, one of our other friends who would sometimes read them out loud during lunch for a laugh, imitating a stupid street slang because *BG* was the only black girl in our school. Jay didn't care if she was watching, broken-hearted and shit. Sometimes she'd write poems for him—haikus, sonnets, and regular rhyming ones—claiming they were her own work even though I saw her copying them off a Tennyson book (which I didn't think Jay could interpret anyway) at the library a couple of times. Jay didn't like her because she was black.

"We're going to break contact now," he told whatever it was we talked to, and rolled the oracle to *Goodbye.* He had already been angry since Luis didn't show up. Every Saturday it was another *quinceñera,* like everyone in his stupid family decided to have babies a week apart, Jay said once, and fifteen years later, they were ready to release them into dicks like horseshoe pitching. If it wasn't a *quince,* it was a wedding, or a wedding of the *quince* from a few weeks before.

I didn't like Jay much, which was probably why we eventually stopped being friends. When he was beaten in video games, he'd throw the controller (which he didn't own) against the wall and screamed as many bad words as he could think of. One time, one of my roommates refused to take a candy bar from him. Jay, in an act of anger, swung his backpack with a full-size combination lock attached to one of the zippers towards his head and ripped it open. Eight or so surgical staples later, most of us stopped being friends with him.

"Man, Jay," Bern Bern said. "I'd be shitting my pants every night if I was neighbors with a hm of goes."

Jay pulled out a pack of cigarettes he stole from his dad and offered them to us. Bern Bern and I didn't know how to smoke, but we each took one anyway. We lit them with the candle we always had burning to make the Ouija experience more real, and to be able to see the stupid answers in the dark. We pretended to smoke them.

"It's holy ground," Jay said. "It's been blessed by God. These people are in heaven now, so there's nothing to fear."

"My grandfather used to say that we should be more afraid of what's alive than what's dead," I said. I couldn't confirm this since he died before I had the chance to have images of him in my memories. I blew into the cigarette filter instead of inhaling it. "So, high school next year." We witnessed the wild breeze and heard the screams of the cicadas, contemplating about future plans we'd never realize.

A few days later, my mom found the Ouija board under my pillow and demanded an explanation. I didn't include Bern Bern in it so he wouldn't be blamed, too, and as she was starting to say that she didn't expect that of me, Bern Bern spoke up and said he helped me make it and we'd use it together.

"I had questions that needed answers," I said.

"What if you end up in hell?" my mom asked. "What if you end up getting haunted? What if the ghosts followed you two here?"

"Well, *tía*," Bern Bern said, "if that ever happens, who you gonna call?"

I stopped trying to understand Bern Bern as a person that day, as we lit the poster Ouija board on fire and watched it turn black and crumble as if the devil's hand were squeezing it and taking it with him. If I tried to create any kind of meaning out of Bern Bern, tried to interpret him in any way like a piece of literature, I'd fail.

PART ELEVEN

The Part About The Theft

Towards the final days of 2004—when our city saw snow for the first time in a hundred years, four fucking inches of it—our store had an employee appreciation lunch shit where the manager set up a grill in the back parking lot, by *la palma*, and he and a couple other employees grilled fajitas—a step up from the dark meat chicken we served our customers on customer appreciation day. It wasn't a feast where we all sat down on a long table and ate together like comrades while we posed for Leo. The store was required to keep running as if it were any other day we weren't appreciated, so that day, each employee went to the back during his lunch hour to have his free lunch. During mine, I tonged a couple of steaks, cut them into smaller pieces on a cutting board spotted with browned blood from the meat not resting long enough, and wrapped them in corn tortillas.

Some of the coworkers grabbed the big pieces of steak and ripped them apart with their teeth before removing the smaller pieces from their mouths to organize into rows across the middle of the tortillas. They reminded me of cavemen who had been vegans their entire lives and somehow ended up trying meat for the first time that day, some of them not even bothering to shoo away the flies landing on their food. It wasn't disgusting, but it was easier to turn the other way. That didn't make their voices go away. They spoke in low-pitched monotones that made no sense in any language—grunts, mumbles, and the kind of sighs you hear from the next stall when you're taking a piss. Someone behind me grunted in anger as he tried to bite a piece of meat off the whole cut. This was how communication worked during this hour. Whenever another employee joined us, they'd all greet him by mumbling his first name, or what sounded like his first name given by the number of grunts equaling to the number of syllables in the their names. Two grunts for me. And then they'd grunt what sounded like asking him to take a seat on the chipped picnic table adorned with a pot of meat, a stack of tortillas, and several salsas and pico de gallo, a language only made clear by their downward arm gestures. The lack of English or Spanish wasn't so much due to chewing with their mouths open or speaking with food in their mouths—though some of them did both simultaneously—but rather due to the success in understanding the vowel sounds they made, to there being meaning behind the grunts. They weren't inhuman. They never talked like this any other time, so it had to do with the food. Or it had something to do with humility, that they were being fed for free by the place they sold hours of their lives to and they didn't want to make a party of it. They wanted to be civilized and not be disrespectful. So they whispered. And they grunted.

Before heading back to work, one of the new guys, George, showed up to eat, and the voices around the picnic table suddenly raised in volume as they all invited him to sit down next to them with a single grunt. He was the new district manager's nephew, working the counter in hopes of advancing in the world of auto parts retail. And why wouldn't he? The company started to branch out like trees in a never-ending spring season, adding extra stores to extra busy cities, stores closer to competing companies, stores closer to the border areas to appeal to the Mexican consumer, or as Plato put it, Corporate America's way of saying, "Welcome, but stay as far away from us as possible." A new store in La Joya to add to the Rio/Roma route, two more stores in Edinburg, two more stores in McAllen, and the one in Hidalgo that would be opening soon, too, which meant no more Wolf. So our old district manager was in control of everything east of McAllen, and our new district manager, a fat man a few people habitually started calling

La Polla when he wasn't around because it rhymed with his last name, was in control of McAllen and everything west of it.

George's was a strange presence in this environment, though. If everyone at the store could be painted with a color, it would be different shades of evil, considering some of us were a bit more evil than others depending on our choice of crime and how dark our hearts became. George, though, was the complete opposite. No gray area or anything. Guy was whiter than bird shit on a black car. The epitome of good. Or he pretended to be because many of us didn't buy it. He always showed up to work earlier than scheduled, and when one of the counter guys asked him why, he said like a fucking band student, Because when you're early, you're on time. When you're on time, you're late, and when you're late, that's unacceptable. And I said, So either way you're fucked? And he covered his ears.

He always combed his gelled black hair straight to the back and had his shirt tucked in, while most of the men from the distribution center entered the store in their white undershirts with their uniform shirts hanging over their shoulders. He had a girlfriend he was planning to marry soon and he said he loved her and that he was looking for a home and could almost afford one he wanted to buy for her. A real fucking catch, this guy. When he would talk about her and their plans, some of the guys at work would ask him, You put it in her, yet? And George would say, No, I couldn't do that to her until we're married. I respect her. And everyone would laugh as soon as he left the room. He was a castaway. He didn't belong here. Refused to be infected with whatever it was our coworkers were carriers of. And I didn't understand how someone could be *that* good. The thing about this guy that topped everything else was that every payday, he would go cash his check before his shift started and buy Blue Bell ice cream cones for the entire store, at least anyone at the time his shift started. He'd roam around from person to person, letting them take their pick between caramel, fudge, or plain vanilla. Every payday. It always felt wrong to take one.

One time, I asked him, Are you sure this is what you should be doing? *Here's* where you want to work?

He said, Why not? I mean, my uncle gave me this job, and it would be disrespectful to throw it back in his face.

During employee appreciation day, he grabbed his plate and sat down, and then put his palms together, bowed his head and closed his eyes to pray. Outside his sight, the guys looked around at each other making sudden upward motions with their heads as if saying, And what's with this freak? Or, more accurately, *Y este, qué?*

"A short."

It's been 365 days to the dot since I've written anything worth writing. My roommates aren't worried. Their parents pay their rent. Pay their phones. Pay their food. It's a state of mind I wish I could be in again. The other day, I was driving to school and remembered a bill was supposed to be paid the day before, a couch purchased at a furniture store. I started running out of breath. They were going to charge a late fee. Or sell the account to debt collectors, and they'd start figuring out different ways to threaten me into paying.

Then I remembered I gave the last payment last month and closed the account.

It's possible my roommates have worries too. Everyone worries. Stress levels are relative, right?

I guess I forgot how good it felt to have time to write something.

It started to feel like a movie I'd watch as a kid over and over, the boss on the phone every time he asked me to come talk to him, the RLS, shaking his leg, shaking my foot, half spinning ninety degrees in the chair. I had started to mind these movies because he was in the habit of playing them during my lunch breaks and escaping for at least an hour was necessary, to think about something other than work. Credits, stop, rewind, play, credits, stop, rewind, play, rinse, repeat. Auto parts purgatory, but closer to hell than heaven. The past week had been half of each, but I couldn't remember where the half heaven came in since I was blinded by the hell caused by The Wolf, his assistant, and another driver doing the lunch runs who were supposed to be sorting out tickets and parts with me, and instead stood around talking while I did everything.

When the boss hung up the phone, he turned his chair to face me and asked if I knew The Wolf was leaving to Hidalgo. Oh, yeah, I thought, there's the half heaven I was thinking of. Which means, he added, that the hub is going to be left without anyone running it. I asked him to push you extra hard because I would like it if you took over the hub.

I spun the chair to face away from him.

If you think about it, he said, there's no one else who can. You'd be doing me a solid, little brother.

To push me harder? I asked. That wasn't pushing. That was more like, "Oh, you go ahead and do all my work for me. I trust you." So why ask me? You know I'd never go for the job.

Why not?

Well. Well, because of classes that's why. I work ten-hour shifts Mondays, Wednesdays, Fridays, and Saturdays so I can have Tuesdays and Thursdays off to go to school. You know this. Hub runs Tuesdays and Thursdays, too.

Yeah, about that, he said. This whole "help you with your tuition" program we have working here? They're not showing that you're even taking any courses. Not since you started working here. You haven't reported it. What's going on there?

Trying them out first, I lied. Before I make the mistake of paying for them, but I'm still going to school.

Lying consumes so much energy. Why do we even do it? It's tiring.

He looked back to his papers, probably thinking about what else he could do. I didn't have to explain myself to him. Even if I wasn't show-ing up to my classes, I couldn't take over the hub. If I did, I'd be here forever. I'd be like all the other guys here and count the days till I hang myself. Writing was my tether to keep me from turning into them. So I told him, What about Rick?

What *about* Rick?

Why can't he run the hub? He's done it before. I think he'd be qualified enough.

You know why. Didn't you see what happened with him last time?

No. Did *you*?

No, he said. But I wouldn't give the hub back to him.

So he made one stupid mistake. What do you think the chances are that he'd be stupid enough to make it again? Here's what I think—and you can feel free to disagree with me on this if you want, I don't give a shit—if you ask me, I think this time off has been good for him. Made him think that he shouldn't take the job for granted, that he should know what he can miss out on. I'm willing to bet that if you were to give him his job back, he'd be thinking about that every single second he does the job. Think it over. I'm going to have a fucking soup because I'm almost out of time.

He didn't say anything as I exited his office and into the back, climbed the stairs up to the second floor, shoes striking metal, and a few more to reach the lounge, which looked like a room out of the 70s. Lower half of the walls covered in bars of paper-thin plywood that looked more oak-colored than they were actual oak. Upper half enveloped in flowery, yellow wallpaper peeling off in several areas, isolated graffiti following the flower stems. Every piece of plaster over our heads had water damage, and through the hums of the refrigerator, the air condition, and the fluorescent lights, we could hear the rats crawling over the ceiling.

George told me, Don't you know it's bad to heat those up in the microwave? It releases toxins that can give you cancer.

Let's hope.

What?

I'm sure it would kill me a lot slower than using one of these glass cups everyone shares to heat the water first.

Rick, Flask, John, and Red were also in the lounge, eating, or having barely eaten and waiting for the hour to be over, or, in Red's case, waiting and drawing sketches of large-breasted naked women. They had been discussing marriage, trying to warn George of all its dangers. When I entered the lounge, John had been telling George not to do it because, When you get married, that's it, you're trapped for the rest of your life and there's no getting out, and then Rick added, It's not like the movies make it seem. You know how the word *marriage* sounds a lot like *mirage*? In fact, I think if you actually mix the letters around—

Nope, I said.

Well, he continued, in movies, marriage is like a mirage, man. It's not real, at least not what you think it's going to be. You don't get to do anything you want to do anymore. At first, I guess, it's okay, but then you kind of both let yourselves go. You don't have to pretend to be another person anymore. Work stresses you out and you don't want to come home and have to fix your own dinner. Then one of my neighbors has been flirting with me a lot, and when you're having this kind of life at home, it kind of makes you want to go for it.

I know exactly what you mean, John said. That's why we're warning you right now, George. It's going to happen to you, too, *güey*. Don't let all the free pussy fool you. Sometimes I've caught myself wanting to cheat on my wife, like I'll think to myself, Hey, she's going to be out of town next week, going to go see her mom and shit, and I'm thinking to myself that's the perfect time to do it. Seems like a great idea and everything. It'll be okay if she doesn't know, and it's a thought that, well, kinda gets you a little excited. So I go into the shower, if you know what I mean, and play a little one-on-one, and here's the weird thing, *puto*, after I'm all done and shit, I suddenly don't feel like cheating on my wife anymore. Like it ain't even worth it.

That's a thing, you know, I said.

What is?

Being clear-headed after you jerk one. Thinking with your head instead of your dick. I think the Japanese even have a word for it.

But it's still cheating, George said, right? To you, you already made this fantasy in your head, and it's like you did it.

He focused on some piece of grime on the table, probably thinking about how he wanted to finish his thought. I thought he wanted to say that the actual orgasm was the feeling of cheating, the feeling they would feel when cheating on their wives, like when you orgasm before a pornography clip is over and the girl's or girls' moans start to sound less pleasing and more like she's being raped as you sit there in regret, especially if it's Asian porn. But why add anything to the conversation? It's better to keep letting the characteristics add on to the definition of a typical auto parts store employee. This was us.

I don't know, Red said. I sometimes wish marriage wasn't about fighting all the time. Every fucking day: "All you want to do is fucking leave me," and, "Fine, then. Leave." We've been together since we were twelve years old. The fuck am I going to go? Yeah, I fuck other chicks sometimes, but she's my only wife.

You guys are fucking crazy, Flask said. I actually love my wife, and I don't cheat because I don't fuck other people. I only let them give me blow jobs or I go down on the girls at the club. Way I see it, it's good practice for me to use on my wife because, think about it, if I get better with them, then that's something I can use to make my wife happier. So everyone wins.

How's that not cheating?

It's not, Red said. You don't get it. We're men. It's in our fucking nature to desire other women. You don't understand that because you're not a real man yet. Maybe you'll know when you get married. When you're married, you get tired of dealing with the same person over and over again.

Some of what you're all saying makes sense, George said, but you guys have to realize how good you have it. You're all taking advantage of the fact that there is someone waiting for you at home, who cares more for you than any other woman will. That's the main reason I want to get married.

That sounds like something a chick would say, John said.

I clocked out later than usual that day because La Polla wanted to make me the same offer the boss had, thought he'd be better at convincing me. He told me, You're getting what, $6 the hour? Well, if you decided to stay and run the hub, we'd be willing to raise it to $10. How does that sound?

I said the offer was appreciated but readdressed the needed time to keep going to school, and before I left the office, I added, You know, Rick used to run the hub before. He was good at it.

Outside, I sat in the truck for a while as I looked on towards *la palma*, where Plato, The Wolf, Red, Güero, and a few others had lined up beer bottles along the wall, and with a slingshot, they shot rocks at them, trying to break them or knock them down at least. Sometimes the sound of glass breaking followed by manly cheers would sneak in through the vents, and then they would grab more bottles and keep on shooting rocks.

I took out my notebook from the glove compartment. The pages were hot. It had been sitting there for months. I wrote down *Employee Appreciation Day* and started with: *We speak different languages.* Then I ripped the small paper out, crumpled it with one hand, and threw it across the seat.

"Vampires suck, anyway."

I tried to start working on a series about vampires, to try to take the genre to a new level, but something keeps telling me I should write more important works. That it's not the time to get involved in the literary vampire.

I need to leave a few pieces of work behind. That's the plan. Pieces to be remembered by, not by the world or mass audiences, but by anyone who wants to give a fuck. It would be nice to leave a decent story behind, even if only two people end up reading it. Even if it never gets *published* published. I want to know I created and finished something worth writing. Maybe not worth reading, but worth creating.

Full of shit, isn't it?

George covering his ears almost every time someone used profanity around him didn't make sense. They'd say *fuck*, or *shit*, or even *damn*, and George would immediately place both hands over his ears as if that would make the bad words go away or would make anyone around him use less profanity. It was more like a late reaction than anything else. Why cover the ears when someone has already said the bad word? It's like putting on a condom *after* you've had the sex. If he could foresee the word coming, if it were possible, and cover his ears before, that'd be understandable. Otherwise, it seemed to do the opposite, like he heard the bad word and he wanted it to stay trapped inside his head.

He might as well have been fucking deaf and blind when Flask, Red, and John dragged him to a strip club for his bachelor party. They chose to take him to one of the clubs out on 107 in the middle of fucking nowhere, one of those BYOB ones.

You know what BYOB means? John asked George.

Bring your own beer?

Yes, that's what it stands for, but do you know what it fucking . . . ? John waited for George to remove his hands and then said, It means that because they don't serve you alcohol here, the girls get to show everything. Full nude, *güey*, pussy and . . .

From the backseat, George leaned forward, trying to hide his nerves from going to a place God wouldn't allow him to go, and he asked, So how exactly does that work? What does one have to do with the other?

John said, I have no fucking clue, but . . . And then he laughed, even though George only heard half of the phrase.

You want to come to the ones way out here, Red said. First of all, they're not as expensive as Stiletto's by the expressway that thinks it's *classier* 'cause it's surrounded by palm trees. Two, there's an understanding between us gentlemen that come to these. We come here because we don't want to run into anyone we know. We want to be, how you say, secret agent about it, and just in case we happen to run into someone we know, which chances are will happen, then there's that understanding I was telling you about. They're here because they don't want to run into anyone. We're here because we don't want to run into anyone. So we know neither of us says shit, because if you . . . And thirdly, and this is a rule for all strip clubs, the golden rule, if you ask me: chicks can't walk in alone. They can't even walk in with other chicks.

They made a U-turn, passing by a fireworks stand, to head back east since the strip club was on the south side of the road separated by a grassy median. Two hours earlier, an ad-less billboard advertising itself would have been shading the tanned walls of the club, a color that matched the skin tones of the girls who danced there. *Pie in the Sky* was painted in black cursive over its door.

Why not? Don't the clubs want their money?

Of course, John said, but if it were your chick looking for you, would you want them to let her in? Of course you wouldn't. That's why these clubs will only allow a girl to go in if she's with a man. So as long as your future wife and her brother don't show up looking for you when you start coming here regularly, you'll be fucking fine, especially if . . .

The parking lot at Pie in the Sky was covered with gravel and the people parked their cars wherever they pleased, sometimes blocking other cars, leaving the people trapped inside longer. A row of four palm trees separated the club from a drive-thru conveniently placed there so people could go buy their alcohol there and take it to the strip club. Flags stabbing the ground advertised sports drinks, micheladas, and corn. An adult video store stood on the opposite side of the club, simply calling itself XXX, with a marquee that read *Buy One, Get One*. Before the gentlemen exited the car, everyone except George reached into their wallets and started taking out dollar bills.

You don't want to waste anything more than a dollar if you have to tip these girls, one of them said. George couldn't tell who because he was trying not to trip on the rocks. As much as they appreciate five's and ten's, he continued, it's not like we're that well off either. George reached for his own wallet before Red grabbed his arm and told him it was his party.

I don't get it, George said. It's full nude. Where are you supposed to put the money?

They laughed while Flask walked to the drive-thru to buy the beer.

Now, John said touching George on the shoulder, the gravel crunching underneath them like pork rinds, I don't want you to pussy out on us and . . .

The first thing George did when they walked through the metal door was cough after being engulfed by the thick haze of cigarette smoke like fog on early morning drives to work, when it's still cold out for a few hours. The small club had two large televisions playing whatever sports they were able to tune into. From far away, it looked like one of them was a pre-recorded football game and the other one was hockey. He expected there to be a center stage, a main place where they'd play a song and they'd feature one girl to dance for everyone, like in the movies he saw between his index and middle fingers. But there wasn't. Only tables and chairs scattered everywhere and several girls doing table dances, either for an individual or for a small pack of men.

They took a seat at a nearby table and waited for Flask to get back. George kept eyeing the floor, not wanting to be the only idiot in the strip club covering his eyes, even though he felt in his heart that he was doing something bad. Flask showed up with a six-pack of longneck Bud Light bottles and opened up the first one with his teeth for George, who said he didn't drink. Tonight you do, Flask said, now drink up or we'll make you chug it with your asshole and you'll get drunk faster. Through George's covered ears, "Drop It Like It's Hot" started sounding like he was trying to listen underwater. All he could hear were faint noises and the bass beats in his body. At that moment, he felt the only thoughts that could make everything right were of his fiancé, Esmer.

Red lifted one of his dollar bills in the air and started waving it for any girl who'd spot him. When an older woman in her mid-thirties showed up, Red said, How about a little dance for our friend here? He's taking the big leap next week.

George thought of meeting Esmer for the first time at church, how they were both assigned to sing psalms in the choir, the first psalm being: "If I take the wings of the morning, and swell in the uttermost parts of the sea; Even there shall thy hand lead me, and thy right hand shall hold me." He looked straight at Esmer and sang it for her, to her, about her. He thought of this as a black G-string bounced in front of him, as long smooth legs ending in stiletto heels tapped up and down the board of the table like a Spanish flamenco.

Esmer wasn't even as pretty as that woman, George thought. She had her good qualities—good hair, the fact that she looked okay without having to wear makeup—but she had her faults, too. There was the acne. She would never wear something like this. She always used the same style of long dresses, and then there was a bit of a weight problem, too, but those were attributes he loved about her. Because all the good qualities outweighed the flaws, especially her religious foundations. She valued the sanctity of marriage, which was something that was getting harder to find. These were the qualities he thought about, the qualities he hoped would keep him glued together.

But there was no going back anymore, not when a pair of nude breasts were pushing into and rubbing against his face, the erect nipples working themselves around his tight closed lips as the nude vagina rubbed against his jean leg.

I drank a Diet Coke for lunch at the front counter because I needed a change of scene, natural lighting mixed with fluorescent, regular people mixed with the uniformed kind. Eating in the hub office was out of the question because The Wolf, even though he'd be leaving soon, didn't understand the concept of a lunch break and would still ask me to complete tasks in the middle of my meal. Plato's office wouldn't work since our lunch breaks had started to become aligned and his employees spent his time away in his office looking at *Hustler* magazines.

George came back from his lunch break carrying a box of oil bottles in his arms. He dumped them in front of the manager and said, I didn't steal these. No one said anything back to him, so he continued, I went out for lunch with Esmer. She picked me up. When she dropped me back off, I was going to my car to get something, and this was in the backseat, under one of my sweaters. I had taken it off because it was cold in the morning and then it got hot. And now I'm bringing this back here because I don't want to be accused of stealing.

The Rio Grande Valley fucked you that way during this time of the year. You'd leave the house early in the morning, shivering inside your thick jacket as you waited for the truck to finish heating up before shifting off park, and by 10:30 in the morning, it was forty-fifty degrees higher.

What happened? Jesse from the front counter said. Figured out it was the wrong oil, or what? But the boss held up his hand and told him to shut up, and then he asked George to talk to him in his office. When they were done, they planned to launch a full investigation, since it was obvious to him that George wouldn't be stupid enough to enter the store again with the item he supposedly stole. The boss asked to see me first, and that time, he let the phone ring and didn't answer it in order to get to the bottom of this problem.

The person I replaced, little brother, he said, was transferred because people were always stealing from the store, under his stupid nose because people had no respect for him. That's not going to happen now. I won't let that happen, and you know I've even cracked down on people I considered my closest friends. So, who do you think could've done this?

Well, I said, the first thing I would do is try to find a reason people would have to go about doing it this way. A motive. George said he found the box in his car? Obviously the real thief is either someone whose shift ends before George's, so he used his car as a place to hold the part and then planned to discreetly remove it on his way out of work. It's either that or someone who has some type of grudge against the district manager. Someone who knew that if George was caught stealing, then the district manager should be more careful about who he offers jobs to.

No, he said. No one here is that smart. It has to be the first thing.

What if Jesse's right? What if he did get the wrong kind of oil?

He slammed his hand on his desk. If only it were a part, I could see what kind of car it goes into. But it's fucking bottles of oil.

That doesn't narrow it down, does it?

He started with the people from DC, asking them if they had seen anything or anyone getting oil and taking it to George's car. Their eyes, already accustomed to studying naked bodies from previous minutes, turned serious, probably at the possibility of George stealing something. Nobody claimed to have seen anything. Same with the hub. Same with the commercial department. The stockers and the front counter. No one knew who could've possibly taken the oil and put it in George's car. When the boss gave up, he said, At least it didn't get fully stolen.

The next day, George asked to be transferred to another store a couple of miles north of us, saying he felt like someone was out to get him here. I feel, he said, like someone is trying to get me fired.

Which was my initial goal, but this was okay, too, I guess. At the other store, he'd have less of a chance of turning into us.

PART TWELVE

The Part About Rebirth

Near the middle of December, at dawn, as I climbed up on the loading dock to get back to work, Rick had shown up earlier to let me
know that he had his job back. He carried tickets in one hand, some
smothered between his lips, and parts with the other. He said not to
worry about doing anything for now, that he was in a great mood
and I should clock in and relax. He probably thought I had power of
influence around here, that if I could make him get his position back
after being accused of positioning himself behind Quique and humping away, then I could probably make more happen for him. Raises,
extra paid vacations, even let him run the whole store. I thought that
up until he told me about what they did most recently at his church:
watch *The Passion of the Christ*.

He asked me, Have you seen it yet?

Can't bring myself to watch it.

He took a seat nearest him, taking a quick glance at the 1980s
clock radio to make sure there was still time before the drivers started
showing up, and he asked, You don't want to see what really happened,
or what?

I've read the book, I said. I don't think I need it acted out for me in
an overdramatized way.

You need to see it, man. It'll change your life forever like it's changed mine. This year, for example, I'm not buying Christmas presents for any of my kids. You wanna know why? Because it's not their birthday. It's Jesus's birthday, and he suffered greatly for our sins. So we shouldn't be spending it forgetting about that.

That's the thing, I said. I don't want to see the movie because of what people are making it out to be. And I guess you can say I also pretty much ruined movies for myself forever, because I can't suspend my belief.

But it's historical.

Not what I mean. Take romantic comedies. I find them hard to believe because, as you've said on more than one occasion, it's not what real life is like. Life is bigger, so I keep telling myself that what I'm seeing on the screen are not real people. Who cares if they're fighting? We know they're going to end up together, and at the end, they do. So we get what we wanted. Our needs are met. Let's watch another. So. Not real. They're actors. People who get overpaid to make me think they're real people. I can see them kissing, and possibly there is a part of them that's enjoying it, but I'm willing to bet most of them grimace and wipe their lips as soon as they cut.

He stood back up and started looking through the rest of the tickets he needed to sort out before asking me, So what does kissing have to do with *Passion of the Christ*?

The actor is an actor, I said. Not Jesus. He's not really bleeding. He's not really being nailed to the cross. How do I put this? I guess what bothers me is that they're supposed to be depicting a real story, but we have no way of knowing if this is exactly the way it happened. Hollywood has a tendency to embellish and exaggerate. Writers always embellish. We're obsessed with lying about ourselves and everything else, making us seem smarter than we are, stronger than we are. In our minds, our life plays out like a movie, with explosions and guys' heads falling off and shit, because the truth is, life isn't all that interesting. If movies were like real life, no one would want to be reminded of that. And you can do your research, as much research as you possibly can, to get as close to the truth, but there are still liberties being taken in how you tell a story, which is why people always end up fighting about interpretations.

But I am a changed man, Rick said again. I'm not going to do anything that will displease the Lord. I'm going to start paying more attention to my wife and kids. I'm going to meet their needs instead of my needs. I'm not gonna spread gossip. It ain't even my business. And you know what else? You've, like, inspired me, too. Next semester, I'm going to enroll in college and go to school. Not too late, right?

Episodic images of Rick started flashing through my medial temporal lobe like a movie, everything he had done up to this point in the story—spreading gossip that possibly ruined people's reputations, humping people at work, using a coolant house to pretend it was his dick. I asked, Are you sure you're going to pull off this change? I mean, it feels like a huge change for you? You should take it little by little. One battle at a time to wean yourself off you.

Of course I can do it. I'm even going to be like George. No more bad words no more. Because when we use words like that, it makes Jesus unhappy, because he doesn't want us thinking or doing stuff like that. So why should I be the one to upset him? I don't need words like that in my vocabulary. I can go about my day, not using a single one. Give me one good reason we need them.

Because they help you emphasize a fucking point when you need to make one?

He shook his head and pushed through the hub office door with me tailing behind him. One of the DC guys walked in with a white bag full of tacos to share with his coworkers, to be the hero of the day, at least until the next person took his turn. Shoe Guy scanned the merchandise while the new inventory specialist, Spider Man, stocked at a slow pace. The guys at work started calling him that because, Shoe Guy said, he looked like the guy from the movie, and also because no one liked him. He had a habit of hiding from Shoe Guy to avoid doing the work, usually in the bathroom, or sometimes he'd clock in at the front counter and then walk around the back after his lunch break to take longer to get back to work, or sometimes he would stand in the aisles with a cart of parts to stock, holding a box in his hand, looking at nothing and waiting for the second hand to finish another turn. Someone caught him sleeping in the bathroom once, head back against the sink.

I caught up with Rick and said, Here's what I think. I don't think

Hey-sús minds so much that we use a bad word every now and then, as long as we're not using them to insult anyone, you dumb shit.

He laughed and spit out the invoices between his lips, sending them all over the floor. Or maybe he didn't have the invoices between his lips. Maybe it's funnier that he did. For comedic effect. Or he didn't laugh. Or he pretended to, but disliked being called a dumb shit, considering he had higher education in his sights. I don't know. You don't know.

But if we're screaming "shit" every time we hit our small toe with the corner of a piece of furniture, that's not a sin. It's not literal shit. And if it was, what is so sinful about talking about shit? It's shit. And screaming "shit" is a manner of expressing ourselves.

So then we don't express ourselves when we sin?

Maybe. Except when screaming "shit" when we hit ourselves, we're not hurting another person. You don't have to be self-conscious here and fear of being struck down because then it's a never-ending downward spiral of fucking cursing. Shit, I said a bad word, and, Shit, I said another one, and Fuck, now I can't stop. And if we start on the path of profanity, it'll lead to the first *goddamn*, which will make us feel too guilty to show our faces at church. Before we know it, we're stealing, coveting, murdering fornicators dishonoring our parents. It's exhausting being afraid to cuss.

You should still try to be a good person, though.

And I agree. But sometimes it's easier to pretend there's no one watching us, to pretend it's all for show, like a movie, to justify all the shit we say and do. I snatched half of his tickets—or picked them up from the floor—and climbed the stairs to retrieve parts from the second floor. Through the metal bars beneath my feet, Red snuck up behind Rick and tried to hump him, screaming, Giddy up, horsie. His pronunciation made it sound like whorsie. Rick pushed him off and said he didn't play like that no more. Because it upset the Lord. So why didn't he just *butt* off.

"Break"

I was supposed to work today, but there is this new kind of paid day we get called "floating day." I don't fucking know the purpose behind it. Don't care. All I know is that you have to take it between December 15 and January 15 or else you lose it and have to wait a year. With one day left in the time window, I took mine today. On a Friday. So two days off for a change.

And I'm sitting here, floating. Wondering if I believe everything I told Rick. I shouldn't even be writing this. I should be working on this stupid short story I've been putting off that might be a good fit for a young adult magazine. About a sandwich artist teenage outcast who gets trapped in an attic with a hot girl at a party and they're abandoned there all night.

I don't even like young adults. It's an oxymoron.

Rick gave me the road back when he was hub manager again, Because, he said, I know how much you hate being in here with everyone, putting up with everyone's—stuff. I have to say, though, that the hub is not going to run as smooth as when you basically ran it for The Wolf, but this is my way of saying thanks.

During my first run on the road, back on the Weslaco route, the cards had a funny way of playing themselves. In Mercedes, the guys greeted me, saying they didn't know I still worked for the company and asked why I hadn't visited them in a long time. I didn't say much, feeling like I either didn't owe them an explanation or it would take me forever to give one, and then they said, "Looks like we have some bad news for you. You're going to have to park out back."

They had an engine, covered in oil and grease which dripped off of it like something out of a horror movie that uses disgust to cover up the fact that it isn't scary. A customer of theirs wanted it sent back to Houston, which had to go through our store, which required the hub to take it back. So one of their youngest employees and I started rolling it onto a type of non-motorized forklift, pushing it on top of the forks. We loaded a palette on the bed of the truck, and my job was to hold the engine on the forks while the other employee rolled the crank to raise them. It took us about fifteen minutes to get the motor on the truck, and another five for me to wash all the gunk off my hands.

The route was running late, but the drive to Progreso made up for it. I made it a point to not think about my writing, not think about anything that had happened in the past year, with The Wolf and Flask and Quique and Shoe Guy, not think about anything, keep a blank mind and listen to the sound of the road, not look at the cars driving in the opposite lane, what color they were, who was driving them, nothing. When I woke up, I was back in McAllen, in my store, not knowing how the hell I had gotten back, wondering if that was all a dream I couldn't remember, but all the Progreso and Donna parts were signed for and delivered.

I take it that's why you're late, Rick said, pointing at the engine. He had my next route ready to go, all the tickets sorted, all the parts put away in boxes, which was a first. He said, If there was another truck, I'd let you take it, so let's unload this engine right now. He screamed for the DC guys to bring around the forklift, which had a chain linked to a hole in one of the forks. Rick jumped on the bed of the truck and started tying the chain around the palette under the engine, figuring it was probably the easiest way to secure it and get it out of there while Plato drove the forklift, moving it slightly forward. When Rick gave him the thumbs up, the forks started rising while Plato peeked through the area over the load apron. There was a crack sound. Rick started yelling, Whoa, whoa, whoa, stop. Stop. Stop. But it was too late. The engine broke through the palette, falling on the bed of the truck a few inches away from Rick's feet. Nobody got hurt, but the bang from the engine hitting the steel must've reached the front counter area, even through the closed doors.

A moment after that, while they were trying to figure out how to go about getting the engine off the truck, Mario showed up from the Pharr route and Rick said to take his truck, which smelled like ass.

Rick's oldest son mowed the neighbors' lawns so he could, according to Rick, start understanding the concept of earning and managing money. With Valentine's Day coming up in a few weeks (and the fact that he wouldn't get any help from Rick to buy his girlfriend a present) and a lawn that needed mowing, I asked Rick if he wanted to ask his son to show up and do it for us.

"This is a nice place," Rick said about our house. "I like the location, too."

"Yeah, the only reason Elle and I can afford it is because we have three other roommates living with us, pitching in for rent and the bills. A fourth friend is actually moving into the garage next week. You want a beer? I think one of my roommates—"

"Nah, I don't drink."

We stood around outside the house, leaning against his van, enjoying the few cold days we had left in South Texas and the constant chirping of thousands of olive sparrows and warblers on the power lines. "I used to drink," he said, "a few years back. Used to live with roommates like you, out in California when I worked over there. In construction. We used to get drunk all the f—reaking time. The truth is, I didn't like who I was back then. That was when my wife and me only had two kids. Needed to start thinking about them. So I gave up drinking because it turned me into a worse version of me."

"You mean there's worse?"

He knew I was kidding, and said, "So. Writer. Next week. Vacation time. Any plans?"

"I had several plans," I said. "I wanted to go to Denton with Elle and one of my roommates and go check out a used bookstore they have in their town square. I went there with Elle once, the year we met. It's nice. I found a couple of first edition Stephen King books, which her mom ended up burning. As it turns out, though, there's no money to go this time, which is kind of disappointing, but kind of not, you know. I should probably stay home, use that time to get writing done, which I haven't done in a while now. It's getting depressing. Life gets more depressing the more you go on without writing."

"That's good," he said. He waited for his son to turn the lawnmower back on and then said, "That's exactly the way it is with me and Fidelia, man. I don't know what to do. Or if I should do anything about it. Like I know she isn't my wife, but I love her."

"Guess we're moving on," I said. "I thought you said you wanted to start following the path of the righteous. You can't pick and choose what counts and what doesn't count."

"That's the thing. I actually know that what I'm doing with her feels right, feels more right than anything else. I know I have my wife and my children, and I love them all, but I also love Fidelia. It's possible to love two women, isn't it?" He looked for some kind of answer from me, but I shrugged my shoulders. "It's like you and your girlfriend. You live together, but you're not married, right?"

"Well, we can't get married in the Catholic church because there are all these rules she has to follow and hoops she has to jump through because she's non-denominational, and I wouldn't want to put her through all those sacraments. Seems like a waste and a checklist. If we get married in a Christian church, my mom says it's a sin anyway, so fuck it. I love her. And maybe *I'm* picking and choosing, modifying the commandments to soothe my conscience, but whatever."

"That's exactly how I feel about Fidelia, though," Rick said. "It doesn't feel like I'm doing something against Jesus."

A car passed by us, a male driver peeking out of his window to see who we were, a neighbor most likely. This was something that bothered me about this neighborhood. The neighbors weren't nosy. It only appeared that way because they were too fucking worried that people would break into their houses and steal all their shit. The other day, I parked the car out front instead of the garage, and someone had broken into it with a piece of steel, pushed it through the top of the window to get the door open, somehow without shattering the window. Stole the stereo and left the metal bar in the car. When I called the police to file the report, a short police officer showed up, one that would make it easy to reach for his gun and beat him with it, the kind of officer that people wished there were more of so they wouldn't get so nervous every time they got stopped for speeding because he didn't look the least bit menacing. I waited for him outside, sitting by the curb, and when he stepped out of his car, I told him what happened and pointed out the tool the drug addict used to break into the car, there, sitting on the driver's seat, untouched. As he was leaving, I asked if he was going to take it, run it for prints or something as I'm sure the guy was most likely in the system. He said, "You watch a lot of TV, don't you? That's not how these things work. This isn't fucking CSI."

"I guess you do what you have to do," I said to Rick, stepping out of the memory. "I mean, I'm happy you want to make positive changes, but what good are the changes when the damage's been done?"

"What do you mean?"

His son was nearly done with the lawn and it was about to get dark.

"Hey, would it be too much trouble if I asked you to give me a ride to work tomorrow? The truck's not working, and I figured I'd use vacation time to get it fixed. So would you mind?"

"Of course not, man," Rick said. "It would be my pleasure."

"The blockage"

If we're supposed to write to learn that we know what we didn't think we knew, then by that logic, every story we have to write is already inside of us. We simply have to move our fingers back and forth and make them come out.

I am starting to think I do not know anything.

When we couldn't fit the new stores to the current routes, we had no choice but to divide them, starting with the Mission/McAllen route. We needed to hire someone new, and Flask recommended Rollie, one of his neighbors from his apartment complex, a decent choice considering he had a lot of experience driving trucks for Budweiser. He took over the remodeled McAllen/Edinburg route, Mario did the remodeled Pharr/Hidalgo, Dago—because Rick couldn't stand his stupidity—was sent off to do the Rio/Roma route, I did the Weslaco one, and another recent hire did the Mission one. Flask and Bern Bern stuck around to do lunch routes and help Rick sort parts.

Every Thursday, Rollie would show up early from his lunch breaks, sometimes fifteen or twenty minutes before his break was over, and he'd walk into the hub office, sit next to the clock radio, and tune in to the local country station. It's George Strait Day, he'd say, and listen to a marathon of his songs, at least until his lunch break was over, and then he'd keep listening in the truck. There was something about the way he listened to the radio, static cutting through the vocals sometimes, that I found off for a Mexican man like him. Up to that point, I was used to everyone else in the store liking Spanish music—norteñas, mariachis, cumbias, tejanas. So for Rollie to sit by the clock radio and listen closely to every single word George Strait sang as if he were preaching to him, I don't know. His eyes reminded me of movies attempting to depict life early in the first half of the century, when families would huddle together in the living room to listen to the radio like a Norman fucking Rockwell painting. Sometimes Rollie would sing along to the songs, trying to recreate the story the songs were telling, but most of the time, he'd sit there and listen. Every Thursday.

One day in February, Rick walked in the office while Rollie was listening and changed it back to the party station. He liked rap and R&B more than anything else, almost everything the local party station played, except reggaetón, according to him, even though I had caught him several times raising the volume whenever the station played Daddy Yankee, though that could've been because Flask was in the room. So with only one radio in the office, they always fought for control of it. I had sworn off local FM radio like alcohol to avoid the temptation of having to call them and bitch about their music selections. I then discovered that you could listen to the iPod on the radio with an iTrip and loaded mine with audiobooks and podcasts, which started to make my job tolerable. I hoped one of the books would eventually lead to some kind of inspiration to get back to writing outside the journal again.

Hey, Rollie told Rick in the office, I was listening to that. It's George Strait Day.

Rick was looking over the invoices remaining to be sorted on the printer and then turned to Rollie and said, George Strait can suck my nuts, and he grabbed them with one hand, gave them a shake, and then left. He had forsaken the idea of being a good person during my time off. No one knew how it happened, if it was sudden or gradual, if he couldn't take it anymore and screamed all the bad words he could think of so everyone could hear because he had been keeping them all bottled up, or if he picked up the phone and started spreading all the gossip he had heard while being good, or if he decided this whole *Passion-of-the-Christ*-changed-my-life shit wasn't him. He had thrown his fake halo away by the time I returned.

Best part of all, he said afterwards, is that I didn't have to tell Fidelia anything about how I was feeling. I figured it's a lot easier this way. Everything can go back to the way it was, and I don't have to break anyone's heart, or go through the trouble of changing my life completely. No guilt. No regrets. And I get to be me. You don't get the feeling that you're being judged for everything you do anymore. Freedom feels so fucking good.

As soon as he was gone, Rollie tuned the radio back to George Strait, and then looked at me and said, It's George Strait Day, before placing his ear closer to the speaker, even though the volume was already turned up. I threw what was left of my soup in the trash and left the hub, walked around to DC, and entered Plato's office. He was there, reading the newspaper and sipping a Coke off a can.

Okay, I said. I have writer's block.

Really? How long have you had it for?

Too long. I tried starting this online journal thing a few months back, to think of as practice, you know, and I don't know. I figured all that writing would build to something better, even lead to some kind of break to get some real writing done.

He put the paper down and asked me what kind of shit I wrote in the journal.

Just the stupid kind. I'm not even trying hard or anything. I guess I figure I shouldn't waste my energy there, so I save my good ideas for my actual writing. Which I haven't been creating much of anyway. Anything I do work on in that area ends up being terrible.

Says who?

I don't know. I've been feeling a little meh from ever writing again, especially discouraged with what I'm working on right now. They're these two companion short stories that I thought would be pretty interesting to turn into film. I wrote the first one already, and I kind of liked it. It was about this daring girl, a play on the manic pixie dream girl archetype, who decided to sit with a man-eating dinner alone because he had been stood up. So they start to pretend they had known each other their whole lives playing along with it—kind of like a reverse *Last Tango in Paris*. I haven't started on the second one yet, but I wrote the first one in one sitting. I gave it to my four roommates to read, expecting more feedback from them. Three of them had only positive comments to say, went on and on about how good it was, and how it would make a great movie. The fourth, this new guy staying in our garage, didn't even bother to comment on it. It's interpretable as negative feedback, but not helpful. Some of the assholes from the writing group would've at least said *why* it's bad.

So, then, why do you think you have writer's block? Plato asked. I know the answer, but I want to see if you can find it.

I can't tell if these talks are like therapy or like dialogue. Given your nickname, the latter's more appropriate. I spit out my thoughts while you ask questions, only in a dialogue you would be agreeing with everything and saying phrases like "how true" and "you're right" and "lay some more of that philosophy on me."

And now you're avoiding the question, he said. Here's the thing. You say that you've been writing in this journal for a few months now, that what you write in it is basically half-assed because you're saving your good ideas for your actual writing. Do you not see what's wrong here?

Certainly not.

You're a baseball player. You haven't been playing a lot of baseball lately, though, but you know you'll play again one day. So, in order for you to be ready when this decides to happen, you start practicing running around your neighborhood, which even though it's still helpful, it's causing you to go backwards. It's helping you forget most of the sport. Then one day, when you actually try to swing at a ball, you begin to wonder why you're always striking out. Sure, you'll be able to dash to first base, but what's the point when you're not hitting anything you swing at? You've forgotten the sport.

Why? Why am I forgetting?

Your journal's the problem. If you're not trying to write well, writing well is not going to come to you. So I'd say either start writing for real on the journal or stop writing on it completely so you can focus on your real writing.

Back in the hub office, Rick was getting ready to leave on his lunch break as soon as Bern Bern returned from doing my route. Hey, Writer, he said as I double-checked that the parts for my route matched the numbers on the invoices, I was wondering if you wanted to come to my church on Sunday. We're going to watch the Super Bowl and make fajitas.

At church? I asked. Watch the Super Bowl at church?

It's gonna be fun.

Don't you usually go to churches to pray or something?

Oh, we'll be praying, but during the commercials.

During the commercials. For the Eagles or the Patriots?

The Patriots, of course.

I'll see what my weekend's like.

John was coming back from his lunch break and had overheard part of the dialogue and told Rick afterwards, Fuck you, *güey*. The Eagles are gonna win. How about it, Writer? You want to make a little bet, *o qué?* Bet you lunch at Whataburger that the Eagles win the game.

Fuck it, I said. You're on. Rick's church is praying for the Patriots anyway.

PART THIRTEEN

The Part About The Nonfiction

I've never been sensitive to other people's pains, never attempted to feel a part of anyone's suffering. I'd probably feel sadder for a dead cat on the side of the road than for another human being. I hate cats. Family members have died before. My father's mother died of muscular dystrophy when I was three. We'd visit her house for breakfast every Sunday after church, and she would try to get me to drink coffee like everyone else after making it in a saucepan. Mom kept taking it away, and all that back and forth made me hate coffee. I tried crying at my grandmother's funeral by creating images in my mind that actually made me sad, but the tears wouldn't come out. Mom's dad got a stroke when I was six. This was also the day Bern Bern found a butter knife buried in my backyard and threw it at my neck, meaning to throw it over the cement wall surrounding our property. Everyone else was at the funeral home, and when I walked over to show my mom the red mark on my neck and asked if it looked okay, she told me to be quiet because we didn't talk during funerals. I'm familiar with death—and getting hurt—as a natural part of life, so during hospital visits, any emotions tend to stay in the car. That's why when Rick told me about John getting a nail hammered through his right hand, "Oh shit" were the only words that escaped my mouth.

Sit down, Rick said, even though he knew I had to leave on the route soon, because I'm going to tell you the story of John. It was Spring Break at South Padre Island, right? If there's one detail you should know about John, it's that every single Spring Break, that's when he gets his vacation week. Every single year. They don't call him "Spring Break" John for nothing.

They didn't call him that.

He takes his other week sometime in the summer, Rick continued, so he can spend time with the family, but on the Spring Break one, he always ax his wife to stay home and not bother him for the entire week. It's his week. Men need alone time, too. And she has to put up with it. Always. I hear he left for the beach as soon as he clocked out of work the Friday before, likes to get there earlier so he can be one of the first people to get there before the traffic builds up on the Queen Isabella. He parties and judges car shows and always brings back Polaroids of naked chicks to share with everyone. So, on his first day there, he parked and realized that he left all of his cash at home. You see, he didn't want to have to bother to use the ATM machine at the island because the previous year, it wasn't working.

You know, it's actually—

So he had to wait in line *again* on the causeway to come back from Port Isabel to use the stupid ATM machine. This year, then, he went ready, at least he thought he was. Heh. He called his wife as soon as he realized he was cash-less, axed her if she'll deposit the money for him so he can check the ATM machine later on, hoping it works this time, and, in the meantime, he axed a guy he knows down there, this guy he sees every year, for money. Ten hundred big ones to get him situated, start checking out the scenes and shit, said he'll pay him back in a couple days. But what "Spring Break" John didn't know was that his wife was done. She decided to take a little vacation, too, and took the thousand in cash John was planning to take to the island. Left with their son to her mom's in San Antonio. Stopped answering her phone when John called. Perfect revenge plan. After a while, John started to freak out because he couldn't pay the guy back, and, yeah, it was a guy he knew from every Spring Break, but also a guy you don't want to mess with. So John had to call his Spring Break short and started to leave the island, but, you know, it's a bitch to get out of there with all the Spring

Break traffic, people from all over the country going crazy and flashing their titties and all, so he waited until early dawn. However, I hear someone who works for the guy he owes money to had been following him, so they ended up catching up to him as he was leaving, pulled their car in front of his, forcing him to stop. Guy walked out of the car in the back and pulled John out of his car, right? He was all tough and said something like, "Where's the money?" in this deep voice, and John told him the story about his wife and said he'll get it for him, but the guy didn't care. One of his guys grabbed John's hand, held it flat against the hood of John's car, and the guy grabbed a nail and a hammer, did the sign of the cross, and then hammered down the nail through his hand, to remind him that he needed to pay for his dues.

Oh, shit, I said, and then left on the route.

John wasn't always the best at dealing with money or coming through with his bets. He never did get me the Whataburger lunch after he lost, but could be that he forgot because I didn't want to be annoying and constantly bring it up. But people talked of other instances when he didn't pay, one of them a little before I was hired. He had been bragging about his new Gorilla Grip Club he bought for his steering wheel, said it was completely anti-theft, no one could break into it. The boss bet him $100 that he could do it in under two minutes and they shook on it. He used a can of freon to freeze part of it before smashing it with a hammer. John complained that he went over two minutes and that he wouldn't pay him, and everyone at work started calling John a pussy. When he couldn't take the insults anymore, he showed up to work with a $100 bill and handed it to the boss. To prove a point, the boss reached for a lighter and set the bill on fire right in front of him.

I tried spending my lunch break in Plato's office to let him know of my decision to stop writing in the journal, and that it felt like matters were getting better, the creative writing was flowing, but before speaking, Red asked, You heard about John?

Yeah. Think I did. About the guy he owed money to?

Plato grimaced and said, You better think again.

I gave him a rundown of what Rick said to me earlier that day, and

Plato said, You see, Red? That's what happens when the fat man starts spreading around gossip.

That's not what happened at all, Red said. You want to know what happened?

You know, I don't care how John's hand—

Well, I'm going to tell you anyways. In Red's version of the story, everything was the same up to the point where John arrived at the island, only there was no money forgotten, no calling the wife. Come to think of it, the only detail that was the same was the island. The truth was, according to him, John was there to judge a competition for tits, which was basically this: A pack of women lined up side by side, some of them in bikinis, some of them wearing nothing except bottoms and white t-shirts, or so Red hears, and then, at some point around the beginning or something, they're judged by looks first. This is done by someone who some local magazine calls an expert on babes, and then by the general audience according to applause volume, but the competition doesn't stop there. Afterwards, Red said they got rid of the uglies and moved on to the pretties.

Now, he said, because the entire audience can't run up to the stage and grab tits, that's where John comes in. His job was to walk up to each of the remaining contestants and cup their boobs, get a good feel for them, their softness, or their firmness, their overall shapes and sizes. He'd judge them from a scale of one to ten, sometimes adding a point-five for laughs. He'd give them a little squeeze to see how good his hand felt when it took hold of them. Then give them points.

According to Red, after the winner was declared, there was a woman who caught John when he was leaving, readying himself to check out the public access beach for any other women flashing their boobs, and the woman claimed she was cheated, that she should've won.

"You're that guy that grabbed my tits, aren't you?" Red said she said. "Well, I think you, like, totally rigged the competition. I think my tits should've won." He made a high-pitched voice when he impersonated her and waved his hand around with every other syllable as if it didn't have any bones in it, an inaccurate but typical personification of women. And you know what John's like, Red said. "Well, I don't know," he said, now in a deep mocking voice. "Maybe I was being a little unfair, but I'm pretty sure I made the right call here. I'll give you the benefit of the doubt, though, so let me feel yours again to make sure." So he stood in front of her and started squeezing her tits again, like when you're checking an avocado to see if it's good. The messed up part was that he did it right in front of her boyfriend, who became pissed, pulled out a jackknife, and stabbed John in the fucking hand.

The stories of John went on like that for the next two or three days, sometimes being changed a bit, sometimes a lot. It was all the workers talked about, which was understandable since it wasn't everyday someone got hurt that way, even if it was the ends and not the means that were nonfiction. V-Lo had one of the craziest versions. In his, there was no Spring Break, no beach. He told anyone who would listen that John had been stealing parts from the company, one by one, since he had started working five years before. The truth was, according to V-Lo, he had been working on a car built with stolen parts. He had found an old Camaro and was rebuilding it completely. Now, V-Lo said, to do that, you need proper equipment, or you'll lose a hand. His accusation caused him to go in for an interrogation, in which he admitted to making it up for laughs.

While passing by Shoe Guy and Spider Man to collect parts for a route, Shoe Guy said to him, That's why you have to know how to handle a lady with your hands. He held his index and middle fingers upward in front of Spider Man, like a closed peace sign, and started gesturing them in a come-here motion. This will make her squirt out of her pussy, he said. If you don't do this for her, you're going to get her angry and she'll stab your hand with a kitchen knife. He burst out laughing and Spider Man chuckled while he scratched one of his pimples with his forefinger and stared at the ground.

Sometimes it was John's left hand. Sometimes the right. In a couple of retellings, he lost his entire hand—once with a hacksaw and then with a meat cleaver "handled" by this strong man. The latter came from one of the guys from the front counter directed at me, while purchasing a Diet Coke. Really? I asked him. A meat cleaver? Did the guy happen to be wearing a hockey mask, too, because I think I might know the guy.

Now you're making shit up.

In the main office, soda in hand, all it took was one look at the boss with a blank expression for him to say, I know. It'll all blow over in a couple of days. When I started leaving, he stopped me and added, Wait, but don't you want to know the truth?

I don't think I can handle the truth. I'll settle for the fictions for now. It's more interesting this way. Keeps the mystery alive. And it remained alive with San Peter's version in the commercial department, which was also about owing someone money. Instead of the island setting, it was at a ranch outside the city limits where John would fight his cocks, which sounded more plausible to me because I recalled a time, while I was working under The Wolf, when John spent an entire afternoon talking to me about his roosters. He wanted me to write something about this type of life, his type of life, how he'd train the roosters for days, keeping the fighters on special diets and on steroids. He followed me through the aisles as I slaved and sorted parts, wiping his own sweat from his shaven head and explaining how the derby works in the fights, how they weigh the roosters, and then match them, how people bet, everything. He wouldn't shut up, at least until I photo-copied "Los Gallos" by Gilb and gave it to him the next day, told him it's been done already, so we'd need a new angle for this writing project. San Peter's angle: a machete through the hand after not paying up on a bet and a severe case of tetanus.

Before leaving on the last run of the day, Bern Bern asked if I had heard about John.

About what, I said, that he died?

His face turned serious and spat out, He died from trying to catch a dart?

Completely unreliable. All of us.

For what it's worth, let me put your mind to bed. Sometimes, when the stores closest to us can't wait another hour for the hub to send them a part they need to sell—or they missed the route taking off to their stores right before putting in an order—they send one of their commercial drivers to come and pick it up at our store. That way they can take it back immediately and the seller from that store makes his commission.

Sometime a little after Rick was promoted back to hub manager, the small branch a couple blocks north of us (the only reason for its existence: to take customers away from the competition next door) hired Lisa as a driver/stocker and to work the counter every now and then. She was the one that came to our store to collect parts, her uniform tucked in tightly to accent her figure, her jeans strangling her legs to accent her ass. It would be an understatement to say we all liked looking at Lisa when she'd stop by considering almost everyone rushed to her aid because we all wanted to be the one to hand her the part, take a close look at her brown eyes and take a whiff of her long ash-blond hair that fell in hair-sprayed curls and smelled like some kind of expensive fake-brand shampoo.

One time, I handed her a carburetor and one of her buttons was unbuttoned.

Sometimes she walked in through the side door, through the commercial department, and even if they were in the middle of some humpfest, they stopped what they were doing and asked her if she stopped by to pick up a part, even if they knew that was the only reason she came to our store. Other times, she came in through the back, the loading dock, and every time she climbed up the stairs, it was as if she did so in slow motion, her boobs jumping a bit like they had hiccups, and all she needed to do upon reaching the top to complete this archetypal imagery was swing her hair around, which she did sometimes, as if five fucking stairs broke some sweat. Shoe Guy greeted her most of the times, always reminding her, while putting his hand on her shoulder, that if there was *anything* she needed, that all she had to do was ask him. When they talked to her, it was creepy like that, especially when Rick talked to her. All he needed to say was, Hi, Lisa, and it sounded like he wanted to take her to the alley and rape her, even if he was smiling. Tone of voice, maybe. Slight sense of nervousness, the bit of saliva that seeped out of his tongue with the elongated S sound in her name. Sometimes they played around with her, used sexual innuendos she never seemed to catch or pretended not to. Innuendos like, I got your part right here. Or, Do you want me to load this shaft on your bed?

She signed my tickets once while I was covering that store one Saturday, wrote *Lisa* right underneath the *Inspected by* and, like a fucking idiot, I said, "Your name's Lisa?" even though it was written on her fucking uniform. She giggled and then continued scanning some merchandise. "That's my sister's middle name," I said.

She never caught on to the innuendos, but it was obvious she knew the effect she had on the workers by the way she looked around from side to side as if she were making sure she was being looked at, knowing how her role in our space defined us all.

One day it was John who had a part for her, even though he wasn't even part of the department. He had actually paid Rick five dollars to let him know when she was going to stop by to pick up a part because John wanted to be the one to give it to her, and as soon as Rick told him, he ran to retrieve the part and waited around the hub office. When she showed up ten minutes later, he was waiting, compressor in hand as if it were a dozen roses. He even said, I believe this is for you, and the strangest part was that it worked. She touched his arm.

When she left, he said to anyone within earshot, I'm going to lick her asshole. Ever licked asshole? I like to get it right here in front of my face and lick it around the edges. He put his hands up in the air and then mimed the spreading of ass cheeks which looked like opening a truck's back window. Then he buried his face in between his hands and waved his tongue around the area. And then with this finger right here, he said, you can massage the ass right here.

That's pretty nasty, someone said. What if she don't wipe it right?

What's wrong with eating a little shit sometimes?

Against the boss's advice, he left his wife and child to move in with Lisa, just like that. As far as anyone knew, it wasn't anything that he had been planning long term. Mid-life crisis, but at 35. His wife wasn't treating him badly or anything. His son wasn't resenting him. He had a nice family, good things going for him, but he decided to be with Lisa.

We all saw her differently after they moved in together. She always wanted it to be him waiting for her with a part. She would speed a little to arrive faster and allow herself five extra minutes to sneak into the back corner of DC, where Brown used to piss to avoid having to walk to the bathroom, to make out and grab each other's junk. The rest of the guys from DC would huddle up between palettes of oil to spy on them and laugh under their breaths. Sometimes the guys from commercial, the hub, and Shoe Guy would join in to check out the show. I saw them once, too, but I tried not to stare too long.

You like her, or what? Shoe Guy asked me as I started to walk away.

I'm not like you guys, I said. I have a girlfriend. But I didn't know why it bothered me. It shouldn't be bothering me.

And that was how it went every day, sometimes two or three times a day.

On his days off, she always talked about him when she stopped by, saying John this and John that, leaving me with a ringing in my head. When she didn't work, she showed up in her pink Victoria's Secret pajamas and tight tank top with food for John, that way everyone could envy their happiness, his upgrade, which lasted for a month until he knocked her up. For a man who doesn't pay much to the people he loses bets to, he was quick to take her to the abortion clinic in downtown McAllen, pushing through the two or three old men outside holding protest signs. How many different arguments he came up with for going through with it, or which one actually ended up working, is unknown. Fiction's required. Some of the guys at work said he tried telling her about all the responsibilities of having a child, that he made up horror stories about his own son, about how he always misbehaved to paint a picture of what a horrible burden having a kid could be. Someone else said that the argument that finally worked was: Think about it, babe. If we do this, it'll be just the two of us, and we'll go places, schedule vacations together and travel, and no one will ever bother us. It's really an awfully simple operation, Lis.

None of these fictions mattered, though. Who knows what version was used. In the end, they still sucked the fetus out. And abortion changes you.

At first, there's a sigh of relief. John and Lisa walking back inside Lisa's small, one-bedroom apartment, guiding her to the nearest couch so she can lie down from the cramping, turning on the television to see what's on that can keep the thoughts trapped in the tube. But then you start to think about it. He starts to look at Lisa, at how beautiful she is, and starts to wonder what the baby would've looked like if they had only waited like he waited for her with parts. Lisa, through almost closed eyes, looks at him and starts to think that their baby would've gone to college and ended up supporting them, and that he'd never have to work at the auto parts store again. And these thoughts, of handsome heartbreaker and classy congressman, keep running through their heads for the rest of the day, rest of the month, sometimes for the rest of their lives, and all it takes is a quick press of the power button on the remote to turn the TV off for him to tell her, "I made a mistake. I'm sorry. I need to go back to my family."

And just like that, the fling was over.

That night, while he slept, Lisa thought it would be a good idea to keep him on the bed forever, so that they could have sex all the time and make baby after baby. So she climbed out of bed slowly and grabbed her mini tool box in the kitchen, looking for the hammer and the biggest two nails she could find. When she entered the bedroom again, she grabbed his right hand and held it against the backboard with the side of her palm, her thumb and forefinger holding one of the nails slightly over the middle of his palm. And then she hit the head as hard as she could.

The visit to the hospital provided the right amount of sympathy from his wife to take him back.

I married Elle the following month. The conventions that come with it would help keep me under control. We didn't tell anyone until a few days later.

PART FOURTEEN

The Part About Literariness

Trevor "Cool Whip" Whippley was destined to be a failure. He moved into the garage the night before a tow truck appeared mysteriously in front of our house at three in the morning to repossess his car with Connecticut plates. He worked at a photo studio a few blocks north of the auto parts store, at least until he couldn't drive himself there anymore, and then I told him I could ask Rick if he would set up a job for him at the store. He met Elle online on some social networking site—I stayed away from them altogether since my breakup with journaling—which is how he came to know all of us at the house. She worked at a different photo studio and Cool Whip thought it would be a good idea to meet her and bring her coffee to work, unaware that she was married. We met while I was picking her up from a shift.

Cool Whip lasted four weeks until he took off his uniform shirt on the last day and hung it over his shoulder as he walked to the manager's office, bright white undershirt glaring with the summer sunlight bleeding through the holes in the cement walls of the warehouse. He told the boss, I'm sorry, but I'm going to have to resign. I'm afraid I cannot function in an environment such as this anymore. It's not suitable for me. Ergo, I feel as if I am forced to be unprofessional here, and I will not be able to handle two more weeks of this rubbish. He exited the store and waited in the truck for me to finish my shift. The boss and a few others laughed at his choice of words for a good thirty minutes.

The first domino fell a little before my return from surveying and mapping out a new delivery route, as even more branches continued to appear across the Rio Grande Valley, to find Rick leaning on the counter of the hub office, pensive and fat ass hanging in the air, as if he wanted it humped to play around. He rested his head on one hand and swung air at his face using sweaty invoices with the other. Summer is the season for suffocation and our summers started in May. Rick was starting to take breaks more than work lately, and right after his raise, too. That probably had something to do with it. There's a study that suggests getting paid more leads to a worse performance or something like that, but that might only be for jobs that actually require you to think. You have it real easy, Writer, he said every time he was not getting work done, as if he thought it was upsetting or something. You're out there on the road, in a truck with A/C, while I'm in here, getting all these parts ready to be shipped in this hot-ass warehouse.

I'm not saying anything. You need a break, take a break. It's fine. As long as we're still running, no?

He kept fanning himself with the tickets. It didn't feel like the room was filled with tension, so I approached him with the clipboard and said, I don't know if the Harlingen route is going to work in the time we had hoped. We're going to need at least fifteen more minutes if we're going to account for construction, traffic, and driving the speed limit.

He called me a motherfucker, he said and then walked to face the A/C unit vent instead of the clipboard. Cool Whip. He called me a motherfucker.

It took a while to process who he was talking about. No one was used to the nickname yet because Rick was the only one in the store who insisted on keeping it alive. Some of the guys in stocking and commercial liked to poke fun by nicknaming other people, too, but they would eventually drop it when it started to get boring. Not Rick, though. If Rick had the money, he'd drive me to the courthouse to get my name legally changed to Writer. Since Cool Whip's last name was Whippley, the only white guy in our McAllen branch—and there's a semen innuendo in there, too—Rick christened him Cool Whip, saying that Trevor was "cool" as his main reason. Sometimes other co-workers would think of an actual whip and thought it had something to do with being *pussy* whipped, doing the whipping motion with their hands every time Cool Whip passed by them.

What happened? I said. I had laughed at first because I thought of the literal meaning of motherfucker, and calling Rick one was like calling his uniform shirt red and the shorts he wore everyday stretchy—in other words, simply another adjective that described who he was. In the literal sense, he fucked his wife (and was starting to get back from lunch a few minutes late because of this, according to him), who happened to be a mother, so, yeah, he was most definitely a fucker of mothers.

He kept calling me *fat*, he said.

There was also something funny about the way he said that word, too. It sounded a bit like *fate*. He stretched the vowel, made it sound like it was disgusting to be that way, and no one likes being fat. I know this. He continued to explain how they argued over the company's newsletter, how Cool Whip kept saying Rick was the guy on page 13 because he was so fucking *fate*. He even remembered the page of the newsletter, as if he wanted me to take a look and see for myself. He looked a bit scared, too, afraid that we would stop being friends because of this whole fight with Cool Whip. So he spoke slowly as if he were desperately trying to prove he was in the right here, and not my roommate.

After that, Rick said, I told him he was the guy on page 18 because he had buckteeth, but I was playing around, you know. I was joking when I told him. You could tell by my tone of voice that I was totally kidding with him.

Trevor does have buckteeth, though, I said, so, yeah, I'd say you probably stuck an insecure nerve with that one.

What, and I'm not insecure about my weight?

We usually avoid those conversations.

So I told him, Rick said, and these were my exact words: Yeah? And you're the one on page 18 'cause you have the buckteeth. That's when Cool Whip said, "Well, you're nothing but a motherfucker." Then he took off on the Rio/Roma route. I'm waiting for him to get back and see what he's going to do. I think he might quit. He looked like he was going to quit. I know you hooked him up with the job and everything, but you believe me, right? I have the newsletter here. As proof of what happened. So you'll take my side if this shit heats up, right?

Everyone was familiar with the company newsletter *Team Spirit*. Every month, corporate would send a pack to each store for the manager to dump in our mailboxes like religious propaganda, short cheap magazines of about twenty-six pages to keep our spirits lifted and our work ethic motivated so we could continue doing a good job and work as a team. With spirit. I liked reading through mine during a lunch break, looking at the letter from the editor, some white guy with a stupid face that looked like he needed two or three copyeditors to say something correctly. Sometimes laugh cynically when he wrote about the "culture value" of working in a company like this, and how we treat everyone around us with respect, and how we build strong, lasting relationships "that keep us together under pressure." The editor hadn't seen our store, the scary masks we all wear to hide something much scarier. It was always funny to read this in the middle of some commotion or a conversation going on in commercial that proved the complete opposite of what the editor thought he saw when working for the company. While V-Lo humped one of his employees and laughed, forming strong, lasting relationships by rubbing his pants against someone. While someone pinched the new fat guy's man tits and yelled "honk" or while someone else waited for something to be dropped—a ticket, a part, a coin—only to stand behind the victim while they bent down to pick it up. Culture value. Workplace *pelados* who feel a constant need to perform for each other. To see who could come up with the most sexual prank or joke. Who could display his fake virility the most. Who had the bigger fiction. The editor would close with a line like: "Respect is the glue that holds us together."

In the "Service Awards" section, they displayed lists of people who had been working a long time with the company, starting with the most years of service and ending with the least, the lists lengthening by the page. The issue that caused the fight didn't have enough employees for a list, so they had to include employees celebrating their third anniversary with the company. In a little over a year, my name would be on that list. I hoped to be out of here before then. This was also the only place in the magazine where the Rio Grande Valley branches were recognized. Photos of our store never made it in there, either because corporate was never willing to send down their newsletter people, or we didn't accomplish much.

So outside the lists of names and letters from the editor, there were also letters *to* the editor from customers usually saying what great service they had (some of which were fiction), a bullshit section about staying healthy in the workplace, to stay hydrated and oxygenated when our job descriptions required us to do the opposite, and then the pictures of other employees from faraway branches tending to a customer, stocking a part, installing wiper blades for a different customer, or smiling in a group or individually at the camera. And since there were no pictures of us, we pretended we were in there by searching for lookalikes every month. Someone in our store would find a fat guy with a goatee, write *Rick* by the picture and an arrow pointing to him. We'd look for cross-eyed black guys and say it was V-Lo because of his dark complexion. A pimpled teenager in the background of a group snapshot was Spider Man. Anyone with glasses was Writer. Anyone with a short mustache and crew cut was *La Gata RIP*, still leaving an impact after being gone for months. One month, a salesman from our neighboring branch in Mission made it to an issue—some award or bonus-less recognition he had won, a gift card for the auto parts store—someone most of us had met in person from working ten minutes away from him. We still thought he looked like Shoe Guy and wrote that in.

We kept the ones that came the closest to looking like one of us, cut them, and pinned them on the bulletin board in the hub office, always hoping to find better ones the following month. Cool Whip found a great one of a fat guy in a Santa suit—some upcoming Christmas in July company bullshit—that looked like Rick and accepted his initiation as one of the auto parts clan by writing Rick's name with a black marker next to it. In retaliation, Rick found one of a bucktoothed white guy from a Mississippi store and tagged it with *Cool Whip*. By the end of the day, Cool Whip had supposedly called him a motherfucker for it.

I can't choose sides yet, I told Rick. I haven't even heard the other side of Trevor's story, so there's no way to make up my mind on the spot. Either way, I have no involvement in this clash, don't care one way or the other.

The printer had been spitting out orders we needed to have ready to go for the next day, and I had no desire to let the last twenty minutes of the shift drown in Rick's gossip. I tore out and divided six invoices before squeezing my way around him towards the exit.

It's not Trevor, he said. It's Cool Whip.

What does that have to do with anything?

How come no one ever gave me a nickname? he asked. Everyone has one except me.

It wasn't the best time to tell him people had been calling him The Whale behind his back for months, most of the time in Spanish—*La ballena*—but sometimes in English.

The hub office door always swung fully open with a bang that echoed all over the loading dock. Dust rained in a few places as the garage door chains slapped against the wall. We were starting to interpret the noises as a sign that Rick's break was over. On the way out to get parts, Bern Bern came in from driving the Weslaco route. He was putting the invoices back in order when he almost bumped into me.

Hey, I said. So were you there when the argument happened?

Rick and Cool Whip? he said and then nodded.

So, what happened? Whose fault was it?

Well, he said, if you ask *me*, Rick was in the office when Cool Whip—But Cool Whip was eating lunch. Those soup humms you guys always bring, heat the microwave. And then, *Rick*, grabbed the magazine to make fun people, and Cool Whip said he was fat.

The day before Cool Whip brought Elle coffee to the studio, at my parents' house in Rio Grande City, my dad, out of the blue, took an interest in my writing. He had never seen any of my writing in high school because I was either afraid he wasn't going to like it or afraid he was going to think it was stupid. The first time we talked about the possibility of me being a writer, he said that the best writing in the world was political, that all good writing is political writing. I thought he was talking about the memoirs written by politicians and ex-presidents, but some years later I looked up the definition for the word and understood what he meant. Sometimes it helps to read a definition like poetry. Dad dropped out of school in sixth grade to work but never stopped reading. Newspapers like *El Mañana* and *El Norte*, sometimes the same story to decipher which political side each writer took. Magazines like *Proceso* and *¡Alarma!* Books like *Vivir para contarla* and *El laberinto de la soledad,* the latter of which he gave me for my thirteenth birthday since he couldn't afford to buy me a present or he forgot it was my birthday, decorated with dog-eared pages, coffee stains, and spine wrinkles. I still hadn't read it. So when he asked me what my writing consisted of, I could've answered him with, "Mostly horror works because I've always wanted to entertain people." He probably would've said, "Entertaining is good. Enlightening is better."

I ended up saying, "I don't know who I am as a writer yet. Or if I should even call myself a writer."

"You're never going to be one if you look at it that way."

In twenty years of knowing him, or thinking I knew him, he never wrote *anything* down, not even part of a grocery shopping list, or something he needed to do, somewhere he needed to be, a math problem to solve something financially. His signature was a cursive capital *A* followed by lifeless scribble. He never wrote reminders. Never wrote me letters. Nothing. He never needed to. He continued asking about my writing. "Is it at least exciting?"

"You mean, like, adventurous?"

"I don't know. Sure."

"Sometimes not a lot is happening," I said. "Sometimes the only action is happening inside the character's head."

"Is plot that important, then?"

"Plot matters."

Coming to a decision to buy him *The Da Vinci Code* for his birthday earlier that year—a new copy of it—is a mystery to me. I had never read anything by Dan Brown, and, if anything, he would probably get a kick from reading something that presented him with a plot that showed how stupid the church was, which was something he always argued about with my mom as if it were the one subject that would cause them to end their thirty-some years of marriage. He never read it. A couple months later, while visiting them again for a weekend, the book was placed in my bookshelf next to all my old Stephen King and Richard Matheson books. He probably felt that's where it belonged. While my parents slept, I started reading it, read it through the whole night, and finished it in the morning. There's a reason you can finish books like that in a single night. I liked it, though. I downloaded the audiobooks for his other three books to listen to at work.

San Peter from work had also been reading Dan Brown books, though in Spanish, at around this same time, and we talked about them at work, sharing reviews and wondering how much of them were real and how much of them were bullshit. He became the one person, outside of Plato, capable of holding intelligent conversations. At least holding what I presumed were intelligent conversations because when Cool Whip caught me listening to *Angels and Demons*, he said, Holy shit. You're actually a step up from *Green Eggs and Ham*.

What do you mean?

What you're reading is shit. They're stupid books. How do you expect their letters to stay ingrained in your mind? You've said you read a lot. Can't you tell a good book from a bad book?

The iPod Mini display read *Now Playing* at the top with *Chapter 5* right below it.

There are some books, he said, that we call genre books, books that follow a specific formula, that stick to that formula, so they don't have much else going on for them. Because they can't break that formula, no one says anything new, or anything different. Then there are the books that are actually written well, that place more value in the writing and its ideas. These are smart books. That atrocity in your device that I'm surprised hasn't made your ears start bleeding is obviously genre work that claims it's actually smart because of the amount of research taken into account to produce it. It lacks any kind of vision.

It's kind of interesting to see the Catholic church's treatment of women, though.

Again, he said, research. You could've gotten the same information, probably better written, too, by doing a search online for Catholic and Chicks—after sorting through the porn, that is.

Part of me didn't care if he thought it was stupid of me to be listening to Dan Brown while he listened to *Lolita*. I wasn't the best treasure hunter when it came to illegal audiobooks, and he swore he'd found a version of *Lolita* actually read by Nabokov. At work, though, books on tape were like listening to a movie with the brightness setting on the television turned all the way down. *Fight Club* poured out of the speakers in the truck a few weeks before, and yeah, in my mind it featured Brad Pitt, Norton, and that chick from the movie. You can't escape the auto parts store with James Joyce. This place fries your brain too much to be able to follow Leo Bloom around Dublin without spacing out and remembering how much you hate your life. Even if Dan Brown was shit to a lot of people, compared to the miasma of daily conversation at work, it's more put together.

I don't see smart or dumb as a difference between everything else I've read and this. There are other criteria you can use to compare books. It seems like different styles of writing, is all. And isn't it possible to have both? To break the formula of genre but still make it, let's say, an adventure story that's written well. It's been done in the past, hasn't it?

Cool Whip didn't say anything and crawled back into the warehouse. It wasn't the first time good writing and genre writing were pulling at me from each arm. Sometimes it felt like comparing cooked vegetables to steak. Both food, but it's not necessarily one or the other. You can have both. In another creative writing class I wasn't signed up for, I turned in a post-apocalyptic novel about two relatives falling in love because they're attracted to each other's DNA, but they're nine generations apart. *The Ninth*. But first, the protagonist needed to get from the present to nine generations later. I even did the math and everything to see what year it would have to be based on when each son or daughter would be born. I'd worry about the means later, and the character disappeared like how I assumed Arnold Schwarzenegger or Michael Biehn must've done so before they appeared in the present time. "This is written well, but it's genre. And I said no genre. *B-*. By the way, you should check to see if you're still registered in my class with the registrar's office. I think you might've been dropped."

What was so wrong with reading something entertaining for fun, giving the mind a rest? Isn't reading still reading? But Plato's words about baseball resonated with me, how the wrong kind of practice will only end up hurting you. It applies to reading as much as it applies to writing. I tried starting a book club to read more and get away from reading crap. Choosing *Ghost Story* by Peter Straub made Cool Whip sigh. He chose *Flatland* by Edwin A. Abbott. Not many people joined it. Mostly my roommates. There were a couple of Elle's friends, a few of my roommates' friends, and one strange girl who somehow ended up at our first meeting in a coffee house in Edinburg. She picked *Oliver Twist*.

"I think I know who she is," Cool Whip whispered while everyone was helping themselves to the cheap pastries purchased for the meeting. "Her name is Blanca, and she had a shaved head before. I thought she had cancer or something, because she was all bones, too, but she was only majoring in Philosophy. I know her from somewhere." It turned out he had developed some photographs of her at the studio he worked at. Nude photographs. At the time, that was one of the few studios in the Valley that offered that type of photo shoot and would actually allow you to develop film containing nudity—which is where John would always develop his South Padre Island pictures. "I remember falling in love with her pictures. I actually kept one of them for myself, told the person who came to pick them up that one of them was stuck in the printer or some shit." After the book club meeting, he walked up to her and said, "I think I've seen you naked."

She left in a hurry and only thanked him for the compliment.

"You never learn, do you?" he said to me. "Peter Straub? It's annoying that you honor these people that think they're great writers when they're anything but. You're only helping them get more money they don't deserve. You're perpetuating the problem with the publishing industry as it continues to set aside books worth promoting, worth printing more copies of."

"Except no one's reading those books," I said, hopeful for Peter Straub.

The book club only lasted that first session. Blanca went first. No one liked her book, so we all became discouraged from ever going back. Cool Whip even called us into the garage and said, "Come and check this out. Here's my review of *Oliver, Twist My Balls*." And then he lit his paperback copy on fire with a lighter.

I wondered what he would do to Straub if he did that to Dickens.

Cool Whip didn't get much of a paycheck the first time around because he owed a lot of money to his parents for child support. He had gotten a girl pregnant in Connecticut and had a daughter. The mother didn't care and left. Cool Whip didn't care and left as far south as the US let him and left the little girl with his parents.

So he thought it was a good idea to accept Rick's invitation to have a free dinner at his house. We drove together in my truck, trying to get through the heavy rain that barely let us see the cars ahead of us. I asked him if we should stop to get something, if it was proper etiquette to pick up a bottle of wine or something when you're going to somebody's house for dinner.

"Do you have money?" he asked.

"I have $2 in my wallet plus whatever change is in the cup holder."

"Then I say fuck that, and let's go eat. My first check was shit."

Rick's wife made meatloaf, mashed potatoes, and carrots, which Rick had been talking about since he invited us the first day of that week, claiming she made the best meatloaf ever. It was okay. But I don't like meatloaf. We both said it was delicious, and I never asked Cool Whip what he thought of it later. We played poker with Rick and his kids for a while, and then Rick walked us out. He stopped us before we climbed in the truck and said he needed to talk to me about something. It had stopped raining as the sun set. Dying flying termites stuck to the pavement around Rick's apartment complex, and we tuned out the steady rattling of the cicadas.

"So I talked to the district manager earlier today," he said. "Axed him for a raise."

"Yeah, I remember you saying something about that."

"I told him that with the new stores opening up and everything, that we were getting a lot busier in the hub. A lot more orders are coming in, which is a good thing. Means the company is making a lot of money. But also means they're gonna be opening up a lot more stores.

So because of that, I told him I'll be needing an assistant hub supervisor, and I told him I wanted that person to be you because you were the most qualified. The best part is that I got you a raise. You're at seven dollars an hour now, and you don't have to mess with your schedule. You can keep going to school."

"But what about driving?" I asked, wondering how forty more cents an hour qualified as the best part.

"What do you mean?"

"Well, it's the only tolerable—"

"Oh, I'd still let you drive," he said, as if it were a clause in the contract he made up on the spot. "Sometimes, I'll let you do the lunch routes, or on Saturdays, when it's not too busy, you can take a route. I'll also let you map out new routes whenever we have to do that. But most of the time, I told him it would be better for you to stay at the warehouse with me, making sure the hub runs smoothly. This also means you'll run the hub by yourself every other Saturday when I'm off. I already told him you'd be willing to do it because it wouldn't conflict with your school schedule."

"Well, thanks and everything," I said, "but can I think about it first?"

"Okay," Rick said. "Are you going to summer school by the way? I think you mentioned you weren't going, right?"

"I'm not planning to."

"Okay," he said, "'cause I'm taking my vacation in early August before the kids go back to school, and you'll be running the hub that week on your own. You'll have someone helping you but you'll have to send him on the lunch routes. Best part is that you'll be getting some nice overtime."

"Yeah, I'll think about it," I said again.

On the way home, I told Cool Whip I didn't want to be Rick's assistant. "I won't be able to listen to my music anymore, or my audiobooks. I won't be able to concentrate on my writing."

"It's not like the audiobooks you listen to have any value to begin with. If your writing is anything like you read, you're better off being the assistant hub manager. This way, you'd have four dollars in your wallet right now."

I talked to Elle about it when we were home. Being in the warehouse all day again, like with The Wolf, I didn't think I could stand it. I barely remembered those months of my life. It would mean going back to that. She said the studio she was working at was written up, and she wouldn't be returning to work anymore.

"It's only a write-up," I said. "I've gotten one of those. Don't quit." But the next morning, she didn't answer the phone calls from her boss, wondering why her studio wasn't running.

After Cool Whip quit and burned his uniform shirts in the backyard, he moved away from the garage and we never saw much of him again. There were awkward moments at work because he was hired on my recommendation, so his quitting was a reflection on me, but they eventually forgot about it and I vowed never to make further recommendations. It was obvious why Cool Whip quit. The newsletter. But it was the way he put it before he walked out on his last day, telling the boss that he couldn't function here anymore. He was too smart to be stuck in a place full of idiots, that if he stayed here longer, he'd become like everyone else, even though he already had a lot of the qualifications to work at the auto parts store: repossessed car, abandoned child from a woman he didn't talk to anymore, and he was an atheist, or at least claimed he was, so there was no fear of godly judgment for doing immoral deeds.

I thought a lot about baseball, about how a place like this was for *me*, who was trying to be a writer and say a smart word or two. If I constantly surrounded myself with idiocy for almost two years, what was *that* going to do to my writing? What was it going to do to my thought processes, to my identity? That's probably the reason for joining the writing group, or why I still attended classes, even if there was no credit. When the entire world around you stinks of retardation, you have to be able to breathe in a little bit of intellectualism to survive. All this bad air can't be good for you. Cool Whip was quicker to sniff it out, and that's why he left. So the baseball analogy applies to everything. Too much of a good thing is bad and too much of a bad thing will fuck you forever.

Cool Whip was a distant memory a few days after he left. That's the way it was. No one brought him up anymore. In the future, something might trigger a memory of him in the store—like the time someone let the air out of his bicycle tires on a day he worked and I didn't and rode it to work. But thirty seconds later, they would forget about him again. I remembered him every time San Peter brought up Dan Brown, like when he asked during a lunch hour one day in the commercial department if I had been reading any other Dan Brown books.

I realized I shouldn't be reading them, I said. It's not good writing, and I think I should be spending my time reading works that are actually going to help me. He writes stupid books, apparently. A lot of people that consider it good are wrong.

Who says they're wrong?

Well, when I started high school, for example, I said, I used to read a lot of Stephen King, and I remember my sophomore English teacher telling me I was wasting my time. I even tried to change his mind by making him read "Secret Window, Secret Garden" but he said there are better ways to show fear of our own writing. I thought reading his work was helping me. I thought I was being academic. You see, these writers, they might think their work is academic and smart, but—

Whoa, whoa, whoa, San Peter said. When did these writers ever say their work is smart? It's the readers who say it. People spend so much time saying this is a good book and that is a bad book, or this is a good writer and this is a bad writer, but none of the bad writers are ever claiming they're good and writing smart books. Do you see McDonald's telling their customers that their burgers are better than the expensive ones at the gourmet restaurant down the road? No. People can think they're better because they're not spending their entire paycheck on a burger, which is something to smile about.

But don't you think availability is affecting how we make choices? The fact alone that there are three McDonald's restaurants within a five-minute-drive from us makes us decide on it. At a bookstore, we can say, "Oh, they have all these extra copies of this bestseller, it must be a good book." We choose McDonald's because they make it easy for us to choose McDonald's. Whereas good books and good restaurants are more difficult to find so no one bothers to find them.

At that moment, Spider Man walked in the room to hide from Shoe Guy, and San Peter continued, Or take this faggot, for instance. Do you think the director of his movie, whatever his *pinche* name is, said this movie is going to turn me into the Fellini of this century? That's why you have to know what you're reading, not so you can know whether it goes in the good pile or the bad pile, but to make up your own fucking opinion about it. In your case, that's why you also have to know what you're going to write, who you're going to write it for. Just don't be surprised if you end up writing about zombies and people don't end up believing you when you say it's the best novel in history.

By zombies, I said, you mean the dead kind that eat flesh, right?

What other kind is there?

PART FIFTEEN

The Part About Method Acting

For a while, all eyes were on me, even if they weren't. It was my fault. Cool Whip had the job because of me, and he didn't last. Time finally moved us on from the tension that had risen from the incident between Cool Whip and Rick. Everyone ended up forgetting that Cool Whip ever existed. One time the boss pulled me aside while running around the warehouse, chasing parts around, and asked me what ever happened to him.

Last I heard, I said, he was working back at the photo place from before.

Probably still developing pictures of naked people and keeping some of them for himself.

Did I tell someone about that?

Rick assigned me two routes a week since becoming his assistant hub manager, most of the time covering for him when he wasn't there or helping him when he was. It wasn't as bad at first, not like it had been with The Wolf, because for being a fat man, Rick moved around and tried to get the work done, tried strategizing sorting the parts so that he could get ten or fifteen parts at a time instead of making several trips.

One of the times I drove after becoming assistant was on the Weslaco route. Elsa came first, and Deedee, the assistant manager, greeted me and asked me what had happened with Rick and Cool Whip. I tried not to stare at the piece of white hair across the middle of her head and said, "You mean Rick didn't give you the details?" It wouldn't be the worst thing in the world waiting at the Elsa store for them to sign the tickets. The store smelled like Fabuloso and looked clean, which was something ours had been missing for a long time.

Deedee crossed her arms, which looked like they were supporting her breasts, and said, "You know he told me all the details, but I want to hear it from you."

"There's not much to tell. It was a stupid ordeal over the stupid magazine. They both ended up saying words that hurt the other's feelings, and Cool Whip quit. End of story."

"Shit," she said. "For being a writer, you suck at telling stories."

"Story of my life."

She signed off on my tickets without even double-checking the parts, repeating that she trusted Rick and that I wouldn't screw her over, and then she sent me on my way to the next store. I had the company credit card assigned to that specific truck because it needed gas. Every truck in the store had its own credit card, which is how the company kept track of how much gas each truck used, and every card had the same code we had to punch in whenever we swiped it: 110278. When the prices of gas started climbing to almost three dollars per gallon, the thieves in the store went from stealing parts to stealing gas, which in the end probably made the most sense. They were too stupid to steal money directly from the card because they knew they'd eventually get caught—two swipes on the same day, a swipe after 5:00 PM, that kind of shit. One of the commercial drivers had gotten fired for telling his wife and a friend to bring his car around to a gas station, park right behind the company truck at the gas pump as if they were in line to pump next, and then he'd pump a little bit of gas into the company truck, have the friend move the truck forward, and then pump the other half a tank's worth in the car his wife drove. It could've worked had it not been for his conscience when all of a sudden he decided to confess and was then forced to quit. One of the hub drivers tried a different approach: buy a container for gas and take it on the road with him, wait until the last route of the day to pump gas, fill up the truck, and then fill up the container. This also would've worked by unloading the container after parking the truck in the parking lot at the end of the shift, then transferring it to their own vehicle and wait until getting home to fill it up with the three or so gallons of gas, which wasn't much, but at the same time, it's like ten bucks. The only problem with that approach was the meetings that would go on at *la palma*, and how they would look on to see who was getting back from the last routes, noticing the bright red gas container in the thief's hand. The only ones who were never caught were the cock-sucking vampires, the ones who would sneak in at night to suck the gasoline out of the trucks with a hose. It was always after closing hours, and the company was too cheap to buy surveillance cameras or hire a security guard.

I stopped at a gas station I'd never stopped at before in the route, probably because of all the times the route mutated, forcing us to change the order we visited each store. I also needed to time out different highways to find the most efficient one for getting to Mercedes from Elsa, so a gas station off 1015 felt right. We usually stopped at the more corporate ones, the bigger Exxon's or Circle K's, because they actually filled their gas pumps with receipt paper and there was no need to have to take more time to walk inside, so in hindsight, who knows why that gas station felt right, with gas pumps that had scratches and holes on their keypads and funny faces and dicks drawn over the sticker of the black state trooper holding up a Texas driver's license card, warning people that if they took off without paying that they could lose it, a warning that started appearing on all gas pumps the second those prices went up. How did they ever expect us not to turn into animals? I swiped the card and entered the code. The display immediately showed CANCELED and asked me to try again. Fuck. The clerk inside was a young girl, about eighteen years old, couple years younger than me, thin, long brown hair, dark complexion, Mexican.

"Well," she asked, "were you going to fill it up?"

"Yeah. The reader kept saying canceled, so."

"Okay, so, like, how much does it usually take to fill it up?"

"I don't know," I said. "Forty?"

She swiped the card on her register and asked me to put in the code on a keypad before handing me the receipt. To my surprise, the truck filled up with \$28, and the display read *SEE CLERK*. Fuck. Should've stopped at another station.

"So do you swipe the card to put the other twelve back in—"

"Nah, sweetie," she said, "this is easier." She pulled out twelve in cash from the register and handed them to me.

On the way to Mercedes, then on to Progreso, and then on the way to Donna, all there is to do is think. The gas card and a receipt for forty dollars in one cup holder and twelve dollars in the other. As far as anyone knew, proof existed that forty dollars were pumped into the truck. There was no paper trail anywhere that it had come out to anything else. I could pocket the cash, and no one would know. For starters, it wouldn't be expected of me. The boss hired family specifically to avoid this kind of problem from happening in his store, even though that wouldn't stop anyone when realizing how much bill money they'd have to spend on a new radiator, telling himself, Wouldn't it be much easier if I had it for free? Besides, no one could prove I took it. It would be like finding a ten-dollar bill in a supermarket parking lot. Does anyone walk around to ask who might've dropped it? Would you? I started fantasizing about everything I could do with the money. Lunch hour was in a while. I could eat a decent meal for once, at the company's expense. Buy a book. *Zombie* by Joyce Carol Oates was on my list because someone had told me she uses gore in an interesting way as opposed to a writer who writes gore for the sake of gore. My dad said *Memoria de mis putas tristes* would change my life, not 180 degrees, but 45 at least, so there was also that. These would basically be free with this money. But in all likelihood, the twelve dollars would probably go to the electric bill, which had gone up since Cool Whip kept leaving the garage door open and then moved out. There was even a moment on the way back to our store when I reached for the three bills and put them in my pocket, and part of me felt I deserved them. But back at the store, I thought if I gave them to Rick, he would keep them for himself. I told the boss what happened, said it was money left over from pumping gas, and he took it, expressionless, naturally, like nothing, like he knew in his mind that it had never crossed mine to take it.

Back in the hub office, right before I clocked out for my lunch break, Bern Bern was coming in from his and told me he forgot to tell me his mom had sent me a lunch plate, saying that it had been a hmm time since I ate her food. After leaving the plate sitting in the car for six hours, it wasn't fresh anymore. It tasted like his old house, like an aftertaste of shit. A small part of me thought I deserved to finish it.

Lou showed up the day after Cool Whip quit, fully equipped with catch phrases and everything as if he had been preparing for this role his entire life. He worked with Rick at Pizza Hut after Quique quit there, and they became best friends forever, at least until Rick quit Pizza Hut, too, after getting his raise at the auto parts store, but then they became best friends again when Lou joined the gang. He immediately became Rick's favorite employee, got all the perks Becky, the Donna whore, did in every store she worked at without ever having to blow, fuck, or be fucked by Rick (as far as everyone in our store was concerned, anyway). Rick even scheduled him to always get out of work at 3:00, so he could have plenty of time to relax before having to go work at Pizza Hut.

The first day, Rick introduced me as his assistant and kept telling him that if he ever needed anything, that I would have him covered.

Okay, Lou said, three-something.

That was his signature line apparently. He didn't speak a lot of English, and according to Rick, Lou once wanted to say "threesome" as a reaction to a conversation they were having, and three-something happened to come out instead and stuck ever since. When he walked into the store in the mornings, hair combed to the side like a schoolboy, the workers at the front eventually started greeting him with "three-something" instead of the usual whatever-the-fuck. Lou also said, 17th Street, o qué? a lot, which was a street in downtown McAllen known for its prostitutes, most of them males, and he'd say them— both fucking phrases—for no reason whatsoever as if he were a broken 80s toy with a string sticking out of his ass.

When it became apparent to us that Lou had a habit of actually picking up prostitutes of either sex, I nicknamed him El Sida, and did so deliberately through casual conversation in the commercial department so V-Lo could take full credit for it. To my surprise, my first and only nickname caught on and everyone started calling him that, or Aids, or three-something, but each nickname had a specific context attached to it. El Sida was used when he wasn't present and we were talking about him. Aids was used when talking directly to him, and three-something was when we greeted him. Within two weeks of working there, he became the first employee to have three different nicknames.

When he first started, Rick made me teach him the Weslaco route because he said I knew it best, like it made any difference. But as soon as you get back, Rick said, you're covering me for lunch. El Sida slept for most of the route, especially in the desolate highways with less traffic. I kept the radio on and didn't have much to say anyway, but the times he'd wake up, he'd start talking about how hard his life was, about how much he needed to have two jobs. Why he thought we were friends was beyond me. Rick had probably said something to him.

"When you have a kid," he said in Spanish, "you have to make sacrifices to provide for them. That's why I still stay at Pizza Hut. It's more money. I deliver pizzas there, so the tips are helpful and they get the bills paid. Oh, but delivering to hotel rooms is the best because sometimes it's girls there, man, and they'll ask if I want a tip or see their tits."

"Which do you pick?"

"Well, the tits, of course. It's all about the tits." He talked about the prostitutes on 17th Street and about a motel in Pharr that charged by the hour, "like a lot of the hookers do. Three-something." He said he'd even pick up guys sometimes, too, when money was extra tight since they usually charged less, and then added, "With a condom, nothing happens." It sounded like a slogan when he said it in Spanish: *Con condón, no se hace nada.* Like something you'd hear at the end of a commercial about cleaning detergent or cooking oil. The way the words worked together, it was rather fitting for that. "You married?"

"It's starting to sound like it's a good thing I am."

"Yeah, me, too. This is her." He pulled out his wallet and showed me a picture of his wife and kid. They were at South Padre Island and had sand on their hair. I didn't have pictures in my wallet. The ink would always stick to the inserts and get discolored.

"And you still pick up guys?" I asked, sounding as if I were interviewing him for a documentary or a talk show.

"Yeah," he said. "I mean, I love my wife and everything, but sometimes, you need something tighter. Know what I mean?" I shook my head. "And a lot of these guys don't care. They need the money, so they bend over and take it, which I don't personally find gay because it feels exactly like doing the same to a woman. So I close my eyes and pretend and take what I came for."

"I've actually heard that concept before," I said, remembering Quique and wondering what he was up to. It wasn't a concept I agreed with, but it had turned out to be common at work. You're only gay if you're the bottom. Or you're the woman because you're the bottom. El Sida seemed like the type that would probably spill everything, considering what he was sharing with a guy he just met. But maybe it was all locker room talk to them.

I wondered what drove these guys to act this way. In the next few weeks, I kept running into El Sida outside of work, mostly at supermarkets and at Target, always with his wife and kid, and it was strange to me how good-looking his wife and daughter were to do that to them. Anyone at work would say he hit the jackpot and wonder how that happened or why him, and after giving him a quick nod as we passed each other in the aisles, I asked myself what she was like at home. Did she treat him like shit? Maybe she didn't fulfill his needs. Didn't justify cheating, though. Cheating varies from person to person, but there are particular rules and circumstances that apply to all of us in general.

Then there was the possibility his wife wasn't to blame, the possibility that he picked up prostitutes for the sake of cheating, for the thrill, to feed the monster, for knowing that you've done it, and once you've done it, you can't stop. It's no different from going through suffering for the sake of art, or putting yourself through a bad or immoral experience for the sake of being able to write about them. When I had started working on the vampire novel that ended up sucking, most of it was going to take place in an underground strip club. Not like *From Dusk Till Dawn*—a classier one. I didn't know what it was like to be in a strip club, other than what they portrayed in movies, so in order for me to be able to write about it honestly and know about it, I had to visit one, get a feel for the lighting, a feel for the smells, the sounds, the customers, everything, or else I'd never know what it's like, or else my work would sound fake, dishonest, artificial. It's probably the same argument Flask and everyone else used about pornography, tried to justify watching it for the sake of it being educational, good practice to use on their wives. And I asked them once, But don't you think it still messes with your mind a bit? Don't you all think that it's possible that it might raise our expectations, that we'll end up thinking our wives should look exactly like the girls in those movies?

We're not that stupid, Writer, Rick said. I'm pretty sure we can tell real and fantasy apart, and then he'd stick his hands out, seeking low-fives for successfully saying something smart.

I know we can, I said, but once you start watching a lot of it, it starts becoming more difficult to start telling them apart. It's like smoking. I'm sure once we start we tell ourselves we can stop whenever we feel like it. Try quitting after a hundred cigarettes, a thousand.

Flask slammed his fist down on the counter and said, Hell, fucking girls are the fucking same with their fucking *novelas*. They think we're these romantic ass pussies that are going to wait on their every word and always be there for them. Talk and fucking talk until they think we're actually listening. It's the same fucking thing. Fantasy. And so we lie so we can get what we need.

And what do we need? I said. I didn't tell them that I'd asked Elle a couple of times if she'd give me permission to go to a strip club, thinking how stupid it sounded of me to say it was for fucking research, even though it was the truth. I even asked her if she'd go with me, that way she'd know I wasn't interested in getting a lap dance or a table dance or that I wasn't going to drool all over the sight of breasts. But she said she didn't want to go, that I could and should take one of our roommates, but there was always a tone, *that* tone, that "I want you to get what you need even though it's fucking me up inside" tone.

"You know what you have to do," one of my roommates said when I talked to him about the novel, "you're going to have to do it behind her back. She's probably better off not knowing. Only way you'll be able to truly write about a strip club."

El Sida waited by the crummy parking lot of the Red Door Inn in Pharr, pacing back and forth and staring down at his wrist as if it had a watch around it, but he had pawned the one his father left him a long time ago to pay for a two-girl experience that ended up lasting him exactly twelve minutes. He reached for the phone in his pocket and saw that he had ten minutes to get back to work and Paris hadn't shown up yet. Maybe it's the rain, he thought. That's what's taking so long. He had already paid for the room. $20 for the lunch hour and had another $50 to give Paris. He remembered when he used to pay more for hookers, sometimes up to $500, before working at Pizza Hut. He'd look through the *Coastal Current* magazine—this newspaper-like booklet from the island decorated with nothing but ads and a team of untalented writers, like a movie critic that would rant on and on about a fake life he lived instead of the actual movie he was reviewing—to find escort ads, went by whoever looked the prettiest in the picture even though she was never the one to show up. Still, to spend an entire night in a hotel with a girl like that, a girl that would do anything in the world if you needed her to—except let you go bareback—and pretend she loved you more than anything in the world if you needed her to. That made him feel important. He had to save the money now, he thought to himself, couldn't be spending so much cash on something that would disappear completely the next day—or the next hour—so Paris had to be enough. He put the phone back in his pocket and immediately felt it vibrate against his leg. He hoped it was Paris as the clouds in the sky started rubbing against each other and crashing.

He's not picking up, Rick told me in the hub office. Goddamnit. He left him a voicemail, for El Sida to let him know he was okay and if he planned to make it back from his lunch break before turning to me and saying, I need you to get ready to go on the route. I hid my happiness and loaded the tote box inside the truck because it sounded like Hurricane Emily was going to show up with rain, and I already had a write-up for letting parts get wet. When everything was ready and it was time for the route to take off, I entered the hub office to let Rick know I was leaving. He turned to face the printer, the invoices coming out one after the other, and then he said, Just give him five more minutes. He'll be here.

But then you risk the route running late, I said. It looks like it's even going to rain, so I'll probably have to take it kind of sl—

Just five more minutes, he said. If he's not here in five minutes, take off in five minutes.

Five minutes from now? Or five minutes after he doesn't get here in the first five minutes? So am I waiting ten minutes?

"Just ten more minutes," El Sida told Paris in the room. They hadn't done anything yet, only lay on the bed and touched each other's faces and talked. El Sida did most of the talking, telling Paris about his job at the auto parts store, how he had been there for almost two months, how hard it was to have to juggle two jobs one right after the other, and then still have to put up with his wife asking him how his day was, which annoyed him. The last thing he wanted to do after getting out of work is talk about work. Paris did most of the listening, only talked to remind El Sida every now and then that he could do anything he set his mind to, that he was strong and could probably handle three jobs if he wanted to. Words El Sida needed to hear. "Just wait," El Sida said, "don't leave yet."

"What do you mean don't leave?" I told Deedee in Elsa on my way out, thick drops of water running down the store's display windows.

"Don't leave yet," she said. "Mercedes needs a part and they caught you barely." She handed me the small part that was probably worth five bucks. I signed off on it without even checking if it was the right part and took off, not forgetting to throw my middle finger at the stupid gas station on the way to Mercedes.

Paris used the same finger on El Sida while performing fellatio on him, stopping sometimes to ask, "Are you sure you still have time? You're gonna be late."

"I'm not fucking paying you to keep track of time," El Sida said. He was always serious when the situation started to get sexual, like with most men, he thought, any man would get pissed if he were interrupted in the middle of these acts. It was only the sex and not the cuddling that made him hate himself. Sometimes he would tell Paris to shut up, to not speak at all, so he could close his eyes and pretend it was his wife doing it—at least back then when she still used to, when he still wanted her to—to hide the self-hatred for doing something wrong. Something out of character. Something not us. But other times Paris, not knowing what else to do, would talk, telling El Sida how big it was because that's usually what the customers wanted to hear. "Okay," El Sida said, "I'm coming."

It had started to come down, and I couldn't see beyond three or four feet in front of the truck after managing to avoid the rain for most of the route. The occasional canals on the route had started to overflow. After Progreso there was no more progress to be made. I parked the truck on the shoulder, turned on the emergency lights, and called Rick. He answered the phone like he always does: Hub office, this is Rick.

"Hey," I said. "I think we have a problem. I'm out here near Progreso, and I'm stuck in the rain. I can't see shit. Don't worry, though. The Donna parts are fine inside the truck. Let them know I'm running even more late. I'm going to wait for this to clear up."

What do you mean? Rick asked. Writer, the route's already running late. You have to keep going, or there will be pissed off customers from other stores not getting their parts. Lou's not back yet. I don't know what's wrong, but there's no one else I can send out on the last route. Wait. You calling me on a cell?

"Maybe you didn't hear me," I said. "I cannot go on. If I do, there's a high chance I won't make it to Donna at all, and the customers won't get their parts anyway."

Maybe you didn't hear me, he said. I don't care. Keep going and finish the route. Turn on the high beams if you have to. But get back here because I'll probably have to send you on the next run, too.

I waited in almost complete silence except for the wiper blades ticking left and right in vain, then said I'd try my best. Five minutes later, I drove towards Donna. When I arrived back at McAllen, the last route was already thirty minutes behind, which meant that if it were me driving again, I'd be clocking out at least thirty minutes late. Luckily, El Sida showed up from his lunch break at the same time I did. Rick asked him where he'd been, not angry, more like glad to see he was okay, and El Sida said, I won't lie. I was with someone. I'm sorry. It'll never happen again. And then he put his head down and started to cry.

Will you go on the route again? Rick said to me.

Whatever.

Oh, and before you go, Rick said, you need to sign this. He handed me a white form. It was a write-up for using the cellphone while on the road. It was in Rick's handwriting, straight and to the point: Employee was on route for hub department. He was carrying a cellphone while on route, which was used to make a call.

I was parked, I said. I was letting you know my situation, which was work-related.

I know, man. But you still used a cellphone. Somebody else sees you and reports you, then it'll be on me. District manager'll probably be on my ass axing why I can't keep my employees in line.

I muttered something under my breath as I walked out of the hub office to leave on the route. It was probably "faggot" but I wasn't sure.

I took my time with the route, figured it was running late anyway and I might as well get the extra paid hour. Rush hour would be over by the time the route concluded, and all of the undesirables would be gone by then. The rain had calmed down for the most part, at least in this region of Hidalgo County, but still came on and off like the last streams at the end of urination. I couldn't remember the last time I was this angry while at work, not like that day, the way it felt like the rage was crawling at my brain and scratching it. Almost crashed twice unable to focus on something as simple as the road. No one talked to me in the Elsa store. There were only two parts for them and the first free guy at the counter signed off on them. I waited in the truck a little bit longer, staring out the window at nothing.

A woman customer came out of the store and got into her car, carrying one of the parts that had just been delivered. A coolant hose shaped like an S. Hoses came in all shapes and sizes. C hoses. J hoses. U hoses. Hoses that could bend. Hoses that couldn't. A few months back, a hub driver from the Brownsville branch was fired because he had started harassing a woman, not too different from this one getting in her car in the Elsa parking lot. He had stopped at another branch to drop off parts, not too different from what I had just done, except while he waited for signatures, he helped a woman find a part for her car in one of the aisles. A coolant hose. The woman was about two decades younger than he was. This woman looked at least a decade older than me. Once the parts were signed for, he waited for her to leave and started following her instead of continuing on the route. He followed her to a gas station and asked her if she would like him to pump the gas for her. Needless to say, she started getting scared, especially when he asked her if it was okay to follow her to her house. I wondered how the write-up would've read if they had decided to warn him instead, but more importantly, why he thought it was okay to deviate from the route to do this. How do our minds convince us that this is okay? The woman at the Elsa store must've caught me looking as she was backing out and waved at me before driving west towards San Carlos. My destination led me east towards Edcouch and, for a second, because of the wave and smile (though I'm no longer sure if the smile was even there, or if it was if it was even an authentic one), I considered going west. Only for a second.

On the way to Mercedes, I wondered what Cool Whip was up to, and if he had seen something in Rick. We had talked about Rick on the way to his house for dinner, when we were discussing if we should spend money we didn't have on a bottle of wine. "Rick's actually pretty cool," he had said, and he wouldn't lie about that. He was always blunt, never worried about hurting feelings, including those he cared about. He was the type of person that wouldn't mind telling the poor Mexican kids whose parents forced to sell candy apples in restaurants to fuck off or violently reach for the door latch from the backseat as the black man asking for church donations approached the vehicle in the middle of a red light.

I stopped at the same gas station off 1015 even though the gas tank of the truck was half empty, parked by the first pump that was open and started walking inside, the rain starting to pour again, dripping from the tips of my hair and turning my work shirt a darker shade of red. The previous Saturday, Rick had told me I wasn't going to drive, but when El Sida didn't show up, he changed his mind. I was wearing cheap khakis for some stupid reason, and they tore right around my taint area while climbing in the truck. I asked Rick if I could go home and get a quick change, that it would only take twenty minutes.

No, he said, the route needs to get going.

The pants kept tearing throughout the day, and I kept stapling them together in the bathroom, the staples pricking at my inner thighs and legs all fucking day, let alone having to practice walking backwards and sideways when stopping by other stores. Didn't complain.

The Tuesday after, while reviewing the hub employee schedule Rick put together every payroll, it showed Rick was giving El Sida three-day weekends every other week while the rest of us were left with days off in between the week and worked every single Saturday. El Sida brought him something to eat every day and they would tickle each other all the time. I made copies of all the schedules since El Sida started working and made a list showing how it had been the last two months. Rick had seen me making the list during my thirty-minute lunch break but didn't know what it was. I pretended to take it to the front while he saw, mostly because he looked curious, so he could think I was showing it to the boss, but I actually wanted a fucking drink to wash down the chile and dried shrimp soup.

Can I talk to you real quick, I asked him when I came back, and showed him the list. So this seems a little unfair, not only to me, but to all our staff that's not your best friend. This is how many days Lou's name pops up for a three-day weekend. Now, I know *I* haven't had one since Cool Whip quit, and that's fine, but it's certainly been a while since some of the rest have either, and they *will* say something if they're not stupid enough to not notice. I know Lou's your best friend and brings you food all the time, which is kind of nice, but would you be willing to give the rest of us three-day weekends if *we* fed you?

He started sweating, even while standing in front of the A/C unit. I wondered if he wanted to hit me. The atmosphere had been starting to gradually change since Rick received his raise. He was doing less and less every day, showing up late in the mornings. He'd clock in El Sida when he thought no one was looking. He started cheating the payroll system by scheduling sixteen hours of overtime and actually clocking in over thirty hours—doubling his OT pay every week. I never said anything because his family needed the money, and I would've done the same if I could, but at that wage, two part-timers could be helping make our jobs easier. After our talk, when he brought up a new schedule, Rollie noticed he had his first three-day weekend in almost three months of not resting even two days in a row. He thanked me and said that if I hadn't said anything, he would've.

At the gas station the same girl manned the counter, same hairstyle, same Willie Nelson playing on the speakers, same everything like self-induced déjà vu.

"You again," she said. "How much this time?"

"Let's go with fifty this time."

She followed the same routine: swipe the card, asked for the code, and gave me the receipt. The gas was barely flowing through the nozzle. I started acting, in case the girl was looking at me, acted like the whole fucking thing was broken. Only fifteen dollars went in. I told her the nozzle was acting crazy.

"Want to try another one?"

"I'm running late already," I said. "It'll have to do for now."

I took Elle out to dinner that night, the sun finally out and lighting the puddles on the McAllen streets like floating paper lanterns. It came out to a little more than $35, but not by a lot. While we waited for our food, she asked me how work was going.

"I don't want to talk about work," I said. "Let's talk about something else."

She never knew about the $35 because she was the type of person that would tell me to return them, because I was afraid she'd think less of me, and because I didn't want her to know who I was. She kept thinking they were earned. What if they were? Given that it always felt like five hours more than what it was. The shit Rick and El Sida put me through didn't justify stealing from the store, but maybe I did deserve this money. This meal. I didn't feel guilty about it. Not that day, anyway. I thought about telling Elle the truth that night as I set my alarm to go back to work the next day, but she was probably better off not knowing I wasn't a good person.

PART SIXTEEN

The Part About The Wishes

Like an earthworm, he slithered into work thirty minutes late in the morning. All the parts ordered the afternoon and evening before were sorted and readied in hopes Rick would take a hint and stop showing up late. Having the parts ready to go was a new strategy. Before, I'd take my time when he wasn't there by 6:30 or even by my own start time thirty minutes after that, and then he'd usually help with the last ten or so invoices. But when that became routine and started slowing down progress, it became easier to fetch them all myself. He had a list of four different excuses he used, rotating them every day he showed up late—fifteen, thirty, sometimes forty-five minutes. Sometimes it was trouble with the van. Sometimes it was dropping off the kids to be picked up by the bus. Sometimes he overslept because he was tired from the day before because he had stayed up all night doing remedial math homework for college. His most popular excuse was when he'd give a big sigh, sometimes a quiet burp escaping from his throat, and say, It's hard raising five kids, Writer. You don't know what it's like. You don't have any kids.

You don't know what it's like—the mantra that haunts every beginning writer.

One Tuesday, he took the day off completely without warning me, and then he told me he needed to take his family back-to-school shopping because his wife didn't know how to do it. It worsened when he started attending college, too, to major in Kinesiology to be a coach of all career choices. He could barely move sometimes. I'm sure he'd have plenty to teach obese Rio Grande Valley kids about avoiding obesity. Most coaches are fat here, anyway. His newfound quest for knowledge also meant leaving earlier so he could have time to eat before going to his classes, something he always denied me when I wanted to have a chance to rest before mine. Running the hub on your own for an entire day was a bitch. I basically did it for The Wolf, but at least he answered the phone and dealt with the workers from other stores. By the time I got home on the days Rick wouldn't show up, there were two heartbeats on each foot and a sweat rash on my chest that was as itchy as it was painful until some skin started to peel off. Literally falling apart. Once I took a white lawn chair into the shower and sat there for a couple hours, hoping Rick wouldn't skip work the next day, and hoping all of this would matter when I cashed my next paycheck. It never did.

Do you need help with the tickets? he asked, and I shook my head. I'll let you do the lunch route today, he said.

When I showed up from that route, it seemed like the entire store was in the hub office, bathing Rick in questions. You could swear he negotiated two-dollar raises for everybody by the way they looked at him when they heard a female from the Pharr branch was transferring to ours. An actual female. Not a mannish one like the one Shoe Guy and Quique obsessed over. Red, Güero, El Sida, and some other guys gathered around Rick, asking discovery questions about Genie. Before the transfer was proposed, Rick had been spreading rumors—as was his custom—that she had been blowing her manager for an easier time at work: better hours, better pay, and some other shit. The channels were never an issue since, according to Rick, the district manager had given her a taste of his dick, too, and so she'd be closer to his office on the second-and-a-half floor by working here. With all of this common background knowledge, the interviews with Rick were limited to questions about her looks.

Oh, they're enormous, Rick said. The workers in the office grew excited as if the third lotto number was a match, too. Rick basked in every second of it, probably thought he was doing us all a favor by getting a hot female onboard our ship. Anything to lay off the fat whale jokes, I guessed. Like he might enjoy the talk of someone else's tits for a change. He meant for her to be an additional assistant, one who would know all routes and cover whoever was off for the day, and he made a good case to the district manager saying we needed another person. It was something he had been meaning to do since Cool Whip left telling the boss he couldn't function in a place filled with so many non-intellectual low lives, taking the copy of the newsletter as proof of that. He didn't want anyone else to see the copy with his name on it, even though the day after he left all the other copies with the bucktoothed redneck in them had *Cool Whip* written over his head.

No, Rick said, she's really fuckable. I mean, by how she looks. She looks like anyone would want to feel her from the inside. I don't know how fuck-*able* she is, though. At least when it comes to you, *jotos*. He tried opening up a round of laughter by giving everyone an "I'm kidding" smirk. It worked. The long ohs and ahs hovered around the pockets of laughter and made it hard to form thoughts.

I sat in the back corner of the office. If Rick wasn't going to get part orders, I shouldn't either. Rick would probably be the last guy in this entire warehouse anyone would be able to fuck. Meanwhile, the orders kept shitting out of the printer behind his ass, oblivious to their urgency to be sorted out and delivered to the other branches.

She's got a kid, though, Rick added. A couple of the guys became discouraged and displayed this through a usual chorus of grunts—no jackpot, after all—and exiting the office. The ones that stayed looked like that wouldn't stop them. Yeah, Rick continued, she's got a little girl, like eight years old. The faces in the room began to lose interest—a comedy routine with the weaker jokes at the end or a novel running on fumes—begging for Rick to come back to tits and fuckability. El Sida kept smiling, though, hanging on to every word.

Oh, three-something, he shouted, punching the guy in front of him on the shoulder. No one ever gave him a lot of hell for not being able to speak much English, which wasn't much of a requirement to function around these parts anyway. Everyone and their dogs spoke Spanish. And if they didn't, odds were someone would be around them to interpret for them. But El Sida knew, as much as everyone else in the office did, what he implied by saying his phrase that time. *That* time he meant "threesome." Which is probably why I was the only one that didn't laugh. Everyone else did. Fuck, they even high-fived to it.

Lou's off tomorrow, Rick said, turning to me, so I'm going to need you to teach her the Weslaco route. Everyone else screamed in unison as if something were going to happen between us in the shitty Ford Rangers they made us drive. Rick shouted with them before continuing, Then we'll keep at it with whoever has days off because I don't trust any other these fuckers with her.

V-Lo walked out of his department and into our office to ask, So how big are we talking about here, extending his arms behind him to measure ass size. Is it bigger than mine?

Rick said before she showed up the next day, I wish I could drive her and show her the route, but I wanted it to be you, Writer. You deserve this. You've earned it, man.

Anything to get the fuck away from here, I guess. I waited for her by the truck, double-checking to see that all the part numbers matched since Rick had recently adopted a habit of making mistakes and blaming me for them. His eyes were on me during this process, as if he was noticing my trust in him was evanescent.

When Genie appeared, she looked like I remembered her from the time I met her in the Pharr store, right before I was written up. She jumped down from the loading dock like the rest of the guys instead of taking the stairs. Rick made a comment about me not being a gentleman for not helping her down and opening the passenger door for her. Where has all the cavalry gone, he said.

Don't worry, she said when she climbed in the truck. You don't have to do any of that shit for me. I'd like to be treated the same as everyone else. She closed the door and studied the chart on the clipboard while I started the truck.

That's admirable, I said. Her red uniform was tightly tucked into her jeans that hugged her hips and were fastened by a belt that was at least three or four inches wide. Her seatbelt disappeared into her breastbone before appearing again by her stomach area leading down to the buckle. Her straight black hair hung in a pony tail over the headrest. She wore pink tennis shoes and light red nail polish. Her skin complexion was a shade or two darker on her left knuckles. She had punched someone recently.

"So is that really your name?" she asked, looking at the embroidery of my uniform while we waited for a 23rd Street light to turn green. "Or is it something you go by because you love the restaurant?"

"No, it's my real name," I said. "It's actually pretty fortunate the uniforms get ordered before Rick gets around to developing a nickname."

She shifted to her left and pointed at her name spelled across her breast and said, "I went with the last name and ordered it right before I divorced that fucker." I didn't know if I should look or for how long. Her shirt was so tight that you could see a small opening between buttons, showing part of her white bra. So I explained to her how the clipboard works, knowing Rick had probably walked back to the commercial office to exit through the side door and see us waiting for the light.

"Pretty basic with that," I said. "For the route, we start off by taking the 281 loop to Edinburg and 107 to Elsa. That's our first stop. From there, straight through on 88 to the Weslaco store, then 83 to the Mercedes one, and all the way around the back roads to Progreso and Donna. I don't know how familiar you are with the highways, but either way, you'll see in a bit. It's actually pretty simple."

"I guess we *will* see," she said.

I settled for a regular radio station, one that played everything, since I thought it would be inappropriate to finish listening to *The Death of Artemio Cruz* in Spanish in her company, which was hard enough to follow from the beginning, let alone three-quarters of the way through. Or even worse, play my song collection for her—hundreds of Ramones, Guns n' Roses, Depeche Mode and The Strokes compiled between several 80s pop songs that seemed out of place. I wasn't ready to be labeled by this.

After the 107 exit to start heading into Elsa, she asked me if Rick was a good person. We drove through long patches of dead grass, frequent palm trees, junk yards, nameless stores that simply advertised construction material for sale, leading to what the natives called the Y because of the way the road curved and split.

"Define good."

"Well, shit," she said. "So. Give it to me straight."

"You're going to be driving a lot," I said, "so it's better if you pretend he doesn't exist. Pretend he's not real. One way or another, the job needs to be done. He won't do anything to make it easier for anyone, so the best thing I do is pretend my job's difficult already. And then I just have to finish it so I can be able to go home at 5:00. The sad part is that I think he usually means well. Maybe he's a good guy. Everything he says and does he thinks it's because he's trying to help someone else. It's unfortunate that it always ends up going the other way."

"How so?" She stretched her legs forward and relaxed into the seat as much as she could, letting out a high-pitched sigh like a wet Disney princess.

"Well, take my position, for example. I was never asked if I wanted to be his assistant. He assumed I wanted to be. He assumed I could use a raise, the extra money, and, yeah, extra money is always nice, but he also knew how much I preferred to do this. Driving. Being out of the store, away from their influence. Let me have my isolation. And he never gave me the opportunity to tell him how I felt about it. I know he only did it because he wanted to help me. At least, I think he did, but if he had actually ax— asked me, I would've said no and kept on driving."

She talked about how they would treat her in the Pharr branch, omitting the blowjob parts from her version of the story, and I couldn't stop looking at how half of her last name disappeared into the middle of her breasts. They were as Rick described them. On the outside of her left breast, *res* was displayed in the white stitching, while in the valley was the first half of her last name, *Casa*, which was Spanish for "house," so I wondered if anyone else had made that connection about that place of her body.

"Do you actually like listening to this crap?" she asked.

"Not really," I said. "Fallout Boy sucks."

"Yeah," she said. "And 'Dirty Little Secret' sucks even harder."

"I didn't know what kind of music you liked, so I thought I'd play a variety station. I mostly listen to alt rock. Mostly."

"Then play the rock station, man." She tuned to it herself and then added, "Oh, I love Velvet Revolver. Did you catch them when they came down here?"

"Front row. Slash was as close to me as you are now."

"My boyfriend is a crew member for this station, so he was able to get us backstage passes for the show. We got to meet and hang out with Slash and Scott Weiland and the rest of the guys. It was a real blast."

"So, you have a boyfriend," I asked like an idiot. Why that stuck to me more than meeting Slash was beyond me. After the show, by the Dodge Arena parking lot, Slash had thrown a towel at the crowd as a souvenir. The guy who caught it immediately stuck it down his pants. Most likely because he didn't want anyone else to take it from him, like when you lick all your food before you eat it in front of your younger siblings (which I don't know what it's like since I don't have any younger siblings). During the show, I caught a guitar pick from the opening band, Shinedown, moments before people asked the security guards between us and the stage to hand them the cigarette butts Velvet Revolver flicked there.

"Well, he's more of an ex-boyfriend. My daughter's father. We don't see each other that much anymore."

I introduced her to the guys in Mercedes before showing her where we left the parts and where those workers left the outgoing ones. One of their counter guys called me back after she walked out and asked if she'd be doing the route from now on.

"I don't know," I said. "I think Rick wants her to know all the routes, just in case."

"Well," the manager said, "tell him to send her on this one from now on."

Everyone else loved the idea and I exited the store to the sound of manly cheers and guffaws behind me.

Genie mostly sang on the back roads to Progreso, along to "Rock'n Me" and she asked if I liked classic rock. It didn't feel like we were on the clock. It felt like we were a couple on some trip somewhere. Part of me wished we were going to the beach instead.

"Sure. Some."

"Then who's this band?"

"The Eagles?"

"No, man. It's Steve Miller. Come on."

After that one, she sang along to "Sex Type Thing" by Stone Temple Pilots before she started talking about sex. We were passing a creek when she said, "All roads lead to sex. I don't think, personally, that there's anything wrong with having casual, promiscuous sex. I enjoy having it as much as I expect other people might, too."

I felt like a cornered male high school teacher speaking to a half-naked senior girl he wasn't allowed to touch, didn't know what to pay attention to more when she said that—that she felt like talking about it while we drove on a lonely road or that she said it right after she sang she knew I wanted what's on my mind. It didn't help that we were less than two feet away from each other, trapped in a moving vehicle with me behind the wheel.

"I don't think it's being slutty or anything. I like going to clubs sometimes to meet guys and have one-night stands, as long as we're both being safe. I mean, sex feels so good, and it's fun, so why should it be so taboo to have it?"

"Nothing happens with a condom," I said, thinking about the one I had in my wallet, and thinking probably only losers carried them in their wallets.

"That's right," she said. "You are totally right. And one more thing . . ."

I took the short cut road I'd usually take to avoid passing through a couple of businesses with a little more traffic. Hardly any traffic ever passed on this short cut, crop fields on each side of the road. Sometimes I would stop the truck there to have a quick lunch when Rick would take my lunch hour away so he could leave home early, forced to mess with Texas there to avoid getting fired for having food in the truck. The managers would write you up even if the truck *smelled* like food. It was more desolate than desolate back there. And I could've stopped the truck. I was wishing for it. For some reason, I knew that if I asked her if she wanted to have casual, promiscuous sex, she'd say yes, and I'm terrible at reading signals. She'd say yes. It's fun. It feels good. There's nothing wrong with it. Hell, we had time to kill. The route was running with perfect timing. No one would see. We could fuck each other like animals and no one would know. And she'd say yes. She seemed like the type of girl who would.

"How about you?" she said. "Do you enjoy casual, promiscuous sex?"
"I'm kind of married," I said.

Sometimes Genie made me wonder what it would be like to live in a world where we could   have sex any time we wanted to, with anyone we wanted to, and for it to be natural, like shaking hands. Whenever she talked about it, she made it seem like it was eating lunch together in the lounge or like saying good morning when you saw each other. It was a need like needing a drink of water. Some of the guys at work cared too much about the idea of sleeping with a used woman they weren't married to. When they absolutely had to, they either had to pretend they were virgins or not think about the fact they weren't. Genie brought up the clichéd feminist argument about it being okay for a man to sleep around but being labeled a slut if a woman did, but to some of these guys, sleeping with a non-virgin was like trying on a shirt at a thrift store. Even if it didn't have scabies, someone else wore it. I wondered if women felt the same way about men.

It was awkward when Rick was around her. One time, on one of her first couple of days, he grabbed her arm lightly and pulled her aside. He said that if any man in the warehouse ever made her feel uncomfortable in any way, to let him know, and he'd kick his ass for her. I'll defend your honor, he said to her.

I was sitting in the hub office by the bulletin board, a picture of a short man with both hands in the air and a black circle drawn around it and *Rollie* written to the side pinned to it. My arms were crossed and I wanted to tell Rick to shut the fuck up.

If anyone here makes me feel uncomfortable, she said, pulling her arm away from his grasp, I'll kick his ass myself.

Every day it was a different incident and they started making their way into my notebook because of Genie. Each page represented a day and the events that would happen with her. One of them was "Day 5" when someone had dared El Sida to give her a lollipop with a flavor called Balls of Fire. He didn't know what it meant and didn't bother to ask anyone. As far as he knew, they wanted to see her put the lollipop in her mouth so they could fantasize about it and pretend it was a dick, but their real intention had something to do with reasoning involving being able to say that she put balls in her mouth. She looked at the lollipop and hurled it against the floor of the loading dock, sending pieces of candy flying in every direction.

I'm here to work, she screamed. I'm not here to put up with your bullshit.

El Sida cowered like a stupid mutt that doesn't know any better. Genie didn't report him. Probably assumed the scene was enough to keep everyone else at bay.

The next day, I was having my lunch in the hub office when Genie asked Rick if he wanted anything from Jack in the Box for lunch, said she'd pick it up for him, either sucking up to him or only being nice. Rick struggled with naming the salad he was asking for (probably because he never ordered them) and wanted to impress her by proving he could make good eating choices.

What's that salad, he asked, with the orange things? Haysan? Asayan? Ashun?

Asian? I asked.

Yeah, he said, the one with the orange slices.

She brought him the Southwest Chicken one because they were out of Ashun, and he left it unopened in the office for a moment while he continued running the department by himself, a scene I started to enjoy more and more every day as he struggled with boxes of parts lined up across both arms. After a few minutes, El Sida showed up with a Whopper for Rick, and he didn't hesitate at all to unwrap it and sink his teeth into it like he had been waiting his whole life for it. Then Genie entered the hub office again, mid bite. He turned to face me to either hide the fact he wasn't eating the salad or hide the fact that he's not the nutritious human being he hoped she thought he'd be or to look for some kind of answer from me, to bail him out, something I could say to make the awkward situation go away. But I stayed quiet and fished for dry shrimp. I don't think Genie even cared.

We were alone on the seventh day while Rick was out on one of his long lunches. Everyone else was out on the routes. Bern Bern felt like going out on a run and she felt like staying in. She talked mostly about Rick, about how ever since she had made him feel uncomfortable by pulling his hand off of her, he had been telling people her sex stories. About how she would sleep with the manager from the Pharr store to get better hours, or how she would sleep with the district manager from there—the one who wrote me up—for the company to give her a raise. I wanted to tell her that Rick had been saying shit about her long before she started working here, but it wouldn't help.

Even if the stories are true, she said, even if it's true I fucked them, I would never do it for those reasons. I'm not a fucking whore. And it's not any of that fucker's business. He's no one to be telling people shit about me. She started to cry as she said this. She was within arm's reach, but I sat there and said nothing even though I wished I could touch her.

A while back, she said, I let a married man go inside me. I feel bad about it. He ended up falling in love with me and his relationship was pretty much ruined, but any relationship where a man chooses to sleep with someone else is pretty much ruined anyway. There were plenty of opportunities for him to stop, for him to say, "No, I shouldn't be doing this," but he didn't. Now, you can spin that any way you want, but that man didn't love his wife anymore. Any man who can do that to his wife doesn't love her anymore, even if he tries to make himself believe that he does, that it's possible to love two people at the same time, it's not true.

Why are you telling me this?

Because we're friends, Writer.

The next morning, the routes were ready to go thirty minutes early thanks to me. The sun wasn't even fully out yet, and already the warehouse was melting from the inside, probably still going from the day before. Rick arrived while I stared at the printer, waiting for more orders to come in and give me something to do. He was late. He asked where the rest of the orders were as if he still didn't think I could sort all of them on my own. I gestured that they were ready to go, and then, like a broken record: I'm sorry I'm late, man. Let me say this. You're lucky you don't have any kids. You don't know what it's like.

He had a fifth kid on the way with his wife, and the biblical -iah names would soon run out and wouldn't get him any closer to God. The prophets would have to write a sequel. The Newer Testament: Testify Harder.

I had to go drop them off at three different schools, Rick said, and my wife couldn't do it because I need the van today to go to school right after this. You're lucky that you don't got kids. He sat down on the chair in the office to catch his breath. So, he added, did you hear about Genie?

I hadn't seen her that much since we talked the day before. The times she did appear, she was always with Rick. He kept reminding her that he'd do everything for her, Anything you need, he said, and then, If the people here in the warehouse give you crap—I'm sorry— act inappopri- inapp- inap-pro-priately with you, if you see that anyone's bothering you, you tell me and I'll report him. He readied her route and loaded all her parts. None of us knew what he expected from her, and definitely never received the same treatment from him. The guys from DC would stand facing her back every time she and Rick spoke. Güero made the most accurate mime interpretation of a blowjob, making his Adam's apple move up and down. Then Red would mime out a correction, highlighting the fact that it was Rick's dick being mimed and would use his thumb and forefinger, pinching them together instead of a whole hand, like smoking a joint.

What, I told Rick, did she quit, too?

No, he said, but you'll never guess what she did. And before any response from me like a bad comedian with worse timing: She moved in with John, that fucking slut, man.

Rick's rumors were shit for the most part, but this one had several ounces of possibility. Shit, was all I said. Rick's eyes lit up, probably upon realizing someone believed what he was saying, or surprised it wasn't being questioned, asking who the source was. He picked up the phone and dialed the store in Elsa to tell Deedee about the new romance that had brewed in our McAllen store. When he hung up, he started calling Mingo in Mercedes, and the calls kept going out. Once while the line was ringing, he turned to face me and said, You're taking Dago's route instead of her today. If she wants to fucking spend time with John, then I'm going to keep that bitch here with me all day. So make sure you leave your cellphone in your truck, and you can start getting the truck ready if you want.

Before doing so, I stopped in the front office to talk to the boss. He was blowing on a cup of coffee. What's up, he said.

I shook my head. Thought better of it and said, Actually, did you hear that John and Genie moved in together? He looked disappointed, but not at the news. His eyes didn't tell me that.

How'd you hear about this?

I made him a face, and he knew the answer without needing it to be said.

So, then, what?

So then, nothing, I said, just thought he'd learn from the first time, is all.

I drove Genie's routes the rest of the week and started feeling guilty doing so. I tried offering to switch with her some of the times so she could take a break from the warehouse, but Rick refused to let her go. I don't want to separate her from her little sweetheart, he would tell me when I'd ask. I want to make it *all* perfect for her. And then he'd tell her, This week, you need to learn where all the parts are in the warehouse. You need to learn what goes where.

I listened to an abridged version of Stephen King's *Desperation* that week, read by Kathy Bates, because it was the only audiobook I could find and put into the iPod. Why was Kathy Bates so crazy about Steve? Or was this another paycheck to her? At least it was free even if it was taking steps back.

On Wednesday, Rick decided to give me a full lunch hour. I asked him what the special occasion was. He laughed, but didn't understand the question. I returned within thirty minutes, already accustomed to shortened or missing lunches, and tried helping out with the orders that kept coming in. But Rick snatched the tickets from my hand and handed them to Genie.

Plato joined me at the loading dock stairs while waiting for the other thirty minutes break to pass by, smoking a cigarette and trying and failing to make shapes with the smoke to make the time go by faster and be back out on the road. He asked me if I knew what Weslaco stood for. He said, It stands for West Louisiana Company. Wes-la-co.

Is that right?

It's what they tell me, he said, and then sat down next to me before asking me how the writing was coming along. Sometimes it's good to have someone on your back asking you that, reminding you that *that* was what you need to be doing, not fucking running around for Rick so he could have an easier life. Can you blame commercial writers for getting paid to do what they love? Look at the fucking alternative. I wanted more people in my life to ask me that, even if I answered the same way I answered him that time: I'm not sure how it's coming along. All I have are notes right now. Might be a good idea to let them sit in the oven a little while longer.

Brainstorming is good for the process, he said. You need to strategize at least a little bit or else you'll jump in without thinking it through and realize you're swimming in diarrhea, not clean water.

You have a way with words, I said and flicked the cigarette to the street. I was getting better at that. Why aren't you a writer?

Don't want to know myself that way.

So, I said, you hear about your employee? That he and Genie are living together now.

He stared at me for a moment like the boss had, same look on his face before asking, Is that right?

It's what he tells me, I said, pointing at the hub.

When Rick called me back into the office, he told me he wouldn't be showing up on Saturday and that I'd have to run the hub because I was the only other person that knew how.

I told him, You mean I'm the *only* person. He laughed, but still didn't understand.

Before leaving on the route, he added, Oh, and don't let Genie go on the route. You make her sort out parts and keep her in the warehouse with you. If she goes out on a route, I'll write you up for insubordination.

How old are you?

Why?

I gave Genie a choice that day. Saturdays weren't the busiest of days anyway. She chose to stay. But don't tell Rick I let you decide, I said.

Don't worry about it, she said. Today's my last day here. I'm not going to be working in this company anymore. It's funny. I've worked at three different branches, and it was this one that finally made me fall off the tree. And it was all Rick. And I didn't even fuck the bastard. So, yeah. I'm quitting.

That's probably a good idea, I said.

My ex-boyfriend hooked me up with a job at the radio station, so I think it's going to be okay. Honestly, dude, I don't know how you've made it so long working for that fucking idiot. How the hell do you put up with that *pelado*? I mean, can't you see him for who he is? He's a fake asshole, Writer. You told me he had good intentions. He doesn't. He does shit for his own convenience, not for anyone else. He's nothing but a fat cunt, is what he is.

I had never heard a girl use that word before. It wasn't as strange as I thought it would be. Nothing like a six-year-old telling his kindergarten teacher to go fuck her mother, which was me, but in Spanish. *Chinga tu madre*, I had said because she wouldn't let me write words on my drawing.

I don't know, I told Genie. I've seen almost every side of Rick, and trust me, there are a lot of sides. Maybe he's convinced himself so much of what he isn't, so the fiction becomes our only wellspring of fulfillment. I guess I've lasted here because you eventually get used to the sides after a while. They become routine. And you stick to routines because they fucking work.

We stepped out of the hub office together so I could light a cigarette. She asked if she could have one, my last one, the lucky one. She removed it from the carton and placed it between her lips, ignoring the lighter and instead leaning towards me so that our cigarette tips could kiss and mine lit hers. Her lips puckered when she blew out smoke.

Some of the other guys, I said, have been here ten years. I can't fucking picture myself working here that long. I'd hang myself the moment I realized it.

I hate him, Writer, she said. He's such a piece of shit. All last week, "Oh, I'll do this for you, Genie. No, Genie, let me get that for you." And this week? Fuck him.

Inside the hub office, the printer started spitting out an order. Whatever the destination, it didn't matter. All the last routes were gone for the day, and the store wouldn't get the part until Monday.

You wanna know something, Writer? Want to know what I did to fuck with his head? Check it out. I got John from DC to play a prank on him with me. We told a few people that we were seeing each other, just to see how fucking jealous Rick would get and how many people he'd tell. Son of a bitch ended up telling everyone. And don't even get me started on how he chose to act out on his jealousy. Dropped his whole fucking—how did the dumbass say it?—cavalry act. Like he thought I was going to fuck him. It was actually pretty fucking hilarious.

That's a good one, was all I could say.

You knew about it, right? About this whole prank.

Yeah. I think Plato told me, went along with it, too. I turned to face the ground to avoid looking at her, even though I wanted to look at her, forgetting about the cigarette between my fingers. Shit, I thought to myself. If this were a fucking movie and there was something in the hub office that could cast a reflection, I thought Rick would be looking back at me.

I'm going to take off already, she said. Is that okay with you?

Sure, I said. Day's practically over anyway, right?

She leaned towards me again and we kissed each other on the cheeks like two idiots before she left the hub office. The cordless phone clinging to my pocket started ringing. I ignored it. She jumped down from the loading dock and then looked up to face me.

Well, Writer, she said, it was great knowing you. I do hope you don't stay here forever. You're too smart for a place like this. And write your book, okay? If you write it, don't forget about me. She raised her fist in the air and said, Death to the Rick. I hate to leave you all alone here. We could've gone far here, together, to make Rick's life miserable, you and me.

Isn't it pretty to wish so?

She climbed in the passenger side of a car that was waiting for her. The phone started ringing again as the car started moving. She threw her uniform out the window, yelling woo-hoo like a motherfucking cliché.

Hub office, I said.

Hey, Writer. This is Mike from Weslaco. I just ordered a part. Did I catch the route?

Sorry, man, I said. Route was already gone.

Fuck, he said and hung up the phone.

PART SEVENTEEN

The Part About Clichés

On the outside, Genie had large breasts, curvy legs, and brown eyes, but it was the words she'd say that were the most memorable to me. The people in the writing group remembered her as a slut. They hadn't changed much since the last time. A year ago? Two? Three? Most of the members were new, but that wasn't much of a change considering they were still having the same unfinished conversations as before, as if I had left them on pause the entire time and forgot about them. The only remaining people from the last time, besides the ever-silent leader, were Toby and Flaco. Daniel and Melissa, who I actually wanted to see, weren't there anymore. Neither was Jeremy. The new people weren't impressive, which made this group unable to move forward because there would always be beginners keeping it from doing so. If memory serves right, one of the new guys was named Martillo—or he reminded me of a hammer—and he refused to write about anything that didn't have vampires in it, which was made clear when the rest of the cast in the circle complained about this one story being about vampires again. His story actually hurt my eyes reading it, and the grammar was terrible. Grammar wasn't usually important to me. That's last draft shit. But when you can't turn your brain off from so much of it being wrong, you can't enjoy the story anymore. The pages grew heavier with every turn. The story had all the elements of a typical vampire story—the garlic, the fucking, the missing reflection, the being killed by sunlight, the youth, everything that Cool Whip had said made genre writing shit. When I spoke up about it during the workshop, to sort of convince myself that I could still think about writing, I told him he should try to aim at writing something a little more original, something no one has seen before. That he could still write about vampires, but try to transcend the genre. Change its direction.

"Like how?" he asked.

"I don't know. It's your story. It's not on me to tell you what to write or how to go about writing it. Your narrative. You make the decisions. It's clear you read a lot of this type of literature."

"I mostly watch movies," he said.

"Right. The 85% dialogue explains that. And it's clear you dig the genre. As much as it would be fun to join in on the conversation, though, I can't help but imagine how great it would be to start one of your own. I would try to say something with this genre that no one else has before."

"I am," he said. "My vampires can actually eat garlic sometimes. They just have some trouble digesting it. They can also walk in sunlight, but they only have an hour—"

"You see," I said. "I don't think that's starting a new conversation. You're only bending the rules of vampirism a little bit and trying to call it your own creation. The originality has to come with the actual characters, not their characteristics. It has to come in the plot. In the craft. You *can* work with this."

There was silence for a while except for pages being flipped back and forth, eyes searching for another flaw to comment on. And then Toby spoke. "So then we're in agreement that this is a crap story," he said. "That we've wasted precious time reading this. That instead of moving forward and making us better readers—or even left us the same way we went in—that it has actually turned us into worse readers."

"Kind of like practicing baseball," I said.

"What's that?" Flaco said.

"Or in this case, more like watching little leaguers playing it when you're looking for professional advice."

"What the hell are you talking about?"

"Nothing. Never mind."

I knew exactly who the other unbearable person was by reading the first paragraph of her work, by knowing what it was going to be about as soon as I read the first sentence: "Jennifer was a smart high school girl who had a crush on Stan, the hot football player who needed help with some English tutoring because Jennifer liked to read books a lot." Her story proceeds at her house, with her parents gone, where they start talking about the book they're reading in class, *Harry Potter and the Sorcerer's Stone*, as if that's the book of choice in high school English classes. Only an idiot teacher would choose that over *The Odyssey*. They start kissing, and then he wants to have sex and she realizes she doesn't want to go that far. But he's a football player and she can't defend herself. So he rapes her. When he pushes himself off the bed—leaving her lying there, looking up at the ceiling because she can't believe what happened to her—he actually pulls out the condom and tosses it at her face (which I thought was the one moment in the story that sounded like something I hadn't read or seen a thousand times). She ends up telling her best friend the next day, the way they always do, who ends up waiting for the guy to finish practice to cut off his dick, because she's an outgoing person like that, one of those rebels. She ends up going to prison, where she's given the death penalty. The protagonist visits her all the time because they'll always be best friends. There's even a moment in the end where they both place their hands against the window while they talk to each other, and they start laughing about the time she cut off the guy's dick a whole four paragraphs ago. All of this in fewer than a thousand words. I summarized the fucking thing in a quarter of that.

Like I said, I knew exactly who she was. She was the reason literary journal readers didn't look past the first paragraph in their submissions. The type of writer that was under the illusion she was a writer. Her parents probably told her she had a talent for it. Her siblings probably told her she was good at coming up with stories, that they could picture everything she wrote like it was a movie. That she should send her work out and get published in newspapers because they had no clue how publishing works. Her high school teacher, to avoid giving her any form of constructive criticism because it's not like high school teachers to actually help you, told her she was creative. And that she showed potential or some bullshit like that. And that she only gave her a *C* because of her grammatical problems because any fucking idiot can grade for grammar over content. She sent lovey-dovey poems out for publication in poetry dot com, which offered to feature her in a book of poetry titled *Untamed Doves* or *Herbal Essences*, and if she wanted to, she could order a copy of that book with her poem in it for only $18.99, plus shipping and handling. When she'd get the book in the mail—the error on the second stanza where she wrote "they're" instead of "their" still *there*—she'd open it up to find her poem published as the first poem in the whole book, in front of all the other ones. Probably because hers is the best one out of all them, right? Totally worth the $18.99, plus shipping and handling. On the other side of town, another poet in the making is jumping with his own copy of *Herbal Essences* in hand because *his* poem is the first one printed, even before "To Mend a Broken Heart" by that person he goes to the same high school with, only he doesn't know that because she didn't pay the extra $19.99 to be included in the contributors list, and she used the pseudonym Whyte Rayne because that was her poet name and you can't write poetry unless you have a pseudonym like Whyte Rayne or Chica Moth like they're ashamed of using their real names.

I didn't share any of this cynicism during her critique, didn't have the balls to say any of this to her. Barely the balls to think it. Martillo was easier to deal with because he actually showed faint signs of hope. This girl—not sure what her non-bullshit name was—looked like she should've realized it was better to walk away before letting an illusion like that take you that far.

I didn't always think creative writing was something you had to be born with. I had sat in classrooms with professors who actually did. You either have the talent or you don't. You can work on it as much as you want, but if you don't have the knack (or the madness from the Muses) you'll never be successful standing next to the madmen. I never thought that. I believed that stupid cliché that writing was only 10% inspiration and 90%—you fucking get it. That even if we had a shitty rough draft, we had the power of revision, to learn from our mistakes and improve, and to use it to discover new ideas about ourselves and about our writings. Fuck Kerouac and his first-draft-best-draft rule. Same sign, same birthday, same goals, and I still don't buy that first-draft shit. I thought there was hope for all of us to say something because there are over six billion minds out there, so there were almost twice as many eyes experiencing life in their own way, always twice as many hands to write those thoughts down. But then I looked at the short story "That Piece of Shit Motherfucker" by this writer again.

The name of a new workshopper was Layla, though she used the name Adelaida in her story, a young white girl that looked like she had recently gotten out of high school but didn't write like it, not like That Piece of Shit Motherfucker did. She was short, small, must've been like five feet—a couple of inches more if you want to be precise—and had dark red hair. If there ever was such a standard that you had to be born a creative writer, she gave me the feeling she was, even if her work was nowhere near perfection yet, let alone good. She had turned in this short story of about 11,000 words or so. Didn't even bother to double-space it for the critical notes because she either didn't want to waste as much paper or didn't want to scare anyone from reading it after judging it by its thickness. She titled it "Perpetual Summer, or some other title that will sound better than this one" and I thought she had started strong. The opening was a couple arguing in a car after the man accidentally ran over a dog, which was executed well for an action scene. I pictured the back roads I was used to driving. Her attention to setting was spot on—the vegetation, the weather, the sounds, the smells—way better than mine by miles. Then it felt like she couldn't stop writing. Like she kept going on with the story as if her fingers were pounding away at the keyboard and the sweat poured down her body. Like a mad writer. They ended up in this small town where some people kidnapped them and left them tied up in some woods. Some of the men from town would bet money to see who could hunt them down and kill them first, except the woods, because so many people had died in them, were believed to be spiritually linked to other woods in other towns, in other years, even. After the critique, when she was allowed to speak, she said she wanted to write a quadrilogy with the four different seasons. "Hence," she said, "the working title. I wanted to have the stories take place during the four different seasons. This one obviously summer. But I'm not sure if it's a project worth pursuing anymore."

I didn't have much to say during her critique. She'd go on to not say much during mine, though that had nothing to do with my silence—despite the routine mentality of "you didn't say shit for me so I won't say shit for you" everyone loved to employ. She'd have my notes and critique when I'd hand my copy to her, though I felt the sudden need to keep "Perpetual Summer, or some other title that will sound better than this one" with me because the other detail I noticed about Layla was that we wore the same uniform. And she held Genie's chapter in her hands.

When they started with mine to close the workshop, Flaco said, "I can't believe you're still working on this. You'd think you'd have some other material by now, or that you'd be finished. You'd think you wouldn't feel much like writing this. How slow do you write anyway?"

I paid no attention to Flaco. How I'm still able to quote him is puzzling to me. He spoke, he speaks in that manner, and there was a comment about my lack of new material, so that is what he must've said. While he spoke, however, my mind kept surfacing thoughts of what Layla would say or what she was thinking. She could see my shirt, so she knew the inspiration for the words she read. She wasn't stupid.

"If I have to say something nice about it," Toby said, "I'd say that I kind of like the progression I'm seeing here with the first-person narrator and his relationship with the antagonist. How he's becoming more and more integrated into the culture he hates. I like that they're not exactly ripping each other's throats yet, but it seems like it'll eventually escalate to that. However, my praise can only go so far."

Of course.

"I found myself absolutely hating this Genie character," he said. "I didn't find her believable at all, and—I don't know. I know we haven't seen you or your work in a long while, But I actually feel sick at the fact that every fucking time you write female characters, you have to make them out to be sluts. Every time. Here's another girl. Slut. Another girl. Slut. Not all girls are sluts, you know. That's, like, your thing. Your mark as a writer. Every female in your fiction is a fucking slut."

He must've used the word "slut" like a hundred more times. He was probably right. It had crossed my mind that I might be under the impression that every girl is a slut. If that was the case, I couldn't help it. Fuck. What if this is what I see when I look at the girls in the valley, the girls at or around work? What if these are only observations? So fucking what? There was probably a part of me that wanted every girl in the world to be a slut like every man is a slut. What would that be like? But Toby's full of shit. These were the characters in my life. Write what you know and all that shit, right? How could I put that in a phrase Toby would understand? I was—and he would most likely underline this with his red pen—a fucking victim of my own environment.

"I don't know," Toby said towards the end. "I found myself hating most of this. There were a lot of clichés, which you actually pointed out yourself *in* the writing a couple of times. Doesn't make them any less cliché. And I honestly think it's about time you start moving on to something else. I don't know how much longer you can take this endeavor. Don't know how much longer you can keep writing about these characters. Maybe you've said all there is to say about them already."

"I didn't think Genie was a slut," That Piece of Shit Motherfucker said.

"Yeah, you wouldn't," Toby said.

The writing group started to feel too familiar. We weren't getting anywhere. Their comments trying to analyze my writing and worrying about aspects having little to do with the craft itself weren't taking me anywhere.

"Does the writer have anything to say?" the leader asked.

"Thanks for your comments, everybody," I said. "But it's the being surrounded by men that makes us see each other as threats. That creates chaos and makes us act without thinking because it's impossible to do both at the same time. We have an undying desire to feel superior to everyone else, to be convinced that everyone else is inferior to us. So we only see what we want to see."

"What does that have to do with Genie?" Toby asked.

"I don't know," I said, and I didn't. I was desperately trying to find five-dollar words for fifty-dollar phrases and take the focus away from the reality in the work.

As the writers and critics began to leave, Layla walked up to me. She said, "Hey, we're wearing the same shirt." Her shirt also read Adelaida, like her name at the top of her story.

"I noticed," I said.

"I started last week. New branch here in Edinburg."

"South 23rd," I said. "The big warehouse store."

"I noticed," she said. "So is it as crazy over there as what you describe in your work? Are people really doing shit like that? Is any of it true?" She saw I was trying to find my words and didn't want to let the silence rest in the air. "Do I need to be thinking about finding another job?"

"Sometimes setting becomes a character," I said. "It's all fiction. Don't worry. I'm inspired by the setting because it's where I'm at every day. Characters are all composites."

"Good. I didn't want my husband to start worrying about me. He works over at the Mission branch. Pretty crazy there, though." Her uniform shirt was not tucked and she wore tennis shoes that looked like Genie's, only she was more attractive than Genie was. Smarter, too. I wanted to tell her nothing written is ever fully true, and I wanted to knock down the marked up copies of her story from her hands the moment she used the word *husband*. "Well, it was nice meeting you. Are you coming next week?"

"Yeah. You bet."

When I exited the building, Daniel was waiting outside like before. I barely recognized him. He looked older. Maybe it was the clothes he wore. New job or something that required him to look more professional, so no more t-shirts of Yoda in different colors that looked like he made himself: "A book by its cover judge not" or "What around comes, around goes" or "When naked, you party, happens shit."

"We need to start another writing group," I said after we caught up. "A smaller one this time, without assholes like Toby or idiots like Flaco in them. What do you think?"

"Yeah. I got tired of all the bullshit that went on in this one. No one actually talked about the writing. Probably didn't even care about the writing. Felt like it was all for show."

"Our writing group," I said, "if we start one, will be everything that that one in there isn't. We'd only need at least one more person, so we can both have a third opinion *and* a number low enough to maintain focus on the task." Not Layla, though.

Quique showed up as if he had finished the longest metamorphosis illusion in history because he hadn't changed at all. Some of the other workers—myself included—looked like they had aged years since the moment Quique left, only harder to notice when you see them every day. Not Quique, though. Same mustache, some short hair, some complexion. He caught me on my way out of the hub office with orders at the loading dock, our old home, and asked me how everything was. Walk with me, I said and started telling him about how the hub office and commercial department had switched places.

Anyone jump the wall, he asked as we climbed up the stairs.

A lot of people have been hired and fired since you left, so no need to mention those. Pansy left for a little bit after you did. Planned to start a rock band and was pretty serious about it. Didn't work out and he's back. The Wolf transferred to another store and they gave Rick the hub supervisor position back. And Brown, you remember Brown?

Did he finally get canned for pissing in the warehouse?

Nope. Stealing car batteries. Well, actually was caught stealing air fresheners, the stupid pinecone ones, and from that investigation, it turned out he had been snatching car batteries, too.

That's pretty retarded, he said. What about Rick? What's new with him?

Quique helped me get the rack and pinion box from the top shelf, which fell to the ground and scared one of the employees from commercial on the first floor. I apologized and said to Quique, Let's not talk about Rick.

What do you mean? Is he a piece of shit now?

I mean you'll see for yourself. Hey, you remember these?

The ropes, Quique said. The fucking ropes. They're still there? I guess nothing *has* changed.

Back in the hub office, he said he'd start working at the front counter the next day, at a better pay than before. Your brother, he said, he's a pretty forgiving guy. He didn't even remember that I jumped the wall before my two weeks were over. Still, man, working at the oil rig, it was horrible. You think this is bad. Yeah, they freaking pay you a lot, but that's because not a lot of people are willing to do it. That shit, man, it gets into your lungs. You get to your bed all tired and shit, and then you start wheezing because you're having a hard time breathing and you want to explode.

It's not so different here, I said, running a pair of fingers through the lining of the steel shelf and showing them to him as if he were ready to take my prints now.

Couple of the guys I worked with had to leave the rig because they actually ended up getting some type of cancer from breathing all those fumes. Company gives them some money for the hospital bills, but they make us sign this contract when we start working. That way we're not allowed to freaking sue the company or anything if it ends up happening. When I noticed it started getting pretty bad for me, that's when I decided it was time to quit, which was a few months ago. Didn't want it to end up happening to me.

Few months ago? I said. What did you do in the mean time?

I met someone, he said. This girl. Don't worry. Nothing happened between us. Wasn't like that. We didn't have sex or anything. We only made out a little.

Y tu wife? Your daughter?

Like I said, Quique said as he sat down, nothing happened between us. Just kissing. It was nice. Like a real relationship, something I missed out on with my wife. We went straight to being parents. Missed the whole dating part. Don't make that face. It's not cheating if you don't fuck.

I calculated how much time there was to sort out the orders that had come out while I was upstairs, figured there was enough. Started separating them before putting them off to the side and the moaning of the A/C unit hung between us. It was working harder as the few cold weeks we get down here were dissipating. Rick would be back from lunch in twenty minutes—scheduled to be, anyway. I faced Quique again and said, I think wives would call investing emotional time with another woman a stronger cheat than physical sex. But what do I fucking know? I guess everyone's different.

Well, that doesn't make sense. Adultery is the sin here. So that's what they should care about the most. I didn't commit that. All we did was kiss.

Adultery is a man-made sin and placed higher up because the thought of our wives sleeping with another man is unbearable, disgusting, the worst. But the thought of ourselves sleeping with another woman is, I don't know. It's bad, for sure, but you notice there is a difference here, even though there shouldn't be. But there is.

So, then, you're going to give me some kind of lecture? On how what I did back at the rig was bad? Nice welcome I get.

No, I said. I don't even give a shit about what you did at the rig. I'm having a conversation.

Well, we didn't do anything wrong. Besides, I don't think it's cheating when it's your own wife's fucking fault. I mean, she's the one that wanted me to get that job, all far away, and make more money. Always fucking fighting with me on the phone.

What does that have to do with it?

Well, I'm saying men have physical needs. Our wives can't expect for us to be so far away from them and not satisfy those needs. If they don't want us cheating, then they should keep us locked up.

But you said you didn't cheat.

You get lonely, man. After a while of being so far away from your wife, you start getting lonely, and you start forgetting what it feels like to have someone close to you. Or, you know, to have someone sleep next to you in bed. He scratched his nose while I put the tickets in order based on where the parts were located in the warehouse.

S'good to have you back, was all I could say.

Quique wouldn't go far in the company, unfortunately, as not many of us do. There is always something that keeps us from going far. Some obstacle—some form of self-sabotaging—will always get in the way. For a lot of us, we steal. We convince ourselves of a fiction that we will starve, or they'll shut off our electricity, our water, lose our home, if we don't take that money or that merchandise to exchange for money. And the reality is that we'll be okay without that money, but we do it anyway. For some of us, we harass. We convince ourselves of a fiction that the way she looked at us, the way she made us feel, the way she kissed me on the cheek, merits touching her, merits kissing her, and following her around all over the city. And the reality is that these actions keep feeding the monster and feeding the fiction. For some of us, we escape. We convince ourselves of a fiction that we are superior to the men who surround us, a fiction that has us believing the longer we stay here, the faster we'll transform into them, a fiction that makes us not want to face the reality. And the reality is, there is no transformation. It's a bridge.

For Quique, it will be bad timing. He'll be at the end of the bridge, working the counter at the store and getting ready for an assistant manager position to eventually manage his own branch. That's his dream on the elementary school wall with the star students. His picture next to kids who want to be doctors, lawyers, Hannah Montana, and on Quique's star, auto parts store manager. All of his good sales will show that he is ready to be an assistant manager at the Edinburg branch.

In the future, he will be waiting for his transfer to go through, trying not to breathe the smoke I'm breathing out on the stairs in the loading dock and stepping aside so it doesn't sink into the fabrics of his clothes. Clementine used to smoke a lot, he will say, referring to the woman he didn't have an affair with, only kissed a lot. Have you ever tried to make out with someone who smokes a lot? It's like doing drugs. Feels so good, but tastes like shit. In the end, feeling beats taste.

That's probably why some people can't handle certain food textures, I will say, even if it tastes good.

I remember the times I would see Luci and she would smell the cigarette in my laundry and ask me about it. It was an easy lie, blame it on the other roughnecks, even though only two of them smoked and we would never hang out. Clementine couldn't get enough of them, though. Do you think if she had blown me, the taste would stick to the skin forever?

I wouldn't know, I will say, and remember trying to wash the fingers I used to hold cigarettes with soaps, dish detergent, creams, and the smell never came off. Good thing I didn't use my left hand to smoke. I'm right-handed, but I read using your left felt like someone else was doing it. It didn't. Eventually, trying with the right did, so I had to stick to southpaw.

In the past, at the beginning of the bridge, he was at a party at a friend's house in San Juan, norteñas and rancheras blaring out of the speakers. It wasn't his scene, but his girlfriend told him she'd meet him there. So he put on his best jeans, ostrich boots, and a long-sleeve plaid shirt, buttoned all the way to the top like David Lynch. But no one at the party said anything. The girlfriend didn't show.

"Hey, Puñetas," Quique said to his friend, who was smoking out of a bong. "Let's get the fuck out of here. This party blows."

"You got a car?"

They ended up leaving with Puñetas's younger brother, Puñal, who was believed to be a closeted homosexual. Quique remembered a different party he had gone to a couple years before. They tell him he was too drunk to go home and was dumped in the host's game room to sleep it off. After a while, Puñal disappeared. No one knew where he went. They say they caught him in the game room, blowing Quique, which Quique will always refuse to believe.

Puñal drove by San Juan's Basilica and Quique did the sign of the cross without thinking about it. The moths and stoneflies flew around the lamp posts in circles, not resisting the temptation to touch the light and get burnt, then fly around again until their next turn. Quique took his girlfriend on a date there once to walk around the grounds. They ended up doing voiceovers for the statues, especially the one of Jesus falling while carrying the cross: "Can't let the side touch the lava." Then they kissed for the first time.

"Hey, Puñal," Quique said. "Can you turn right up on Stewart? Pass by Mary's house? She said she'd be at the party."

In the future, Quique will be filling out his new application on a clipboard while he's following me around because he wants to make sure he "sounds smart."

You think I'm the best person to be helping you with this application, I will ask him as I remove a Borg Warner box filled with switch boxes and start looking for the number that matches the one on the invoice in my other hand. I'll sniff hard at the air because it's the only way to get air into my lungs and I don't want to breathe through my mouth.

You're the only one in here who's not an idiot, and it's not like you try to hide it.

Ramos might say that that means I'm trying to hide the opposite.

Who the hell is Ramos?

Mexican critic.

That's another thing, Quique will say. What should I put here? How do you identify yourself? Are you Latino, Chicano, Hispanic, Mexican-American? Or are you too busy being educated and pretending to be white?

How do I pretend to be white?

You're always reading. You're always writing. You hardly ever speak Spanish.

Spanish is a white language, dumbass.

In the future, I will continue grabbing brake rotors out of the shelf, yellow labels facing forward, because they'll continue to rust and continue to stop working, no matter how many times we try to resurface them. They'll always give out eventually. And we won't be able to stop.

So what would you put, then?

The truth is, I will never identify with any of those labels. I won't deal with people who want to pressure me into saying any of those options, to embrace the idea my father was born here and my mother was born there. To be political and pretend I'm oppressed and write some poetry shit about it. To find that writing niche and then maybe be published because some white editor thinks I'm all fucking exotic, even though there's always going to be someone who's a better writer and more oppressed. And he'll be too busy wondering who he is. Is he Mexican? Or is he American? Like it's such a fucking dilemma. Does he really want to know? Put on a Gold Cup final between Mexico and the US. By the end, he'll have his fucking answer.

I would write Mexican, I will say, and be done with it. Though when we desire to be what we picture a Mexican or an American to ideally be, we have to lie to ourselves because that's the only way we'll be happy with the myth.

Over on the other side of the bridge, Puñal said, "Hey, man. Isn't that your girlfriend over there?" He pointed to a petite woman with her arms wrapped around a taller man with his head shaved, leaning against the hood of a car.

"That fucking bitch," Quique said.

"What are you going to do?" Puñetas said.

"Nothing," Quique said. "Let's just go. Bitch isn't worth it."

"Oh, no one is going to fuck with my friend," Puñal said and pulled out a gun from under the seat.

"Stop, man," Quique said.

The past happened so fast. Quique did not remember Puñal's mouth on him, but he remembered him parking the car, getting down, and shooting the guy. After that moment, Quique exited the car and walked in the opposite direction. Because he failed to report it, he was on probation for ten years because it was a lot easier to plead guilty. It's always easier to plead or to pretend that we're not.

The issue with the past is that the future will always come. When the ten years will finish, this incident will come out on record, and before Quique has a chance to transfer, the company will have to let him go. It's one thing to be a degenerate, and it's another to be convicted for it.

In the present, I don't know how to feel about this situation: Quique has had a good while working at the front counter. No one likes working with him, though. They even change his nickname to La Rata because he steals everyone's customers to get the commission. He listens in to the customers asking other coworkers for a part, and if he knows it's an expensive part, he starts charging them at his station while the other coworker goes to the back to retrieve the part. One day, no one wants to sell me a Diet Coke at the front counter because of their cash ticket average, so I stand there and wait.

Smokey the Bear, the heavy smoker, is talking about tattoos while the store's empty because Flask has been showing off his new ones. Flask moved from working for the hub to working at the front counter because he had gone behind the manager's back to ask the district manager directly for a raise, claiming he needed one to get his family and new house on track. The district manager didn't like being asked, but instead of giving him a raise, he moved him to the front counter where he'd have a chance to make better commission. Smokey the Bear says that his father wouldn't ever let him get tattoos, first of all, because you couldn't donate blood.

So, he says, my old man would say that if I'd be driving with my wife somewhere and had an accident, that I could never give her my blood to save her life because of the tattoos, told me she'd die before they found other blood to give her, all because of me.

So what? Flask says. That's why they have all these other people donating blood left and right.

That's right, Quique says, looking at Smokey. I mean, I was even thinking it would be pretty cool to get a barbed wire right here. He rolled up his sleeve and ran a finger around his upper arm before adding, I was thinking I could be wearing a muscle shirt somewhere and scare some people off. Nothing big, though, like you, Flask. I don't want ink to replace my clothes. Just something small.

Yeah, 'cause you're probably used to having small things, faggot.

Hey, asshole, Quique tells Flask, just because I let you put your small thing in my mouth, don't mean I'm a faggot.

Alright, I announce. I'm going to leave two dollars on this counter here as a sign that I'm paying for this shit, and I'm going to walk away. Whoever decides to charge me can keep the change.

I remember one time, Smokey continues, when I tried to give myself a tattoo with some paint. You know, like a henna tattoo. I must've been like sixteen or some shit at the time. So my dad walks in, and pow, he punches me right in the fucking jaw. Told me branding was for fucking animals.

Well, I say, finally joining in, we *are* fucking animals.

Well, Quique says, *mammals* to be exact, dumbass.

The rest of the guys start laughing. The condensation from the drink starts to slip between my fingers. Part of me wants to explain to Quique I meant behaviorally. That it would be like me saying, We're all humans in some sense, and then for Quique to say, Well, Mexicans, to be exact, dumbass. Part of me wants to tell him that he should go back to college and learn to fucking listen. But I don't say any of this, because it caught me by surprise, because I didn't expect it. So I dump my money on the counter and leave them thinking it was a good joke, the lingering laughter ringing in my head.

When I tell Bern Bern about it at the end of my lunch break, about how I didn't know how to feel about it, I don't think he understands a fucking word I say, but I notice I refer to Quique as La Gata for the first time.

PART EIGHTEEN

The Part About The Parts

Rick's writing teacher was blind in one eye, smoked during class, and drove a motorcycle. He had been waiting since he started college to take this course because he wanted to have more in common with me, thought that if he learned how to write, that the situation would be okay between us because we could have conversations about writing. On the first day, he sat behind a girl that looked about twenty years old, in a skimpy blouse showing off her pierced stomach and a little bit of cleavage. Rick also made it a habit to drop objects from his desk—a pen, a piece of paper, his *Everything's an Argument* book, anything—to bend down and check out her Aerosmith logo tattooed right above her ass. He tried to start making conversation with her, asking her if she had heard anything about the teacher, and the girl shrugged and turned back around. Rick didn't pick up on her disinterest, either by choice or ignorance, and he kept looking at the back of her head, big smile on his big face, waiting to see if she'd say something else. She didn't. So he did.

"I'm Rick," he said. "What's your name?" But the teacher entered the room before she could make up her mind about answering him back.

The teacher walked in, smoking cigarette sticking out of her mouth as if she were some deadbeat in the darkest corner of a bar, laid her black helmet depicting a silver eagle spreading its wings down on the desk, sat on the chair, and placed her crossed legs next to the helmet. She sat there in silence for about ten or so minutes, looking out into space, sighing every once in a while, smoke leaking out of her nose and covering her face. Sometimes she'd breathe it in again as if she wanted it to stay inside her. The students started whispering to one another, wondering if it was some kind of test, something she did to all of her classes. Maybe they were supposed to walk out. Or they were supposed to take out some paper and start writing. No one knew.

Rick leaned forward in his desk and asked the girl, "What's with her? What are we supposed to do?"

She looked over her shoulder, not fully turning around, and said, "Seriously, guy, stop talking to me. You're starting to creep me out."

"You're pretty," Rick said. "Do you have a favorite Aerosmith song?"

The teacher decided to speak when she finished her cigarette and lit another one. "Abortion," she said, her voice croaking like a dying frog, cigarette still sticking out of her mouth and conducting with her lip movements. "Take out something to write with and write on, and write me an essay about abortion. Tell me what you think."

A couple of students started asking questions before writing. Someone said, "How long does it have to be?"

"As much space as you need to think."

"How many paragraphs?"

"Do you think in paragraphs?"

"What if we think both ways?" Rick asked.

"Then I'd say you're full of shit."

She called time a few minutes later, told everyone to write their names on it so she'd know who to give credit to, and pulled out a red marker from her jacket pocket after collecting the papers. "Shirley," she called out. "Let's see. Pro choice. Okay. You get an *A*. Michael: you're against abortion, little religious man, so you get an *F*." And she went on like that, for whatever reason. "Take this as a lesson," she said. "If you agree with what I agree with, you'll find that you'll be doing well in this course, even if you think you're the worst writer in the world. Just show me that you can think right. If our thoughts clash, then you probably won't be doing as well as you hope. One more thing. I'm impressed by big words."

"You mean like an extended vocabulary?" Rick asked and smiled.

"Exactly. Very good. In this world, all it takes is an extended vocabulary to impress people. Usually because you'll intimidate them with your higher words, and they'll always agree with anything you have to say, even if they don't know what you're saying. So start studying those thesauruses and learn to use the big words."

After class was over, Rick told the girl in front of him that it was nice to meet her. She didn't say anything back. He decided to follow her, thinking he could casually walk around campus falling back a few steps behind her, pretend his van wasn't parked on the other side. Besides, it was dark outside already and it wasn't like he would be too noticeable. She was or pretended to be on her cellphone the entire time. Sometimes, she'd start to turn around and Rick would hide like an idiot behind a bush or by a building corner. He felt like he wanted to know everything about her, to have her for himself. It was his second semester in college, and he thought he could use a fresh start and meet new people. Meet smart people. Or, *intellectuals*. He felt happy for thinking of that word. She climbed in a red Dodge Neon and drove out of the parking lot. Rick tried to memorize her license plate number, failed, and called it a night.

I decided to fake take Theatre Appreciation that same spring semester upon realizing I hadn't read any plays outside of Shakespeare, ever, while speaking with one of my roommates, Blas, about censoring books. He had been writing an argumentative essay on it in which he decided to argue against book censorship and claim all books should be available to everyone. I told him some required reading shouldn't be required because high school students don't have the mental capacity to deal with them. A lot of students wind up doing stupid shit in the name of film and literature.

"But don't you think that it's a lot better to read a book where the character goes through drug addition in lieu of going through the drug addiction yourself?" We were driving towards the university, taking Jara Chinas Road north towards 107, surrounded by tall, dried grass at each side that would probably turn to powder in our hands, the heat creating illusions of wetness in the spots where the road curved.

"No," I said. "If anything, reading about drug addiction, even if it's painted in the darkest shade of negative, would probably drive you to try drugs so that you can fully understand the work of literature. I would."

"But what about, let's say, sex?" Blas asked.

"What about it?" We passed by a dead oak tree, a victim of a brush fire, with branches sticking out in every direction, like it was missing a trunk and couldn't wait to spread out. A row of dead mesquites followed.

"Come on. Look at all the bullshit they gave us in high school health class, how they made us watch that video with the baby being born that probably messed up all of us for life, and the awkwardness of the teacher having to explain sex to us in some fashion that wouldn't end up with any of us suing her."

"Kind of helped she was attractive. But still, I think I see what you mean here. Instead of having someone awkwardly explain sex to us, let the students see the actual act of sex in literature, that way they see the intimacy between the characters and they actually know what sex is supposed to be like, instead of committing a series of errors that will lead them to dropping out of high school anyway. Question is, though, is this method of sexual education going to have a reverse effect? Are sexual relationships exactly the way they're depicted in fiction?"

"I don't think it will have a reverse effect. I'm still working out the details on that."

I turned right on 107, a straight shot to the university, and then said, "Here's my problem with required literature. A lot of students will end up building the wrong connections. Take *Romeo and Juliet*, for instance. We're all forced to read it freshman year in high school. Fourteen, fifteen years old. Think about how the teenage mind works at that age. We're always thinking about sex, wanting to have sex, wanting to be in love with the pretty girl but can't build the confidence to tell her or talk to her about it. We're all star-crossed lovers. Her popular friends won't have anything to do with our nerdy friends. She's too busy fucking the asshole while telling us to wait forever. We have this play about teenagers, which is obviously something everyone that age is supposed to relate to. Then we get to the end of the play. Now, of course we're going to think this is a tragedy. This is no way for any of us to go. However, at the same time, it sends us a message. It's not saying it's okay to commit suicide, but it's saying it's natural to do so for love. If anything, it's romantic to kill yourself for the person you love. Then you have people like our old high school friend who gave you those stitches on your melon with the combination lock, who would actually cut himself with staples because God couldn't give him a girlfriend. *He* ends up reading this play his freshman year and wants to do *something* to get the attention of this otherwise unattainable girl that never noticed him. And what's the best way to let her know of his torment and pain? How will Jeremy speak in class today? That's why I don't think high school students should read about these subjects."

"So if *Romeo and Juliet* makes you want to kill yourself, why is the suicide rate so low at our old high school?"

"Because no one fucking reads it if they can't fail anyway. Those who try don't speak Shakespeare. So I say the required books should be pre-chosen, not by whether or not they're classics. Okay, all literature comes from older literature, but people are still writing great shit today. They should be pre-chosen by content. And keep the books about drug addiction, and sex, and suicide in the library. Those students who actually want to read, the students who actually have the mental maturity to read the material, will seek them out."

So when the Theatre Appreciation teacher—a tall man that introduced himself as an actor and sat cross-legged on his desk—asked us why we were interested in taking his class, most of us said because it fit into our schedules or because we had to take it as a basic or because we also wanted to be actors, and when he got to me, I said because I was tired of thinking Shakespeare was the only playwright who ever lived.

I bought the textbook the first day, which was a collection of popular plays throughout history to appreciate, and started flipping through it to see if there were any Mexican playwrights in it. There weren't any. Most of them were either European or American, and the writer who came closest to what I was looking for was Federico García Lorca and the book contained his play *The House of Bernarda Alba*. I read it all the first night and found myself torn into different pieces. Not because it wasn't written well, but because I couldn't stop writing my thoughts on the margins and pointing out all the similarities between the play and

The Virgin Suicides by Eugenides. Even on the character list at the beginning, I ended up writing *Cecilia* next to Adela, *Lux* next to Martirio, *Bonnie* and *Mary* next to Magdalena and Amelia, and *Therese* next to Angustias. The resemblance in themes, in plot, in characters, in almost everything almost angered me, and what seemed unfair to me was that it felt like García Lorca was the plagiarizer and not the other way around because I read Eugenides first.

"But didn't you say that all literature derives from older literature?" Blas had said.

"Yes, but it takes the fun away when you notice you've read this story already."

I told myself that I'd have to give *Bernarda Alba* a second chance, and chose it as the play I wanted to do my presentation on, even though it wouldn't be for a grade anyway, but it was fun to pretend. Besides, I figured I could get away with it for a while since the instructor didn't believe in grades for drama because it was all subjective anyway, that he could never put a grade on our vision, as long as we gave it a shot and acted it out, not sit around with our hands on our dicks and read off the script. If we did that, then he'd start recording grades.

He paired me up with Layla from the writing group, who was taking the class as her basic but was one of the students who said they wanted to act, and said that the best way to understand a play was to hear it acted out, otherwise, they would only be words on a page—completely meaningless if no one speaks them, acts them, becomes them. Layla sat in front of me and turned to face me. We re-introduced each other, now that we were in our civilian clothing, as she called it. She wore her red hair down for the first time and a Black Eyed Peas Monkey Business tour t-shirt with 2005 tour dates on the back. She smiled with her mouth and with her eyes. They would squint a bit when she smiled wider.

"Nice shirt," she said. For a moment, I forgot what I was wearing and looked down at the red lines running down the Chivas jersey.

"Thanks. You, too," I said, though I didn't mean it. I didn't listen to the Black Eyed Peas. "Did you go to a concert, or . . . ?"

"Yeah. With my friend. In Houston. My husband wouldn't go with me. He doesn't like this kind of music. Says it's not 'real' music. Just noise."

"All music is real music," I said, thinking that probably sounded stupid. "I've faced similar battles with books. But I can understand when some music can get tiresome. They actually gave me a write-up for something related to that once."

"How the heck does that happen?"

"Long story."

"You'll have to tell me about it someday."

When she started reading some lines, I couldn't stop looking at her. It was like she was talking to me when she told me to leave her alone, as Adela, that what she did was her business and she'd do whatever she wanted with her body, and to stop looking at her. I turned the other way, but then I'd meet her eyes again. Then she said her body would be for whoever she wanted.

It went on like that for almost the entire hour and fifteen minutes of class. Other than reintroductions, she didn't say anything else to me that didn't come from the words in the play, like she refused to get out of character, and yet it seemed like everything was coming from her with the way she read it. I asked her if she had written the play herself.

'Sorry," I said. "It was a stupid joke."

"It wasn't a joke," she said. "You never liked jokes. There was something else that was boiling up inside you that was bursting to get out. Say it."

I'd do anything to have you for myself.

Then Layla said there was no end to what an evil tongue would tell, and I wondered why, out of all the sisters in the play, she had to play the part of Adela.

At work, Rick couldn't stop talking about his writing class, up to the point where he wouldn't let me do our labor. Kept saying that he had finally stumbled upon the conundrum to writing good: an extended vocabulary. You see, Writer, he said, it doesn't matter what you say. It's all about the words you utilize to say it. Using big words and shit will make people automatically think you're smart because they won't understand you. So if they can't comprehend, that means they must be of lower intelligence, so they'll be intnimi- intidi- intimi-dated by your words and surrender to them and not bother with them.

That's horrible, I said as I typed my password to clock in, using the same password since they started making us clock in with the computers: *PoetryIsShit*. The point of writing is for it to be read. That's how communication works. Besides, you never know when this is going to backfire on you and you'll end up using them wrong and sounding like an idiot.

Well, Rick said, sitting down and using invoices to fan the sweat dripping from his beard, that's what my teacher addressed to the class when it commenced. That writing is only about big words. I even used some in class myself and utterly flabbergasted her.

I sighed and left the hub office, invoices in hand. Pretty sure you can use *flabbergasted* as a verb the way Rick used it, but there was still something off about how he said it, like he said it without it being the first word he thought of using. It still seemed like the perfect word for Rick linguistically. You had *flabber* at the beginning, which reminded me of something fat did, as in "I hate the way your belly flabbers like that." And then *gasted* at the end, which reminded me of gas or something ghastly, like Rick. So Rick could flabbergast whoever he wanted.

He kept hounding me all over the warehouse, finding me in the aisles, waiting to see if I removed a large part off a shelf so he could plan to have his face planted on the other side of it, chin resting on the dust forming morsels of mud like lovers in a library, wanting to talk about writing and the process of composition. He asked, When you brainstorm, do you do like the web thing, or an outline, or a timeline, or some type of model? How do you brainstorm? I've found it works better to have a web. How do you do it? Do you make bubbles or boxes? Does it even matter?

I told him I made lists of words, phrases, and sentences. Told him I knew what I wanted to say, so, even while I was working, I'd write down a sentence or two that I knew I'd use in the actual text in some form. Those sentences usually triggered something when I went back to them. I'd ask myself why I wrote them. And that probably doesn't make any sense to you, does it?

When he returned from his lunch break (late), he started asking me about audience, if it was always a good idea to please them so that they'd give you a better grade.

No, I said. Think for yourself because even if the teacher has the power of the grade, he shouldn't command all of your choices. I handed him the invoices that were still left to sort and started clocking out. *PoetryIsShit*. He was starting to get bothered by my lunch breaks, which left him alone in the hub. He kept following me, starting to write notes on a clipboard like I was being interviewed. The idea here, I said, is to have your own opinions and be able to defend them, but still maintain an open mind to listen to the opposing side, even allow yourself to be convinced by it. Otherwise, you'll never be able to think.

In the days that followed, every time he walked back in from sorting parts, he asked me more questions. Sometimes I'd stop listening and he noticed and said, Okay, I can see I'm boring you. And then he'd fetch more parts.

A lot of the times, I was thinking about Layla instead of paying attention to his questions. She had acted out a few lines from other plays, some of them not as dramatic as when she played Adela, but it always felt like she was talking directly to me, even though she wasn't even looking in my direction. Near the middle of the semester, we were assigned to either write a response to a one-act play or write one of our own. He said it didn't have to be 100% original, that it could be adapted from another work we admired, so I wrote a one-act play adaptation of T. Coraghessan Boyle's "Modern Love". The play was titled "Full Coverage" and I spent an entire weekend writing it, thinking of Layla every time Breda Drumhill spoke, thinking that must be exactly the way Hollywood writers felt like when they wrote parts for specific actors in mind.

The two of us performed it the following Thursday in class since it was only meant to last twelve minutes. She was a natural and grasped Breda's germaphobic character, sounding as if she were climaxing every time she mentioned another disease (I added extras). I was, however, especially good at narrating, which there was plenty of in my adaptation because one of the strongest devices in the work was the narrator's voice and the way he decided to tell the story. It wouldn't have been right to lose that in the play. So at various times in the play, Layla's character froze, and then my character would face the audience and narrate. This became essential in the treatment of one of the main scenes of the story—the scene where Breda makes the narrator wear a full-body condom. An explanation as opposed to acting it out in front of the class. I hid all the other minor characters in the story through the use of narration or phone calls, manipulating the dialogue in such a way where it was clear to the audience what the person on the other side of the phone line was saying. So in the end, it only had to be me and Layla on the stage, and when it came to the parts where we had to kiss, we placed the back of our hands over our mouths and leaned towards each other. Instead of our lips touching, the palms of our hands would clap together like a couple of amateur idiots, which wasn't the real thing, of course, but the emotion was still there because feeling the back of my hand with my lips was alien to me. It felt like it was okay, because we were so close to kissing, but in the end, not close enough.

Sometimes Blas and I would sit outside somewhere in the university to look at people and take turns telling each other their backstories, who they were and what they had done even though we knew nothing about them. We thought it was a good way to come up with characters and stories. "Your turn," he said once. We were sitting in the center island of a circular driveway, having to sit in the sun since the shady part was covered with fire ants. "What about her over there?"

It was Layla. Probably on her way to Theatre Appreciation.

"She, uh," I started to say, but then she waved at me.

"Nope," Blas said. "That's cheating. Have to pick someone else now."

Thank God.

He reached into his backpack and pulled out an index card with seven words written on them. "Here," he said. "I read about this. I figured you could use this since you said you've been having a hard time coming up with something different to write about. Use these as a means to jumpstart the writing flow. You should write some down for me, too." I don't remember if I ever did, or if I did, what the words were. His words were *boat, stars, ring, seagulls, drink, book,* and because Blas considers himself a funny guy, *butter.*

I studied the index card during Theatre Appreciation while other people were doing their one-act plays. Most of them weren't interesting anyway. I opened a notebook and started thinking of ways to write a story about Layla to make me forget about her because I didn't know what else to do, to make myself understand that she didn't give a shit about me. I wrote down a few sentences and phrases about a story where the protagonist would lure an ex somewhere and kill her, and even though there wasn't anything close to a rough draft, it didn't feel like it would make her go away. Psychologists always say that writing is a good form of therapy, that writing about something helps us put our issues into perspective and we can wrestle them with more ease. I thought that writing about killing Layla would make her disappear forever, believe in the fiction, like some kind of symbol or metaphor. You kill her and you kill the idea. But after looking at my notes and at her, her neck within reach, it would take more than murder. The story had a Spanish title—"*Tomar y beber*"—because the title reminded me of going to church with my mom as a kid, and Layla was a religion. The first half of the first draft looked like this:

It's that time of the year, in late October, when you can freeze to death in the absence of light, but still burn alive at sunrise. In my case, I blow out smoke every time I exhale, and it's not only the Marlboro Light I'm smoking. I'm down to my lucky cigarette, as most people call it, the one you're not supposed to give away, and I know I'll be craving another sooner than later. For some fucked up reason, the craving is worse (or better?) when you know you don't have any within reach.

The sea breeze isn't helping much, but the stars look great in the marina sky. You can't get these stars in the city—not these kind, anyway.

I sit in the deck of my boat, otherwise known as my porch these days, enjoying the noisy silence only harbors can create. The sound of water rubbing against the boat as if it's afraid to make a full splash, the occasional screaming of trains in the outskirts of the city, and the sound of bending boards form the soundtrack of my life. The train doesn't bother me as much as it used to. I sleep through it now. Then there's the sound of a tall bottle of tequila that I slam down on the wooden table I've set up on the deck every time I take about a shot's worth of drink. I have the actual shot glass with me, but I never use it anymore. In drinking, there are three approaches: moderation, excessiveness, and carelessness. With me, it's the last, and not in the absence of being careful way, but in the absence of caring, period. Besides, it tastes much better from the bottle. Nothing like nicotine to relax your mind and a decent amount of alcohol to relax your heart.

I hear the sounds of footsteps approaching (high heels are kind of hard to miss on a plank wood surface).

"Liam?" she calls out before she appears right in front of my boat. Five years, and Adela looks more beautiful than ever. I don't recognize her at first. It's either the alcohol or how her hair was blond the last time I was able to breathe in that scent of flowery shampoo. Now it's long and black, yet still as bright. Her face gives it away. Those deep brown eyes that buzz me like no drink can and wide smile that could calm my nerves faster than the strongest kind of Kools.

"Adela," I say, standing up from my chair, trying not to give away the fact that I had been drinking a lot. It's not like she'll be able to tell, anyway, since I doubt kissing her lips is anywhere in the agenda for tonight, before or after the coffee I invited her over for. "I was beginning to think you wouldn't make it."

"Had a little trouble finding the place," she says as she starts getting closer to the boat. I walk up to the edge of the deck and extend my hand to help her aboard. I notice the diamond ring as I hold her hand and the pier's light reflects off of it and straight into my eyes. She was engaged to someone else, and why shouldn't she be. We're both in our thirties, and she still looks as great as the day we first met.

I had pawned my wedding ring four years ago when I had given up hope that she would come back—and when I couldn't afford more drinks. It's such a boring cliché to turn to alcohol at the end of a relationship, and I'd regret doing so if it didn't help. It never managed to drown any sorrow for me after Adela left. Alcohol only sinks the sadness and supplies it with an oxygen tank so it never actually drowns. Once the alcohol wears off, the sorrow comes back up to the surface. *I'm back, you bastard*, it says. *Now cry yourself to sleep again.*

"I missed you," I tell her. I can tell I can't hide my nervousness. She adjusts her dark red dress, pulling the skirt part down to her knees to hide her legs and her sleeves to hide the shoulders I used to kiss.

"Me, too," she says, probably only to say it. I want to tell her to relax, but I don't know if it will make her feel more anxious, more afraid of something. She always used to get mad when I told her to calm down, even when I was right and there was something really wrong. She looks as if it's difficult for her to keep a smile on her face for a moment, and any movement I make, like brushing back a lock of her hair away from her face, causes her to flinch. As if I were abusive or something. "How about that coffee?" she asks, taking a short step back.

Coffee is the last thing on my mind, but anything to be able to share a few words with her again, tie loose ends and explain the unsaid. I avoid grabbing her hand again and start walking towards the main door, otherwise known as my front door these days, expecting her to follow me. After nicotine, alcohol, and now, caffeine, I begin to wonder what else I'll be poisoning my body with by the end of the night.

When Theatre Appreciation finished, I waited in the room to see if there would be another class afterwards, which was always made clear when new students walked in after my classmates walked out. Layla was putting her books away before she turned to face me, adjusting the strap of the red dress she was wearing.

"Are you staying?" she asked. "Class is over."

"Yeah, if the room's empty next class. I need to get this story out."

"I know the feeling. I'll leave you to it, then."

I saw her from the corner of my eyes until the moment she turned left at the door, disappearing into the crowd of students. Five minutes of waiting for more people to appear were enough while I thought about what I had written so far and what was left to write. I didn't care much for the story but knew where it was headed. I wished Layla could read what I have so far and tell me what she thinks. Also wished she didn't. I wished I could stop thinking about Layla. And as I clutched the blue pen with my right thumb, index, and middle fingers, also wished I couldn't. I continued writing:

At this point in my life, I'm sure I can afford to live inside a warm apartment by myself in the heart of the city, away from the water, the train, and the seagulls.

The fact of the matter is that I like my home having the kitchen, dining table, sofa, and bed all in the same room. When you live alone and without dependents, you don't require much, and you can't stand to look at vast, empty apartment space for fear that you might end up relating to it and become friends.

"I'm sorry for the mess," I say, as Adela shuts the door behind her. "I haven't had a chance to clean up the place." I wait for her to say something, but she doesn't, so I make my way to the couch and start removing dirty clothes that have been piling up for about two weeks, revealing my comfortable Chesterfield—which serves as my own version of the Freudian couch where I tell all my problems to Jack Daniels— making a new temporary hamper out of my unmade, twin-sized bed. A flare gun rests alone after I'm done disrobing the couch, and Adela gasps after I reach for it.

"What the heck is that?" she asks.

"I use it for emergencies," I say. She looks at me as if I intend to use it on her. I place the gun in one of the drawers by the small television adjacent to the sofa. "Have a seat," I say. "I'll get started on the coffee."

"What have you been doing these past five years?" she asks without the slightest sound of interest as she practically tiptoes to the sofa. "I mean," she takes a look around my home, "are you happy here?" She sits down on the edge of the sofa farthest from me, about ten feet away from the bed.

"I'm doing okay, I guess." Sure, I'm comfortable with where I live, but God knows I haven't been happy for five years. "I make enough to survive, working for a magazine, mostly handling and trying to get sponsors. Other than that, take another look around. I'm an open book." An open book with torn pages and those still bound together, scrawled and in the wrong order, and I don't want to be this anymore. I open the fridge to search for milk, but with the exception of a six-pack of beer and a stick of butter, everything in there is spoiled and more than likely poisonous. *Everything is poison*, as Paracelsus said, *there is poison in everything. Only the dose makes a thing not a poison.* The new bottle of creamer will do fine for tonight. "How about you? Who's the lucky guy?"

She looks down at her hand, noticing her ring as if she had forgotten it was even there, and then she hides it between her legs like I hadn't seen it. "You always paid attention to detail, didn't you, Liam Hes?" she says more than asks. "I'm okay, too." She sounds like she's trying to not sound happy, probably out of sympathy. "His name is Michael."

"Michael?" I ask. "Michael, as in the attorney who handed me the divorce papers, Michael?" She nods. I refrain from making any kind of comment on that to avoid making this meeting more awkward that it already is, not letting it build up inside me.

I search for a knife in one of the counter drawers to cut the seal off the new creamer but can't find it. Pocketknife from my jacket will have to do, but Adela gazes at me with the same expression she had when I had the flare gun. When I cut the seal of the creamer open, she lets her breath go and sighs with relief.

I pour the coffee into two cups and set them up on the table. Adela stands up before I say anything, walks over, and takes a seat. I begin to think that looking her up and asking her to visit and have some coffee was a bad idea. Shouldn't have called her, but need the answers. Answers to the questions that temporarily disappear with alcohol and nicotine, yet still rise from the dead as soon as my nervous system read-justs to its regular state. If there's such a state.

"Will you excuse me? I'll be right back," I say to her. "Would you mind grabbing that whiskey bottle from that cabinet behind you and pour a small amount in my cup. Just fill it up to the rim. I still take my coffee black."

"Sure," she says, getting up from her chair as I step outside onto the deck. The night is brighter and colder. I look over at the edge of the boat and picture Layla standing right on the pier where I saw her for the first time in five years.

Adela sits still as I enter, looking up briefly at me, then back down at her cup of coffee, evident that her lips have not made contact with the rim of her cup. The small bottle of whiskey is not in sight, but my cup of coffee is full. She must've placed it back in the cabinet.

"I didn't know you started drinking with your coffee," she says.

"It's not as bad as it used to be." Truth is that I had never touched alcohol before Adela left. We didn't even have champagne at our wedding because I never saw myself as a person who drank or would ever drink. When you're seven years old and your father dies from alcohol poisoning, you're more than likely going to be ordering virgins the rest of your life. My mother left him because of the alcohol, and he started drinking larger quantities until it killed him. Unfortunately, you never know how good something is until you try it for yourself.

"So what's up with you tonight?" I ask her. "I know it's been long since the last time we saw each other and that you—that we didn't leave on good terms. But I keep getting this feeling like you're afraid of me. First with the flare gun and then with the knife. Now, it looks like you're not even going to try the coffee. Should I drink it first? Here."

"I'm sorry, Liam," she says. "I wanted to see you, too, and see how you've been, but the more I thought about it on the way over here, the more I kept telling myself that it was a bad idea. I wouldn't blame you for holding this huge grudge. I wouldn't. And I know the way I left was wrong. I'm even more scared knowing I was the cause of you drinking. You have quite the collection in that cabinet."

I take a long sip from my coffee as she tells me this, not minding the hot liquid burning my tongue and throat. My mouth goes numb for a while, and then I taste the coffee more bitter than it should be. There is the flavor of black coffee—a taste I've hated my entire life— the sweet taste of Wild Turkey Bourbon, and then there's the aftertaste. A taste of bad cough syrup. So that's what it tastes like. I smile at Adela, though I can't even feel my lips tightening the muscles to produce the smile. The cup is half empty.

"Why *did* you leave?" I ask. "That's the only thing in my life that I've never been able to piece together. What happened?" I drink the rest of the coffee and don't feel the heat of it anymore. My face sweats and I use the back of my hand to wipe my forehead.

"You didn't do anything," she says.

"I know that." I cringe as my stomach begins to feel as if someone has repeatedly kicked it with all his might. The pain disappears after a while, and my entire body begins to feel numb and weak. I try to pick up my cup of coffee, but it feels as if it weighs a ton. It breaks as it falls on the hardwood floor. Feels like drowning. My chest begins to hurt when I breathe.

"Liam, what's wrong?"

I have thought of this moment for a long time—the final moment before I die. I fall off the chair and hit the floor, the shards of porcelain probably cutting and stabbing against my back. I don't feel any of that, though. The left side of my chest begins to squeeze tightly together, and my lungs feel as if they're panicking, looking for oxygen that isn't there. My throat and nasal passage begin to close as the last amount of air enters my body.

My senses begin to disappear. The last image I see is Adela getting up from her chair and rushing over to my side when I hit the floor. Then I begin to black out completely. The last sound I hear is the sound of sirens approaching over the sound of a seagull flying over the sea and the train again. The last scent I smell is her hair as she places her ear against my chest and probably realizes she won't be hearing anything in there. The last feeling I feel is her hands pressing against my chest, trying to get my heart going again.

The last thought I have are of her fingerprints on the bottle of poison that killed me. Then I feel nothing.

I hated my story for a lot of reasons. Number one: Because it flopped with my new writing group, which I was actually okay with. There were three of us after I had tracked down Melissa and asked her if she wanted to join. Like Daniel, she also looked like a completely different person—healthier, her hair was longer, her glasses were thicker. They didn't care much about the characters, which made sense. You add distance in fiction within fiction and make it difficult to convince yourself of the events. It doesn't matter what happens to the characters because in the end it's only words.

Daniel told me the narrator dying in the end didn't work because how could he be dead *and* be able to narrate.

"Well," Melissa said, "I think that's why it's in the present tense. That way we look at this story, not as something that happened already, but something that is happening as we read it. So, in a sense, I think it kind of works. But I can see what Daniel means. There's something about it that feels a bit off. Like it's missing something. Is this about anyone?" She gave a quick glance at Daniel, as if asking if it was okay for me to answer her, which never stopped being cumbersome in workshops.

"Don't worry," Daniel said. "In our writing group, we should recognize it's important for the authors to join in on the conversation about their work. Even though other people may think they're trying to change our opinions, I think we'll be okay with sticking to our guns and be productive. So." He turned to face me. "Can we ask if this is about anyone in particular."

"No," I said. "She's fiction."

They asked about specific elements having to do with the actual writing, constructive comments, which made me wish I were fully listening to them. But I kept thinking about the second reason why I hated my story: it didn't work. Earlier that day, while on campus, I spotted Layla coming my way. Like an idiot, I took out my cellphone and pretended to be on a call, pacing around my area, and then finished the call when Layla was right by me. I said hello and started walking with her.

"I wouldn't get so close to me," she said, with a smile on her face. "I just got out of Racquetball and I probably stink."

"You do know there are available showers for after class, right?" I thought about her taking a shower.

"My coach is mean, though. He lets us go like right at the end of class, so I only have a chance to change and bolt it to Poli-Sci. That's why we're walking so fast right now. Do you have a class right now?"

"Nah. I'm waiting for my friend to get out of his Philosophy class so we can take off. I'm his ride."

"That's nice of you," she said. "So what happened with the story you were writing? I haven't seen you in writing group in a while. You disappeared."

"I'm actually meeting with a new group tonight, a smaller group. See how that goes."

"That sucks," she said. "I liked reading your writing."

"Seriously?"

"Yeah. Your work is pretty good."

"You seem to be the only one who thinks so, then."

We circled around the campus library, not saying anything for a while. There were a million words I wanted to say to her, but I couldn't. She was married. And I was married. Eventually, she broke the silence.

"Remember when we acted out the play you adapted? During the kissing scenes when we would put our hands in the way so that we wouldn't actually kiss."

"I remember."

"I actually wanted to kiss you. For real."

"What if," Daniel said, "you tried changing the point of view a little bit? Write it on a more objective point of view, kind of like a surveillance camera or the fly on the wall. I think this way, it might help you narrate it better."

"But one of the best aspects about this," Melissa said, "is that narrator's voice. And we'd be losing that by switching to objective."

"I don't think I can write in objective," I said.

"Why not?" This came from Daniel.

"I don't know. I guess I always end up feeling a mental connection to my characters. I always have to think in my work and express those thoughts, because a lot of times, especially in real life, it's easier to express thoughts than to actually come out and say them. I'm a reflectionist."

"Well, in that case," Daniel said, "why not try . . ."

Number 3: The previous day at work, Rick had shown up late in the morning. He said he stayed up all night working on an assignment, that he would start needing to leave earlier from work on Tuesdays and Thursdays so that he could have time to focus on his school work. Don't worry, though, he said, I'll make up the hours missed by getting out later all the other days. Maybe show up an hour earlier some of the other ones.

Like today?

He asked me if I could look over his draft, that I could do it during lunch and that I didn't have to clock out so I could get paid the hour. I told him I didn't know.

Please, he said. I had such a hard time with it last night. The teacher told us to reflect on our class so far and write about the thing we've had the hardest time with. I brainstormed a lot. I tried webs, maps, charts, outlines, everything, and I couldn't come up with anything. It's hard to write about writing. So I ended up writing about something else I've had the hardest time with in her class.

His essay ended up being about how he had a hard time starting a conversation with the girl that sits in front of him, that she always ran away whenever he tried to approach her, that she didn't even know he existed, that she probably thought he was a pervert when he only wanted to have an honest conversation with her. That she accused him of being married and then never talked to him again.

"One more thing before we move on to the next one," Melissa said. "Were you debating about what name to use with Adela? Or did you change it to Adela? Because I think you forgot to change one in here. I went ahead and marked it in my copy. You ended up writing Layla instead of Adela."

We moved on to Daniel's piece after mine, and I commented on opening directly with dialogue. "We don't know what's going on," I said. "Who's talking? What's happening? Where are we? What's the context? I don't think there's anything incorrect or improper about it, but I'm not a fan of opening a text with dialogue."

PART NINETEEN

The Part About The Brothers

"I don't know what I'm doing there anymore," I told my brother over lunch. He had invited me to drop off some ads at the local newspaper office because he was selling a boat and some tools, and then we went out to eat at Fuddruckers. I wouldn't let him pay for my food. While sitting across from him, I noticed for the first time in a long time that we were brothers. Without knowing it, we ended up ordering the same thing: the southwest burger with avocado, we both cut it in half with a steak knife and fork before starting to eat it, we both drenched it in green jalapeño Tabasco sauce, we both grabbed red onion rings to eat on the side (not add to the burger), we both dipped our fries in spicy mustard sauce. He probably didn't take notice of it. "You always were the fucked up one in the family," he said to me a lot.

"Why? What's wrong?" he said. We were sitting by a collection of Ramones memorabilia. Pictures, posters, and framed vinyls.

I couldn't tell him anything. Couldn't tell him that Rick had been showing up late almost every morning, or that he had been asking El Sida to clock him in on time when his lunch break was supposed to be over so he could show up late from it guilt-free because he was at home screwing his wife or off somewhere else. Couldn't tell him about the favoritism, about how he punished me by not letting me drive whenever I'd bring one of the issues to his attention. Couldn't tell him any of this. They'd call me a rat for the rest of my time there. So I made something up. The truth was, I didn't care about Rick's methods and actions. I needed to get out of there, but I couldn't tell him that either.

"It's starting to get in the way of school," I said. He looked concerned. "No, my grades aren't going down, but it would help if I had more time to focus on it."

"So, we'll cut your hours," he said.

"Rick already did that. I'm down to thirty a week. If I cut more, then I won't be able to pay the bills."

"And you think that's a problem that's going to go away with you quitting?"

"I can look for another job that might pay a bit more and won't leave me as drained every time I clock out. Something in an office. A video store clerk. I don't know. Somewhere where I won't have to deal with as many coworkers. It's about time I move along and try something new. I've been working for you almost three years, and it's going to keep on adding up until I'm there forever." And become someone I don't want to become.

"Here's the thing," he said and pulled out documents from a bag. "I shouldn't even be showing you this, but look at these numbers. You see these? These are the store numbers in the area. Now, twice a year, we do inventory." During inventory, people from all over the region's stores would get together and check every single part in the warehouse—mostly managers, stockers, and people that could leave a store fully functional without having to be in it. The last time we had an inventory done was a few weeks ago. The Wolf was there, and he looked at me as if he had told me all along, that "I told you so" stare. I asked him why he never came back. "These numbers over here are the reports for missing parts, most likely parts that are unaccounted for or stolen. You would think that with a store our size, the biggest one in the area, and therefore, the one with the highest number of employees and number of parts available for stealing, our missing parts rate would be higher, right? But it's not. It's actually the lowest. Yes, stealing does happen, but do you want to know why my store has the lowest?" He squeezed an onion ring to make it look like two French fries together and dipped it in the mustard. "It's not because I hire family and my family tells me everything that's going on. It's because the other workers think my family will tell me what's going on. I like to think that I have eyes everywhere. With you in the hub. With Bern in the loading dock and commercial. With Flask in the front counter. I like my employees to *know* I have eyes everywhere. And I'm not hoping for all that to fall apart."

We mirrored each other as we sipped our drinks at the same time and rolled our tongues around our mouths to scrape off the taste of onion.

"So how much longer do you need my eyes for?"

"I can't answer that," he said. "All I can do is ask you, from one brother to another, to please stick around and not quit. I like having you around as much as I like managing the number one store. So will you stay?"

When we returned to his truck and started driving back to work fifteen minutes late, which he told me not to worry about, he told me we had another problem at work. That someone had told the regional manager about us being siblings. "I heard," he said, "that it was coming from the stupid manager from the store up the street, and when the district manager asked Rick, he freaked out like a pussy and said, 'I don't know. Maybe. Pretty sure they are.' Don't worry about this. I'll deal with it. In the meantime, if anyone approaches you and asks, we aren't brothers. We're nothing."

If Layla had kissed me for real, if our hands weren't covering our mouths, she might be able to see the small white scar between my upper lip and nose that I've had since I was ten years old. I used to play with action figures when I was a kid, mostly Teenage Mutant Ninja Turtles, even though I had probably only seen two episodes of the actual show because I have no memory of them now when I try to bring the pieces back together. That's why I eventually wanted to become a writer, because I'd make up different stories every day and acted them out with the action figures, repeating my favorites. Sometimes my characters would get captured by the enemy and then get burned alive when they refused to offer them any kind of information. I do remember dumping a plastic GI-Joe in kerosene, hanging him from the clothesline outside, and setting him on fire with a match. He never talked. I used to get into the stories, but as I kept aging and the toys kept breaking or burning (which didn't happen all that much), time kept shortening. I must've had about four action figures left by the time I was scarred, and I was playing with them on the living room floor. I was reenacting a movie I had seen recently, only from the antagonist's point of view. Stories were much more interesting being inside the villain's head, or to see the hero become a villain. My brother sat on the couch next to my mom—we're twelve years apart, so he must've been twenty-two years old at the time—and he kept throwing a baseball back and forth between each hand. I was quiet for the most part. I never felt the need to actually speak out what was happening with the figures since everything was happening in my head. I heard my brother call my name and I turned to face him. From three feet away, he threw the baseball at me with all his might, and it struck right where I have the scar. I cried, smoldering inside, and when my parents asked him why he did it, he said he thought I'd catch it.

We visited our house in Mexico every weekend, and the following year, my dad thought it was about time to teach me how to drive. We went out to my dead grandfather's ranch, where I used to climb the windmill all the way to the top when no one was looking, and he sat me on his lap because I couldn't reach the pedals. I moved the steering wheel slightly in each direction, like when learning to ride a bike and trying to keep your balance, thinking that was how you kept the vehicle driving straight. My brother rolled his eyes from the passenger side. After a few seconds, I started driving a little too far into the right side of the road. A branch from a mesquite tree scraped across the windshield, right in front of my brother, and then swung inside the truck, striking him on his upper lip and right cheek. It didn't scar, but his look might as well have. Looked at me like I was an idiot.

I asked him a few weeks later if I could quit again, and he said, Here's the thing. You're too good an asset to this company. You're a good worker, and that's why you can't quit. And you're my brother. You're supposed to have my back.

I thought we were nothing, I muttered and left his office.

My roommates kept asking me what happened to Rick. They said we used to be good friends and now we had become enemies. I thought about that word for a while before I answered them. Enemy. I told them that sometime after Trevor quit, Rick started a slow transformation. He started getting more comfortable with his job. He started letting the power, whatever the hell kind of power it was, get to his head. He started making me and whoever else do the work for him while he fled to one of the other offices and gossiped with those coworkers. He started eating through his lunch break without clocking out. El Sida and Genie happened, too. It was no one's fault, I told them. It was all a bridge. We're all getting there sooner or later, unless we jump off.

Lately, he was in the habit of assigning me the Weslaco route since every time he put someone else to run it, they were always fucking up two or three times—forgetting to drop off parts, picking up the wrong ones, and the list went on. When I showed up from my last route one Friday, he said he wasn't going to be there the next day. I'd rather have you out on the road, he said, but go ahead and do whatever you want. You can stay here and send someone else on the route, or go yourself. I don't care anymore. It's your call. And with that coldness in early August blowing in both directions, our friendship disintegrated.

I used deductive reasoning to decide that it would be best for me to stay there that Saturday since I was the only one in the store with the full training to handle running the department *and* the pissed off coworkers from other stores when drivers would fuck up. I sent El Sida to Weslaco, and when Rick came back on Monday, he complained to me because he had promised El Sida that he would be staying in the warehouse. I wish I could write you up for that, he said.

You told me to make a decision, and I did. And guess fucking what. Not a single mistake was made.

Bern Bern said El Sida had gone crying to Rick on Saturday because I sent him on the route, and then Rick told Bern Bern that he didn't know why I sent him out, that it should have been me because that was what he had ordered me to do. Then Rick added, I'm going to send Writer on the Weslaco route from now on and make him clock out for lunch so that he'll get paid less.

He messed up with the schedule the following day because he

ended up running the department by himself. When I came back from my second run and told him that I was going to take my lunch, he said, Don't clock out. Just take twenty or thirty minutes to eat something real quick. I'll need you with the rest of the hour to help me.

No, I said. I think I'll take my full hour. I have a friend's story that I need to read anyway.

Please, he said. Think about it. You'll be missing out on the paid hour, and you're practically getting a thirty-minute break for free since you don't have to clock out.

What's another six dollars? I asked. I'll still clock out. Next time you say something, you should try meaning it. We didn't say a word to each other the rest of the week, except for when he told me that I wouldn't be going out for lunch anymore, just run the Weslaco route four times straight.

Sorry if you don't like it, he said, but with budget cuts, I don't have anyone else to help me here.

I asked him anyway the following week, when I returned from the first run, if there would be anyone to cover my lunch route that day.

Sorry, he said. I need Lou here with me, so I got no one to cover you. I even had to ax one of the stockers to do the Rio route for us. The hub needs to keep running, too. Are you angry?

Do I seem like it? I didn't. I wasn't.

Look, he said, if it means so much to you to have a stupid hour off, I'll do your last run so you can clock out an hour earlier.

It's fine, I said. I can do all four runs.

Are you sure? He always asked this, to confirm that it was, in fact, *I* who had made the decision and not him. Cold silence. I took this and the fact the boss thought I was a great asset to the company into consideration when I decided to pick up a burger in Elsa before heading to Weslaco. I wasn't even hungry. I wanted to be written up.

My first mission was to drive a little on the shoulder from time to time and let other people in traffic see me driving with one hand and eating with the other. When they would pass me, I'd raise my cup in the air and smile like an idiot. Most of them would smile back. Some would wave. But no one in the rearview mirror started dialing or writing down the number on the bumper sticker of the truck to report me.

To be sure, I went with Plan B. In the busy Weslaco store with the burger still in my left hand and the cup in my right (I didn't have any parts to drop off that time), I greeted everyone I could on my way to check the back for outgoing parts. I knew they knew the rules. When the night and weekend manager saw me, he pulled me aside. We never got along. The pieces never seemed to fit every time we encountered each other, one of those situations, I guessed, when we expected the other one to say hello first, never did, so we assumed we didn't like each other for not wanting to greet each other or wanting to be greeted. A couple months before, he started complaining about the parts we would deliver, claiming they were boxed wrong or we were boxing damaged, used parts. He opened an accumulator in front of me one day, looked at the brand new part, and asked how he would know if it was the right part if the part number was not printed on the part itself. I don't know, Roland, I told him. Compare it with the customer's broken one? We don't box them ourselves. Why don't you write the parts company a fucking letter?

He asked me why I was late, not taking his eyes off the cup. I held it closer to his face and said, What's it look like?

Don't you know that you're not supposed to have food in the truck?

I nodded and waited for him to say something else. I supposed he was waiting for me to say something—this fucking shit again—an explanation, or some kind of reaction, but I didn't want to offer one. He straightened himself and said, Well, I bet the district manager would love to hear about this. And I said, Sing it to him, as I exited the store.

I talked to my roommate Blas on the cellphone from Mercedes to Progreso and from there to Donna. We didn't have much to talk about, and though it was on roads where regular company drivers couldn't see me on the phone, you never knew if the district managers or pissed off employees were driving around the area. As a closing note, I threw my food trash away in front of everyone at the Donna store, but all of this was in vain. The only result that had come out of this was Roland's call to the boss. When I returned, he ordered Rick to tell the stores the last route would run a bit late so he could talk to me.

What are you doing? he asked.

What do you mean?

You know you can't have food on the road, he said.

I wasn't allowed to have a lunch break. I'm entitled to one, so I picked up some food.

Yeah, but you didn't have to get it down and eat it in another store.

Would you have preferred I eat it while driving? On the expressway where there are plenty of cars to run into while I'm reaching for a fry that slipped from my fingers?

You know what I meant, he said. I'll see what I can do about lunch breaks, but in the meantime, look, just behave, okay? I have enough problems to deal with.

So can I quit?

Seriously, he said. Don't do this now.

Alright, I said. I'm sorry.

Before you go, he said, there's a training thing I want you to go to in a couple weeks. The company is finally updating these old computers and we're getting new ones with a new program. Each store has to send a representative to become familiar with the program and then come back and teach us. For efficiency.

But you do know I don't even use computers here, right? I don't deal with the customers.

You're probably the only person here that will be good at teaching us how the new system works when it gets here. I don't trust anyone else to.

I don't know.

Look, it's two days. Company pays for everything and pays you for the two days. And you get to not be here for those two days.

The rest of the days before the training, Rick started checking my pockets for a cellphone every time before I would leave on a run, making me lay out all its contents on the hub counter like I was about to pass through a metal detector. He would apologize after every time and say he was trying to cover his ass.

The week before I was to leave to go to Houston for the new computer system workshop, the front tire exploded on my way to Donna. The truck swerved from left to right. It was lucky there were no cars around and I was able to control the truck enough to leave it parked on the shoulder. My first impulse was to check my pockets for my phone to alert Rick of the situation and that the next route would probably run late while I changed the tire. My pockets were empty, though.

I sat in the truck for five minutes, letting a song finish and the next one play—"A Pain That I'm Used To" by Depeche Mode—before I stepped out and inspected the damage. A huge chunk of the tire was littered across the road several meters back. I walked over to get it out of people's way first and threw it into the bed of the truck before I started searching for the spare. It wasn't there. They usually hooked it up right underneath the bed of the truck, but it wasn't anywhere. I crawled under the truck, looking for it in every inch of its insides in vain. There was no spare at all. Fucking Rick, I said to myself.

I looked in both directions, watching the road disappear on each side, trying to decide which way would lead me to a phone first, the sound of the wind slapping against the rows of corn. It was right in the middle of Donna and Progreso. I decided to walk back to Progreso, leaving the truck locked and parked on the shoulder, mumbling the lyrics to the Depeche Mode song because I knew I was a terrible singer.

"Did I ever tell you I wanted to be a singer when I was little?" Layla asked me once, near the end of the spring semester. I think that was the last time I saw her. She was wearing her uniform that day. Probably had work that night. *Adelaida* stitched by her breast. We had been talking to each other more and more after every class.

"I don't think so," I said. "I won't even try. Spare people the agony."

She laughed. "When I was little, I told my mom I wanted a microphone for my birthday. I told my whole family, 'I'm going to be a singer.' My voice was so high-pitched, though. I was so weird."

"And now?"

"I'm still weird," she said.

"No. I meant, what's the goal now? What's the dream?"

"Given my personality," she said, "I don't think singing is in the cards for me. Writing as a job would be nice."

"Wouldn't it?" Before I knew it, we were left alone in the classroom. Everyone else had left and the noise and traffic in the hallway had dissipated as well. "I should get going, then."

"Seriously?" she asked. "That sucks." She looked off to the side and adjusted her glasses. We had texted each other about wanting to kiss, without our hands in the way. We both thought today would be the day, our knees almost touching, but our words always spoke louder in text than they did face-to-face.

"I don't know if—" But before I could finish, she reached for my face and pulled it towards hers. When she stopped kissing me, without saying a word and looking like she couldn't believe she did that, I kissed her again.

A few yards out, I started running, hoping I would get somewhere sooner, but after a mile or so, I stopped, tried to catch my breath, and started walking again, feeling nowhere closer to Progreso. Fucking Rick, I said to myself again.

My brother and I used to watch this movie with Hulk Hogan a lot when I was a kid. I would ask him repeatedly to rewind it and play it again. He didn't seem to mind since that meant he could go make out with girls while I watched the movie. I think it was called *No Holds Barred* or something like that. Hulk Hogan's character's name was Rip, and for some reason, he reminded me a lot of my brother. Most of the time, my friends and I would watch movies and we'd point to the main character, usually a martial artist, and we'd say, "I'm him" or "I'm that guy." Even if the guy was Chinese and we couldn't be more Mexican. With this movie, I wanted my brother to be Hulk Hogan. On his bed, he had three stickers on his backboard with his initials, R. F. P. One day, when he wasn't home, I scraped off the two horizontal lines on the F to make it look like an *I* because I thought it would be like Hulk Hogan's character in the movie. He became angry and asked everyone in the house, all of his friends, who had done it, and in the end, no one ever confessed. I saw a cartoon much later on where the camera was panning over a cemetery and some of the tombstones had the letters RIP. Someone told me what it really meant.

I walked east for almost two hours before someone offered me a ride. I didn't care if he was a serial killer or a gay rapist. I wanted out of that situation. He dropped me off at the Progreso store. Rick didn't pick up the phone in the hub office. No one did. My brother answered his cellphone and I told him what happened.

"Why didn't you put in the spare?"

"I checked. There's no spare in the truck."

"There should be a spare," he said. "You're probably being an idiot."

The day after my return from the training, I let the writing group know that I couldn't work on the book anymore. "It's too much," I said. "And it's starting to feel like the more I write about it, the more it never goes away."

"Why do you want to make it go away?" Daniel asked. "I think some of your best writing is about the auto parts store. For the longest time, my main and only issue with it was that it never seemed personal to you. It felt like the narrator was only an observer, like it wasn't about him. It was about everything else that was going on around him. And then you hit us with this chapter about your brother, about testing communication, and some of the previous chapters before this, and we see what you've been building up to all along. The fall of man at his own hand. It would be crazy for you to stop."

He wore a US soccer jersey and chewed on a Mexican hamburger which had avocado, salsa, and an actual slice of ham in it. I wondered sometimes if the salsa would get on his copy of my chapter as he flipped through the pages to go over his notes, which were usually made up of questions that gave me a sense of direction for revision once I actually thought about answering them. A teenaged boy approached us with a small poster of himself in boxing gear, the lamination tearing and folding at the edges, and asked if we could donate money so he could go compete. Daniel spoke for all of us and said not right now.

"I think it would be crazy for me to *not* stop," I said.

"I'm going to have to agree with Daniel on this one," Melissa said, which was strange considering they always disagreed on everything about my work. She liked how I used ellipses to illustrate George covering his ears when someone would say a bad word, and Daniel said it was only going to confuse the readers—even though he used ellipses all the fucking time for dramatic pauses. He felt the part about stealing the money at the gas station was a beautiful, wonderful ending. She thought it seemed redundant. He said George was unbelievable as a character, that he was too good to be true. She said she had known people like that.

"I found myself trying hard to not be like the Bolaño quote you mentioned in that early chapter," she continued, "the one about how your friends are nice instead of honest. I felt like you might think that of me, but the truth is, I didn't have that many complaints about these last few chapters. Honestly. I like some of the methods of storytelling you're using there. Time jumps, weaving flashbacks, messing with tense and point of view. Why would you want to stop?"

"I want people to look at these people I'm writing about, to look at us and how twisted we all are. How, at first glance, we seem like the simplest and nicest guys, or at least we pretend we are when we're in front of other people, that's the part we decide to play, but deep down, we're all fucking twisted." We had a saying when I was a kid, whenever someone would fuck up, like if I dropped a plate of food or something, the entire family would chant, *Tenía que ser Shoney, y siempre será Shoney. Por eso México no progresa, porque Shoney se le atraviesa.* And it's this sense of keeping Mexico or Mexicans from progressing that has us culturally divided into a high culture and a low culture. Educated and non-educated. Gentlemen and *pelados*. Good books and bad books. We lacked the self-awareness necessary to be civilized enough to not have to resort to dick jokes. We *are* inferior. "We shift shapes before our eyes and play all these different parts in front of different people, and what fucking for? What is it that we're hiding from people? What is that we're trying to make them believe about us? Who are we trying to make them think we are? Who do we *want* to be? I need to stop writing about them. I need to stop writing about me."

"One thing you might want to watch out for, though," Daniel said, "now that you mention it, is your audience. Who makes up your audience for this? Do you want anyone to be able to read it? Or, with all its cerebralness throughout, are you looking for an audience made up of avid readers or creative writers? Because that can end up hurting this in the end."

"I disagree," Melissa said. "I think there's something here for everyone. Different people will get different things from this, and I think that's actually good."

We had started meeting in study rooms at the university library before the silence started forcing us to be silent, and we ended up moving our meetings to restaurants, where we let our comments to each other become juxtaposed with the noise. I liked this group more than the other one. We were more honest with each other. We cared about the same things, the important things, and actually supported each other. But I couldn't convince them that I had to stop writing the book, that it was all doomed to crumble. I guessed what got to me the most is how much they liked the characters I had grown to hate over the last three years, which confused me for the most part because it wasn't so much that they liked the characters, but rather the way they were written.

We all had our personal assholes to battle in our writings, constantly asking ourselves if our nonfiction was fiction and if our fiction was nonfiction, if we lied when we told the truth or told the truth when we lied. Melissa wrote nonfiction embedded with lies. Daniel wrote fiction embedded with truth. I couldn't tell the two genres apart anymore.

"You started at the end," Daniel said. "You're not at the end yet. So how can you stop?"

"Because there is no end," I said. "As much as I try to end it, it doesn't seem to. I've tried many times to get out, and something keeps me there."

"So then why start at the end?" Melissa asked.

"I don't know," I said. "Bolaño wrote one day that the visceral realist walks backwards. They're looking at some point in the horizon, but they're moving away from it instead of walking towards it. Straight into the unknown."

"Have you ever heard of the Ouroboros?" one of them asked. I don't remember who it was. Or if it was even asked. I think I imagined it.

PART TWENTY

The Part About the Chains

Sometime around July 15, 2003, I was younger, dumber than I am now, and in prison. Not *imprisoned*. I worked at a prison, in the commissary at the Starr County Detention Center, where most of its residents were awaiting trial. My goal was to use the job to save money for my first semester of college. Once or twice a week, they would let the prisoners of different cell blocks go to the square courtyard in the center of the complex to play basketball and ask us, through a thick window with a small metal door on its lower half, if they had any funds in their accounts, if their families had dropped off any money for them. If they had nothing, they would each get what they were entitled to—a few sheets of paper, a ballpoint pen, and two stamped envelopes, which made me always think how much writing I could accomplish if I murdered someone. All that time and peace to write. Depending on the cell block they put me in, it wasn't like I would be running out of writing material. When I related these fantasies to my mom, she gasped and said, "So much writing you'll do when someone in there kills you, too." And I said, "Then at least I won't have to worry about writing or anything else anymore."

If they had money, they could find it all inside. There was an entire list of shit they could buy—Cokes, chips, Corn Nuts, tuna packets, cheese dips, candies, power bars, other groceries in non-lethal packaging, more stamped envelopes, more paper, more pens. The orders went out quickly with me at the helm. I'd check the ledger to see who had money or didn't, and then I sorted all the items into plastic bags before they were next in line like I was born to do this kind of work. A master of sorting.

Sometimes, the cholo prisoners in gangs would try to get my attention, always asking me about my shirt, where I bought it, who designed it, and if they could have it. I recognized a few people from school. One of them in particular had never returned a copy of my best friend's *Mortal Kombat II*. He recognized me, too, and asked me how this girl we went to school with was doing as if I kept up with all these people.

They grouped them in the cell blocks based on what they had done, allegedly. All the gangsters were together, which were mostly made up of armed robbery. All the murderers were together. All the trustees were together. All the potheads and the cokeheads were together. All the illegals were together. All the girls were together. There was one woman with man-like qualities that was obviously the leader of the block. She always had money in her account, so there was always large quantities of all these items on her list. The one detail my boss always laughed at was that she always asked for three summer sausages, which were pretty thick. He said one day, "She doesn't exactly eat them, if you know what I mean." He was an obese man with a thick mustache and hair combed back. His uniform pants would disappear into his crack and there was no way of knowing where his back started. "Well, at least not at first."

I never saw why they needed the commissary other than the writing material and the occasional craving for a soft drink. It was a garden of earthly delights in there. The food they were served daily was a hundred times better than the food they served us in the cafeteria in high school. It seemed kind of backwards. We were served shit that looked like food. Prisoners were given real food. Real beef. Real nuggets. Real everything. And it's a whole meal, too. Most of it was thrown away because even if they didn't want the side, they would take it anyway. Because it was theirs and they were entitled to that side.

Sometimes during lunch breaks, I'd get on the computer to look at mugshots as if I were trying to identify a suspect for a case, everyone who had ever been a prisoner there. I found some idiots that disappeared from high school my senior year, looking drunk in their pictures. My old manager from when I used to work at a sandwich restaurant had been imprisoned for possession of marijuana with intent to sell. Then I found a mugshot of one of my high school teachers. I remembered him one year when he had walked in on a Monday morning with a huge black eye and him telling us that he had slipped coming out of the shower and his eye had landed on the door knob. It was around this same time that he was evading arrest while driving drunk.

I write July 15, 2003, because that's the day Bolaño died, though at the time, I had no clue who he was and that's what I was doing with my life. I won't say that this is also the day I decided to be a writer, because it would be fucking pretentious of me and anti-poetic to imply that his soul managed to somehow find its way into my mind and infiltrate it. But I do know for a fact that around this time—with cholos asking me for my shirt and women making each other their bitches with summer sausages—I could look around and see that the world didn't need my help, or fiction's help, to make it look fucked up. It was already doing that on its own.

The guards in the prison somehow managed to discover that I wanted to be a writer, and they also asked me if I could write a book about them one day. "There are a lot of stories inside these walls," one of them said. Too bad I was only there for two or three months before I was given the opportunity to lose my mind. It was as if, like the prisoners, I was awaiting my arraignment. And my sentence was serving time at the auto parts store.

I also won't be able to pretend to have the ability to engage Bolaño's work in conversation. I don't have the ability or thoughts on that level of sophistication, but here are my two cents.

Before Theatre Appreciation class finished, the instructor gave us the ultimate test if we ever wanted to be liberated from ourselves. He said that when we look at a play, we shouldn't look at the characters and decide which one is the perfect part for us. Which one is most like us. He said we should look at all the roles in the play, all the parts, at all the characters, and see ourselves in each one, because all we had to do was act out a character a little bit, and then we could decide if it was out of character for us at all. "So that's your assignment," he said. "You have to do something that's out of character for you. Do anything that you wouldn't normally do. Do this many times, and it will lead to yourself."

"What are you going to do?" Layla asked me after class.

On the drive home, I realized it was the same with writing. Every character in your work, to some extent, is a version of you. They're committing actions that are normally out of character for you, but they're still you experiencing those actions—kidnapping a lesbian, getting probation, being written up, nailing a hand, covering your ears—because they're your own creation. And it's the same with nonfiction. Sure, it may be about other people who aren't you, quoting them on words that they said, but they still have to pass through your filter. It's the truth as you see it. To them, what the guys at the auto parts store said, how they said it, why they said it, might be a completely different reason than what I'm perceiving. So by bending that a bit, I'm making them my own personal version of who they are. Every character, then, is a composite character of me and him, as if we're a part of each other. Or it's more like a reverse composite character. You write fiction and you're splitting yourself off into parts. Everyone is you.

What's out of character isn't what I did. That was my character all along. What was out of character was telling Rick about it.

I came back from another route and Rick was waiting for me in the office. He said he had gotten a write-up for half-assing his truck inspection on the one I got a flat on. He had written on the inspection sheet that there *was* a spare in the truck, that he didn't know why it wasn't there after.

I tried calling you first, I said, but you were gone already. I didn't know who else to call. I *needed* to do something, and—

Don't worry about it, Writer, he said. I understand. It's just that I've never gotten no write-up before. It feels pretty bad, like they'll use it as a reason to get you fired.

It's not so bad. You learn to get used to them.

How did the training go?

I did something, I said. There was no one else in the hub office. Everyone was out driving, and my route wouldn't leave for another twelve minutes. I had the time to be out of character, and I tried to get past the fact Rick looked interested, excited to hear more gossip, or to be a part of the circle again. I didn't give him the full version, though, because it wasn't only my story. I didn't write it alone.

Layla's store had sent her as their rep to the training and we ran into each other as we were checking in at the hotel. I told Rick her name was Elisabeth and that she worked at some branch in north Texas, not specifying the city and pretending not to remember. If I had said even Dallas, he would probably start making phone calls to every branch in Dallas looking for Elisabeth the second I left back on the route.

I met Layla for a drink at the hotel bar that first night. We didn't get carded even though I had turned 21 a few months back and she was 20. She wore glasses and her uniform because she thought she'd need it for identification purposes for the shuttle that brought us to the hotel. I didn't feel like wearing mine anymore, so I didn't.

"How's your writing coming along?" she asked as she stirred the ice cubes in her drink with a straw. She fished out a small one and sucked on it to let me answer.

"It's not," I said. "I want to be done already, but it feels like I'm unable to stop. Like driving with broken brakes. It's becoming routine. Have you ever looked up the definition for *enemy* in the dictionary? One of the examples used there is 'routine is the enemy of art.' As in routine is actively seeking to weaken or harm our ability to create art. I thought about that when we were given our last assignment in Theatre Appreciation."

"I haven't written anything in a while. It feels like I'm constantly working on the same works. Revising and revising and revising. Never able to move on. Then these long periods of time go by where I'm not even sitting down to write anything."

"It's depressing, isn't it," I asked, wondering if we were ever going to talk about our kiss. "And the more you go on without writing, the more depressing it gets. Makes you wonder if you should even be bothering with it at all."

"Makes you wonder if you're going to be working on the same four projects for the rest of your life and never going to be able to start something new." We looked off to the side and noticed other company employees also wearing their uniforms. It was strange seeing white and black people in those uniforms, like they only existed in magazines. In our world, everyone was Mexican. "You remember the play we acted out?" she asked. "How we acted out those disease names, and it kept getting more and more intense, like we were having sex?"

And now I was thinking about fucking her.

"Writer's block," I said.

She spit out an ice cube into her cup and grinned. "Authorial intrusion," she said.

"Tell, don't show."

"Ooh. Purple prose." She held on to the edges of the table with each hand, and I felt her foot rub against my ankle. No one was looking at us, even though she was selling it.

"Stating the obvious."

"Bad, unrealistic dialogue."

"Unnecessary description."

"Yes," she said. "Plagiarism."

"Passive voice," I said, and then together, "Clichés." She laughed for a while and was still laughing when the hotel waiter came to serve us and I asked for another round.

"I feel like I need a cigarette," she said. I offered her one and she said she was joking. "That was fun." We sat quietly for a while. There's a rare moment that writers or artists feel sometimes, when they see something, or watch something, or hear something, or do something—probably what García Lorca meant by *duende*—and you get this incredible itch in your brain and hands and fingers that makes them want to dance with the keyboard. Layla gave me that itch. Like I could write and it would have a purpose.

It reminded me a bit of when I used to write cheesy poems in high school. I never wrote them down for anyone in mind. Poetry has never been in my blood. I used to write them for other guys who wanted to give them to girls they wanted to fuck. I'd sell them for $5 each, guaranteed to be one of a kind. They rhymed, of course, but the haikus yielded the highest income based on amount of labor required. They had to rhyme. That was how they said they got their panties real wet. Meanwhile there I was, writing wetness-inducing poetry with one hand and whacking off with the other. I wrote this epic once about nice guys finishing last when I was a freshman. Four pages, single spaced. Thirty-stanza'd motherfucker of a poem. Sold that one to Pete, a drummer, for $20 so he can give to Roxanne, a girl I ironically had a crush on in middle school the year before, but she never put on the red light.

"So," she said, catching her breath. "How do you break the routine?"

"You do something you wouldn't normally do," I said. "Isn't that it? Immersive writing. Put yourself through something so you can write what you know."

Sometimes I would walk across campus alone, and I thought she was walking in front of me, there, a few feet in front of me. It wasn't her. It was some other student, but with the same hair that fell like red ocean waves. And in the hotel lobby, I am having a difficult time holding a conversation with her. I know I shouldn't be thinking what I'm thinking, but I'm wondering if she's thinking the same thoughts as I stumble through my words. I wonder if she isn't having the same thoughts.

"And what don't you know?"

I don't know if I can accept who I was always going to be. At the other side of the bridge.

We had sex the night before we were going to come back home.

We could've been doing this the whole time, I asked her.

We would've skipped the trainings, she said. Then we'd have a lot of explaining to do.

That night, as we removed our clothes, she noticed I left my socks on and asked, "Are you one of those guys that likes to keep his socks on when he has sex?" Then I took them off. We stayed quiet for the most part, figuring our words would most likely keep us from continuing. Sometimes words ruin situations. I could feel we were both tense at first. She picked up on it, too, and asked if she should turn on the radio.

"Go ahead," I said, and she almost tripped over one of our shoes.

"You never told me what kind of music you listen to, did you?" She tuned to a station that was playing "Hey You" by Pink Floyd and then climbed back up on the bed and we continued to kiss until the next song played.

"I know who this is," she said. "Don't tell me. Don't tell me. It's The Eagles, right?"

"Good job," I said, even though it wasn't. We had a strange playlist as we had sex, and I was trying not to focus on it. After Steve Miller Band, they played AC/DC's "Hells Bells" and then they played Carly Simon's "You're So Vain" and then "Every Breath You Take" by The Police and then "Bad Moon Rising" by CCR. And then I wasn't even hearing the music anymore, only her breathing while her thighs pressed against my ears.

We lay in bed for a while after we were done, not saying anything at first as the music came back into focus. "Crazy" by Aerosmith and then "Crazy On You" by Heart. I remembered what Quique said about loneliness. You get lonely, he had said. And after a while of being so far away, you start getting lonely, and you start to forget what it's like to have someone close to you. But it wasn't loneliness. It was something else.

John or Flask or Red—I forget who the fuck it was, it was all of us—said the feeling goes away after you reach orgasm. That you get this sudden burst of clarity and stop thinking with your dick. But even still, from my peripheral vision, I could see her body and my thinking hadn't changed in any way.

What did we do? she asked.

I don't know, I said. I don't have the words for it right now. I knew it never felt like it was out of character.

I told Rick she gathered her things and walked down to her room to shower. I spent the entire night running the scene in my head, trying to create a justification for what had happened, like any other worker at the auto parts store.

But it wasn't cheating, Rick said.

The fuck you mean it wasn't?

It's only cheating if you have sex with the person locally. You were like six hours away, in a different area code. So it's okay. You're going to be fine.

It's not cheating if in my mind I wanted it to happen again?

Of course not, man. Not if it's only in your mind. Why are you so worried about this?

I regretted telling Rick about it. It was supposed to be liberating. It was supposed to help me break character. To lead me to myself. It didn't do any of that. But I sure as hell could write about it now, couldn't I?

On the ride back home, I don't know. The best way to put it is that music started following me everywhere. Not entire songs, but certain lines and lyrics. It started when the radio alarm went off that morning, still tuned to the same station, and it was a Santana song, one that advised I had to change my evil ways. And the music didn't stop.

I knew songs had to be left open to interpretation and you could make whatever meaning you want out of them. It all depends on how you decide to read a line or a verse, like looking for the number 23 in everything, or all the fucking Beatles conspiracies. But I started to feel like a mouse inside a maze with traps when I started connecting with them, when lines started triggering certain memories. As people, we like to see metaphors and symbols in everything we see, give every incident some kind of meaning or purpose. Most of the time, there is nothing to interpret.

Rick commanded me to cover his lunch break the day after I told him about my encounter with Layla—or Elisabeth—as if the whole experience had never happened. We had been at it again because he had opened his mouth and told his wife about what happened.

He said, Man, it's my wife. I don't keep anything from her. Besides, who's she gonna tell?

That's not the point, I said.

He had also told the district manager that my brother and I were related, and they had started investigating it. I may be out of here sooner than planned, which at the moment the plan was two lifetimes.

I'll be back in an hour, Rick said. This time I promise to be back on time. That way you take lunch and then go on the last Weslaco route.

When he left for lunch, I tuned the radio station in the hub office to the rock station, and "Layla" of all fucking songs by Eric Clapton was playing. I had heard that song many times before, and yet it felt like the first time I heard "Layla" as a lyric in the chorus. I guess I always thought it was "Hey, yeah" or something. I looked out the hub window and saw Rick as he talked to people on his way to the front. I wondered how long he'd take. In the loading dock, Plato was telling Shoe Guy off because he was using the fork lift to raise the palette with the parts for the second floor with the chain still attached to one of the forks. He was supposed to remove it first. Afterwards, Shoe Guy stepped off the forklift and made a hand gesture asking Plato to suck it, forming an *X* with his arms and pulling them towards his crotch.

I took a seat and wiped the sweat off my forehead with my shirt sleeve, wondering who still said suck it. Seemed like the insult had died off along with thumb biting. I thought about when I flew back from Houston, looking into the oaks surrounding the McAllen airport, the buildings, cars, and people slightly increasing in size as the plane moved closer. As the life I'd have to face drew closer. Moment of truth, I said to myself. Wife would be waiting for me. Friends would be waiting for me. Parents would be waiting for me. Brother would be waiting for me. But the moment of truth never happened.

Fiction is better.

When music started talking to me, God kind of stopped. I used to pray every night before going to sleep. Never asked him for anything. It never felt right doing so, like asking Santa Claus for shit. I only talked. Said how my day went or goals I was looking forward to, even though God was supposed to be all-knowing, so I was probably stating the obvious. If I were him listening, or pretending to listen, I imagine it would be a long series of uh-huhs. After the training, it started to feel like I was talking to myself. Like no one was listening. Or like no one wanted to listen anymore. It could've been guilt, even though I was still waiting to feel at least a little guilty. Never happened. So I stopped talking altogether, admitting I was alone. I even tried writing for a while, typing down the prayers up on the computer, but nothing ever came out. It felt like writing without an audience. Forced. Unreal. Not me.

Now I simply thought about whatever story I was working on or some shit like that before falling asleep. Started counting down from a thousand to force the sleep to come, and then started counting up again when the countdown wasn't enough.

I told the boss I needed to quit before matters worsened.

Why, bro'? Seriously. I thought you never wanted to leave this place.

I need to, that's why. Isn't that enough?

But the computers come next week. Who's going to teach us how to use them if you're not here? You're the one that went to the training, so you're the one who knows how they work.

It's always going to be something, isn't it? If it's not this, it's that I'm a good asset, or that I'm your eyes and will let you know if anyone is stealing. I'm going to be here forever, aren't I? I wanted to cry, but I kept myself from doing so. I thought it best to go back to the hub office and go back to what I did best.

Hub office, I said. How may I help you?

"Hey, Writer," Mingo from Mercedes said. "Can you check to see if you have a starter? 6785."

Just a second. While I did that, I looked at all the other coworkers, wondering how much value they placed into everything they did here, if our jobs were so fucking important for this world when they obviously weren't.

Rick had been gone for more than an hour when Quique stumbled into the hub office. I was already used to not listening to his promises anymore. He took a seat and ate from a bag of mixed nuts he had purchased from the vending machine. He stretched out his hand and offered some to me. I said I was okay. He sat there for a while as I looked out through the plastic window towards DC, watching Red, Güero, and John smoking cigarettes underneath a palette of batteries, sharing *albures* and laughing at some dirty story about one of them, probably John since he had the most stories.

Rick not back yet? Quique asked before making it seem like he was drinking out of the bag of nuts. I shrugged my shoulders. Hasn't he been gone for more than an hour?

Wow, I said. It's like you're following a script now. I take it the next question is "Aren't we usually allowed only one hour for lunch?" And then "Shouldn't you be out to lunch now instead of him?" And then "Aren't you going back on the road in twenty-five minutes?" And then "So you're not having lunch? Didn't I ask all these same questions yesterday and the day before?"

Alright. Calm down, queer.

Now, just because I let you suck my dick, I said, that doesn't mean I'm a queer. I stood in front of the printer, tapping my foot at it and waiting for more orders to come out so I could get the fuck out of the office and out of my mind already. Quique grabbed a Coke and started spitting the unsalted nuts into it after he sucked the salt from them.

Perfect lunch, he said.

I looked at my watch again and said, Damn it. Where the fuck is he?

Fucking fat ass probably eating everything in the fridge, Quique said. Probably eating the fridge, too. His wife and the kids. The dog. He's eating everything. What a fucking fat ass.

He stood up and dusted his pants before walking up to the computer to clock back in. Through the small window, I saw him run into Rick in the warehouse. They stopped to talk to each other, but it looked like he didn't care about whatever Quique had to say to him. He slammed the door when he walked in and messed up his password to clock in three times before getting it right. And it was all numbers. His birthdate probably.

Sorry I'm late, Writer, he said. I know I said I'd be back early, but something happened. I know there's no time for you to go to lunch, but I'll try to make it up to you this week. I'll let you leave an hour early on Friday.

We're shorthanded on Friday. Lou has the day off.

Oh, yeah, he said. Fuck. Shit, shit shit, shit. We'll work something out for you to leave early on Saturday, then.

Lou also has the day off Saturday.

Well, we'll figure something, okay?

I'll try not to wrestle with my mind too much, I said.

I think my wife might be cheating on me.

And?

What do you mean "and?"

I mean, don't you cheat on her like all the fucking time? *Locally?* Why would this even surprise you?

This is different, he said. He started saying some other bullshit about how a wife was supposed to be loyal to her husband, no matter what. That it was okay for us to fuck other women because it was good practice for when we fucked our wives. But when a wife was fucked, it was like someone else had had her. The same old bullshit I had been hearing from everyone the past three years. I didn't say anything, and he realized his explanation wasn't enough. When you have sex with another woman, he said, you can wash off your dick. Clean it up. Good as new. Like nothing happened. But you can never wash the sex off a woman. Because that shit's inside of her. It's impure. And adultery. You know what I mean, right? You get what I'm saying? You understand why I'm like this?

It's adultery for everyone, I said. Can't you see that?

I heard the chair's legs creak below him after he sat down. He heard it, too, and made a face like he hoped I didn't, like farting in class.

You know, he said, changing his tone a bit. One day, you're going to get out of this place.

I told him I wasn't so sure about that, that it would be a miracle if I could even go out for lunch nowadays.

Seriously, he said. I mean it. You're different than the rest of us here, even if you don't think so. You're smarter. You're more cultured. More educated. You're not like us. And you're going to get out of here. One day you're going to write a book about all of us.

My mind split into three paths, three impulses. My first impulse was to tell him: I'm not a fucking writer, okay? I'm only under the illusion I am. Why would anyone listen to anything I have to say? Why should they care? I'm not a writer. I'm an assistant fucking hub coordinator, is what I am. So don't count on a book because you probably have a better chance at writing your *Back to the Future* fan fiction than I have at getting my words out there.

My second impulse was to tell him: Yeah, I probably won't. No offense, but you guys are idiots. It's people like our coworkers why this country think our ethnic group is made up of idiots. You put our culture to shame. We're degenerates in every sense of the word. Degenerating our generations. I'm not saying I'm not like you guys. God knows I'm a fucking *pelado*, too. I know because he doesn't listen to us. After all, I work right here, right? Probably rubs off. But in all honesty, I can't picture anyone wanting to read a piece of literature about a bunch of pieces of shit.

I went with the third impulse. Yeah, maybe.

He sat there a while longer, thinking hard about it, about what the book would look like (would it have chapters that focused on the different characters, or would it be one long narrative?) and the kinds of descriptions I would use (will the characters be painted as being the upstanding people they think they are, or will the truth be written?). He wondered if he'd be famous because I'd write about him. For the bad reasons. Because there weren't that many good.

I hated him. More than any other person in the store. I hated everything about him. Everything people said about him was right. He *was* a fat cunt.

Take a break, he said in the office after a while. I'll go get these parts. It took him a moment to get up from the chair. It actually came up with him a bit.

Don't worry, I told him. Give me the fucking tickets. What's three more parts?

I left him sitting in the hub office, trying to put shit into perspective in his head. The commercial office door was open, and inside V-Lo was initiating one of the new guys by humping him doggy-style. You like that? he said. You fucking like that? The other characters in there cheered him on and laughed so hard that I pictured their tonsils coming out of their mouths, probably still thinking that the work we did here was important work.

And why *wouldn't* they think that, I asked myself as I climbed the stairs, avoiding the grease on the yellow railing. For most of us, this is all we have going for us. We may not be teachers or politicians, or anything else that actually *is* important, but the way we must see it, we're all parts in this machine that provides some type of service for people. We sell them parts so they can fix their ways to get somewhere. A lot of us need this. We need to feel like the work we do matters. Otherwise, we'd probably end up hanging ourselves.

Coolant hose. 14358.

If we can't find meaning in our work, we go off and try to find meaning elsewhere—through church, through family, through experiencing shit only to be able to write about it because in some way, this shit's worth writing about. Someone needs to write this shit.

CV-shaft. 60-163.

I take it back. We don't put our culture to shame as much as we do ourselves, because there were all types of races at the training in Houston, and we're all the fucking same. It doesn't matter what the newsletter thinks our culture is. It's not Mexican culture, or white culture, or black culture, or even Puerto Rican culture. It's part of the work culture. We're people that somehow feel forced to have a stupid job like this, prancing in this fucking garden, and with that job comes these parts we have to play. For some, it's asserting dominance, or asserting manhood, but for most, we're just fucking around. If we play the parts we play at home, we get ridiculed for it and humped in the ass. So we play the part of the piece of shit. The part everyone in the store plays to feel this sense of belonging, thinking it might make all of this more bearable.

But that's me trying to justify this fucked-upness and use it as a lame excuse for doing the stupid shit I do.

Belt. 7088.

I stop in front of the forklift on the second floor. I have to stop whining about all this crap because all this wandering around for days is getting me nowhere. My second impulse is right. Who the fuck would want to listen to this? I reach a bit to touch the chain hanging off the fork and I get a bunch of oil and grime on my hand.

Ah, shit, I say, and I rub it against my right pant leg, creating this giant black stain that reaches down almost to my knee. I can't help but think I look a little more important now, like someone that helps people.

Part of me feels more like a man.

THE END